Praise for the novels of #1 *New York Times* bestselling author Debbie Macomber

"Debbie Macomber tells women's stories in a way no one else does."

—*BookPage*

"Macomber is a skilled storyteller."

—*Publishers Weekly*

"Whether [Debbie Macomber] is writing lighthearted romps or more serious relationship books, her novels are always engaging stories that accurately capture the foibles of real-life men and women with warmth and humor."

—*Milwaukee Journal Sentinel*

"Bestselling Macomber...sure has a way of pleasing readers."

—*Booklist*

"Macomber is a master storyteller."

—*Times Record News*

"With first-class author Debbie Macomber, it's quite simple—she gives readers an exceptional, unforgettable story every time, and her books are always, always keepers!"

—*ReadertoReader.com*

"No one writes better women's contemporary fiction."

—*RT Book Reviews*

DEBBIE MACOMBER

Navy Grooms

mira

mira

ISBN-13: 978-0-7783-3123-0

Navy Grooms

Copyright © 2018 by Harlequin Books S.A.

The publisher acknowledges the copyright holder of the
individual works as follows:

Navy Brat
Copyright © 2004 by Debbie Macomber

Navy Woman
Copyright © 2004 by Debbie Macomber

PLEASE RECYCLE
THIS PRODUCT IS RECYCLABLE

Recycling programs
for this product may
not exist in your area.

Also available from Debbie Macomber and MIRA Books

Blossom Street

Cedar Cove

The Dakota Series

The Manning Family

Christmas Books

Heart of Texas

Midnight Sons

Alaska Skies
  (*Brides for Brothers* and
  The Marriage Risk)
Alaska Nights
  (*Daddy's Little Helper* and
  Because of the Baby)
Alaska Home
  (*Falling for Him,*
  Ending in Marriage and
  Midnight Sons and Daughters)

This Matter of Marriage
Montana
Thursdays at Eight
Between Friends
Changing Habits
Married in Seattle
  (*First Comes Marriage* and
  Wanted: Perfect Partner)
Right Next Door
  (*Father's Day* and
  The Courtship of Carol Sommars)
Wyoming Brides
  (*Denim and Diamonds* and
  The Wyoming Kid)
Fairy Tale Weddings
  (*Cindy and the Prince* and
  Some Kind of Wonderful)
The Man You'll Marry
  (*The First Man You Meet* and
  The Man You'll Marry)
Orchard Valley Grooms
  (*Valerie* and *Stephanie*)
Orchard Valley Brides
  (*Norah* and *Lone Star Lovin'*)
The Sooner the Better
An Engagement in Seattle
  (*Groom Wanted* and
  Bride Wanted)
Out of the Rain
  (*Marriage Wanted* and
  Laughter in the Rain)
Learning to Love
  (*Sugar and Spice* and *Love by Degree*)

You...Again
  (*Baby Blessed* and
  Yesterday Once More)
The Unexpected Husband
  (*Jury of His Peers* and
  Any Sunday)
Three Brides, No Groom
Love in Plain Sight
  (*Love 'n' Marriage* and
  Almost an Angel)
I Left My Heart
  (*A Friend or Two* and
  No Competition)
Marriage Between Friends
  (*White Lace and Promises* and
  Friends—And Then Some)
A Man's Heart
  (*The Way to a Man's Heart*
  and *Hasty Wedding*)
North to Alaska
  (*That Wintry Feeling* and
  Borrowed Dreams)
On a Clear Day
  (*Starlight* and
  Promise Me Forever)
To Love and Protect
  (*Shadow Chasing* and
  For All My Tomorrows)
Home in Seattle
  (*The Playboy and the Widow*
  and *Fallen Angel*)
Together Again
  (*The Trouble with Caasi* and
  Reflections of Yesterday)
The Reluctant Groom
  (*All Things Considered*
  and *Almost Paradise*)
A Real Prince
  (*The Bachelor Prince*
  and *Yesterday's Hero*)
Private Paradise
  (in *That Summer Place*)

Debbie Macomber's
  Cedar Cove Cookbook
Debbie Macomber's
  Christmas Cookbook

CONTENTS

NAVY BRAT

For Marcia, Catherine, Kathy and Pam and others like them, who've picked up the pieces of their lives and taught me the meaning of the word *courage*.

Special thanks to

Gene Romano,
Senior Chief Journalist, Naval Base Seattle

Barbara Davis,
Kitsap County Community Action Program

and

The Olympic College Women in Transition Group

Plus

navy wives

Rose Marie Harris

Jan Evans

One

He was the handsomest man in the bar, and he couldn't keep his eyes off her.

It was all Erin MacNamera could do to keep her own coffee-brown eyes trained away from him. He sat on the bar stool, his back to the multitiered display of ornamental liquor bottles. His elbows were braced against the polished mahogany counter, and he nonchalantly held a bottle of imported German beer in his hand.

Against her will, Erin's gaze meandered back to him. He seemed to be waiting for her attention, and he smiled, his mouth lifting sensuously at the edges. Erin quickly looked away and tried to concentrate on what her friend was saying.

"...Steve and me."

Erin hadn't a clue as to what she'd missed. Aimee was in the habit of talking nonstop, especially when she was upset. The reason Erin and her co-worker were meeting was that Aimee wanted to discuss the problems she was having in her ten-year marriage.

Marriage was something Erin fully intended to avoid, at least for a good long while. She was focusing her energies on her career and on teaching a class ti-

tled Women in Transition two evenings a week at South
Seattle Community College. With a master's degree
clutched in her hot little hand, and her ideals and enthusiasm high, Erin had applied to and been accepted
by the King County Community Action Program as an
employment counselor, working mainly with displaced
women. Ninety percent of those she worked with were
on public assistance.

Her dream was to give hope and support to those
who had lost both. A friend to the friendless. An en-
courager to the disheartened. Erin's real love, however, was the Women in Transition course. In the past
few years she'd watched several women undergo the
metamorphosis from lost and confused individuals
to purpose-filled adults holding on tight to a second
chance at life.

Erin knew better than to take the credit or the blame
for the transformation she saw in these women's lives.
She was just part of the Ways and Means Committee.

Her father enjoyed teasing her, claiming his eldest
daughter was destined to become the next Florence
Nightingale and Mother Teresa all rolled into one te-
nacious, determined, confident female.

Casey MacNamera was only partially right. Erin certainly didn't see herself as any crusader, fighting against
the injustices of life.

Nor was Erin fooling herself about finances. She
didn't intend to become wealthy, at least not monetarily.
Nobody went into social work for the money. The hours
were long and the rewards sporadic, but when she saw
people's lives turned around for good she couldn't help
being uplifted.

Helping others through a time of painful transition
was what Erin had been born to do. It had been her

dream from early in her college career and had followed her through graduate school and her first job.

"Erin," Aimee said, her voice dipping to a whisper, "there's a man at the bar staring at us."

Erin pretended not to have noticed. "Oh?"

Aimee stirred the swizzle stick in her strawberry daiquiri, then licked the end as she stared across the room, her eyes studying the good-looking man with the imported ale. Her smile was slow and deliberate, but it didn't last long. She sighed and said, "It's you who interests him."

"How can you be so sure?"

"Because I'm married."

"He doesn't know that," Erin argued.

"Sure he does." Aimee uncrossed her long legs and leaned across the minuscule table. "Married women give off vibes, and single men pick them up like sonar. I tried to send him a signal, but it didn't work. He knew immediately. You, on the other hand, are giving off single vibes, and he's zeroing in on that like a bee does pollen."

"I'm sure you're wrong."

"Maybe," Aimee agreed in a thin whisper, "but I doubt it." She took one last sip of her drink and stood hurriedly. "I'm leaving now, and we'll test my theory and see what happens. My guess is that the minute I'm out of here he's going to make a beeline for you." She paused, smiled at her own wit, then added, "The pun was an accident, clever but unintentional."

"Aimee, I thought you wanted to talk...." Erin, however, wasn't quick enough to convince her friend to stay. Before she'd finished, Aimee had reached for her purse. "We'll talk some other time." With a natural flair, she draped the strap of her imitation-snakeskin

handbag over her shoulder and winked suggestively.
"Good luck."

"Ah…" Erin was at a loss as to what to do. She was
twenty-seven, but for the majority of her adult life she'd
avoided romantic relationships. Not by design. It had
just worked out that way.

She met men frequently, but she dated only occa-
sionally. Not once had she met a man in a bar. Cocktail
lounges weren't her scene. In her entire life she'd probably been inside one only a couple of times.

Her social life had been sadly neglected from the
time she was in junior high and fell in love for the first
time. Howie Riverside had asked her to the Valentine's
Day dance, and her tender young heart had been all
aflutter.

Then it had happened. The way it always had. Her
father, a career navy man, had been transferred, and
they'd moved three days before the dance.

Somehow Erin had never quite regained her stride
with the opposite sex. Of course, three moves in the next
four years—unusual even for the navy—hadn't been
exactly conducive to a thriving relationship. They'd
been shuffled from Alaska to Guam to Pensacola and
back again.

College could have, and probably should have, been
the opportunity to make up for lost time, but by then
Erin had felt like a social pygmy when it came to dealing with men. She hadn't known how to meet them, how
to flirt with them or how to make small talk. Nor had
she acquired a number of the other necessary graces.

"Hello."

She hadn't even had time to collect her thoughts, let
alone her purse. Mr. Imported Beer was standing next to
her table, smiling down on her like some mythological

Greek god. He certainly resembled one. He was tall, naturally. Weren't they all? Easily six-four, she guessed, and muscular. His dark hair was neatly trimmed, his brown eyes warm and friendly. He was so handsome, he might well have posed for one of those hunk calendars that were currently the rage with all the women in the office.

"Hi," she managed, hoping she sounded a whole lot less flustered than she was feeling. Erin knew herself well, and she couldn't imagine what it was about her that had attracted this gorgeous man.

Few would have described Erin as a beautiful sophisticate. Her features were distinctively Irish, comely and appealing, but she wasn't anywhere close to being strikingly beautiful. Naturally long curly chestnut-red hair, straight white teeth and a smidgen of freckles across the bridge of her Gaelic nose were her most distinctive features. She was reasonably attractive, but no more so than any of the other women who populated the cocktail lounge.

"Do you mind if I join you?"

"Ah…sure." She reached for her glass of Chablis and held on to it with one hand. "And you are…"

"Brandon Davis." He claimed the chair recently vacated by Aimee. "Most folks call me Brand."

"Erin MacNamera," she supplied, and noticed several envious stares coming her way from the women in the crowd. Even if nothing came from this exchange, Erin couldn't help being flattered by his attention. "Most folks call me Erin."

He smiled.

"Is it true? Was I really giving off vibes?" she asked, surprising herself. Obviously it was the wine talking. Generally she wasn't even close to being this direct with a man she didn't know.

Brand didn't answer her right away, which wasn't any wonder. She'd probably caught him off guard, which was only fair, since he was throwing her completely off balance.

"My friend was saying men in bars pick up vibes like a radar detector," she explained, "and I was wondering what messages I was signaling."

"None."

"Oh." She couldn't help being disappointed. For a moment there, she'd thought she'd stumbled upon some latent talent she hadn't known she possessed. Apparently that wasn't the case.

"Then why were you staring at me?" He'd probably ruin everything by informing her she had a run in her nylons, or her skirt was unzipped, or something else thoroughly embarrassing.

"Because you're Irish and it's St. Patrick's Day."

So much for padding her ego. Naturally. It was the in thing to be seen with an Irish girl on a day that traditionally celebrated her ancestors.

"You're not wearing green," he added.

"I'm not?" Erin's gaze dropped to her blue striped business suit. She hadn't given a thought to it being St. Patrick's Day when she'd dressed that morning. "I'm not," she agreed, surprised she'd forgotten something so basic to her heritage.

Brand laughed lightly, and the sound of it was so refreshing, Erin couldn't keep from smiling herself. She didn't know a whole lot about this sort of thing, but her best guess suggested Brand Davis wasn't the type of man who lounged around bars picking up women. First of all, he didn't need to. With his good looks and innate charm, women would naturally flock to him.

She decided to test her suspicion. "I don't believe I've seen you here before." That wasn't too surprising. Since this was her first time at the Blue Lagoon, the chances of their having crossed each other's paths at the bar were pretty slender.

"It's my first time."

"I see."

"What about you?"

It took Erin a second to realize he was asking her how often she frequented the cocktail lounge. "Every now and again," she answered, striving to sound urbane, or at least a tad more sophisticated than she'd been at age fourteen.

The waitress stepped up to the table, and before Erin could answer one way or the other Brand ordered two more of the same. Generally, one glass of wine was Erin's limit, but she was willing to break a few rules. It wasn't often she ran into a Greek god.

"I'm new to the area," Brand explained before Erin could think fast enough to formulate a question.

She looked at him and smiled blandly. The wine had dulled her senses, but then, making small talk had always been difficult for her. She wished she could think of some intelligent comment to make. Instead, her gaze fell on a poster on the other side of the room, and she blurted out the first thing that came to her mind.

"I love ferries." Then, realizing he might think she was referring to leprechauns, she felt compelled to explain. "When I first moved to Seattle, I was enthralled by the ferryboats. Whenever I needed to think something over, I'd ride one over to Winslow or Bremerton and hash everything out in my mind."

"It helps?"

* * *

Whatever you do, don't let her know you're navy. Casey MacNamera's voice echoed in Brand's mind like a Chinese gong. The MCPO—masterchief petty officer—was a good friend of Brand's. They'd worked together for three years early in his career, and they'd kept in touch ever since.

As soon as Casey had learned Brand had been given his special assignment at Naval Station Puget Sound at Sand Point in Seattle, the old Irishman had contacted him, concerned about his eldest daughter.

She's working too hard, not taking care of herself. Give an old man some peace of mind and check up on her. Only, for the love of heaven, don't let her know I sent you.

Personally, Brand wasn't much into this detective business. But, as a favor to his friend, he'd reluctantly agreed to look up Erin MacNamera.

He'd been ready to enter her office building when she'd stepped outside. Brand had never met Casey's daughter, but one look at that thick thatch of auburn hair and he'd immediately known that this woman was a close relative of his friend. So he'd followed her into the Blue Lagoon.

He studied her for several minutes, noticing little things about her. She was delicate. Not dainty or fragile, as the word implied. Erin MacNamera was exquisite. That wasn't a word he used often. Her gaze had met his once, and he'd managed to hold her look for just a second. She'd stared back at him, surprise darkening her eyes, before she'd jerked her gaze away. When he'd stepped up to her table, she'd been flustered, and she'd striven hard not to show it.

The more time he spent with her, the more he learned

about her that amazed him. Brand wasn't entirely sure what he'd expected from Casey's daughter, but certainly not the enchanting red-haired beauty who sat across from him. Erin was as different from her old man as silk was from leather. Casey was a potbellied, boisterous MCPO, while his daughter was a graceful creature with eyes as shiny and dark as the sea at midnight.

Another thing, Casey had warned. Remember, this is my daughter, not one of your cupcakes.

Brand couldn't help grinning at that. He didn't have cupcakes. At thirty-two, he couldn't say he'd never been in love. He'd fallen in love a handful of times over the years, but there had never been one woman who'd captured his heart for more than a few months. None that he'd ever seriously considered spending the rest of his life with.

Be careful what you say, Casey had advised. My Erin's got her mother's temper.

Brand didn't feel good about this minor deception. The sensation intensified as they sat and talked over their drinks. An hour after he'd sat down with her, Erin glanced at her watch and flatly announced she had to be leaving.

As far as Brand was concerned, his duty was done. He'd looked up his friend's daughter, talked to her long enough to assure her father, when he wrote next, that Erin was in good health. But when she stood to leave, Brand discovered he didn't want her to go. He'd thoroughly enjoyed her company.

"How about dinner?" he found himself asking.

Twin spots of color appeared in her cheeks, and her eyes darkened slightly as though she'd been caught off guard. "Ah...not tonight. Thanks anyway."

"Tomorrow?"

Her silence didn't fool him. She appeared outwardly calm, as if she were considering his invitation, but Brand could feel the resistance radiating from her. That in itself was unusual. Women generally were eager to date him.

"No thanks." Her soft smile took any sting out of her rejection—or at least it was meant to. Unfortunately, it didn't work.

She stood, smiled sweetly and tucked her purse under her arm. "Thanks for the drink."

Before Brand had time to respond, she was out the door. He couldn't remember a woman turning him down in fifteen years of dating. Not once. Most members of the opposite sex treated him as if he were Prince Charming. He'd certainly gone out of his way to be captivating to MacNamera's daughter.

Who the hell did she think she was?

Standing, Brand started out the cocktail lounge after her. She was halfway down the block on the sidewalk, her pace clipped. Brand ran a few steps, then slowed to a walk. Soon his stride matched hers.

"Why?"

She paused and looked up at him, revealing no surprise that he'd joined her.

"You're navy."

Brand was shocked, and he did a poor job of disguising it. "How'd you know?"

"I was raised in the military. I know the lingo, the jargon."

"I didn't use any."

"Not consciously. It was more than that…the way you held your beer bottle should have told me, but it was when we started talking about the ferries crossing Puget Sound that I knew for sure."

"So I'm navy. Is that so bad?"

"No. Actually, with most women it's a plus. From what I understand, a lot of females go for guys in uniform. You won't have any problems meeting someone. Bremerton? Sand Point? Or Whidbey Island?"

Brand ignored the question of where he was stationed and instead asked one of his own. "Most women are attracted to a man in uniform, but not you?"

Her eyes flickered, and she laughed curtly. "Sorry. It lost its appeal when I was around six."

She was walking so fast that he was losing his breath just keeping up with her. "Do you hate the navy so much?"

His question apparently caught her by surprise, because she stopped abruptly, turned to him and raised wide brown eyes to study him. "I don't hate it at all."

"But you won't even have dinner with someone in the service?"

"Listen, I don't mean to be rude. You seem like a perfectly nice—"

"You're not being rude. I'm just curious, is all." He glanced around them. They'd stopped in the middle of the sidewalk on a busy street in downtown Seattle. Several people were forced to walk around them. "I really would be interested in hearing your views. How about if we find a coffee shop and sit down and talk?"

She looked at her watch pointedly.

"This isn't dinner. Just coffee." Unwilling to be put off quite so easily a second time, Brand gifted her with one of his most dazzling smiles. For the majority of his adult life, women had claimed he had a smile potent enough to melt the polar ice cap. He issued it now, full strength, and waited for the usual results.

Nothing.

This woman was downright dangerous to his ego. He tried another tactic. "In case you didn't notice, we're causing something of a traffic jam here."

"I'll pay for my own coffee," she insisted in a tone that implied she was going against her better judgment to agree to talk to him at all.

"If you insist."

The lunch counter at Woolworth's was still open, and they shared a tiny booth designed for two. While the waitress delivered their coffee, Brand reached for a menu, reading over the list of sandwiches. The picture of the turkey, piled high with lettuce and tomato slices between thick slices of bread, looked appetizing, and he reluctantly set it aside.

"Officer?" Erin asked, studying him while he stirred cream into his coffee.

"Adding cream to my coffee told you that?" Casey's daughter ought to be in intelligence. He'd never met anyone quite like her.

"No. The way you talk. The way you act. Lieutenant j.g. would be my guess?"

He was impressed again. "How'd you know that?"

"Your age. What are you, thirty? Thirty-one?"

"Thirty-two." This was getting to be downright embarrassing. He'd climbed through the ranks at the normal rate of speed and received a number of special assignments over the years. Since the navy was considering closing down its station at Sand Point, Brand had been sent by the admiral to conduct a feasibility survey. His duties in the area would last only a few weeks. Most of that time had already been spent.

"I take it you weren't raised in the navy?" Erin questioned.

"No."

"I might have guessed."

She sure as hell was batting a thousand with those guesses of hers. Her eyes briefly met his, and Brand was struck once more by how hauntingly dark they were. A spark, a hint of pain—something he couldn't quite name—touched an emotional chord deep within him.

"Listen," she said softly, regretfully, "it's been interesting talking to you, but I should have been home an hour ago." She was ready to stand when Brand reached across the table and gripped her hand.

The action was as much a shock to Brand as it was to her. She raised her head a fraction of an inch so that their eyes could meet. Hers were wide and questioning, his...he didn't know. Unrelenting, stubborn, he guessed. Brand wasn't thinking clearly, and hadn't been from the moment he'd followed her into the Blue Lagoon.

"We haven't talked."

"There isn't any need to. You weren't raised in the military. I was. You couldn't possibly understand what it's like unless you were carted from one corner of the world to another."

"I'd love it."

Her smile was sardonic. "Most men do."

"I want to see you again."

She didn't hesitate, didn't think about it. Nor did she delay answering. "No.

"I apologize if I'm bruising your ego," she added, "but frankly, I promised myself a long time ago to stay away from men in the military. It's a hard-and-fast rule I live by. Trust me, it's nothing personal."

Brand sure as hell was taking it personally. "I don't even tempt you?"

She hesitated and smiled gently before tugging her hand free from his grasp. "A little," she admitted.

Brand had the feeling she was saying that to cater to his pride, which she'd managed to bruise every time she'd opened her mouth.

"As far as looks go, you've got an interesting face."

An interesting face. Didn't she know handsome when she saw it? Women had made pests of themselves in an effort to attract his attention for years. Some of his best friends had even admitted they hesitated before introducing him to their girlfriends.

"I'll walk you to your car," he said stiffly.

"It isn't necessary, I—"

"I said I'd walk you to your car." He stood and slapped two dollar bills on the table. Brand liked to think of himself as a tolerant man, but this woman was getting under his skin, and he didn't like it. Not one damn bit. There were plenty of fish in the sea, and he was far more interested in lobster than he was in Irish stew.

Erin MacNamera wasn't even that attractive. Hell, he wouldn't even be seeing her if he wasn't doing a favor for her father. If she didn't want to see him again, fine. Great. Wonderful. He could live with that. What Erin had said earlier was true enough. Women went for guys in uniform.

He was attractive. He wore a uniform.

He didn't need Erin MacNamera.

Satisfied with that, he held open the glass door that led outside.

"This really isn't necessary," she whispered.

"Probably not, but as an officer and a gentleman I insist."

"My father's an enlisted man."

She announced the fact as if she were looking for some response.

"So?" he demanded.

"So... I just wanted you to know that."

"Do you think that's going to make me change my mind about walking you to your car?"

"No." Her hands were buried in her pockets. "I... just wanted you to know. It might make a difference to some men."

"Not me."

She nodded. "My car's in the lot near Yesler."

Brand didn't know Seattle well, but he knew enough to recognize that that area of town wasn't the best place for a woman to be walking alone at night. He was glad he'd insisted on escorting her to her car, although even now he wasn't completely sure of his motives.

They turned off the main street and onto a small, narrower one that sloped sharply down to the Seattle waterfront.

"You park here often?" As prickly as she was, Erin would probably resent his pointing out the all-too-obvious dangers of the area.

"Every day, but generally I'm gone shortly after five. It's still light then."

"Tonight?"

"Tonight," she said with a sigh, "I met you."

Brand nodded. He found the parking lot, which by now was nearly deserted. The spaces were tightly angled between two brick buildings. The entire lot was illuminated by a single dim light.

Erin pulled her keys from her purse and clenched them in her hands. "My car is the one in the back," she explained.

Brand's gaze located the small blue Toyota in the rear of the lot, facing a two-story brick structure. Once more he was forced to swallow a chastising warning.

"I didn't want to say anything earlier, but I'm grateful you walked with me."

A small—damn small—sense of satisfaction filled him. "You're welcome."

She inserted the key into the driver's door and unlocked her car. Pausing, she glanced up at him and smiled shyly.

Brand looked down on the slender young woman at his side and read her confusion and her regret. The desire to pull her close was so strong that it was nearly impossible to ignore.

"I'm sorry the navy hurt you."

"It didn't. Not as much as I led you to believe. I just want to be on the safe side. For the first time in my life I have a real home with real furniture that I purchased without thinking about how well it would travel." She hesitated and smiled. "I don't worry about being transferred every other year, and—" She hesitated again and shook her head as though to suggest he wouldn't understand. "I apologize if I wounded your ego. You're really very nice."

"A kiss would go a long way toward repairing the damage." Brand couldn't believe he'd suggested that, but what the hell. Why not?

"A kiss?"

Brand nearly laughed out loud at the shocked look that came over her features. It was downright comical, as if she'd never been kissed before, or at least it had been a good long while. Not taking the time to decide which it was, he cradled her face between his large hands.

Her mouth was moist and parted, welcoming. Her eyes weren't. They were filled with doubts, but he chose to ignore her unspoken questions, fearing that if he took the time to reassure her he'd talk himself out of kissing her.

Brand wanted this kiss.

If Erin had questions, he was experiencing a few of his own. She was his friend's daughter, and he was risking Casey's wrath with this little game. But none of that seemed to matter. What did concern him was the woman staring boldly up at him.

Tenderness filled him. A strange tenderness, one he didn't fully understand or recognize. Slowly he lowered his mouth to hers. He felt her go tense with anticipation as their lips clung.

She was soft, warm and incredibly sweet. He opened his mouth a little more, slanting his lips over hers as he plowed his fingers through her thick hair.

Her first response was tentative, as if she'd been caught unprepared, but then she sighed and sagged against him. She flattened her hands over his chest, then flexed her fingers, her long nails scraping his sweater.

Gradually she opened to him, like a hothouse flower blossoming in his arms. Yet it was she who broke the contact. Her eyes were wide and soft as she stared up at him. A feeling of surprise and tenderness and need washed through him.

"I...was just thinking," she said in a lacy whisper.

Just now, thinking could be dangerous. Brand knew that from experience. He silenced her with a kiss that was so thorough it left them both trembling in its aftermath.

Once again, Erin was clinging to him, her hands gripping the V of his sweater as if she needed to hold on to something in order to remain upright.

"The rules you have about dating military men?" he

asked, rubbing his open mouth over her honeyed lips. "How about altering them?"

"Altering them?" she echoed slowly, her eyes closed.

He kissed her again for good measure. "Make it a guideline instead," he suggested.

Two

As an adult, Erin had made several decisions about how she intended to live her life. She followed the Golden Rule, and she never used her credit cards if she couldn't pay off the balance the following month.

And she didn't date men in the military.

Her life wasn't encumbered with a lot of restrictions. Everything that was important and necessary was wrapped up in these relatively simple rules.

Then why, she asked herself, had she agreed to have dinner with Brand Davis? Lieutenant Davis, J.G., she reminded herself disparagingly.

"Why?" she repeated aloud, stacking papers against the edge of her desk with enough force to bend them in half.

"Heavens, don't ask me," Aimee answered, grinning impishly. After a day spent interviewing job applicants, talking aloud to oneself was an accepted form of behavior.

"I'm supposed to meet him tonight, you know," Erin said in a low, thought-filled voice. If there had been an easy way out of this, she'd have grabbed it.

If only Brand hadn't kissed her. No one had ever told

her kissing could be so...so pleasant. First her knees had gone weak, and then her formidable will of iron had melted and pooled at her feet. Before she'd even realized what she was doing, she'd mindlessly walked into Brand's trap. It was just like a navy man to zero in on her weakest point and attack.

Rolling her antique oak chair away from her desk, Aimee relaxed against its rail back and angled her head to one side as she studied Erin. "Are you still lamenting the fact you agreed to have dinner with that gorgeous hunk? Honey, trust me in this, you should be counting your blessings."

"He's military."

"I know." Aimee rotated a pen between her hands as she gazed dreamily into the distance. A contented look stole over her features as she released a long-drawn-out sigh. "I can just picture him in a uniform, standing at attention. Why, it's enough to make my heart go pitter-patter."

Erin refused to look at her friend. If Aimee wanted Brand, she was welcome to him. Of course, her friend wasn't truly interested, since she was already married to Steve and had been for a decade. "If I could think of a plausible excuse to get out of this, I would."

"You've got to be kidding."

She wasn't. "You have dinner with him."

Aimee shook her head eagerly. "Trust me, if I were five years younger I'd take you up on that."

Since Aimee's marriage was going through some rocky times, Erin didn't think it was necessary to remind her friend that dating wasn't something that should interest her.

"Relax, would you?" Aimee admonished her.

"I can't." Erin tucked her stapler and several pens

neatly inside her desk drawer. "As far as I'm concerned, this evening is going to be a total waste of time." She could be doing something important, like…like laundry or answering mail. It was just her luck that Brand had suggested Wednesday night. Tuesday was the first class for the new session for the Women in Transition course. Thursday night was the second session. Naturally, Brand had chosen to ask her out the one night of the week when she was free.

"You're so tense," Aimee chastised. "You might as well be walking around in a suit of armor."

"I'll be okay," Erin said, not listening to her fellow worker. She stood and planted her hands against the side of her desk before sighing heavily. "This is what I'm going to do. I'll meet him just the way we arranged."

"That's a good start," Aimee teased.

"We'll find a restaurant, and I'll order right away, eat and then make my excuses as soon as I can. I don't want to insult him, but at the same time I want him to understand I regret ever having agreed to this date." She waited for a response. When Aimee didn't give her one, she arched her brows expectantly. "Well?"

"It sounds good to me." But the look Aimee gave her said otherwise.

It was amazing how much a person could say with a look. Erin didn't want to take the time to dwell on the fact, especially now, when she was thinking about the messages she'd given Brand the night he'd kissed her. Apparently she'd encouraged him enough to ask her out to dinner a second time.

Erin didn't want to dwell on that night. It embarrassed her to think about the way she'd responded so openly to his touch. Her face grew hot just remembering. She shouldn't think about it—she was running late as it was. Reaching for her purse, she checked her watch and hurried toward the elevator.

"Don't get started in the morning until we've had a chance to talk," Aimee called out after her.

They generally clocked in at eight, reviewed files and then spent a large portion of the day with job applicants or meeting with prospective employers. Sometimes she wasn't back in the office until after four.

"I won't," Erin promised without looking back. Walking briskly, she raised her hand in farewell.

"Have a good time," Aimee called out in a provocative, teasing tone that attracted the notice of their peers.

This time Erin did turn back to discover her co-worker sitting on the edge of her desk, her arms folded, one leg swinging. A mischievous grin brightened her round, cheerful face.

But Erin wasn't counting on this evening being much fun.

Once outside the revolving glass door of the tall office complex, Erin paused and glanced around. Brand had said he'd be waiting for her there. She didn't see him right away, and she was beginning to think he wasn't going to show.

It must have been wishful thinking on her part, because no sooner had the thought entered her mind than he stepped away from the building and sauntered toward her.

His gaze found hers, and Erin was struck afresh by what a devilishly handsome man Brandon Davis was. If she wasn't careful, she might find herself attracted to him. She wasn't immune to good looks and charm, and they seemed to ooze from every pore of his muscular body.

"Hi," she greeted stiffly. Her defenses were in place

as she deliberately kept her eyes trained away from his smile. It was compelling enough to dazzle the most stouthearted. Erin hadn't had enough experience with the opposite sex to build up a resistance to a man like Brand.

"I wasn't sure you'd show," he said when he reached her side.

"I wasn't sure I would, either." That was stretching the truth. She was a navy brat. Responsibility, promptness and duty had been programmed into her the way most children were taught to brush their teeth and make their beds. No one could live on a military base and not be affected by the value system promoted there.

"I'm glad you did decide to meet me." His eyes were warm and genuine, and she hurriedly looked away before she could be affected by them.

"Where would you like to eat?" To Erin's way of thinking, the sooner they arrived at the restaurant, the sooner she could leave. She wanted this evening to be cut-and-dried, without a lot of room for discussion.

"Ever been to Joe's Grill?"

Erin's gaze widened with delight. "Yes, as a matter of fact, I have, but it's been years." Since she was ten by her best guess. Her father had been stationed at Sand Point, and whenever there was something to celebrate he'd taken the family out to eat at Joe's. Generally restaurants weren't something a child would remember, but it seemed her family had a special place in each of the cities where they'd been stationed through the years. Joe's Grill had been their Seattle favorite.

"I asked around and heard the food there is great," Brand said, placing his hand at her elbow.

She felt his touch, and although it was light and impersonal it still affected her. "You mean the guys from Sand Point still eat there?"

"Apparently so."

A flood of happy memories filled Erin's mind. For her tenth birthday, Joe himself had baked her a double-decker chocolate cake. She could still remember him proudly carrying it out of the kitchen as if he'd been asked to give away the bride. Visiting the restaurant had crossed her mind half a dozen times since she'd moved to Seattle, but with her hectic schedule she hadn't gotten around to it.

"Joe's Grill," she repeated, fighting the strong desire to fill in the details about her birthday and the cake to Brand. Her eyes met his, and mutual smiles emerged, despite Erin's attempts to the contrary. She had to keep her head out of the clouds when it came to dealing with this handsome lieutenant j.g. Reminding herself of that was apparently something that was going to be necessary all evening.

Brand's car was parked on a side street. He held open the passenger door for her and gently closed it once she was inside.

He did most of the talking as he drove to the restaurant. Every once in a while Erin would feel herself start to relax in his company, a sure sign she was headed for trouble. She'd give herself a hard mental shake and instantly put herself back on track.

When Brand eased the vehicle into Joe's crowded parking lot, Erin looked around her and nearly drowned in nostalgia. She swore the restaurant hadn't changed in nearly twenty years. The same neon sign flashed from above the flat-topped roof, with a huge T-bone steak lit up in red and Joe's Grill flashing off and on every two seconds.

"As I recall, the steaks here are so thick they resemble roasts, and the baked potatoes were larger than a boxer's fist." She was confident that was an exaggeration, but in her ten-year-old mind that was the way it seemed.

"That's what my friend said," Brand said, climbing out of the car.

The inside was much as Erin remembered. A huge fish tank built into the wall was filled with a wide variety of colorful saltwater fish. The cash register rested on top of a large glass display case full of tempting candy and gum. Erin never had understood why a restaurant that served wonderful meals would want to sell candy to its customers afterward.

The hostess escorted them to a table by a picture window that revealed a breathtaking panorama of Lake Union.

Erin didn't open her menu right away. Instead, she looked around, soaking up the ambience, feeling as if she were a kid all over again.

"This reminds me of a little place on Guam," Brand said, his gaze following hers. "The tables have the same red tablecloths under a glass covering."

"Not..." She had to stop and think.

"The Trattoria," Brand supplied.

"Yes." Erin was impressed he'd even heard of it, but then he probably had since everyone stationed on Guam ate there at one time or another. "They serve a clam spaghetti my father swore he would die for. My mom tried for years to duplicate the recipe and finally gave up. Who would ever believe a tiny restaurant on the island of Guam would serve the best Italian food in the world?"

"Better even than Miceli's in Rome?" he probed.

"You've been to Miceli's?" she asked excitedly. Obviously he had, otherwise he wouldn't have mentioned it. The fresh-from-the-oven-bread was what she remembered about Miceli's. The aroma would drift through the narrow cobblestoned streets of the Italian town like nothing Erin had ever known. Her stomach growled just thinking about it.

"I've been in the navy nearly fifteen years," he reminded her.

Mentioning the fact that he was navy was like slapping a cold rag across her face and forcing her back to reality. Her reaction was immediate. She reached for the menu, jerked it open and decided what she intended to order in three seconds flat. She looked up, hoping to catch the waitress's eye.

"I can't decide if I'm hungry enough for the T-bone or not," Brand remarked conversationally. He glanced over the menu a second time before looking to her. "You've decided?"

"Yes. I'll have the peppercorn filet."

Brand nodded, apparently saluting her choice. "That sounds good. I'll have the same."

"No," Erin said, surprised by how adamant she sounded. "Have the T-bone. It's probably the best of any place in town. And since you're only going to be in Seattle a few weeks, you really should sample Joe's specialty."

"All right, I will." Brand smiled at her, and Erin's heart started to pound like a giant sledgehammer, a fact she chose to ignore.

The waitress arrived to take their order, and Brand suggested a bottle of wine.

"No, thanks, none for me," Erin said quickly. After what had happened the night they'd met, she'd considered living her entire life without drinking wine again. It was probably ridiculous to blame two glasses of Chablis for the eager way she'd responded to Brand's kisses. But it was an excuse, and she badly needed one. She certainly wasn't looking for a repeat performance. Her objective was to get through this dinner, thank Brand and then go her own way. Naturally she wanted them to part with the understanding she didn't ever intend to date him again. But she wanted to be sure he realized it was nothing personal.

The conversation that followed was polite, if a tad stilted. Erin's hand circled the water glass, and her gaze flittered across the restaurant, gathering in the memories.

"I made a mistake," Brand announced out of the blue, capturing her attention. "I shouldn't have reminded you I'm navy. You were enjoying yourself until then."

Erin lowered her gaze to the red linen napkin in her lap. "Actually, I'm grateful. It's far too easy to forget with you." As she spoke, Erin could hear a thread of resentment and fear in her own voice.

"I was hoping we might be able to forget about that."

"No," she answered, softly, regretfully. "I can't allow myself to forget. You're here for how long? Two, three weeks?" She asked this as a reminder to herself of how foolish it would be to become involved with Brand.

"Two weeks."

"That's what I thought." Her gaze drifted toward the kitchen in a silent appeal to the chef to hurry with their order. The more time she spent with Brand, the more susceptible she was to his charm. He was everything she feared. Appealing. Attractive. Charming. She was beginning to hate that word, but it seemed to fit him so well.

He asked her about the places she'd lived, and she answered him as straightforwardly as she could, trying not to let the resentment seep into her voice. Her answers were abridged, clipped.

Their meal arrived, and none too soon, as far as Erin was concerned.

Brand's steak was delicious. As delicious as Erin had promised, cooked to perfection. He didn't know what to make of Erin MacNamera, however. Hell, he didn't know what to make of himself. She'd made her views on seeing him plain enough. He didn't know what it was about her that affected him so strongly. The challenge, perhaps. There weren't many women who turned him down flat the way she had.

The challenge was there, he'd admit that, but it was something else, too. Something he couldn't quite put his finger on. Whatever it was, Erin was driving him crazy.

They'd agreed to meet outside her office building, and Brand had half expected her to stand him up. When she had shown, he'd noted regretfully that it wasn't out of any desire to spend time with him. At first she'd been tense. They'd started talking, and she'd lowered her guard and been beginning to relax. Then he'd blown it by reminding her he was in the navy.

From that point on he might as well have been sitting across the table from a robot. He'd asked her something, and she'd answered him with one-word replies or by simply shrugging her shoulders. After a while he'd given up the effort. If she wanted conversation with her dinner, then she could damn well carry it on her own.

It didn't come as any surprise to Brand that she was ready to leave the minute they finished. He collected the bill, left a generous tip and escorted Erin to the car.

"Are you parked at the same lot off Yesler?" he asked once they were in traffic.

"Yes. You can drop me off there, if you don't mind."

"I don't." Brand noted that she sounded downright eager to part company with him. This woman was definitely a detriment to his ego. Fine, he got the message. He wasn't exactly sure why he'd even suggested this dinner date. As Erin had taken pains to remind him, he would be in Seattle only a couple of weeks. The implication being that he'd be out of her life forever then. Apparently that was exactly what she wanted.

In retrospect, Brand was willing to admit why he'd asked her out to dinner.

It was the kiss.

Her response, so tentative in the beginning, so hesitant and unsure, had thrown him for a loop. If Casey was ever to find out Brand had kissed his red-haired daughter, there would be hell to pay. The sure wrath of his friend hadn't altered the fact Brand had wanted to kiss Erin. And kiss her he had, until his knees had been knocking and his heart had been roaring like a runaway train.

What had started out as a challenge had left him depleted and shaken. Numb with surprise and wonder. Erin had flowered in his arms like a rare tropical plant. She was incredibly sweet, and so soft that he'd been forced to use every ounce of restraint he possessed not to crush her in his arms.

This dinner date was a different story. She could hardly wait to get out of his car. Fine. He'd let her go, because frankly he wasn't much into cultivating a relationship with a woman who clearly didn't want to have anything to do with him.

He pulled off First Avenue onto the lot and left the engine running, hoping she'd get his message, as well.

Her hand was already closed around the door handle. "Thank you for dinner."

"You're welcome," was his stiff reply. His tone bordered on the sarcastic, but if she noticed she didn't comment.

"I'm sorry I was such poor company."

He didn't claim otherwise. She hesitated, and for a wild moment Brand thought she might lean over and gently kiss him goodbye. It would have been a nice gesture on her part.

She didn't.

Instead she scooted out of the car, fiddled with the snap of her purse and retrieved her key chain, all while he sat waiting for her. When she'd opened the door to her Toyota, she twisted around and smiled sadly, as if she wanted to say something more. She didn't, however. She just climbed inside resolutely.

Brand had to back up his car in order for her to pull out of the parking space. He did so with ease, reversing his way directly into the street. She came out after him and headed in the opposite direction.

His hand tightened around the steering wheel as she drove off into the night.

"Goodbye, Erin. We might have been friends," he murmured, and regret settled over his shoulders like a heavy wool jacket.

Once he was back at his room in the officers' quarters, Brand showered and climbed into bed. He read for a while, but the novel, which had been touted as excellent, didn't hold his interest. After fifteen minutes, he turned out the light.

He should have kissed her.

The thought flashed through his mind like a shot from a ray gun.

Hell, no. It was apparent Erin didn't want to have anything to do with him. Wonderful. Great. He was man enough to accept her decision.

Forcefully, he punched up the pillow under his head and closed his eyes.

Before he realized what he was doing, a slight smile curved his lips. She should count herself lucky he hadn't taken it upon himself to prove her wrong and kiss her again. If he had, she would have been putty in his hands, just the way she had been the first time. Erin MacNamera might well have believed she had the situation under control, but she hadn't. She'd been tense and uneasy, and for no other reason than the fear that Brand was going to take her in his arms again.

He should have. He'd wanted to. Until now he hadn't been willing to admit how damn much he had longed to taste her again.

Brand rolled over onto his stomach and nuzzled his face into the thick softness of the pillow. Erin had been feather-soft. When she'd moved against him, her breasts had lightly cushioned his chest. The memory of her softness clouded his mind.

Burying his face in the pillow added fuel to his imagination, and he abruptly rolled over. He firmly shut his eyes and sighed as he started to drift off.

It didn't work. Instead, he saw Erin's sweet Irish face looking back at him.

Her eyes were an unusual shade of brown. Man-enticing brown, he decided. With her curly red hair and her pale, peach-smooth complexion, her eye color was something of a surprise. He'd expected blue or green, not dark brown.

Beautiful brown eyes...so readable, so clear, looking back at him, as if she were suffering from a wealth of regrets just before she'd climbed into her car.

Brand was suffering from a few regrets of his own. He hadn't kissed her. Nor had he suggested they see each other again.

Damn his pride. He should have done something, anything, to persuade her. Now she was gone....

Sleep danced around him until he was on the verge of drifting off completely. Then his eyes snapped open, and a slow, satisfied smile turned up the edges of his mouth.

He knew exactly what he intended to do.

Erin remembered Marilyn Amundson from the first session of the Women in Transition course on Tuesday evening. The middle-aged woman with pain-dulled blue eyes and fashionably styled hair had sat at the back of the room, in the last row. Throughout most of the class, she'd kept her gaze lowered. Erin noted that the woman took copious notes as she outlined the sixteen-session course. Every now and again, the older woman would pause, dab a tissue at the corner of her eyes and visibly struggle to maintain her aplomb.

At nine, when class was dismissed, Marilyn had slowly gathered her things and hurried outside the classroom. Later Erin had seen a car stop in front of the college to pick her up.

It was Erin's guess that Marilyn didn't drive. It wasn't unusual for the women who signed up for the course to have to rely on someone else for transportation.

Most of the women were making a new life for themselves. Some came devastated by divorce, others from the death of a loved one. Whatever the reason, they all shared common ground and had come to learn and help each other. When the sessions were finished, the classes continued to meet as a monthly support group.

The greatest rewards Erin had had as a social worker were from the Women in Transition course. The transformation she'd seen in the participants' lives in the short two months she taught the class reminded her of the metamorphosis of a cocoon into a butterfly.

The first few classes were always the most difficult. The women came feeling empty inside, fearful, tormented by the thought of facing an unknown future. Many were angry, some came guilt-ridden, and there were always a few who were restless, despairing and pessimistic.

What a good portion of those who signed up for the course didn't understand when they first arrived was how balanced life was. Whenever there was a loss, the stage was set for something to be gained. A new day was born, the night was lost. A flower blossomed, the bud was lost. In nature and in all aspects of life an advantage could be found in a loss. A balance, oftentimes not one easily explained or understood, but a symmetry nevertheless, was waiting to be discovered and explored. It was Erin's privilege to teach these women to look for the gain.

"I was wondering if I could talk to you?"

Erin paused. "Of course. You're Marilyn Amundson?"

"Yes." The older woman reached for a tissue and ran it beneath her nose. Her fingers were trembling, and it was several moments before she spoke. "I can't seem to stop crying. I sit in class and all I do is cry.... I want to apologize for that."

"You don't need to. I understand."

Marilyn smiled weakly. "Some of the other women in class look so...like they've got it all together, while I'm a basket case. My husband..." She paused when her voice faltered. "He asked me for a divorce two weeks ago. We've been married over thirty years. Apparently he met someone else five or six years ago, and they've been seeing each other ever since...only I didn't know."

This was a story Erin had heard several times over, but it wouldn't lessen Marilyn's pain for Erin to imply that she was another statistic. What she did need to hear was that others had survived this ordeal, and so would she.

"I'd...gone out shopping. The bus stops right outside our house, and when I returned home, Richard was there. I knew right away something was wrong. Richard only rarely wears his suit. I asked him what he was doing home in the middle of the day, and all he could do was stand there and stare at me. Then...then he said he was sorry to do it this way, and he handed me the divorce papers. Just like that—without any warning. I didn't know about the other woman.... I suppose I should have, but I... I trusted him."

Erin's heart twisted at the torment that echoed in the other woman's voice. Marilyn struggled to hold back the tears, her lips quivering with the effort.

"Although this may feel like the worst moment of your life, you will survive," Erin said gently, hugging her briefly. "I promise you that. The healing process is like everything else, there's a beginning, a middle and an end. It feels like the whole world has caved in on you now."

"That's exactly the way I feel. Richard is my whole life...was my whole life. I just don't know what I'm going to do."

"Have you seen an attorney?"

Marilyn shook her head. "Not yet... My pastor suggested I take this course, and find my footing, so to speak."

"In session twelve a lawyer will visit the class. You can ask any questions you like then."

"I wanted to thank you, too," Marilyn went on, once she'd composed herself. "What you said about the balance of things, how nature and life even things out... well, it made a lot of sense to me. Few things do these days."

Erin reached for her coat, slipping her arms into the satin-lined sleeves. She smiled, hoping the gesture would offer Marilyn some reassurance. "I'm pleased you're finding the class helpful."

"I don't think I could have made it through this last week without it." She retreated a few steps and smiled again. This time it came across stronger. "Thank you again."

"You're welcome. I'll see you Tuesday."

"I'll be here." Buttoning up her own coat, Marilyn headed out the classroom door.

Erin watched the older woman. Her heart ached for Marilyn, but, although she was devastated and shaky now, Erin saw in her a deep inner strength. Marilyn hadn't realized it was there, not yet. Soon she would discover it and draw upon the deep pool of courage. For now her thoughts were full of self-condemnation, self-deprecation and worry. From experience, Erin knew Marilyn would wallow in those for a while, but the time would come when she'd pick herself up by the bootstraps. Then that inner strength, the grit she saw in the other woman's weary eyes, would come alive.

As if sensing Erin's thoughts, Marilyn paused at the

classroom door and turned back. "Do you mind if I ask you a personal question?"

"Sure, go ahead."

"Have you ever been in love?"

"No," Erin answered, regretfully. "Not even close, I'm afraid."

Marilyn nodded, then squared her shoulders. "Don't ever let it happen," she advised gruffly, yet softly. "It hurts too damn much."

Three

The envelope arrived at Erin's office, hand-delivered by the downstairs receptionist. Erin stared at her name scrawled across the front and knew beyond a doubt the handwriting belonged to Brand Davis. She held the plain white envelope in her hand several moments, her heart pounding. It'd been two days since her dinner date with Brand, and she hadn't been able to stop thinking about him. She'd been so awful, so aloof and unfriendly, when he'd been trying so hard to be cordial and helpful.

When he'd dropped her off where she'd parked her car, she'd practically leaped out of his in her eagerness to get away from him. Exactly what had he done that was so terrible? Well, first off, he'd been pleasant and fun—horrible crimes, indeed—while she'd behaved like a cantankerous old biddy. She wasn't proud of herself; in fact, Erin felt wretched about the whole thing.

"Go ahead and open it," she said aloud.

"You talking to yourself again?" Aimee chastised. "You generally don't do that until the end of the day."

"Brand sent me a note." She held it up for her friend's inspection as though she were holding on to a hand grenade and expected it to explode in her face at any moment.

"I thought the receptionist looked envious. He's probably downstairs waiting for you right now."

"Ah…" That thought didn't bear contemplating.

"For heaven's sake," Aimee said eagerly, "don't just sit there, open it."

Erin did, with an enthusiasm she didn't dare question. Her gaze scanned the short message before she looked up to her friend. "He wants to give me a tour of Sand Point before the opportunity is gone. You know there's a distinct possibility the navy may close down the base. He says I should have a look at it for nostalgia's sake."

"When?"

"Tomorrow… You're right, he's downstairs waiting for my answer."

"Are you going to do it?" Aimee's question hung in mid-air like a dangling spider.

Erin didn't know. Then she did know. Longing welled deep within her, not a physical longing, but an emotional stirring that left her feeling empty inside. She didn't want to have anything to do with this lieutenant j.g., didn't want to be trapped in the whirlpool of his strong, sensual appeal. Nevertheless, she had been from the first moment they'd kissed, despite her best efforts.

He paralyzed her; he challenged her. He was everything she claimed she didn't want in a man, and everything she'd ever hope to find.

"Well?" Aimee probed. "What are you going to do?"

"I… I'm going to take that tour."

Aimee let loose with a loud cheer that attracted the attention of nearly everyone in the huge open room.

Several people stuck their heads out from behind office doors to discover what was causing all the excitement.

Shaking on the inside, but outwardly composed, Erin took the elevator to the ground floor. Brand was waiting in the foyer. He had his back to her and was standing in front of the directory. He wore his dress uniform, and his hands were joined behind his back, holding his garrison cap.

He must have sensed her presence, because he turned around.

"Hello," she said, her heart as heavy as the humid air of the rainy Seattle morning.

"Hi," he responded, his own voice low and throaty.

She dropped her gaze, unexpectedly nervous. "I got your note."

"You look surprised to hear from me."

"After the way I behaved the other night, I didn't expect to... I can't understand why you want anything to do with me."

"You weren't so bad." His lazy grin took a long time coming, but when it did it contradicted every word he'd spoken.

She found his smile infectious and doubted any woman could resist this man when he put his mind to it—and his mind was definitely to it!

"Are you free tomorrow?"

"And if I said I wasn't?" She answered him with a question of her own, thinking that was safer than admitting how pleased she was to see him.

"I'd ask you out again later."

"Why?" Erin couldn't understand why he'd continue to risk rejection from her. Especially when she was quite ordinary. Erin wasn't selling herself short. She was a warm, generous person, but she hadn't been with him.

Yet he'd returned twice now, enduring her disdain, and she had yet to understand why.

Gradually she raised her eyes to his. And what she viewed confused her even more. Brand was thinking and feeling the same things she was, the same bewilderment, the same confusion. The same everything.

The smile faded, and his face tightened slightly, as if this were a question he'd often asked himself. "Why do I keep coming back?" He leveled his gaze on her. "I wish the hell I knew. Will you come to Sand Point tomorrow?"

Erin nodded, then emphasized her response by saying, "Yes. At ten?"

"Perfect." Then he added with a slight smile, "There'll be a pass waiting for you at the gate."

"Good," she said, taking a step back, feeling nervous and not knowing how to explain it. "I'll see you tomorrow, then."

"Tomorrow."

It wasn't until Erin was inside the elevator, a smile trembling on her lips, that she remembered Marilyn's parting words from the night before.

Don't ever fall in love, Marilyn had warned her, it hurts too damn much. Erin felt somewhat comforted to realize she was a long way from falling in love with Brand Davis. But she would definitely have to be careful.

"Well, is it the way you remembered?" Brand asked after a two-hour tour of Naval Station Puget Sound at Sand Point. He'd given her a history lesson, too. Sand Point had originally been acquired by King County back in 1920 as an airport and later leased to the navy as a reserve. Brand had explained that only a few hundred men were based there now, support personnel for the base at Everett. Brand was assigned to the admiral's staff—SINCPAC, out of Hawaii—and sent to do an independent study in preparation for the possible closure of the base.

Erin had been on the base itself only a handful of times as a child. It amazed her how familiar the base felt to her, even though it had been sixteen years since she'd moved away from the area.

"It hasn't changed all that much over the years."

"That surprises you?"

"Not really." What did catch her unawares was the feeling of homecoming. There had never been one single base her family had been assigned to through the years that gave Erin this sort of abstract feeling of home. From the time she could remember, her life had belonged to the navy. Her father would receive shipping orders, and without a pause her family would pack up everything they owned and head wherever her father's commanding officer decreed. Erin had hated it with a fierceness that went beyond description. Nothing was ever her own, there was no sense of permanency in her life, no sense of security. What she had one day— her friends, her school, her neighbors—could be taken from her the next.

Brand's fingers reached for hers and squeezed tightly. "You look sad."

"I do?" She forced a note of cheerfulness into her voice, needing to define her feelings. Brand had brought her here. For the first time since she'd left her family, she'd returned to a navy base. She'd agreed to Brand's suggestion of a tour with flippant disregard for any emotions she might experience.

The wounds of her youth, although she knew she was

being somewhat melodramatic to refer to them that way, had been properly bandaged with time. She'd set the course of her life and hadn't looked back since. Then, out of the blue, Brand Davis had popped in, determined, it seemed, to untie the compress so carefully wrapped around her heart.

As she stood outside the Sand Point grounds, she could almost feel the bandages slackening. Her first instinct was to tug them back into place, but she couldn't do that with the memories. Happy memories, carefree memories, came at her from every angle. The longer she stood there, the longer she soaked in the feelings, the more likely the bandage was to drop to her feet. Erin couldn't allow that to happen.

"I'd forgotten how much I enjoyed living in Seattle," she whispered, barely aware she was speaking.

"Where were you stationed afterward?"

Erin had to think about it. "Guam, as I recall.... No, we went to Alaska first."

"You hated it there?"

"Not exactly. Don't get me wrong, it wasn't my favorite place in the world, but it was tolerable.... We weren't there long." The sun actually did shine at midnight, and the mosquito was teasingly referred to as the Alaska state bird. Actually, Erin had loved Alaska, but they'd been there such a short while.

"How long?"

"Four months, I'd guess. There was some screwup, and almost overnight we were given orders and shipped to Guam. Now that was one place I really did enjoy."

"Did you ever take picnics on Guam?"

Erin had to think that one over, and she couldn't actually remember one way or the other. "I suppose we did."

"And how did you enjoy those?"

Erin glanced in Brand's direction and studied him through narrowed eyes. "Why do I have the funny feeling this is a leading question?"

"Because it is." Brand grinned at her, and the sun broke through whatever clouds there were that day. "I packed us a lunch, and I was hoping to persuade you to go on a picnic with me."

"Where?" Not that it mattered. The question was a delaying tactic to give her time to sort through her scattered feelings. A tour of Sand Point was one thing, but lying down on the grass feeding each other grapes was another.

"Anywhere you want."

"Ah?" Her mind scurried as she tried to come up with the names of parks, but for the life of her Erin couldn't remove the picture of Brand pressing a grape to her lips and then bending over to kiss her and share the juicy flavor.

"Erin?"

"How about Woodland Park? If you haven't visited the zoo, you should. Seattle has one of the country's best." That way she could feed the animals and take her mind off Brand. The choice was a good one for another reason, as well. Woodland Park was sure to be crowded on a day as bright and sunny as this one.

Erin was right. They were fortunate to find parking. Brand frowned as he glanced around them, and she could almost hear his thoughts. He'd been hoping she'd lead him to a secluded hideaway, and she'd greatly disappointed him. He might as well become accustomed to it. Erin had agreed to see him again, but she absolutely refused to become romantically involved.

"Just who do you think you're kidding?" she mut-

tered under her breath. Her stomach had been tied up
in knots for the last hour while she'd replayed over and
over again in her mind this ridiculous scene about them
sharing grapes. For all she knew, he might have brought
along apples, or oranges, or omitted fruit altogether.

"You said something?" Brand asked, giving her an
odd look.

"No…"

"I thought you did."

She was going to have to examine this need to talk
out loud to herself. As far as she could see, the best tactic was to change the subject. "I'm starved."

"Me too." But when he glanced her way, his gaze
rested squarely on her mouth, as if to say he was eager
to eat all right, but his need wasn't for food.

Her beautiful Irish eyes were moody, Brand decided.
Moody and guarded. Brand didn't know what he'd
done—or hadn't done—that disturbed Erin so much.
From the moment they'd driven away from the naval
station, he'd toyed with the idea of asking her what was
wrong. He hadn't, simply because he knew she'd deny
that anything was troubling her.

Brand wasn't pleased with her choice of parks for
their picnic. The zoo was a place for family and kids.
He'd be lucky if they found five minutes alone together.
But then, that was exactly the reason Erin had chosen it.

Brand, on the other hand, wanted seclusion and privacy. He wanted to kiss Erin again. Hell, he needed to
kiss Erin again. The thought had dominated his mind
for days. She was so incredibly soft and sweet. He swore
he'd never kissed another woman who tasted of honey
the way she did. The sample she'd given him hadn't
been nearly enough to satisfy his need. For days he'd

been telling himself he'd blown the kiss up in his mind, way out of proportion. Nothing could have been that good.

"Anyplace around here will do," she said.

He followed her into the park, his gaze scanning the rolling green landscape and falling on a large pond. The space under the trees near the shore looked the most promising. He suggested there.

"Sure," she responded, but she sounded uncertain.

Brand smoothed out the gray navy-issue blanket on the lawn and set the wicker basket in the center of it.

"If you'd said something earlier, I would have baked brownies," Erin said, striving, Brand thought, to sound conversational.

"You can next time." The implication was there, as blatant as he could make it. He would be seeing her again. Often. As frequently as their schedules allowed. He planned on it, and he wanted her to do the same.

"What did you pack for us?" Her voice sounded hollow, as if it were coming from an abandoned well.

"Nothing all that fabulous." Kneeling on the blanket, he opened the basket and set out sandwiches, a couple of cans of cold pop, potato chips and two oranges.

Erin's gaze rested on the oranges for the longest moment. They were the large Florida variety, juicy, she suspected, and sweet.

"Do you want the turkey on white or the corned beef on whole wheat?"

"The turkey," she answered.

Next Brand opened the chips and handed her the bag. She grabbed a handful and set them on top of a napkin. For all her claims about being famished, Brand noted, she barely touched her food.

He sat, leaning his back against the base of the tree,

and stretched his long legs out in front of him, crossing his ankles. "You're looking thoughtful."

Her responding smile was weak. "I… I was just thinking about something one of the women in my class told me."

"What was that?"

Her head came up, and her gaze collided with his. "Ah…it's difficult to explain."

"This class means a lot to you, doesn't it?"

Erin nodded. "One of the women has been on my mind the last couple of days. She hasn't centered herself yet, and—"

"Centered herself?"

"It's a counseling term. Basically, what it means is that she hasn't come to grips with who and what she is and needs to brace herself for whatever comes her way. Right now she's suffering from shock and emotional pain, and the smallest problem overpowers her. Frankly, I'm worried."

"Tell me about her." Brand held out his arm, wanting Erin to scoot close and rest her head on his chest. He'd been looking for a subtle, natural way of doing so without putting Erin on red alert.

He was almost surprised when she did move toward him. She didn't exactly cuddle up in his arms, but she braced her back against his chest and stretched her legs out in front of her. His arm reached across her shoulder blades.

"She's taking my class because after thirty-odd years of marriage her husband is leaving her. From what I understand there's another woman involved."

"I didn't know people would divorce after staying married for so many years. Frankly, it doesn't make a lot of sense."

"It happens," Erin explained softly, "more than you'd guess."

"Go on, I didn't mean to interrupt you. Tell me about..."

"I'll call her Margo. That isn't her name, of course."

Brand nodded. It felt so good to have Erin in his arms. He'd been fantasizing about it for days. The hold wasn't as intimate as he would have liked, but with this sweet Irish miss he'd need to go slowly.

"She's in her early fifties and never worked outside the home. All she knows how to be is a homemaker and a wife. I'd venture to guess that she's never written a check. I know for a fact she doesn't drive. At a time in her life when she was looking forward to retirement, she needs to find a career and make a home for herself."

"What about children? Surely, they'd stick by their mother at a time like this."

"Two daughters. They're both married and live outside the state. From what I can remember, one lives in California and the other someplace in Texas. Margo's completely alone, probably for the first time in her life."

"How's she handling it?"

"It's hard to tell. We're only two classes into the course, but as I said before, she's shaky and fragile. Time will help."

"My parents were divorced." Brand seldom spoke of his family, and even more rarely of the trauma that had ripped his life apart at such a tender age. "I was just a kid at the time."

"Was it bad?"

He answered her with a short nod. Without a doubt, it was the worst ordeal Brand could ever remember happening to him. His whole world had been shattered. He'd become a weapon to be used against one parent or the other. And he'd only been eleven at the time. Far too young to understand, far too old to cry.

"I rarely saw my father afterward. Every time he and my mother were in the same room together, they'd start arguing. My guess is that it was easier for him to move as far away as possible than to deal with her."

"So when he divorced your mother, he divorced you, too?"

Once again, Brand responded with a short nod. His life had been filled with one trauma after another after his father had moved out of the state. A year or two later, when his mother had remarried, all communication and child support had stopped. Brand had been made to feel guilty for every bit of food he ate or each pair of shoes he outgrew. While attending college, he'd become involved in the officers' training program offered by the navy. His life had changed from that moment forward. For the better.

Brand found security and acceptance in the navy. What the military had given him, it had taken away from Erin. He understood her complaints well. She hated moving, never planting roots or building lasting relationships. Brand thrived on the security. The navy was his home. The navy was his life. No one would ever take that away from him. There would always be a navy. Budget cuts hurt, bases were being closed down all across the country and military spending was being decreased, but he was secure, more secure than he had been since childhood.

"But I have a feeling about Margo," Erin continued. "She's far stronger than she realizes. That knowledge will come in time, but she may travel some rough waters before this ordeal is finished."

"You're strong, too."

Erin leaned her head to examine his face, and Brand took advantage of the moment to press his hands gently to her rosy cheeks. Her eyes found his, and he read her confusion as clearly as he viewed her eagerness. She wanted this kiss as much as he wanted to kiss her.

Gently he pressed his mouth to hers. The kiss was deep and thorough, his lips sliding across hers with unhurried ease and a familiarity that belied their experience. Slowly he lifted his head and drew in a deep, stabilizing breath. A bolt of sizzling electricity arched between them.

"Oh, damn," Erin whispered, sounding very much as if she were about to weep. Her eyes remained closed, and Brand was tempted to kiss her moist lips a second time. In fact, he had to restrain himself from doing so.

"Damn?"

"I was afraid of this." Her words were hoarse, as if she were having trouble speaking. Her eyes fluttered open, and she gazed up longingly at him. Irish eyes. Sweet Irish eyes.

"Don't be afraid," he whispered, just before he kissed her a second time. And a third. A fourth. His hands were in her hair, loving the silky feel of it as he ran his fingers through the lengthy curls.

Gradually he felt her opening up to him, like the satin petals of a rosebud. Either she'd had poor teachers or she was inexperienced in the art of kissing. Brand didn't know which, didn't care.

Positioned as they were against the tree, he couldn't get close enough to her. The need to cradle her softness grew until every part of his body ached. He wanted her beneath him, warm and willing. Open and sweet.

With their mouths joined, he rolled away from the tree, taking her with him. Erin gave a small cry of

alarm, and when she opened her mouth he groaned
and thrust his tongue deep into the moist warmth.

She rebelled for a moment, not having expected this
new intimacy. It took her a second to adjust before she
responded, meekly at first, by giving him her tongue.
They touched, stroked and played against each other
in an erotic game until Brand deepened the kiss to a
level neither of them would be able to tolerate for long.

Her hands clenched his shirt, and Brand wondered
if she could feel how hard and fiercely his heart was
beating. He could feel hers, excited and chaotic, pounding against his chest. Her pulse wasn't the only thing
he could feel. Her nipples had pearled and stood out.
The need to slip his hand under her sweater and fill his
palm with her breast ate at him like lye. He couldn't...
not here.

He longed to feel her and taste her. Sweet heaven, if
he didn't stop now he'd end up really frightening her.
He probably had already. He was as hard as concrete
against her thigh. The way they were lying, there wasn't
any way he could hide what she was doing to him. Only
years of training and self-discipline kept him still. He
longed to rotate his hips to help ease the terrible ache
in his loins.

He kissed Erin again, struggling within himself to
take it slow and easy. His mouth gentled over hers, in
sharp contrast to the wild, uncontrolled kisses they'd
shared seconds earlier. She groaned and moved against
him, causing Brand to moan himself. His innocent Irish
miss hadn't a clue of the torment she was putting him
through. Dear heaven, she was sweet. So warm and
moist.

Brand had fully intended to cool their lovemaking,
but he made a single tactical error that was nearly his

undoing. Just because a kiss was gentle, it didn't make it any less sensual, or any less devastating.

By the time Brand lifted his head, he was weak, depleted, yet at the same time exhilarated. Shocked eyes stared up at him. He smiled and noted how the edges of her delectable mouth quivered slightly.

She raised her hand, and her fingertips grazed his face. Her touch was as smooth and light as a velvet glove. Unable to resist, Brand kissed her again.

"Are you going to say damn again?" he teased.

Her grin widened. "No."

"But you should?"

She nodded, then closed her eyes and slowly expelled her breath. "I don't know how this happened."

"You don't?"

"I'd hoped…"

He pressed a finger across her lips. "I know what you hoped! You couldn't have picked a more public place and for obvious reasons, which I fear have backfired on us both. As it is, I may have to lie on my belly the rest of the afternoon."

"You will?" As the meaning of his words sank into her brain, Erin's cheeks blossomed with color. "I… I shouldn't have said anything." As if she needed something to occupy her hands, she reached for one of the oranges, peeling it open. She held out a dripping slice to him. "Want one?"

Sitting with his legs folded in front of him, Brand nodded. He thought Erin meant to hand it to him, but instead she leaned forward to feed him personally. Her eyes were locked with his. A second slice followed the first, but when the juice flowed from the edge of his mouth she bent toward him and licked it away.

When her tongue scraped the side of his lips, Brand's

heart went still. She offered him another slice, but he took it from her fingers and fed it to her. He watched as she chewed and swallowed, and then he leaned forward to kiss her. She tasted of orange and woman. He deepened the kiss and was gratified when she opened up to him in excited welcome. His tongue swept her mouth in slow, even strokes, conquering as it plundered.

Erin looped her arms around his neck and melted in his arms. "I promised myself this wouldn't happen."

"And now that it has?" He angled his head to one side and dropped a series of long, slow kisses on her neck, working his way under her chin and to her ear. "Do you want me to stop?"

"No."

The satisfaction that one word gave him was worth a thousand from anyone else. "Let's get out of here."

"Why?" How afraid she sounded.

His mouth hovered a scant inch from hers. "Because there are other places I want to kiss you, and I don't think you'd appreciate me doing so in public."

His lips inched back to hers in breath-stealing increments. The closer his mouth edged toward hers, the choppier her breath became.

"Brand... I don't think this is such a good—"

He silenced any protest with a hot, need-filled kiss. She welcomed his tongue, and was panting by the time he dragged his mouth from hers.

"Come on," he said, vaulting to his feet. He reached for her hand, pulling her upright. "Let's get out of here."

"Where...will we go?"

"Your place."

"Brand... I don't know."

He turned and planted his hands squarely on her shoulders, his eyes refusing to release hers. "I'm not going to make love to you, yet. That's a promise. We need to talk, and when we do, I want it to be in private."

She might have had objections to the high-handed manner in which he was issuing orders, but she didn't voice any. Nor did she speak while he drove to her house in West Seattle, although the ride took nearly thirty minutes. The only words she did manage were to relay her address and give directions once he was in the vicinity.

It wasn't until he helped her out of the car that she did chance a look in his direction. Brand had to smile. Her eyes seemed so round and wide, an aircraft carrier could have sailed through them.

"He said yet, you idiot." She repeated the sentence two or three times once they were inside the house. Brand found it amusing the way she talked to herself. Without telling him what she was doing, she walked, as if in a daze, into the kitchen and started assembling a pot of coffee.

Brand hadn't a clue what she was mumbling about. He wasn't interested in coffee, either, but since she hadn't asked him, he didn't say so.

"There's something you should know," he began. Then he changed his mind. This wasn't the time. He needed to taste her again.

"What?" She sounded as though she were coming out of a coma.

"Come here first."

She walked over to him as though she were sleep-walking, her steps sluggish and her look disoriented.

"Kiss me first," Brand whispered, "then I'll tell you."

As if she were in a stupor, she planted her hands on his chest, then stood on tiptoe and brushed her lips lightly over his. Unable to hold himself back any longer,

Brand wrapped his arms around her, pulled her close and buried his face in her neck, savoring her softness.

For the last several days he'd been wondering what it was about Erin that preyed so heavily on his mind. After kissing her, he understood. He felt strong when he was with her. Strong emotionally. Strong physically. When they were together, he became another Samson. She gave him a feeling of being needed.

She needed him, too. She'd never admit it, of course, never deliberately tell him as much, but it was true.

"You said we needed to talk," she reminded him. With what seemed like a good deal of effort, she moved away from him.

"Yes," Brand answered softly, and rubbed a hand along the back of his neck. "What are you doing every day for the next four days?"

"Why?" A worried look dominated her face. Then her eyes, which had been so gentle and submissive only seconds before, flashed to life with a fire that all but scorched Brand. "You don't need to tell me. You're only going to be in Seattle four more days."

Four

"Why are you so angry?" Brand demanded, not understanding Erin. He was being as honest as he knew how to be with her, and she was looking at him as though he'd just announced he was an ax murderer.

"You know... You know..." She walked over to the cupboard and slammed two ceramic mugs down with enough force to crack the kitchen counter. "From the beginning you've known how I feel about navy men."

"I didn't mislead you," he reminded her in as reasonable a tone as he could muster. "You knew from the first I was on a short assignment."

Grudgingly she answered him with an abrupt nod.

If Brand was upset about anything, it was the fact that he'd waited so long to do as his friend Casey Mac-Namera had asked and checked up on the old man's daughter. If Brand had contacted her the first week he'd arrived in Seattle, a lot of things might have worked out differently.

"Here's your coffee." The hot liquid sloshed over the edges of the mug when Erin set it on the glass table top.

He pulled out a beige cushioned chair and sat. His

hands cupped the mug while he waited, giving Erin the time she needed to sort through her feelings.

It took her far longer than he expected. She paced the kitchen ten or fifteen times, pausing twice, her eyes revealing her confusion and her doubt. Both times she glared at him as though he'd committed unspeakable crimes. After a while, her brisk steps slowed, and she started talking to herself, mumbling something unintelligible.

"Am I forgiven?" Brand asked when she sat in the chair across the table from him.

"Sure," she answered, giving him a weak smile. "What's there to forgive?"

"I'm pleased you feel that way." Because of the abrupt switch in her behavior, Brand didn't feel as confident.

"Meeting you has…been an interesting experience" was all she'd say.

Brand felt the same way himself. "Can I see you tomorrow?"

"I'm busy."

Brand frowned, and a sinking sensation attacked the pit of his stomach. "Doing what?"

"I don't believe that's any of your concern."

Oh, boy, here it comes, he mused. "But it is. If you're attending church services, then I'll go with you. If you've promised a friend you'd help them move, then I'll cart boxes myself." If Erin thought the Irish could be stubborn, she had yet to butt heads with the German in him.

"Brand, please don't make this any more difficult than it already is. I can't change who I am for you. I told you from the first I don't want to become involved with anyone in the military, and I meant it. I don't know why you can't accept that. And I don't even want to know. You're leaving, and when it comes right down to it, I'm glad. It's for the best."

"I'm stationed in Hawaii. It's not all that—"

"I have no intention of flying off to the islands for an occasional weekend, nor can I afford to, so don't even suggest it."

"The only thing I was going to suggest was the two of us getting to know each other better." He strove to sound casual, although there wasn't a single bone in his entire body that was indifferent to Erin. She affected him far more strongly than any other woman he'd ever known. Generally he was the one seeking an out in the relationship.

Erin sipped her coffee, more relaxed now. Centered was the term she'd used earlier, and he could see it in her. She'd made her decision, and neither hell nor high water would sway her from it.

"Will you see me again?" He didn't like asking a second time. It went against his pride, but he was learning that when it came to Erin MacNamera he was willing to give more than with anyone else.

Her nod took a long time coming, but when it did, Brand felt the tension ease.

"On one condition," she added.

"Name it."

Her beautiful dark eyes found his, and he noted how lost and bewildered she looked. "What is it?"

"No more...of what happened today in the park."

"You don't want me to kiss you again?" Brand was sure he'd misunderstood her. They were just beginning to know each other, learn about each other, and it seemed ridiculous for them to put their relationship into a holding pattern now.

"I'm offering you my friendship, Brand, nothing more." He wanted Erin for more than a friend, but saying so would likely cut off any chance he had with her. If those were the ground rules she was setting, then far be it for him to argue with her. He fully intended to do whatever he could to change her mind, but she'd learn that soon enough.

"All right," he said, grinning at her. "We'll be friends."

"No more of that, either," she countered sharply.

"What?" Brand hadn't a clue what she was talking about.

"That smile. The navy could launch missiles with that smile of yours."

Was that a fact? Brand mused. He'd have to remember that and use it often.

Agreeing to this dinner date wasn't one of her most brilliant moves, Erin decided later. Brand was scheduled to fly out of the Whidbey Island Naval Station early the following morning. They'd talked several times by phone, but she hadn't seen Brand since their date on Saturday afternoon.

Erin hated admitting what a good time she'd had with the lieutenant j.g. They'd toured Sand Point and had a picnic at Woodland Park Zoo, although the only animal she'd encountered was of the human variety. And something else had happened Saturday, something she kept trying to forget and couldn't.

Brand had kissed her senseless.

It caused her cheeks to burn every time she thought about the way she'd abandoned herself in his arms. No one had ever told her kissing could be so wonderful... especially the way Brand was doing it. She felt achy and restless every time she dwelled on it. Her heart would start to beat, slow and sluggish, and the heat would start creeping through her. A warm excitement would fill her, and she could find no way of explaining it. The heat started low in her abdomen and grew into an achy restlessness that disturbed her beyond anything she'd ever experienced.

Then her breasts would start throbbing the way they had when he'd pressed her against the blanket and whispered there were other places he longed to kiss her, too. It had been all she could do not to ask him to take her nipples in his mouth... She wished he had—which was a crazy idea, since they'd been in a public place.

It wouldn't have stopped there. Erin knew that as well as she knew her own name.

Brand awoke carnal instincts in her. She'd never guessed she was capable of feeling sensual sensations as strong as this. Erin had always assumed she knew herself well. Apparently that wasn't the case after all. Not if Brand could evoke such an overwhelming reaction in her with a series of wet kisses.

The doorbell chimed, and, inhaling softly, she braced herself, walked across the living room and opened the front door to Brand.

"Hi." His gaze gave her an appreciative sweep. "Are you ready?"

She nodded. Damn, it was good to see him again. She hated to admit that much, and she gave herself a quick mental shake. Somehow, someway, she was going to get through this evening, and once she did it would be over between them. He could go his way and she could go hers, and never the twain would meet.

Once they were in the car, Erin suggested a Mexican restaurant that was less than a mile from her house.

The food was good and cheap. All Erin was looking to do was to survive this evening with her heart intact.

The walls of the El Lindo were made of white stucco and decorated with several huge sombreros in bright shades of turquoise and gold. Erin studied the pictures on the wall, which were displayed in wide, bulky frames, in an effort to avoid looking at Brand. She dared not allow her eyes to meet his for fear of reviving memories from their last encounter.

"So where are you headed to next?" she asked, making sure her voice contained just the right amount of friendliness. A tortilla chip commanded her full attention as she dipped it in salsa.

"Probably San Francisco."

"When?" It felt good to have the upper hand in the conversation, Erin mused.

"Soon. A month or two from now, maybe less. Have you been there?"

"I don't think there are more than a handful of naval bases where I haven't been." She made light of the fact, when in reality it was a source of fierce bitterness. The comment was made with just enough sarcasm for Brand to recognize she wouldn't return to that lifestyle again for anything or anyone in the world, including him. He must have gotten the message, because his face tightened into a frown.

Erin ordered the cheese-and-onion enchiladas, her favorite, and Brand asked for the chili verde. Both dinners were excellent, and they lingered over coffee, talking about a variety of bland but safe subjects. Brand told her about his two best friends, Alex Romano and Catherine Fredrickson. Like him, Alex was a surface warfare officer. Catherine was an attorney. All three had been stationed in Hawaii for four years.

When Brand pulled into the driveway in front of her house, her hand was already on the handle. She had a farewell, so-glad-we-had-this-chance-to-meet talk all prepared, but she wasn't allowed to say one word of it.

Brand reached across the seat and gripped her hand. "Invite me in for coffee."

"We just finished having a cup."

"Invite me in anyway."

"I…don't know if that's such a good idea."

"Yes, it is. Trust me."

"All right." But she wasn't pleased about it.

She led the way into her compact home. Buying a house was one of the first things she'd done after being hired for the Community Action Program. The payments were high, but Erin didn't mind the sacrifice, because for the first time in her life she didn't have to worry about being forced to move. No one was going to casually announce it was time to relocate. She didn't need to worry that everything she owned was going to be stripped away from her almost overnight.

For the first time in her life, she was planting roots. They weren't as deep as she wanted, not yet, but she intended for them to be. This home was hers and hers alone. It was her security, her defense, her shelter. Falling crazy in love with a navy man would threaten everything she'd strived to build for herself in the past several years, and she adamantly refused to allow it to happen.

Once they were inside, Erin turned on the lights and pointed to the bulky stuffed chair angled in front of the television. "Make yourself comfortable. Would you like some coffee?"

"Please."

Brand followed her into the kitchen. "We've avoided the subject all evening," he said, standing directly behind her. He wasn't actually pinning her against the counter, but he made it plain he could if he wanted to.

"We don't need to talk about it."

"We do," he countered swiftly. "I'm leaving. Trust me, I don't want to go, but I am. It's part of my job. I don't know when I'll be back, but I will be."

She tried to look as uninterested as she could. "Look me up when you do," she said flippantly.

Brand frowned anew. "Erin MacNamera, that wasn't nice."

"I apologize." She didn't completely understand what she'd said that was so wrong. If Brand thought she was going to sit around moping for him, he was dead wrong.

Yes, she enjoyed his company, and when he left she'd miss him for a while, but after a week or so she wouldn't give him more than the occasional fleeting thought.

"Kiss me," Brand instructed.

Erin's heart went still. She'd prefer leaping off the Tacoma Narrows Bridge to granting Brand Davis the privileges she had the day of their picnic. He might as well ask her to light a stick of dynamite and wave it around for everyone to see what a fool she was.

She tried to break away from him. "I can't... I have no intention of kissing you."

"Just once, to say goodbye."

"Brand..."

His hands drifted up and down her lifeless arms, bringing her against him. Erin didn't know who moved, him or her.

"If you won't kiss me, then you leave me no choice but to kiss you." He angled his head to one side and placed his moist, hot mouth over hers.

The kiss was unbearably good; it was all Erin could

do not to melt at his feet. Somehow she managed to stand stiff and straight, not granting him an inch.

Brand appeared unconcerned by her lack of response. He drew her wrists up and placed her hands around his neck, then locked his own arms tight around her waist, lifting her against him.

Erin didn't want to respond, had promised herself she wouldn't, but before she knew what was happening her lips had parted and her tongue was eagerly searching out his. If only he weren't so gentle. So tender and generous. Erin felt as if she were drowning in sheer ecstasy. She moaned, and the sound seemed to encourage Brand all the more.

He kissed her again and again, and it was even better than his lovemaking had been in the park. Even more wonderful, and she hadn't thought that was possible. Brand's kisses were long and deep, and before she knew it Erin was clinging to him mindlessly.

He released her slowly, letting her slide down his front. Once her feet were firmly planted on the floor, his hand closed over her breast. Erin whimpered—it was a soft sound of pleasure—as he battled with the buttons of her silk blouse, peeling it open. He unfastened her bra and filled his palms with her lush fullness. His sigh went through her like a spear, and as hard as she tried, she couldn't keep from reacting.

Her nipples were so hard, they burned and throbbed and ached in a way she'd never experienced until now. Her hands were in Brand's hair and her head was thrown back as she squirmed against him. She wanted his mouth on her breasts, just the way she'd imagined. Just the way she'd dreamed about for the past two nights.

As if reading her thoughts, Brand gave her what she yearned to experience, drawing her nipple into his moist, warm mouth and sucking lightly, then strongly, then lightly again. A sensation of pleasure so hot it bordered on pain flashed through her like lightning. It was all Erin could do to hold still. If he continued this much longer, she'd be climbing the walls. Literally.

The sensation was incredible, beyond description. She wanted him, needed him. Soon her own fingers were busy. She was so impatient, she nearly ripped the buttons off his shirt. It became imperative that she do to him what he was doing to her. She didn't know if this was something women did to men, but she longed to return the pleasure he was giving her.

With her arms wrapped securely around his neck, she nuzzled the hollow at his throat, sliding her tongue back and forth in lazy circles while she fiddled with the opening on his shirt. Once it was free, she spread it back from his shoulders.

Erin had never seen a man as close to perfect as Brand. He was stronger than anyone she'd ever known. And he smelled so good, of spice and bay rum. He'd probably sprayed himself with an aphrodisiac before meeting her for dinner, but Erin was beyond the point of caring.

Brand's muscular body felt hot to the touch. She was unable to keep her hands still. They roamed up and down the sides of his waist, then over the lightly haired planes of his broad chest until she inadvertently touched the tight buds of his nipples. When she did, she was gratified by the shudder that went through him, starting with a rippling motion in his massive shoulders and working its way down.

"Erin," he pleaded, "no more."

She ignored him. After all, he ignored her, and fair was fair. Her mouth fastened over the tight pearl of his nipple, and she gave him the same treatment he had given her. He tasted as wonderful as he smelled.

"Erin," he pleaded a second time. She paused long enough to sigh, loving the sound of his voice, so low and husky. It spurred her on more powerfully than any words he might have said.

"We've got to stop before it's too late," he warned, working his hands between them.

Her response was to curl her fingers more tightly in the hair on his chest and tug lightly.

"Erin."

This time something in his voice did capture her attention. His hands were on her shoulders, and he heaved a giant breath as he wrapped his arms around her waist. Erin buried her face in his neck, embarrassed by the things she'd done and allowed him to do.

She rarely cried, but she felt the salty wetness coat her cheeks.

"Casey would shoot me dead if he knew how close I've come to making love to you."

Erin abruptly broke away from him, her eyes clouded with confusion. She nearly stumbled, finding herself off balance. Nevertheless, she glared up at Brand. "How did you know my father's name is Casey?"

Brand closed his eyes slowly, as if he'd inadvertently allowed a top government secret to pass from his lips. "That's a long story."

Erin jerked away and turned her back to him while her fingers frantically worked to assemble her bra and blouse. Her hands were trembling so badly, it made the task nearly impossible. When she'd finished, she walked across the room and removed her mug from the table, simply because she needed something to cling to. She felt as if she were being beaten by an invisible force, shaken so hard her teeth were rattling.

"How do you know my father?" she demanded a second time, and her voice trembled as severely as her fingers.

"We're friends. We worked together a few years back, hit it off, and have kept in touch ever since," Brand announced, looking none too pleased. If anything, he looked downright irritated. "When Casey learned I was flying into Seattle for this assignment, he asked me to check up on you. Apparently he's worried that you're working too hard. Your father's a good man, Erin."

That wasn't exactly the way Erin would have described him at the moment. He was a meddling, interfering old fool who couldn't keep out of her life!

"So Dad sent you out to spy on me?" she demanded coolly.

Brand nodded reluctantly.

"When we met at the Blue Lagoon...it wasn't by chance?"

"Not exactly. I followed you there."

Erin closed her eyes and placed her hand over her mouth. "Dear heaven."

"I know it sounds bad."

"Bad?" she cried. "You... I was set up by my own father!" She started pacing, because standing still was impossible. Turning abruptly, she glared at him with eyes she was sure conveyed her feelings exactly. "What about everything else? The kissing, the...petting. Did Dad ask you to indoctrinate me into—"

"Erin, no." He expelled his breath sharply and jammed his fingers into his scalp with enough force to remove a fistful of hair. "Okay, I made a mistake. I should have told you the first night that your father and

I are friends. If you want to condemn me for that, go ahead, I deserve it. But everything else was for real."

Erin didn't know whether she believed him or not, but at this point it didn't matter. She crossed her arms and glared at the ceiling, trying fruitlessly to gather her thoughts and make sense of what had happened between them.

"I liked you the minute I saw you," Brand admitted slowly, "and the feeling has intensified each and every day since. I don't know what's happening between us. It's crazy, but I feel... Hell, I don't know what I feel, other than the fact I don't want to lose you."

"That's what I can't make you understand," she cried. "You lost me the minute I realized you were navy."

"Erin..."

"I think you should go." The lump in her throat made it impossible for her to speak distinctly. When Brand didn't budge, she pointed the way to the door. "Please, just leave."

Brand hesitated, then nodded. "All right, I can see I've really messed this up. At the rate I'm going, I'll only make matters worse. I'll try to give you a call before I leave tomorrow."

She nodded, although she hadn't a clue what she was agreeing to.

"I've got your address."

Once more she moved her head, willing to concede anything as long as he would get out of her home, her safe haven, and leave her alone. She felt shocked as she rarely had been. Shaken and hurt. To the best of her knowledge, her father had never done anything like this before. Once she got through with him, she would damn well make sure he wouldn't again.

Brand paused at the front door. "I'm not saying goodbye to you, Erin." He stood there for the longest moment without moving. His eyes were filled with regret. It seemed that he wanted to say something more but changed his mind.

Erin looked away, not wanting to encourage him to do anything but leave her in peace. Or whatever was left of that precious commodity.

The door closed, and she glanced up to discover that Brand was gone. A breath rattled through her lungs as she continued to stare into space.

It was over. Brand Davis had left.

Brand closed his eyes as he listened to the message on Erin's answering machine for the tenth time. He was paying long-distance rates to speak to a stupid tape recorder. Not that it had done any good. Not once had she returned his call.

She hadn't even tried.

He'd contacted her every day since he'd returned to Hawaii, but he hadn't spoken to her yet. It didn't seem to matter what time of the day he phoned, she wasn't home. Or if she was, she wasn't answering.

He'd tried writing, too. Brand wasn't much of a letter writer, but each night since he'd been back he had sat down faithfully and written to Erin. Not just short notes, either. Real letters, sometimes two and three pages each. He wrote about things he'd rarely shared with long-time friends. He wasn't revealing deep, dark secrets, just feelings. Feelings a man wouldn't easily convey to another human being unless that person was someone special. Erin was more than special. Until he'd left Seattle, Brand hadn't realized how important Casey's daughter had become to him.

Ten days into his letter-writing campaign, he had

yet to receive so much as a postcard from her. It didn't take a master's degree for him to figure out that his sweet Irish rose had no intention of answering his letters, either.

Rarely had Brand felt more discouraged. He was frustrated enough to contact Casey MacNamera.

"Casey, you old goat, it's Brand," he said, speaking into the telephone receiver. The long-distance wire hummed between them. Casey had retired in Pensacola, Florida.

"Well if it isn't Face Davis, himself. How you doing, boy?"

"Good. Real good." Which was only a slight exaggeration.

"I take it you told Erin about me asking you to check up on her. Good grief, that girl nearly had a conniption right on the phone. I don't think I've ever heard her more shooting mad. Nearly shouted me ears off, she did." The potbellied MCPO paused to chuckle, as if the whole matter were one of great amusement.

"I didn't mean to give it away," Brand said by way of apology. "We sort of hit it off... Erin and me." He paused, hoping Casey would make some comment either way. He didn't.

"That oldest girl of mine has got a temper on her. If you ever cross her, the best advice I can give you is to stand back and protect yourself from the fireworks."

"Speaking of Erin," Brand said, delicately leading into the purpose of this call, "how is she?"

"I can't rightly say." Casey paused and chuckled again. "She didn't get around to telling me anything about her health. She was far more concerned about giving me a solid piece of her mind."

"Did she say anything about me?"

Casey paused. "Not really. Only that she didn't appreciate the fact I'd sent you her way."

"I appreciated it."

"You did?" Casey's voice lowered suspiciously. "What makes you say that?"

"Erin and I dated two or three times. You've done yourself proud, you old goat. Erin's a wonderful woman."

"She's not your type."

Brand was about to take offense at that. "Why isn't she?"

"I thought you liked your women sleek and sophisticated. Erin's not like that. Not in the least. The girl's meat-and-potatoes."

"I like Erin. In fact, I like her a whole lot. I hope that doesn't offend you, because I intend to see more of her."

Brand expected a long list of possible responses from Casey. It didn't include laughter, but laugh was exactly what Casey MacNamera did. In fact, he burst into loud chuckles, as if Brand had just told the funniest joke of the year.

"Good luck, Brand. You're going to need it with my Erin. That woman's stubborner than a Tennessee mule. I don't want to discourage you, but she won't have anything to do with someone in the navy."

"I plan to change her mind."

"As far as I can see, you've got a snowball's chance in hell of ever doing that. Now, before I forget it, tell me how it is you got chosen for this cushy assignment. I should have known that handsome face of yours was going to get you a boondoggle one of these days. Where you headed to next?"

"San Francisco." And none too soon, as far as Brand

was concerned, because the city was only six hundred miles from Seattle. And that was a hell of a lot closer than Hawaii.

"Oh, please, don't let there be another letter from Brand," Erin prayed aloud as she pulled into her driveway. For twenty days straight, she'd received a letter from him every day.

Twenty days.

She walked up to the mailbox on her porch and lifted the lid. Two flyers and a bill. There wasn't a letter.

Unreasonably disappointed, she sorted through everything again, and then stuck her hand back inside the mailbox. It was there, tucked down in the back.

Erin didn't know whether she should be upset or relieved. What did it matter? She'd been of two minds from the moment she'd met Brand Davis.

Two minds and one heart.

Opening her front door with her key, Erin walked inside her home and slapped everything down on the kitchen counter. Making herself a cup of tea, she leafed through the flyers and set the bill aside.

Once the tea was made, she reached for Brand's letter, opening it with her index finger. She counted five pages. Five long, single-spaced, handwritten pages. Wouldn't he ever stop?

"Oh, please, make him stop writing," she pleaded once more as her gaze hungrily scanned each word, canceling out her prayer.

When the first letter had arrived, Erin had righteously marched to the outside garbage can and tossed it inside. She'd refused to read a single line of what that deceiver had written. From there, she'd made herself dinner, muttering sanctimonious epithets directed at the lieutenant j.g. and then headed off to her Women in Transition class, feeling downright pious about having tossed out the letter.

The feeling hadn't lasted long.

At nine-thirty, when she'd returned from class, she'd reached for her flashlight and, without a pause, started rooting through the garbage until she found the envelope.

She'd called herself every word for fool that she could think of in the days since. As much as she hated to admit it, each night she rushed home, eager for word from Brand.

She was living in a fool's paradise. Nothing would come of this. First off, she had no intention of ever answering him.

Nor did she intend to see him again. Their differences were irreconcilable, as far as she could discern. There were no compromises for her and Brand. He was military, and she adamantly refused to fall in love with someone in the armed services—especially someone in the navy.

Each and every time they'd been together, they'd hashed over their differences. There was no way to arbitrate this issue, no meeting in the middle. Nothing he could say would change her mind. Nothing she could say would alter his. Rehashing their differences would only be a waste of time and energy, and Erin had enough on her mind as it was.

The phone rang just as she was turning the last page of his letter. He was giving a humorous account of something he and his friend Alex had done. Without thinking, she reached for the receiver, not giving a thought to letting the recorder answer for her as had been her habit of late.

"Hello," she said softly.

"Erin? Erin, is that really you?"

It was Brand, and he sounded absolutely amazed that she'd answered the phone.

Five

"Ah…" Erin stammered, resisting the urge to replace the receiver and escape talking to Brand. That would be a coward's way of handling the situation. She and Brand were bound to have a showdown one time or another, and the longer she delayed the confrontation the more difficult it would be.

"Okay, just listen," Brand said, speaking with authority, his voice slightly high-pitched, his words rushed. "I've got everything I want to say all planned."

"Brand, please…"

"You can tell me whatever it is you want when I'm finished, okay?"

She nodded, closed her eyes, then whispered, "All right."

"You asked me once why I continued to ask you out. Do you remember that?"

"Yes." She did, all too well.

"I thought I had it figured out before I left Seattle. I liked you from the first. You're a caring, warm, generous woman, and anyone spending time with you would soon realize that. I noticed it long before the day at the zoo when you were telling me about the older woman in your class who's going through such a difficult time. You barely knew her, yet you sincerely cared about her and her problems."

"What has all this got to do with anything?"

"Just be patient. I'm coming to that."

Erin was so stiff, the muscles in her lower spine were starting to ache. She stood and pressed her hand to the small of her back and paced, walking as far as the telephone cord would stretch and then back again. She longed to rush him along, longed for this to be over as soon as possible. How painful it was, how much more difficult than she'd thought it would be.

"I realized shortly after our picnic that being with you makes me feel strong and good. Strong emotionally, strong physically. I realize that doesn't make a whole lot of sense to you right now. I'm not even sure I can explain it any better than that. Maybe later I can, but for now it isn't the most important thing." Brand paused and inhaled a single, choppy breath. He was speaking so fast that it was difficult for Erin to understand him. And the long-distance hum wasn't helping matters any.

"Brand…"

"Let me finish."

Erin's mind filled with enough arguments to sink a battleship. "All right." Only she wished he'd hurry so she could say what needed to be said and be finished with it.

"The last three weeks away from you have taught me some valuable lessons. I've written you every day."

She didn't need to be reminded of that. Every single message he'd mailed her was neatly stacked on her desk. She'd reread them so often, most had been committed to memory.

"Sitting down and putting my thoughts on paper

has cleared up a lot of the confusion I've been feeling since I returned to Hawaii. It hit me almost immediately that..." He hesitated, as though he were fearful of her response. "I'm in love with you, Erin."

"In love with me?" she repeated, as though in a trance.

"I know you don't want to hear that, but I can't and won't apologize for the way I feel. For the first time in my life, I'm in love. I thought I was a hundred times before, but this is different. Better. Did you hear me, Erin? I love you."

Erin squeezed her eyes closed. Of all the things he had to say, all the nonsensical, absurd, foolish things... why, oh, why, did he have to tell her that?

"Say something," he pleaded. "Anything."

All the arguments she had lined up in her mind fell like dominoes, crashing against one another, tumbling into nothingness. She was left speechless.

"Erin, sweetheart, are you still there?"

"Yes." Her voice rose an octave above its normal range. "I'm here."

"I know it's something of a shock, blurting it out like this over the phone, but I swear to you I couldn't hold it inside another second. Haven't you noticed how I've signed my letters recently?"

She had. She'd preferred to ignore the obvious, even when it was slapping her in the face.

"A relationship won't work with us... We're too different."

"We'll make it work."

Just the way he said it, without leaving room for doubt, caused Erin to wonder if it was possible. Was loving someone enough to alleviate all the problems? Was it enough to gain a compromise where there wasn't

one? Maybe it was, after all. Brand sounded so confident, so convinced.

Erin's hold tightened around the telephone receiver.
"I don't see how."

"Erin, sweetheart…damn, I wish I was there right
now. It's hell being so far away from you."

"You'll always be away from me." The truth was as
cold and lifeless as ice water. How easy it was to forget
he was navy. For a moment, just the slightest moment,
she could feel herself lulled into believing a relationship was possible for them. If she allowed this false
thinking to continue, he'd talk her out of everything
that was important to her, everything she'd struggled
to build. In the nick of time she realized what she was
doing and pulled herself up short.

"I'll be away, yes," Brand argued, "but not all the
time, and when we're together I'll make up for lost
time."

"No."

"What do you mean, no?"

"Claiming you love me doesn't change anything."
The words were easy enough to say, but she wasn't
completely sure they were true. What she had to do
was pretend they were and pray he didn't challenge her
with a lot of questions.

"It does as far as I'm concerned."

"Brand, I'm sorry, I really am, but I can't see where
discussing this is going to make a difference. You love
the navy. I don't. You want to stay in the service, and
I'd rather leap off a cliff naked than involve my life with
anything that has to do with the military. We can talk
until we're blue in the face, but it isn't going to change
who or what we are."

Her words were greeted by a strained silence.

"You'd prefer to leap off a cliff naked?" Amusement echoed behind his words.

Perhaps it wasn't the best way to explain her feelings, but it was one of the worst things she could think of doing, although she had to admit it was nonsensical.

"Sweetheart, listen to me."

"No, please, I can't. It won't do any good. The best thing you can do for the both of us is forget we ever met. It isn't going to work, and prolonging the inevitable will only cause us both more pain."

"I love you. I can't—"

"You're not listening to me," she cried, hating the way her voice trembled. "You never have listened to me, and that's the problem."

Once more Brand was silent, and this time the lack of sound seemed to throb between them like a living thing.

"All right, Erin, I'm listening."

She drew in a tattered breath and started again. "What I'm trying to explain is the plain truth, as painful as it is to accept. It will never work between us. Neither of us can adjust our needs because we happen to be physically attracted to each other."

"I'm more than physically attracted to you."

Erin decided the best thing to do was ignore that statement. "I'm honored that you would feel as strongly about me as you apparently do. Personally, I think you're wonderful, too, but that doesn't make everything right. It just doesn't…even though that's what we want."

A moment passed before he spoke. "In other words, you're saying you don't love me. Or, more appropriately phrased, you won't love me."

"Yes."

He used a one-word expletive that was meant to

shock her, and did. "You're in love with me, Erin. You can deny it if you want, but it's the truth."

"I imagine your ego chooses to believe that. If that's the case, then all I can say is fine, believe what you want." She might have sounded as confident as a judge, but on the inside she'd rarely been more unnerved.

"Say it to me, then."

Erin closed her eyes and swallowed tightly. "Say what?"

"That you don't love me." A strained silence passed before he demanded it of her again. "Say it!"

God help her, Erin couldn't do it.

"Be sure and put enough emphasis on the words to make it believable," he advised, "because I know you're lying, if not to me, then to yourself."

"You have such colossal nerve." She tried to make her statement sound as if she were highly amused by his attitude.

"Say it," he demanded a third time.

A moment passed before she was able to do as he requested. She tried to speak once, but when she opened her mouth she felt her throat start to close up, and she aborted the effort.

"Erin?"

"All right, if you insist. I don't love you."

"Do you mean it?" he asked her softly, sounding almost amused.

If only he didn't make it so damn difficult. She was furious with him, furious enough to put an end to this torment. "Yes, I'm sure. Now kindly leave me alone."

"As you wish." His voice was incredibly low, filled with so many emotions that she couldn't identify them all. "Goodbye, my sweet Irish rose. Have a good life— I sure as hell plan to."

The line was disconnected while she stood holding on to the receiver. For the longest time Erin didn't move. She stood exactly as she was, the phone pressed to her ear, the drone of the line buzzing like angry, swarming bees around her.

The wetness that spilled onto her face came as a surprise. She raised her hand, and her fingertips smeared the moisture across the high arch of her cheek.

"I will have a good life," she choked out. "I promise I will."

"I hate to keep troubling you," Marilyn said, stepping up to Erin's scarred desk. The class had been dismissed for the evening, and Erin was sticking the leftover handouts inside her leather briefcase.

Over the past several weeks, Erin had been keeping close tabs on Marilyn, charting her progress. The older woman had looked something like a baked apple when she'd first come into class. Shriveled up and burdened by the weight of her problems. She'd worn the same dress and the same pair of shoes and little, if any, makeup. All that had gradually changed over the weeks. Marilyn had hired an attorney, gotten a part-time job with a department store and signed up for driving school. She walked a little taller and held her head higher. The going hadn't been easy. Subject to depression and fits of rage, she'd recently confessed to Erin that she'd destroyed one entire wall of the family home.

"It's no trouble, Marilyn. It's always good to talk to you."

"I just wanted you to know I got my driver's license this afternoon."

"Congratulations!"

Marilyn's grin went from ear to ear. "I didn't ever

think I'd be able to do it, but the examiner who gave me the road test was very understanding." Excitement lit up her eyes. "I don't mind telling you, I was nervous in the beginning. I backed out of the parking space the wrong way and then went over the curb on the way out of the parking lot. I thought for sure the examiner was going to fail me, but then I got to thinking about the things you've been saying in class, and I decided to make the best of it."

"And you passed?"

"By two points. They didn't exactly throw a parade in my honor, and the examiner did talk to me two or three minutes afterward, suggesting that I take it nice and easy for a while, which I intend to do. When he told me I'd passed the test, I got so excited, I nearly kissed the man."

The picture that scene presented in Erin's mind was amusing enough to bring a smile to her lips. She hadn't been doing a lot of smiling lately. Not since her phone conversation with Brand.

Over and over she'd played back their discussion in her mind. There were better ways of handling the situation with Brand. Yet she'd accomplished what she'd set out to do. Her methods hadn't been the best, but then, she'd never handled anything like this before.

A few days after speaking to Brand for the last time, she'd sat down and written her father a letter hot enough to blister the mailman's fingers. She'd poured out her outrage, claimed he'd insulted her intelligence and her sense of pride and demanded that he stay out of her life.

In the morning she'd tossed the letter into the garbage, where it belonged. Her father couldn't be blamed because she'd fallen in love with Brand Davis. As much as she'd like to fault her overprotective parent, all he'd done was ask Brand to check up on her. Everything else that had happened was strictly between her and the lieutenant j.g.

Feeling pleased for Marilyn, Erin drove back to her house, showered and readied for bed. She hadn't eaten anything before class, and an inspection of the freezer disclosed one frozen Salisbury steak entrée with sick-looking watery mashed potatoes and cubed carrots. The entrée looked as though it might have been left by the previous owner of the house.

Unable to shake the melancholy feeling, Erin hadn't taken the time to buy groceries that weekend. And she didn't want to traipse into the local grocery store in her flannel nightgown at this late hour.

It was either the entrée or a can of lima beans.

"Why would you buy lima beans?" she asked herself aloud. "You don't even like them."

The habit of talking to herself was becoming more pronounced, she noted, wondering what she should do about it, if anything.

Standing in front of the microwave in her bare feet, her hair wet and glistening from her shower, Erin watched the digital numbers count down. The smell of the Salisbury steak wasn't proving to be all that promising.

The timer on the microwave dinged at the same time as the doorbell chimed. It took Erin a second to realize the direction of the second bell. Her gaze swiveled from the microwave to the front door and then back again while her mind raced.

No one she knew would be visiting this time of night. But then, it wasn't likely that a burglar would announce himself, either.

Walking barefoot across the carpet, she squinted and

peered out the peephole to find an eye from the other side looking back at her. She leaped back and placed her hand over her heart. She'd have recognized that eye anywhere.

Brand.

"Come on, Erin, open up. I'm in no mood to be left standing on your porch."

Pulling back the dead bolt, Erin yanked open the door. She held on to the knob and resisted the urge to launch herself straight into his arms. That fact alone answered every question she'd been taunting herself with the last two days.

Brand walked inside and set down his bag. He looked like hell. Worse. As if he'd been dragged under a car or forced to sleep in an upright position for three nights straight. A two-day beard darkened his face, and his eyes were bloodshot.

"What's that god-awful smell?" he demanded.

"My dinner." She couldn't keep from staring at him. Even though she'd never seen him look worse, he was still the most incredibly handsome man she'd even seen in her life. Incredibly wonderful, too.

"What are you doing eating dinner this late?"

"What time is it?"

"Hell, I don't know. I just spent the last twenty hours on every conceivable means of transportation you can name. For all I know, it could be noon sometime in July."

"It's April."

"Fool's Day, no doubt."

"No." As hard as she tried, she couldn't stop staring at him. Even now, while they were carrying on a two-way conversation, she couldn't be entirely sure it was really him and not some figment of her imagination.

She resisted the urge to reach out and touch him, which was even more powerful than the need to be in his arms.

"What are you doing here?"

His eyes met hers. "I don't know anymore. I asked myself that same question about the time I was on my third means of military transport."

"How long is your pass for?"

"Four days, but to be honest, I don't know how much of that time is left. Maybe I should just say what I want to say and be done with it, then get the hell out of here."

"Do you want something to eat?" That she should offer him anything was something of a joke, considering that she was warming a prehistoric frozen entrée for herself.

"Not if you're planning on serving the same thing you're eating. It smells like..." He left the rest unsaid, because it was apparent what he meant.

"I'll order a pizza." Somehow that made perfect sense to Erin. The fact that he was with her, standing inside her home, didn't, but she hadn't figured out a way to deal with that just yet.

"I think I should sit down," Brand announced unexpectedly. He walked across her carpet and lowered himself onto the sofa, which was against the outside wall. Then he paused and looked around, as if he couldn't quite believe he was with her.

"I'll just be a minute," she said, walking backward, thinking he might vanish if she took her eyes away from him. The flyer she'd received in the mail a few days earlier from a national pizza chain was pinned to her bulletin board along with the discount coupon. With that in hand, she punched out the phone number and ordered a deluxe pepperoni pizza.

By the time she returned to the living room, Brand was sound asleep on her sofa.

Brand woke not knowing where he was. He sat bolt upright, kicking aside several blankets, and glanced around him. He still didn't know. The feeling was an eerie one.

Exhausted, he rubbed a hand down his face and gave his eyes time to adjust to the thick darkness, then slowly, thoughtfully, reviewed what he did remember.

In a flash it came to him. He was at Erin's house.

Erin. If anyone had told him even two months ago that he'd go through so many trials to get to a woman, he would have sworn they were nuts. If he'd ever doubted his love for her, making it from Hawaii to Seattle by way of Japan and Alaska proved otherwise.

And for what? He wasn't going to be able to talk any sense into her. Nothing had worked yet, but that wasn't going to stop him. Casey had claimed she was as stubborn as a Tennessee mule, and the old man was right.

But, damn it all, Brand couldn't turn his back on love and simply walk away. The way he figured it, he had only one chance with her, and that was face-to-face.

Standing, he turned on a couple of lights and noted the time. Five a.m. He found his suitcase and showered.

By the time Erin stirred, he had a pot of coffee brewed.

"Good morning," she said, standing in the doorway. She raised the back of her hand to her mouth and yawned loudly. "There's some leftover pizza in the refrigerator if you're hungry."

"You should have woke me."

"What makes you think I didn't try."

"I wouldn't wake up?"

"The entire Third Infantry couldn't have stirred you."

He felt a bit sheepish about that. "I'm sorry. I didn't mean to crash at your place."

"Don't worry about it. If nothing else, you've given my neighbors a reason to introduce themselves." Yawning once more, she made her way into the bathroom.

It was difficult for Brand to keep his eyes off her. She was disheveled and warm from her bed. Without the least bit of trouble, his imagination kicked into gear. It was much too easy to picture himself in bed with Erin. He could feel her cuddled up against him, her warm, pale skin caressing his. He would put his hands on her breasts and lift them so that they filled his palms. Her nipples would tighten even before he could graze them with his thumbs.

Brand's breath became quick and shallow, and he half closed his eyes, savoring the fantasy. Desire throbbed through him, tightening the muscles of his thighs and his abdomen.

He felt a deep, almost painful sense of yearning for her. Not a physical need. Hell, what was he thinking? Yes, he did need her physically. He'd never wanted a woman as bad as he did Erin. But what he was experiencing now was a higher plane of yearning, a profound longing. An emotional, spiritual craving he'd never understood fully until this moment. It troubled him, knowing how much was at stake in this brief time with Erin.

A few minutes later, she returned to the kitchen, dressed in a dark blue business suit. The skirt was straight and emphasized her long legs and the rounded curves of her hips and buttocks. The jacket was tailored, and the shoulders were padded. Brand poured her a cup of coffee in an effort to break the spell she had over him.

"Thanks," she whispered, pulled out a chair and sat down.

"I suppose you're wondering what I'm doing here?" he asked, realizing he sounded defensive. He was treading on thin ice with Erin, and he knew it. One wrong word and he could lose her, and that was what Brand feared most.

"I can't help wondering why you came." She braced her elbows against the glass tabletop and poised the mug of steaming coffee in front of her lips.

Brand fully intended to answer her, launch into his campaign of reason, but for the life of him he couldn't take his eyes off her mouth. Those sweet, delectable lips of hers were driving him insane.

"Would you mind if I kiss you first?"

She lowered her head so fast it was amazing her chin didn't collide with her coffee mug. "I don't think that would be a good idea."

"Why not?" he questioned softly. He pulled out the chair next to her, twisted it around and straddled it.

"You know why," she countered swiftly.

His sweet Irish rose looked so professional and imperturbable that it was enough to challenge any red-blooded male. He couldn't help himself. He pressed his index finger under her chin and raised her gaze to his. Then he leaned forward slightly and gently brushed his mouth over hers.

She released a soft sigh, and when Brand moved back he noted that her eyes remained closed and her mouth was moist and ready for further exploration.

Brand was willing, more than willing to comply.

He took her mouth again, applying a subtle pressure. He heard her coffee mug hit the table, but if it spilled or not he didn't know. Erin moaned and parted her lips for him, inviting the investigation of his tongue.

It was amazing, Brand thought, that they could be so intimate while sitting in chairs and leaning toward each other.

Her hands were braced against his shoulders and his were in her hair as he slowly rotated his mouth over hers, molding her lips with his, deepening and demanding even more from her.

Erin didn't disappoint him. She'd learned her lessons well.

Somehow Brand managed to get them into an upright position. Her arms locked around his neck, and she was squirming against him in the most tantalizing way, with a hunger that matched his own. Brand groaned, tormented by a heavy load of frustration.

Brand didn't know what he'd expected when they started, certainly not this fire that threatened to consume him. He'd felt rock-hard and aching from the moment their lips had met, and the pressure wasn't getting any better, only worse.

When he couldn't tolerate it any longer, Brand jerked his head back and battled for control. After dragging several deep breaths through his lungs, he bent forward and pressed his forehead to hers.

"I… I told you that kissing wasn't a good idea," she reminded him in a husky whisper. "Now you know why."

"I knew it before, but that didn't stop me." He smiled to himself as he opened his eyes enough to study her. Hungry desire was on her face. Her eyes, her nose and her delicate chin all seemed pronounced with it. Her carefully styled hair was tousled from his roving fingers, and her pink lips were the color of rose petals moist from the dew.

Her arms remained fastened around his neck, her fingers buried in his nape. Neither of them seemed capable of movement, which suited Brand just fine. He'd dreamed about holding Erin just like this a thousand times since he'd left.

"Call the office and tell them you need the day off," he told her. "Make any excuse you want, but spend the day with me."

She nodded, her eyes closed. "Aimee's furious with me."

"Why?" He couldn't resist the temptation to kiss the very tip of her nose.

"She thinks I'm a fool to let you go."

"Luckily, I didn't believe you. You do love me, don't you, Erin MacNamera?"

She took a long time answering, much longer than he deemed it should take to admit the truth.

"I shouldn't have anything to do with you."

"But you will." He made it sound as much like a command as he dared.

"I don't know," she sobbed, and her soft, slender body shook. "I just don't know. I can't believe how much I've missed you since you've been gone. I... I thought I could put you out of my mind, and then you started sending me those beautiful letters. Every night there was one waiting for me. I prayed and prayed that you'd get discouraged when I didn't answer. Yet I'd hurry home every night and be so grateful to hear from you again."

It might have been a little egotistical on his part, but Brand was damn proud of those letters.

"Tell me you love me, Erin," he urged, bringing her

back into the shelter of his arms. "Let me hear you say it. I need that."

She bent her head against his throat and began to cry softly. "I do love you, so damn much. And you're navy."

"It could be worse," he whispered close to her ear. He'd never loved her more than he did at this moment.

He cradled her until she sniffed and gently broke away from him. "We'll spend the day together?" Her eyes avoided his.

"All day."

"Good." She smiled up at him shyly, then started to unfasten her suit jacket. Brand didn't fully comprehend what she was doing until she pulled the white silk blouse free of her waistband.

"Erin?" His voice shook noticeably. "You're undressing."

"I know." She still wouldn't look him in the eye.

His Adam's apple worked up and down his throat a couple of times. "Is there a particular reason why?"

"Yes."

It seemed every muscle in his body went tense at the same moment. She wanted to make love. He wasn't going to argue with her: good grief, he'd been thinking about the same thing from the moment she'd walked out in her flannel nightgown, all tousled and sweet this morning.

"You're sure?" He had to ask! A man shouldn't question a woman's willingness, even though he fully suspected Erin was a virgin.

"I'm s-sure."

The ache in his loins intensified.

"I...didn't know men questioned a woman about this sort of thing." Her voice quivered slightly.

"Normally…they don't, but there are certain factors we need to decide."

"Can't we do that later?" The zipper in the back of her skirt made a snakelike sound as she glided it open. She slipped the straight skirt over her hips and let it drop to her feet. Then she carefully lifted it from the floor and folded it over the back of the chair.

"You want to talk later?" he repeated. If she removed her teddy, there wouldn't be time to wait for anything. She resembled a goddess, her skin so pale it was translucent, so creamy and white. He couldn't resist her. Hell, he didn't even know why he was putting forth the effort. This was the woman he planned to love for the remainder of his life. The woman who would mother his children.

"You'll go slowly?" she asked, her voice liquid and warm.

Brand tenderly brought her into his arms. "Yes, we'll go slow, real slow. Are you sure you don't want to wait?"

"For what?"

"For us to marry." The way he figured it, they could have everything arranged within a month or so.

"Married?" Erin cried. "I—I never said anything about the two of us getting married."

Six

Erin couldn't have shocked Brand more had she announced she was an alien from Mars. "I...thought, I...assumed we'd...you know." The last time Brand had stammered like this had been in the third grade. He couldn't seem to get the words past his tongue without twisting and misshaping them.

"I'd assumed...you wanted to make love." Erin's cheeks were a shiny fire-engine red.

"I do." He couldn't argue with her over that point. He'd been half out of his mind with wanting her from the day they'd gone to the zoo. These lengthy weeks apart had intensified the longing.

"If you want to make love, then why are you standing here arguing with me over a silly thing like us being married?" She folded her arms around her middle and rooted her gaze on everything in the kitchen but him.

"We're not arguing." At least not yet. It took Brand a few more minutes to gather his wits. In an effort to do so, he had to look away from Erin. Having her this close, and this willing, was temptation enough. He couldn't glance her way and not ache inside. His hands longed to touch her, hold her, give her everything she was asking for and more.

Her head was bowed, and the way she was standing with her arms shielding her waist brought out every protective instinct Brand possessed.

"If we're not arguing, then why are we...you know— waiting?"

Brand was asking himself the same question. Oh, hell, who did he think he was kidding? He wanted her. One sample of her willingness wasn't nearly enough to satisfy him. She was so damned beautiful, standing in the middle of the kitchen in her teddy, her skin so pale and baby soft. There were so many places yet to taste her and caress her, so much to teach her and for her to teach him.

The physical frustration was growing more painful, and try as he might, Brand couldn't get the picture of what she was offering him out of his mind.

He yearned to fill his palms with the lush heaviness of her breasts and take her nipples into his mouth and have her nourish him in ways he had yet to fully appreciate or understand. He wanted her legs wrapped tight around his waist and to bury himself so deep in her moist heat that he'd reach all the way to her soul. He yearned for all of those things with a hunger that was threatening to consume him, and in that instant he knew he couldn't have them.

"Get dressed, Erin."

Shocked, she blinked, and he recognized the flash of pain as it lit her beautiful brown eyes.

"Why?" she demanded.

"I believe we have a stalemate here, my dear." He strove to sound unaffected, casual, but it was a front, and a fragile one at that.

"Do you mean to tell me you refuse to make love to me simply because I'm not ready to marry you?"

"Not exactly. We're not ready to make love—not when there's so much left unresolved between us." If she didn't hurry and do as he asked and get dressed, she just might learn how precariously weak his principles actually were.

"Wh-what do you mean?" She reached for her blouse, and Brand swallowed a tight sigh of relief. He was already beginning to question his decision. He'd hurt her, shamed her for making herself vulnerable to him, and that was the last thing he'd meant to do. Hell, he thought he was being virtuous and noble.

He brought her into the circle of his arms and drew his fingers through her hair. "I didn't mean to embarrass you," he whispered. "I love you, Erin."

"You're a—a wart on a woman's pride."

He struggled to hide a grin, not daring to let her know he was amused. "You're right," he agreed.

"Any other man would have been glad to make love to me."

"I'd be glad, too."

"Then why aren't you?"

Brand didn't know how to explain to her what he found so confusing himself. He wanted her. Needed her. Craved her. There didn't seem to be any answers to the questions that plagued him.

Holding her certainly wasn't helping matters any. The peaks of her soft breasts were pressing into his chest, and their rich abundance felt soft and swollen. Every time she breathed, her chest would nuzzle his and he'd experience an added degree of torment. She must know what she was doing to him, because she seemed to be breathing so hard and so often.

Unable to stop himself, he kissed her throat, pushing back her hair and twisting the length around his fist. Erin moaned softly. She removed her arms from around his waist, rotated her shoulders back and forth a couple of times, and before Brand realized what she'd done, her blouse lay on the floor.

"Kiss me there," she pleaded softly in a siren's voice. He was a sailor and he knew he should know better, but when she beckoned, he felt powerless to resist.

"There," she repeated.

She didn't need to explain where she meant. Brand knew. He found her breasts through the silk teddy, his tongue lapping the excited peak, drawing it into his mouth and sucking gently. Erin arched and whimpered, and when she did, her hips rubbed against the hot swell of his manhood.

Brand groaned and lost himself in her body, thoughtlessly throwing his concern and fears into a forty-knot wind. The delicious heat of desire was the only direction he needed. Slowly he slid his hand past her waistband and into the silky crevice between her thighs.

His thumb caressed the dewy mound until she softly cried out and arched upward, silently begging for what her virgin mind had yet to grasp. His finger located the apex of her femininity and slipped inside the folded layers of her heat.

She was hot and moist, and Brand groaned, or at least he thought he did. Maybe it was Erin. Perhaps both of them. It didn't matter. What did matter was the way she closed her legs convulsively around his invading hand, her hips jerking awkwardly in abruptly, frantic movements. Brand calmed her with a few whispered words of instruction then moved his hand, slowly at first, not wanting to injure or frighten her.

"Brand?" His name was a husky question on her lips.

"It's all right, sweetheart," he assured her. "It only gets better after this."

His finger slid smoothly through the moist heat as she gently rolled and swayed her hips, seeking her own satisfaction. Lightly he pushed and explored, going deeper and deeper, again and again. In and out, in an age-old rhythm.

Her hands tightened into a painful grip at his shoulders. Her long nails dug into his flesh as she arched and, with a strangled moan, tossed back her head and panted, cried out as release exploded within her.

There was no such deliverance for Brand, however, and his body throbbed with frustration and denial. He held her for several moments more until her breathing had calmed. Then he broke away from her, walked over to the sink and braced his hands against the edge as he drew in deep, even breaths.

"Brand?" Erin's silky smooth voice reached out to him. "Thank you… I never knew… I've never done anything like that with a man. I've never…"

His smile was weak at best, and when he spoke, his voice was husky and low. "I know."

"You did?"

He nodded.

"Can I do anything like that…for you?"

Brand shook his head fast and hard, the temptation so strong it nearly consumed his will. Nearly all his worthy intentions had been destroyed as it was.

"Can I?" she repeated.

He squeezed his eyes closed and shook his head. For good measure, he added verbally, "No."

"You're sure?"

Hell, no, he wasn't sure of anything at this point, but

his mind was beginning to interject cool reason, and he took hold of it with both hands. How easy it would be for him to set aside their problems and make love to her until she saw matters his way. Once they'd crossed the physical barriers, Brand was certain, he could convince her to marry him. If he'd been a different kind of man, he might have done it, but Brand was convinced he'd hate himself for manipulating her, and eventually so would Erin. He couldn't risk that.

Once he'd composed himself, he turned around and held out his hand to her. She slipped into his embrace, her arms cradling his middle.

"Why?"

Once again Brand didn't require an explanation. She was asking why he hadn't made love to her.

"We're not ready."

He felt her lips form a smile against the hollow of his throat. "You could have fooled me."

Brand eased her away from him, holding her at arm's length, his hands braced against her shoulders. "We'll make love when we've reached a compromise. I'm not going to fall into the habit of settling our differences in bed, and that's exactly what would happen. I'm not looking to have an affair with you, Erin. I want a permanent relationship."

Her shoulders sagged, and her head dropped. "There isn't any compromise for us."

"There is if we want it bad enough."

Erin felt herself weakening against the powerful force of Brand's personality. If only Brand weren't so incredibly stubborn. He claimed he didn't want them to complicate their feelings for each other by hopping into bed with one another. Good grief, a woman was sup-

posed to be the one seeking commitment. If she wanted
to make love, which she obviously had, then he should
"damn the torpedoes" and comply with her wishes. But
oh, no, he wouldn't do that! He had to complicate everything by being decent and honorable.

If she'd had her way, they'd be in bed this very moment. She was so eager to relinquish her virginity that
she'd practically thrown herself at him. Erin's cheeks
grew pink as she remembered the way she'd begged
him to make love to her. She'd never been so brazen
with anyone in her life. Not even in her wildest fantasies with Neal.

Neal was her make-believe lover. Okay, it was
silly—stupid, even—but during college, she and her
best friend, Terry, had read several books about setting goals and achieving dreams. Each and every one
of those self-help books had claimed that one had to
learn to visualize whatever it was one wanted in life.

One Saturday afternoon, when they were bored and
lonely, convinced they were destined to live their lives
alone, Erin and Terry had conjured up the perfect husband. Terry had named her lover Earl, and Erin had
chosen Neal, because she liked the sound of the name
on her tongue.

Last summer Terry had met and married a man she
claimed was exactly like the one she'd created. Erin had
flown to New Mexico for the wedding.

Brand, however, had little in common with her dream
lover. Both men were tall, dark and handsome, naturally. If it were the physical attributes that concerned
her most, then Brand would fill the bill perfectly. In
fact, he was more attractive than anything she'd ever
expected in a man.

Neal, however, had roots buried so deep they reached

all the way to the center of the earth. He was from a well-established pioneer family. His great-great-grand-father had battled Indians and helped settle the area—not Seattle in particular, but any area.

He'd been born and raised in the same house. A home built on a corner, bordered by a tall, fenced backyard. Erin didn't know why she'd decided on the corner house with the fenced yard, but it had a nice secure feel to it.

Once they were married, she and Neal would buy a house themselves, and it, too, would be on a corner. Once children arrived, they'd fence it, as well.

Her ideal man would have been popular in school, and his senior-class president. He was well liked and trusted by all who knew him. As for his profession, Erin saw him as a banker or an attorney or something equally stable. If he was offered a huge promotion, if it meant moving, he'd never accept it. His home and his extended family were everything to him. He wouldn't dream of uprooting his wife and children for something as fleeting as a career opportunity.

Neal wasn't wealthy. Money had never concerned Erin much, although it would be nice if he did happen to have a healthy savings account, since she tended to live paycheck-to-paycheck.

For the past several years, whenever Erin had dated someone new—which she hated to admit hadn't been that often—she'd compared him to Neal. Her ideal man. The visualization of her dream husband.

Although Brand and Neal might be relatively close in physical attributes, they were worlds apart in every other area.

"What did you just say?" Brand asked, nuzzling her ear with his nose. They were sitting on the sofa, watch-ing an old television movie. Most of the day had been spent walking around the Seattle Center, the site of the 1962 World's Fair, and talking. Although they'd talked for hours on end, neither of them had spoken about their situation again or discussed their options.

"I said something?" Erin asked, surprised.

"Yes. It sounded like 'Tell Brand about Neal.'"

"I said that out loud?" She scooted away from him and sat on the edge of the cushion, pressing her elbows into her knees. This habit of voicing her thoughts was growing worse all the time. Nothing was sacred anymore.

"Who's Neal?"

"A...friend," she stammered, not daring to look at him. If she were to let Brand know that Neal was just part of her fantasy world, he'd book her into the nearest hospital and request a mental evaluation.

"A friend," Brand repeated thoughtfully. "Competition?"

"In a manner of speaking."

"Why didn't you mention him before now?" Brand's voice had tightened slightly.

It seemed the perfect opportunity to pretend Neal was real, but that would mean lying to Brand, and Erin didn't know that she could do it. She'd had such little practice at telling lies, and Brand would probably see through it in a second.

"I haven't seen Neal in a while," she answered, stalling for time. She had to think fast, milk this opportunity for all it was worth and prove to Brand that she wasn't as naive or as guileless as he seemed to believe.

"So he's a friend you haven't seen in a while?"

"That's correct. Are you jealous?"

"Insanely so. Do I need to worry about him?"

"That depends."

"On what?" he demanded.

"Several things." She stretched and, leaning back, relaxed against him, tucking her feet beneath her.

It was all the invitation Brand needed. His hands stroked the length of her arms as he buried his mouth against her hair and said, "I'm not too worried."

"Good. There's really no reason for you to be."

Brand slipped his mouth a little higher and nibbled at her earlobe. At the heated flow of tingling pleasure, she carefully edged away from him, unfolding her feet.

Brand caught her by the shoulders and brought her back against him. He pushed his fingers through her hair, lifting it away from the side of her neck, and kissed her there, his tongue moist and hot.

"As I said before," Brand murmured against her throat, "I'm not concerned."

"Maybe you should be. He's got a steady job. Roots."

"So do I."

A tiny smile edged up her lips. "Perhaps, but your roots are shallow and easily transplanted. Maybe you should consider Neal competition."

"Is that so?" He twisted her around and pressed her back against the sofa cushion, poising himself above her. His eyes held hers, reading her as best he could. Erin didn't dare blink.

Slowly he lowered his head to the valley between her breasts and flicked his tongue over the warm flesh. His fingers laid open her lacy bra with a dexterity that should have shocked her, and in fact, did.

Erin clasped his head and sighed with welcome and relief as his mouth latched hungrily on a nipple and feasted heavily. The things he did to her breasts felt so good, so wonderful. To have him come to her like this, as if he were familiar with every part of her womanly body, as if the passion and the intimacy they shared made everything right. She arched and buckled beneath him, having trouble thinking coherently. He didn't help matters any by transferring his attention to the other breast.

Brand made everything feel right. Such thinking was bound to lead her into trouble. Erin might as well believe she could walk on water or leap off a tall building without the least bit of worry as have him make love to her like this.

As nonsensical as it was, having Brand touch her caused all the problems in the world to fade from view. All the conflict between them shriveled up and died a quick and silent death. With her breasts filling his mouth and his hands creating a magic and a heat that threatened to bring her to that earth-shattering sensual explosion, there was no room for anything but feeling. No room for doubt. No room for fear. No room for questions.

His kiss raked her mouth while his hands shaped and molded her breasts, lifting them so that the hardened, excited peaks rubbed against the rough fabric of his shirt. She longed to feel her flesh against his, and she worked toward that end, nearly tearing the material as she tugged it free from his waist. After she popped one button, Brand pushed her eager hands aside and unfastened the few remaining buttons himself. With his help, she was able to peel off the only barrier between them, thin as it was.

Brand lowered himself to her, and the sensation of her warm, heated flesh against the masculine roughness of his hard chest caused her to close her eyes and cry out in pleasure.

Brand subdued her whimper with a kiss, plunging

his tongue deep in her mouth. His hips moved against hers, telegraphing his urgent need for her. Erin wanted him, too, and instinctively countered each of his movements with one of her own.

Pressing her hand between them, she stroked the hard outline of his maleness. Brand groaned against her mouth, and when he drew in a deep breath, she could feel the rumbling in his chest against the softness of her breasts. She reached for the snap of his jeans, but he pushed her fumbling hand aside and released it himself.

He kissed the side of her jaw and teased the seam of her lips with his tongue. "You're proving to be too much of a temptation."

"Me? Really?" She couldn't help sounding surprised. As far as she knew, she'd never enticed a man. Certainly not to the point of arousal Brand had reached. It made her feel beautiful when she knew she wasn't, and powerful when she'd never experienced a weakness more profound.

Slowly, as if her hand weighed a great deal more than it did, he lifted it away from him and pinned it between them, flattening her palm against his chest.

"Now," he said, drawing in a slow, even breath, "reassure me."

She frowned. "About what?"

"Neal."

Her face relaxed into a slow smile. "Neal is… Let me put it this way…" No, she decided, it was too difficult to explain. "You don't need to worry about him."

"He wants you, doesn't he?"

She lowered her lashes and shook her head. "No. I shouldn't have said anything. It was a slip of the tongue, remember? Not meant for your ears."

"I don't care. I want to know who he is."

"Trust me, you don't need to worry about him. I promise."

"Is he married to someone else?"

She was beginning to regret the whole episode, especially since she'd known from the first that she wasn't going to be able to pull it off and she'd persisted anyway. Brand deserved the truth, no matter how unflattering it was.

"Neal isn't real. I made him up a long time ago when I wrote down a list of the personality traits I wanted in a husband. I shouldn't have carried it this far— It was a poor joke."

"What?" Brand exploded. After a shocked moment, he laughed, then kissed the curve of her shoulder and lightly bit her skin.

She yelped, though he hadn't hurt her.

"That's what you deserve."

"I couldn't help it. You fell into my hands."

"That isn't the only thing we fell into. Sweet heaven, Erin, either we resolve something soon, or I'm going back to Hawaii unfit for military service."

The reminder that he would be leaving within a few hours robbed them of laughter and fun and shared passions like a thief in the night.

Slowly, reluctantly, he eased himself off her and then helped Erin into a sitting position. He continued to hold her for several minutes, his chin resting against the crown of her head.

Neither spoke. But the silence wasn't an uneasy one. Both of them seemed not to want or need to fill the void with idle chatter. Perhaps because they were afraid of what there was to say.

He was leaving, and it was something Erin had to accept. If they were to continue their relationship, it would be something he'd do countless times. Soon she'd end up keeping tabs on the times they said goodbye.

Later, Brand insisted on taking her to a plush restaurant. The food was excellent. They talked some more, but once again they avoided the subject that was uppermost in their minds.

"So how's Margo?" he asked over coffee when a sudden silence fell between them.

"Margo... Oh, I'd forgotten I'd told you about her. She's doing better than I expected," Erin said, and then added, "but she's having her share of problems, too. Mostly she's having a difficult time dealing with her anger. A few weeks back I recommended she attend an anger-management course."

"Has she always had trouble with that?"

"Apparently not, but we're not dealing with someone with a hot temper. What Margo is experiencing is rage. There are times when she literally wants to kill her husband for what he's done to her and their marriage. As more and more of the details of his 'other life' come into play, she's having to face head-on the deception and the pain, and that isn't easy for anyone. She feels betrayed and abandoned, in addition to being confused and lost. There was one bright spot, however. She got her driver's license recently, and I believe once she experiences the freedom a car will give her she's going to adjust a whole lot better."

Brand sipped his coffee, his eyes warm and thoughtful. "Doesn't being around these women affect you?"

"How do you mean?"

"Your attitude?"

"Toward marriage?"

Brand nodded.

"I've seen plenty of good marriages, my own mother and father's included. I—"

"Just a minute," Brand interrupted. "You mean to say your parents, who've been married how many years?"

"Thirty."

"They've been married thirty years and they're happy."

It didn't take a genius to see where Brand was leading the conversation. "You can stop right now, Brandon Davis. My mother is a special kind of woman. She thrived on adventure, and don't let anyone kid you, transporting everything you own from one port to another is an adventure, mostly the unpleasant variety."

"She liked it?"

"Liked isn't the word I'd use. Mom accepted it. When Dad announced he had shipping orders, she'd simply smile and dutifully do what had to be done, without question, without regret."

"I see. And you—"

She raised her hand. "Don't even ask." A short silence fell over them. "We're doing it again," Erin said after several tension-filled moments.

"Arguing?"

"No," she answered, her coffee capturing her attention. "We've done it almost the entire length of your stay."

"Done what?"

"Talked about everything else." After he'd first arrived, they'd discussed their relationship only briefly. It was something of a wonder how they'd masterfully avoided the subject for as long as they had. They'd talked about her Women in Transition class, her job with the King County Community Action Program and

Marilyn—alias Margo—at length. Even Aimee and her troubled marriage had entered into their conversation.

Sometimes they'd spend hours on a single subject. Brand was an easy person to talk to. He listened and seemed genuinely interested in every aspect of her life, sharing her love and concern for others.

In retrospect, she understood their reluctance to discuss their own relationship, or rather their lack of one.

"There's no solution for us," she said, swamped with melancholy. They couldn't continue to fool themselves. Sooner or later they'd be forced to face the impossibility of their situation. Brand was one hundred percent navy. As it had been with her father, it was with him. The military was far more than his career; it was his life.

"Of course, there's a solution," Brand countered.

"You could leave the navy and find work here in Seattle," she offered, but even as she spoke, Erin realized that plan wasn't feasible. Brand would be miserable outside of the military, just as unhappy as she'd be as part of it.

He mulled over her suggestion for a time. "I wish settling in Seattle was that easy, but it isn't."

"I know," she answered bitterly. Glancing at her watch, she moved her gaze from her wrist to him. "Shouldn't we be leaving?"

Brand looked at his own watch. "We still have time."

Erin wasn't convinced of that. But she wasn't as worried about Brand making his transport plane as she was about having to tell him goodbye. This time was going to be far more difficult than the first, and the third even more heart-wrenching than the second. It would go on and on and on until they were both so much in love and so wretched they'd be willing to agree to anything just to end the heartache.

"There'll never be any easy answers for us," she whispered through the tightening knot of truth. "One of us will end up giving in to the other and spending the rest of our lives wishing we hadn't."

"You're right," Brand announced abruptly. "Now that you mention it, I believe it is time we left." He stood and slapped his linen napkin on the table.

Erin noted how tense the muscles of his jaw had become. Silently she did as he asked, excusing herself while he paid the tab.

Once she was inside the powder room, Erin leaned against the sink, needing its support. If she didn't compose herself, she was going to break down and weep right there.

She had to put an end to this torment for both their sakes. Brand didn't seem to want to listen to reason. From everything he'd said, he seemed to believe a magical, mystical fairy godmother would swoop down out of the heavens and declare the perfect solution and they'd all live happily ever after. It simply wasn't going to happen.

By the time she reappeared, Brand was standing outside waiting for her. The night was cool, the stars obliterated by a thick overcast and the threat of rain hung heavy in the air.

Brand greeted her with "I think it would be best if we said goodbye here."

Her heart objected loud and strong, but she didn't voice a single doubt. "You're probably right."

"Well," he said after expelling his breath. "This is it."

"Right," she returned. "Have a safe trip."

"I will."

How stiff and unemotional he sounded, as if they were little more than acquaintances.

"Are you sure you don't want me to go to the airport with—"

"No."

She nodded, feeling wretched. This was worse than she'd ever believed it would be. Her throat had closed off, and she couldn't have carried on a conversation had her life depended on it. One-or two-word replies were all she could manage.

"Yes," he countered, just as quickly. "Come with me. God help us both, Erin. I can't bear to say goodbye to you like this."

Seven

The phone was ringing when Erin walked in the door that evening. She rushed into the kitchen to answer it, her heart racing like a steam engine. She frantically prayed it was Brand and that he wouldn't give up before she could make it to the phone. All the while she was dashing across the house she cursed herself, because she was famished for the sound of his voice, eager to accept each little crumb he tossed her way, despite all her vows to the contrary.

She'd gone to the airport with him, kissed him good-bye, then stood and waited until his plane had taxied down the runway and shot into the sky, taking him away from her. Like a fool, she'd stood there for what seemed like an eternity, her heart aching, while she chided herself for caring so damn much. Now she was doing it all again. Running through her own home, risking life and limb in an effort to reach the phone, praying it was Brand who was trying to contact her.

"Hello," she answered breathlessly, nearly tearing the phone off the wall in her eagerness to get to it in time. While her breathing returned to normal, she was forced to listen to a twenty-second campaign from a professional carpet-cleaning company.

By the time she replaced the receiver, Erin was shaking with irritation. Not because she was angry with the salesperson, but simply because the caller hadn't been Brand.

He'd left two weeks earlier, and she'd heard from him twice by phone. A handful of letters had arrived, and although she treasured each one, she found something important was lacking in this second batch. Something Erin couldn't quite put her finger on. Each letter was filled with details of his life, but she felt Brand was holding back a part of himself from her, protecting his heart in much the same way she was shielding hers.

She'd written him a number of times herself, but she'd always been careful about what she told him. Anyone reading her letters would assume she and Brand were nothing more than good friends.

After he'd left the second time, she'd battled with the right and wrong of continuing a long-distance relationship. Over the years she'd repeatedly promised herself she wouldn't allow this very thing to happen, yet here she was involved with a navy man! Her principles had vanished like topsoil in a flash flood. Past experience had taught her that Brand wouldn't give up on her, and frankly, she hadn't the strength to sever things on her own.

Her plan was to subtly phase herself out of his life. But the strategy had backfired on her. Each day she found herself hungering for word from him, convinced this separation was far more difficult than the one before.

Erin dreamed of Brand that night. He'd come to her when she was in bed, warm and cozy, missing him dreadfully. Slipping under the covers, he'd reached for her, his eyes wide with unspoken need. His kisses were hot and hungry as he buried his mouth in hers.

In the beginning, Erin had tried to hold back, not wanting the kisses to deepen for fear of where they would lead. Gradually, without Brand ever saying a word, she felt herself opening to him. She was lost in the wonder of his arms, and he seemed to be equally absorbed in hers. Both seemed on the brink of being found, of discovering heaven.

His body had moved over hers, his skin hot to the touch and as smooth as velvet. The clothes that had been a protective barrier between them seemed to melt away. Bare, heated skin had met bare, heated skin, and they'd both sighed at the mysterious joy found in such simple pleasure.

His hands caressed her, his touch light and unbelievably gentle. His kisses robbed her of her sanity, and when he moved above her, she parted her thighs and moaned in welcome.

"Do you like this?" he whispered close to her ear.

"Oh…yes," she assured him.

His hands cupped her buttocks while his kiss raked her mouth. By the time he finished, Erin was panting and weak with longing. "Make love to me," she pleaded. "Brand, please, don't make me wait…not again."

In response, he lowered his sleek, muscular body to hers. Thrilled and excited, Erin opened to him, wanting him so badly she clawed at his back, needing him to hurry and give her what she craved.

To her dismay, he didn't enter her. She squirmed and closed her legs around the hot staff of his manhood, arching and buckling as he began to move, sliding be-

tween her thighs, the friction moistened by her excitement and need.

"Brand," she pleaded again, her voice hoarse as she
clutched at him, breathing hard and fast. "Give me what
I want."

"No…" His voice was that of a man in torment.

"Yes." She thought to outwit him, and she rotated her
hips so that his thrust met the apex of her womanhood.
If he were to continue, penetration couldn't be avoided,
and he would fill her the way she craved. Arching her
neck, she lifted her hips, coaxing him to completion,
wanting him so much she couldn't think clearly.

"Please," she begged, tilting her hips higher and
higher, but he stopped short. "I want to feel all of you.…
Oh, Brand…"

"No…no…" He sounded like a man pounding against
the gates of heaven, lost for all eternity. "We can't… It
isn't right, not now, not yet. Soon," he promised. "Soon."

"We can…we must."

Her cries and pleas seemed to have no effect on him,
and try as she might with her body, pushing her hips
forward, inviting him, even demanding that he give her
what she sought, did no good.

He was full and hard, and he teased her until a violent release delivered her physically from the prison
of unfulfilled desire. She lay panting, her eyes closed,
physically relieved but emotionally starving.

It was then that Erin had woken.

For a long while, she stared up at the ceiling, her
head spinning, her heart pounding. She'd never been
one to put a lot of stock in dreams, but this one had been
so vivid, so real, that she couldn't help being affected.

This was the way it would be with Brand. It wasn't
that he'd cruelly refuse to make love to her, but he'd

never be able to satisfy the deep inner longings of her soul.

She required more than he could ever supply.

And they both knew it.

Each day that followed, Erin reassured herself nothing good would be accomplished by loving Brand. She'd made a decent life for herself, and she wasn't going to leave the only security she'd ever found because a few hormones refused to let her forget she was a woman.

She repeated the same tired arguments to herself in the mirror every morning and then went about her day. But when the nights arrived, her dreams were filled with loving Brand. Not all her dreams were wild sexual romps. When they did come, she found herself left frustrated and miserable. More often, her nights would be full of memories of him and the scant time they had spent together. Brand and she would be walking, hand in hand, along the beach together, talking, laughing, appreciating the love they'd discovered in each other. Then Brand would take her in his arms and kiss her until her mouth was moist and swollen. His eyes would delve into hers while his hands tenderly brushed the red curls from the side of her face.

They'd kiss, and their lips would cling, then kiss again, slowly, lazily, savoring each other.

Each morning, when Erin woke, it was the ending.

Each night, when she climbed beneath the sheets, was the beginning.

Stunned, Brand sat at his desk, reading over the same words two and three times. He felt numb. He'd been assigned duty aboard the command ship USS *Blue Ridge*. The *Blue Ridge* was the flagship of the Seventh Fleet and was being deployed in the western Pacific. Tour of duty—six months.

This couldn't have come at a worse time for him. Without a doubt, he knew he was going to lose Erin.

There wasn't a damn thing he could do about it.

A feeling of helplessness and frustration engulfed him like a tidal wave.

He'd left Seattle with matters unsettled, but that couldn't be avoided. He'd continued to write her every day since, and all he'd gotten in return were chatty letters that didn't say a damn thing about what she was feeling or thinking. He might as well be corresponding with a troop of Girl Scouts. Reading Erin's letters was like reading the newspaper. Just the facts, listed as unemotionally as possible. She even signed off with "Best Wishes." Well, Brand had a few wishes of his own, but Erin didn't seem to be interested in fulfilling any of those.

"Six months," he said aloud. It might as well be an eternity. Erin would refuse to wait for him; she'd made that clear from the first. She'd start dating other men, and the thought produced an ache that cut through his heart and his pride.

Although Brand had made light of it when she'd brought up this Neal character, he'd been jealous as hell. When he'd learned Neal was a figment of her imagination, the relief he'd felt was overwhelming.

Erin was a rare jewel, undiscovered and unappreciated by those around her. At first glance, few would have declared her beautiful. Her hair was a little too red, her nose a bit too sharp, her mouth a tad too full, for her beauty to be considered classic. But upon closer examination, she was a precious pearl, worth selling everything he owned to possess.

Brand understood from the things she'd told him how seldom she dated. She was endearingly shy. Warm, gracious, caring.

And Brand loved her.

He loved her so much he hadn't been able to function properly since he'd returned from his evaluation assignment at Sand Point.

He had to tell her about being assigned sea duty, of course, and he tried doing so in a letter several times. After attempting to phrase it a number of ways, jokingly, seriously, thoughtfully and playfully, Brand resigned himself to contacting her by phone.

He delayed it, probably longer than he should have.

He announced it flat out, without preamble.

And waited.

"Well," he said, speaking into the receiver. "Say something."

"Bon voyage."

"Come on, Erin, I'm serious."

"So am I."

She had this flippant way about her when she was upset and trying not to show it. Brand had anticipated it and allowed for her sarcasm, but she was precariously close to angering him.

"You want me to act surprised?" Erin questioned. "I can't find it in me. We both knew sooner or later that you'd get your shipping orders. You are in the navy. You should expect sea duty."

"I want you to wait for me." There, he'd said it. He hadn't softened it with romantic words or sent the message attached to a dozen red roses. Just the plain truth. These were going to be the longest months of his life, simply because he'd never left a woman he loved behind until now. He didn't like the feeling. Not one damn bit.

Erin didn't respond.

"Did you hear me?" he asked her, raising his voice. "I want you to wait for me."

"No." She said it so matter-of-factly, as if the answer took little, if any, thought or consideration.

That pricked Brand's pride, but he should have been used to it by now with Erin. Offhand he could have named two or three women who would have broken into tears when they learned he'd been assigned sea duty. In a few cases, the women had promised undying faithfulness and loyalty. They'd stood on the pier weeping as he'd pulled out of port, and they'd been there happy and excited upon his return. Brand hadn't expected the same reaction from Erin—in fact, hysterical women were a turnoff as far as he was concerned—but he needed something more than what Erin was offering him.

"So in other words you plan to date someone else?" he demanded.

"Yes."

"Who?"

"That's none of your business."

"The hell it isn't." His voice was raised and angry. "I'm in love with you, Erin MacNamera, and—"

"I didn't ask you to love me. I'm not even sure I want you to love me. Go ahead, go off and play navy for the next six months, but I'm telling you right now, Brand Davis, I won't sit home twiddling my thumbs waiting for you."

When Erin replaced the telephone receiver, there were tears glistening in her eyes. She hated being weak, hated the emotion that clogged her throat and knotted her fists at her side.

So Brand would be spending the next six months

sailing between Hong Kong, the Philippines and several other exotic ports. Great. She was pleased for him. Happy, even.

It was the end for them. It was over. Done. Finished.

At first, when she'd answered the phone, the excitement she felt hearing Brand's voice had taken the sting from his words. He must have known how she would react to his news and been worried about telling her, because he'd barely answered her greeting before launching into the dreary details of this six-month assignment. To be fair, he hadn't sounded any too pleased about going out to sea himself, but that didn't change anything.

He'd leave without a qualm and without question. Why? Because the navy owned him the way it did her father and everyone else she'd grown up with, and she hated it.

But the United States Navy would never own her again. Never!

Brand had paused after telling her—waiting, it seemed, for some response from her. Her reaction had been immediate, but she'd shared damn little of it with Brand. When reality had begun to sink in, a deep sense of anger, loss, resentment and fear had crowded in around her like teenagers against the stage at a rock concert.

It was the same indescribable sensation that had come over her every time her father had announced he'd received a new assignment and they'd be moving.

Those identical emotions stormed at her once again. She felt like a casualty of a major disaster. Homeless. Lost emotionally and physically. Wandering around in the blue haze of insecurities that came when everything familiar, everything comfortable, had been pulled out from under her feet.

Erin had thought to escape that feeling for the rest of her life. She couldn't, wouldn't, allow Brand to drag her back into that crazy lifestyle.

"I'm going to miss loving you," she spoke into the stillness of the room.

She would miss Brand. As silly as it seemed, she'd miss the loneliness of waiting for his calls. The joy of his coming and the pain of his leaving. All those were part of the man she had to learn to stop loving.

The following morning, Erin called in sick. Unfortunately, it was Aimee who answered the phone.

"You don't sound sick," her friend announced first thing. "In fact, you sound as if you've sat up all night crying. I can hear it in your voice."

"I... Just write me down as sick, would you? Tell Eve I've got the flu, or make up some other excuse." She finished by hiccuping on a sob.

"Aha! So I was right, you have been crying. What's wrong, sweetie?"

"Nothing."

"You think you're fooling me? Think again, girl!"

"Come on, Aimee," Erin mumbled. "Be nice. I don't want to talk about it."

"It must be Brand. What did he do that was so terrible this time? Send you roses? Tell you you're beautiful?"

"He's going out to sea for six months," she blurted out, as though someone should arrest him for even considering leaving her feeling the way she did. "He hasn't had sea duty in two years. He met me, and wham—the navy puts the kiss of death on anything developing between us. I...couldn't be more pleased.... It couldn't have come at a better time."

"You don't mean a word of that. Listen, I've got a light schedule this morning. How about if I drop in and we have one of our heart-to-heart talks. It sounds like you could use one."

"All right," Erin agreed, "only...hurry, would you?"

Aimee arrived around ten. Erin was dressed in her housecoat and her fuzzy pink slippers with the open toes. Her mother had sent her the shoes the Christmas before last, and just then Erin needed something from home.

She carried the tissue box with her to the door, blew her nose and then carelessly tossed the used Kleenex on the carpet.

Aimee walked into the house and followed the trail of discarded tissues into the kitchen. "Good grief, it looks like you held a wake in here."

"The funny part is," Erin said, sobbing and laughing both at the same time, "I don't even know why I'm crying. So Brand's going off to sea. Big deal. It isn't like I didn't anticipate he would. He's navy."

"You're in love with him is why." Standing on tiptoe, Aimee reached inside Erin's tallest cupboard and brought down a teapot. "Sit down," she said, pointing toward the table. "I'll brew us some tea."

"There's coffee made."

"You need tea."

Erin wasn't sure she understood, but she wasn't in any mood to question her friend's illogical wisdom. If Aimee wanted to brew her a strong cup of tea, then far be it from her to argue.

"I've learned something important," Erin announced once Aimee had joined her.

"Oh?" Her co-worker reached across the table for the sugar bowl and added a liberal amount to Erin's cup. "Tell me."

"I've decided falling in love is the most wonderful, most…creative, most incredible feeling in the world."

"Yes," Aimee agreed with some reluctance. "It can be."

"But at the same time it's the most destructive, painful, distressing emotion I've ever experienced."

"Welcome to the real world. If it were only the first part, we'd all make a point of falling in love regularly. Unfortunately, it involves a whole lot more."

"I always thought it was roses and sunshine and sharing a glass of expensive wine while sitting in front of a brick fireplace. I had no idea it was so…so painful."

"It can be." Aimee held the delicate china cup with both hands. "Trust me, I know exactly what you're going through."

"You do?"

Her friend nodded. "Steve moved out of the house last weekend. We've decided to contact our respective lawyers. It's going to be a challenge to see which one of us can file for the divorce first."

Erin couldn't hold back her gasp of surprise. "You didn't say anything earlier in the week."

"What's there to say? It isn't something I want to announce to the office, not that you'd spread the word. The way I figure it, everyone's going to find out sooner or later anyway, and personally, I prefer later."

"How are you feeling?"

Aimee gave an inelegant shrug. "All right, I guess. It isn't like this mess happened overnight. Steve and I haven't been getting along for the last couple of years. Frankly, it's something of a relief that he's gone."

Erin could understand what her friend was saying. The break with Brand had been inevitable. She'd delayed it too long as it was, hoping they'd come up with a solution, a means of compromise, anything that would make what they shared work.

"What we need is a plan of action," Aimee announced with characteristic enthusiasm. "Something that's going to get us both through this with our minds intact."

"Shopping?" Erin suggested.

"You're joking? I can't afford panty hose until payday, and on the advice of my attorney I dare not use the credit cards."

"What, then?" Everything Erin could think of involved money.

Gnawing at the corner of her mouth, Aimee mulled over their dilemma. "I think we should start dating again."

"Dating?" Erin sounded doubtful. "But you're still married, and I'm not interested right now... Maybe later."

"You're right. Dating is a bit drastic. It sounds simple enough, but where the hell would we find men? The bowling alley?"

"But I don't think we should rule out casual relationships," Erin qualified. "Nothing serious, of course."

"Next month, then. We'll give ourselves a few weeks to mentally prepare for reentering the dating scene. We'll diet and change our hair and get beautiful all over again and wow 'em."

In a month Erin might consider the idea, but for now it left her cold. "What about now? How are we going to get through...today?"

"Well..." Aimee paused. "I think we're both going

to have to learn to survive," she said, and her small voice quavered.

Erin handed her a fresh tissue. They hugged each other, promising to support one another.

"Love is hell," Erin blubbered.

"So is being alone," Aimee whispered.

Brand stood in front of the telephone and stared at the numbers for a long while. He'd had a couple of drinks, and although his mind was crystal-clear, he wasn't sure contacting Erin was the thing to do, especially now.

Damn it all, the woman had him tied up in knots a sailor couldn't undo. He was due to ship out in a few days, but if he didn't clear up this matter with Erin, it would hang over his head for the entire six months. He couldn't go to sea with matters unsettled between them the way they were.

More than likely she'd slam the phone down in his ear.

What the hell? It was either phone her or regret the fact he hadn't. Brand had learned early in his career that it wasn't the things he'd done that he regretted, it was the things he hadn't done.

"What's the worst that can happen?" he asked himself aloud, amused that he'd picked up Erin's habit of talking to herself.

He answered himself. "She can say no."

"She's as good as turned you down before," his other self argued.

"Quit talking and just do it."

Following his own advice, Brand punched out the numbers that would connect him with his beautiful Irish rose. The phone rang seven times before she answered.

"Hello." She sounded groggy, as if he'd gotten her out of bed. The picture of her standing there in her kitchen, her hair mussed and her body warm and supple, was enough to tighten his loins.

"Erin? It's Brand."

"Brand?" She elevated her voice with what Brand felt certain must be happiness. She loved him. She might try to convince herself otherwise, but she was crazy about him.

"Hello, darling."

"Do you have any idea what time it is?" she demanded.

"Nope. Is it late?"

"You've been drinking."

Now that sounded like an accusation, one he didn't take kindly to. "I've had a couple of drinks. I was celebrating."

"Why'd you call me? You sound three sheets to the wind, Lieutenant."

Brand closed his eyes and leaned his shoulder against the wall. If he tried hard enough, he might be able to pretend Erin was in the same room with him. He needed her. He loved her, and, damn it all, he wanted her with him, especially when he wasn't going to be able to hold or kiss her for six long months.

"Brand," she repeated. "I'm standing here in my stocking feet, shivering. I'd bet cold cash you didn't phone because you were looking for a way to waste your hard-earned money, now did you?"

"I love you, darling."

His words were met with silence.

"Come on, Erin, don't be so cruel. Tell me what you feel. I need to hear it."

"I think we should both go back to bed and forget we ever had this conversation."

Brand groaned. "Come on, sweetheart. I never realized how stingy you are with your affections."

"Brand…"

"All right, all right, if you insist, I'll tell you why I phoned. On… hold on a minute, will you?" He set the phone down on the table, then climbed down on one knee. It took some doing, because the floor insisted upon buckling under his feet. He didn't drink often, and a few shots of good Irish whiskey had affected him far more than he'd realized.

"Brand, what the hell are you doing?"

"I'm ready now," he whispered. Drawing in a deep breath, he started speaking once more. "Can you hear me?"

"Of course I can hear you."

"Good." Now that it had come time, Brand discovered he was shaking like a leaf caught in a whirlwind. His heart was pounding like an automatic hammer. "Erin MacNamera, I love you, and I'm asking you on bended knee to become my wife."

Eight

Standing on the bridge, a pair of binoculars clenched tightly in his hands, Brand stared at mile upon mile of open sea. The horizon was marked by an endless expanse of blue, cloudless sky. The wind was brisk, carrying with it the scent of salt and sea. Taking in deep breaths, Brand dragged several lungfuls of the fresh air through his chest.

This was his second week sailing the waters of the Pacific. Generally Brand relished sea duty. There was a special part of his soul that found solace while at sea. He felt removed from the frantic activity of life on the land, set apart in a time and place for reconciliation with himself and his world.

Brand was grateful for sea duty, especially now, with the way matters had worked out with Erin. These next few months would give him the necessary time to heal.

Erin was out of his life. But he still loved her. He probably always would feel something very special for her. He'd analyzed his feelings a thousand times, hoping to gain perspective. He'd discovered that the depth, the strength, of his love wasn't logical or even reasonable. She'd made her views plain from the day they met, yet he'd egotistically disregarded everything she'd claimed and fallen for her anyway. Now he had to work like hell to get her out of his mind.

She'd flatly turned down his proposal of marriage. At first, after he'd asked her on bended knee, she'd tried to make light of it, claiming it was the liquor talking. Brand had assured her otherwise. He loved her enough to want to spend the rest of his life with her. He wanted her to be the mother of his children and to grow old with him. She'd gotten serious then and started to weep softly. At least Brand chose to believe those were tears, although Erin had tried hard to make him believe she was actually laughing at the implausibility of them ever finding happiness together.

She claimed his proposal was a last-ditch effort on his part, and on that account Erin might have been right. The fear of losing her had consumed him from the moment he'd received his orders. Rightly so, as it had worked out.

So Erin was out of his life. He'd given it his best shot, been willing to do almost anything to keep her, but it hadn't worked. In retrospect, he could be pragmatic about their relationship. It was time to move on. Heal. Grow. Internalize what he'd learned from loving her.

One thing was sure. Brand wasn't going to fall in love again any time soon. It hurt too damn much.

The breeze picked up, and the wind whipped around his face. He squinted into the sun, more determined than ever to set Erin from his mind.

Erin's philosophy in life was relatively simple. Take one day at a time and treat others as she expected to be treated herself. The part about not dating anyone in the military and not overcharging her credit cards was

an uncomplicated down-to-earth approach to knowing herself.

Then why had she bought a grand piano?

Erin had asked herself that question ten times over
the past several days. She'd been innocently walking
through the mall one Saturday afternoon, browsing. She
certainly hadn't intended to make a major purchase. Innocently she'd happened into a music store, looking for
a cassette tape by one of her favorite artists, and paused
in front of the polished mahogany piano.

There must have been something about her that
caught the salesman's attention, because he'd sauntered
over and casually asked her if she played.

Erin didn't, but she'd always wanted to learn. From
that point until the moment the piano was scheduled to
be delivered to the house, Erin had repeatedly asked
herself what she was doing purchasing an ultraexpen-
sive grand piano.

"How many credit cards did it take?" Aimee had
asked her, aghast, when she heard what Erin had done.

"Three. I'd purposely kept the amount I could bor-
row low on all my cards. I never dreamed I'd spend that
much money at one time."

Running her hand over the keyboard, Aimee slowly
shook her head. "It's a beautiful piece of furniture."

"The salesman gave me the name of a lady who
teaches piano lessons, and before you know it I'll be
another Van Cliburn." Erin forced a note of enthusiasm
into her voice, but it fell short of any real excitement.

"That sounds great." Aimee's own level of zeal was
decidedly low.

In retrospect, Erin understood why she'd done something so crazy as to buy an expensive musical instrument on her credit cards. The two men who'd delivered

the piano had explained it to her without even knowing her psychological makeup.

"I hope you don't intend to move for a long time, lady," the short, round-faced man had said once they'd maneuvered the piano up her front steps.

Getting the piano into the house had been even more of a problem. Her living room was compact as it was, and the deliverymen had been forced to remove the desk and rearrange the furniture before they found space enough for the overly large piano.

"If you do decide to move, I'd include the piano in the sale of the house," the second man had said to her as he used his kerchief to wipe the sweat from his brow. His face had been red and glistening with perspiration.

"I don't plan on moving," she'd been quick to assure them both.

"It's a damn good thing," the first had muttered on his way out the door.

"If you do plan on moving out of the area, don't call us," the second had joked.

Brand had been gone one month, and Erin had maxed out three credit cards with the purchase of one grand piano. It didn't matter that she couldn't have located middle C on the keyboard to save her soul. Nor did it concern her that she'd be making payments for three years at interest rates that made the local banks giddy with glee. What did matter, Erin discovered, was that she was making a statement to herself and to Brand.

She had no intention of ever leaving Seattle. And she certainly wasn't going to allow a little thing like the United States Navy stand in the way of finding happiness. Not if it meant leaving the only roots she'd ever planted!

If Erin was actually in love with Brand—and that

if was as tall as the Empire State Building—then she was going to force herself to fall out of love with him.

The piano was symbolic of that. Her first move had been to reject his marriage proposal. Her second had been to purchase the piano.

Friday night Erin and Aimee met at a Mexican restaurant and ordered nachos. They'd decided earlier in the day to make an effort to have fun, drown their sorrows in good Mexican beer, and if they happened to stumble across a couple of decent-looking men, then it wouldn't hurt anyone if they were to flirt a little. For fun, Aimee had promised to give Erin lessons in attracting the opposite sex.

"We can have a good time without Steve and Brand," she insisted.

"You're absolutely right," Erin agreed. But the two of them had looked and acted so forlorn that they'd had trouble attracting a waiter's attention, let alone any good-looking, eligible men.

"You know what our problem is?" Aimee asked before stuffing a nacho in her mouth.

Erin couldn't help being flippant. "Too many jalapeños and not enough cheese?"

Aimee was quick to reply. "No. We're not trying hard enough. Then again, maybe we're trying too hard. I'm out of touch… I don't know what we're doing wrong."

For her part, if Erin tried any harder, the bank was going to confiscate her credit cards. As it was, she was in debt up to her eyebrows for a piano she couldn't play.

"We're trying," Erin insisted. She scanned the restaurant and frowned. It seemed every man there was sitting with a woman. Aimee was the one who claimed this place was great for meeting men, but then, her friend had been out of the singles' world for over a decade. Apparently everyone who'd met there had married and returned as couples.

"Oh, my—" Aimee gave a small cry and scooted down so far in the crescent-shaped booth that she nearly slid under the table.

"What is it?"

"Steve's here."

"Where?" Erin demanded, frantically looking around. She didn't see him in any of the booths.

"He just walked in, and…he's with a woman."

Erin had never met Aimee's husband, but she'd seen several pictures of him. She picked him out immediately. He was standing against the white stucco wall with a tall, thin blonde at his side. Tall and thin. Every woman's nightmare.

"You can't stay under the table the rest of the night," Erin insisted in a low whisper. "Why should you? You don't have anything to hide."

A tense moment passed before Aimee righted herself. "You're absolutely right. I'm not the one out with a floozy." Riffling her fingers through her hair, Aimee squared her shoulders and nonchalantly reached for a nacho. She did a good job of masquerading her pain, but it was apparent, at least to Erin, that her friend was far more ruffled than she let on.

As luck would have it, Steve and his blonde strolled directly past their booth. Aimee stared straight ahead, refusing to acknowledge her husband. Erin, however, glared at him with eyes hot enough to form glass figurines.

Steve, tall and muscular, glanced over his shoulder and nearly faltered when he saw Aimee. His gaze quickly moved to Erin, and although she could have been imagining it, Erin thought he looked relieved to discover that his wife wasn't with a man.

His mouth opened, and he hesitated, apparently at a loss for words. After whispering something to his companion, he returned to Aimee and Erin's table.

"Hello, Aimee."

"Hello," she answered calmly, smiling serenely in his direction. Erin nearly did a double take. Her coworker had been hiding under the table only a few seconds earlier.

"I... You look well."

"So do you. You remember me mentioning Erin MacNamera, don't you?"

"Of course." Steve briefly nodded in Erin's direction, but it was clear he was far more interested in talking to his wife than in exchanging pleasantries with Erin. "I...thought I should explain about Danielle," he said, rushing the words. "This isn't actually a date, and—"

"Steve, please, you don't owe me an explanation. Remember, you're divorcing me. It doesn't matter if you're seeing someone else. Truly it doesn't."

"I thought you were the one divorcing me."

"Are we going to squabble over every single detail? It seems a bit ridiculous, don't you think? But technically I suppose you're right. I am the one filing, so that does mean I am the one divorcing you."

"I don't want you to have the wrong impression about me and Danielle. We—"

"Don't worry about it. I'm dating again myself."

"You are?" Steve asked the question before Erin could. He straightened and frowned before continuing. "I didn't know... I'm sorry to have troubled you."

"It was no trouble." Once more she leveled a serene smile at him, and then she intentionally looked away, casually dismissing him. Steve returned to the blonde bombshell, and Erin stared curiously at Aimee.

"You're dating yourself?" Erin muttered under her breath. "I never expected you'd lie."

"I fully intend to date again," Aimee countered sharply. "Someday. I'm just not ready for it yet, but I will be soon enough and—" Her voice faltered, and she bit mercilessly into her lower lip. "Actually, I've lost my appetite. Would you mind terribly if we called it an evening?"

"Of course I don't mind," Erin said, glaring heatedly at Steve, who was sitting several booths down from them. But when it came right down to it, Erin didn't know who she was angriest with—Aimee, for pretending Steve didn't have the power to hurt her any longer, or Steve, who appeared equally afraid to let his wife know how much he cared. As a casual observer, Erin had to resist the urge to slap the pair of them.

The dreams returned that night. The ones where Brand climbed into bed with Erin, slipping his arms around her and nestling close to her side. There was little that was sexual about these romantic encounters, although he kissed her several times and promised to make love to her soon.

Erin woke with tears in her eyes. She didn't understand how a man who was several thousand miles away could make her feel so cherished and appreciated. Especially when she'd let it be known she didn't want anything more to do with him.

It got so that Erin welcomed the nights, praying as she drifted off to sleep that Brand would come to her as he often did.

Reality returned each morning, but it didn't seem to

matter, because there were always the nights, and they were filled with such wonderful fantasies.

The letter from her father arrived a couple of weeks later.

"I received word from Brand," her father wrote in his sharply slanted scrawl. "He claims there's nothing between the two of you any longer and that's the way you want it. He was frank enough to admit he loves you, but must abide by your wishes. I couldn't believe my own eyes. Brand Davis is more man than you're likely to find in five lifetimes, and you refused his proposal? I feel I'm the one to blame for all this. I should have kept my nose out of your business. Your mother would have my hide if she knew I'd asked Brand to check up on you when he was in Seattle. To be honest, I was hoping the two of you would hit it off. If I were to handpick a husband for you, Erin, I couldn't find a better man than Brand Davis. All right, I'm a meddling old man. Your mother's right, who you date isn't any of my damn business.

"You're my daughter, Erin," he continued, "and I'll love you no matter what you decide to do in this life, but I'm telling you right now, lass, I'm downright disappointed in you."

"I've disappointed you before, Dad, and I'm likely to do so again," Erin said aloud when she'd finished the letter.

Tears smarted her eyes, but she managed to blink them back. Her father rarely spoke harshly to her, but it was apparent he'd thought long and hard about writing her this letter. It wasn't what he'd said, Erin realized, but what he'd left unsaid, that cut so deep.

Feeling restless and melancholy, Erin went for a drive that afternoon. Before she knew it, she was halfway to

Oregon. Taking a side route, she drove on a twisting, narrow road that led down the Washington coast.

For a long time she sat on the beach, facing the roaring sea. The breeze whipped her hair around her face and chilled her to the bone, yet she stayed, conscious every second that somewhere out in the vast stretch of water sailed Brand, the man she was dangerously close to loving. She could pretend otherwise, buy out every store in Seattle and act as foolish as Aimee and her husband, and it wouldn't alter the fact that she loved Brand Davis.

Wrapping her arms around her bent legs, Erin rested her chin on her knees and mulled over her thoughts. The waves clamored and roared, putting up a fuss, before relinquishing and gently caressing the smooth, sandy shore. Again and again, in abject protest, the waves raged with fury and temper before ebbing. Then, tranquilly, like velvet-gloved fingers, the waves stroked the beach, leaving only a thin line of foam as a memory.

For hours, Erin sat watching the sea. In the end, before she headed back to Seattle, she hadn't reached any conclusions. She was beginning to doubt her doubts and suffer second thoughts about her second thoughts. Why, oh, why did life have to be so complicated? And why did she find the grand piano an eyesore when she walked in her front door?

Brand found order in life at sea. Internally his world felt chaotic as he struggled with his feelings for Erin. Each day that passed he grew stronger, more confident in himself.

Gradually the routine of military life gave him a strong sense of order, something to hold on to while time progressed.

Admittedly, the first weeks were rough. He found himself short-tempered, impatient and generally bad company. He worked hard and fell into his bunk at night, too tired to dream. When he did, his nights were full of Erin.

Erin at the zoo. Erin standing in the doorway of her kitchen dressed in a sexless flannel nightgown. Erin with eyes dark enough to trap a man's soul.

He had to forget her, get her out of his system, get on with his life.

"You still hung up on MacNamera's daughter?" Brand's friend Alex Romano demanded a couple of days before they were due to dock in Hong Kong.

"Not in the least," Brand snapped, instantly regretting his short-fused temper. He smiled an apology. "Maybe I am," he admitted with some reluctance.

Alex answered with a short laugh. "I never thought I'd see the great Brand Davis go soft over a woman. It warms my heart, if you want to know the truth."

"Why's that?" Brand wasn't in the mood to play word games with his friend, but talking about Erin, even with someone who'd never met her, seemed to help. She'd dominated his thoughts for so long, he was beginning to question his own sanity.

"For one thing, it points out the fact you're human like the rest of us. We've all had women problems one time or another. But never you. At least until now. Generally women fight between themselves to fall at your feet. Personally, I never could understand it, but then I'm not much of a ladies' man."

"Ginger will be glad to hear that." Alex and Ginger had been married for ten years and had three toddlers. Brand was godfather to the oldest boy. Although Brand was sure Alex didn't know it, in a lot of ways he was

envious of his friend, of the happiness he'd found with
Ginger, of the fact that there was someone waiting for
him at the end of his sea duty. There was a lot to covet.

"So?" Alex pressed. "What you gonna do about Mac-
Namera's daughter?"

Brand expelled his breath in a slow, drawn-out exercise. He'd asked Erin to marry him, offered her his
heart on a silver platter, and she'd turned him down.
She hadn't even needed time to think about it.

"Not a damn thing," he answered flippantly.

"Oh, dear," Alex said, and chuckled, apparently
amused. "It's worse than I thought."

Maybe it was, only Brand was too stupid to admit it.

Hong Kong didn't help. During three days of shore
leave, all he could do was think of Erin. He sat in a
bar, nursing a glass of good Irish whiskey and thinking he should take up drinking something else, because
Erin was Irish. Damn little good that would do. Everything reminded Brand of Erin. He walked through the
crowded streets, and when a merchant proudly brought
out a piece of silk, the only thing he could picture was
Erin wearing a suit made in that precise color.

The sooner they returned to sea, the better it would
be.

He was wrong.

They'd sailed out of Hong Kong when her letter arrived. Brand held it in his hand for a long moment before tucking it in his shirt pocket to read later. He felt
almost light-headed by the time he made it to his cabin,
where a little privacy was afforded him.

Sitting at the end of his berth, he reached for the envelope and carefully tore open the end before slipping
the single sheet from inside.

Dear Brand:

I pray I'm doing the right thing by writing you.
You've been gone several weeks now, and I
thought, I hoped, I'd stop thinking about you.

What's troubling me most is the way our last
conversation went. I'm feeling terribly guilty
about the way I behaved. I was heartless and un-
necessarily cruel when I didn't mean to be. Your
proposal came as a shock. My only excuse is that
it caught me unaware, and I didn't know what to
say or how to act and so I pretended it was all a
big joke. I've regretted that countless times and
can only ask your forgiveness.

I bought a grand piano. I've never had lessons
and can barely play a single note. Everyone who
knows me tells me I'm crazy. It wasn't until after
it was delivered that I realized why I'd done anything so foolish. It was an expensive but valuable lesson. I'm taking classes now on Saturday
mornings. Me and about five preteens. I strongly
suspect I'm older than my teacher, but frankly I
haven't gotten up enough gumption to ask. I don't
know if my ego could handle that.

The others seem to find me something of a
weirdo. None of them would be there if their parents weren't forcing them to take lessons. I, on the
other hand, want to learn badly enough to actually pay to do so. The kids don't understand that.
In four months, when you return, I should be well
into book 2, and I hope to impress the hell out of
you with my rendition of "Country Garden" or
something swanky from Mozart. At the rate I'm
progressing, I might end up playing in a cocktail
lounge by age forty. Can't you just see me pound-

ing out "Feelings" to a group of men attending an American Legion convention?

Oh, before I forget, you'll be pleased to know Margo is coming along nicely. She has her own apartment now and found a full-time job selling drapes at the JCPenney store. The difference in her from the first time she walked into the class until now is dramatic. She's still struggling with the pain and an occasional bout of anger, but for the most part she's doing so well. We're all proud of her. I thought you might like to hear how she's doing.

Although I've written far more than I thought I would, the real purpose of this letter is to apologize for the way our last conversation went. I can't be your wife, Brand, but I'd like to be your friend. If you can accept my friendship, then I'll be waiting to hear from you. If not, I'll understand.

Warm wishes,
Erin

Brand read through the letter twice before neatly folding it and replacing it inside the envelope. So she wanted to be friends.

He didn't. Not in the least.

He wasn't looking for a pal, a buddy, a sidekick. He wanted a wife, a woman who would stand at his side for the rest of his life. Someone to double the joy of the good times and divide the burden of the bad. When his ship pulled into port, he wanted her standing on the dock with the other wives and families, so eager to see him she'd be jumping up and down, hoping for a glimpse of him. When he walked down the gangplank, he wanted her to come rushing to his arms, unable to wait a second longer.

Erin wasn't offering him any of that. She had some milquetoast idea about them being pals. Well, he wanted no part of it. If she wanted a buddy, then she could look elsewhere.

Disgusted with the whole idea, Brand tossed her letter on his bunk. Erin MacNamera was going to have to offer him a whole lot more than friendship if she wanted any kind of relationship with him.

For a solid week, Erin rushed home from work to check her mail. She didn't try to fool herself by pretending she didn't care if Brand answered her letter or not. She did care, more than she wanted to admit. The way she figured it, he'd received her letter a week earlier. He'd take a few days to think matters over, and if everything went according to schedule, she'd have a letter back by the end of the following week.

No letter had arrived. At least not from Brand. Junk mail. Bills. Bank statements. They'd all made their way to Erin's address, but nothing from the one who mattered most.

"You might as well face it," she admonished herself. "He has no intention of answering your letter."

"What did you expect?" she asked herself a few minutes later. She knew what she'd expected. Letters. Hordes of them, filled, as they had been before, with humorous bits of wisdom that warmed her heart.

No such letters arrived. Not even a postcard.

Erin had never felt more melancholy in her life.

Erin's one-page letter had arrived exactly one month before. And for precisely thirty days Brand had been taking the letter out and reading it over again. Then he would methodically fold it and slip it back inside the envelope. After reading it so many times, he'd memorized every line.

At first keeping the letter was a show of strength on his part. He could hold it and touch a part of Erin. It felt good to be strong enough to stand his ground. He was unwilling to settle for second best with her. He wanted her heart… All right, he was willing to admit he needed more… He wanted her love for him to be so strong she was willing to relinquish everything. Frankly, he wasn't about to settle for anything less.

It was all or nothing, and that was the way it was meant to be. He was tired of going to her on bended knee. Tired of always being the one to compromise and give in. If anyone was going to make an effort to settle their differences, it would have to be Erin.

Besides, the way Brand figured it, Erin needed this time apart to realize they were meant for each other. She'd had two months to forget they'd ever met, and apparently that hadn't worked. Hadn't she said she'd been trying to forget him? She'd also claimed it wasn't working. Brand figured he'd let time enhance his chances with his brown-eyed beauty. She was his, all right; she just had to figure that much out for herself.

Nevertheless, Brand watched the mail, hoping Erin would write him a second time. She wouldn't, but he couldn't keep from hoping.

It wasn't Erin he heard from, but her father.

Dear Brand:
I'm sorry I haven't written in a while, but you know me. I never was much good at writing, unless it's something important. This time it is. I owe

you an apology. Forgive an old man, will you? I
had no business setting you up with my daughter.
That was my intent from the beginning, and I suspect you knew it. My Erin's a stubborn lass, and
I thought if anyone could catch her eye, it would
be your handsome face.

When I heard what happened, I wanted to
shake that daughter of mine, but she's her own
woman and she's got to make her own decisions,
and her own mistakes. I just never thought my
Erin could be such a fool. I wrote and told her as
much myself.

She isn't happy. That much I know for a fact.
She has this friend, Aimee—you might have met
her yourself. Apparently, Aimee and her husband
have split, and so the two girls are in cahoots. To
my way of thinking, no good's going to come of
those two prowling around Seattle, looking for
new relationships. Erin's a sweet thing, and I can't
help worrying about her, although she wouldn't
appreciate it if she knew. She'll do just fine. She's
not as beautiful as some, but when she puts her
mind to it, she'll find herself a catch that will
make this old man proud. Frankly, the wife and I
are looking forward to some grandchildren.

The last time we spoke, Erin mentioned she'd
written you. Seems a shame things didn't work
out between the two of you. A damn shame.

Keep in touch, will you? Give Romano and the
others my regards.

Casey

Erin and Aimee were in cahoots? Brand definitely
didn't like the sound of this. Not in the least. He read

the letter a second time, and the not-so-subtle messages seemed to slap him in the face. Erin was unhappy and looking for a new relationship. If Aimee weren't involved, that fact wouldn't concern him nearly as much. Alone, Erin was a novice in the ways of attracting men, but with Aimee spurring her on, anything could happen.

Brand liked Aimee, he just wasn't sure he could trust her. The other woman had made a blatant effort to catch his eye that first afternoon when he'd followed Erin into the Blue Lagoon. He had the feeling that if he'd paid her the least bit of attention she would have run out of the place with her tail between her legs, but that wasn't what concerned him now. The fact that the two of them were out prowling around looking for action did trouble him.

Damn it all. This could ruin everything. Casey mentioning grandchildren hadn't helped matters, any, either. Damn it all, if Erin was going to be making love, it would be with him. If she was so keen on having children, then he'd be the one to father them, not some… stranger.

"I brought along something for us to drink," Aimee said as she walked in Erin's front door. "Friday night," she grumbled, "and we're reduced to renting movies."

"Don't complain. We're going to have a good time."

"Right." Erin carried a large bowl of popcorn into the living room, having to weave her way around the piano.

"I hope you rented something uplifting—something that's going to make us laugh and forget our troubles. You know, these might be difficult times for us, but we've got a whole lot to be grateful for."

"I do." Erin couldn't help but agree.

"By the way, what movies did you rent?"

Erin picked up the two videos and read the titles. "*Terms of Endearment* and *Beaches*."

Nine

July was half spent, and summer had yet to make an appearance in the Pacific Northwest. The skies had been overcast all afternoon, threatening rain. Erin had been running behind schedule most of the day and had gone directly from work to her Women in Transition class at South Seattle Community College.

By the time she arrived home, she was hungry and exhausted. By rote, she carried the mail into the house with her and set it on the counter as she searched the cupboards for something interesting for dinner. Chicken noodle soup was her best option, and she dumped the contents of the can into a saucepan and set it on the burner while she idly sorted through her mail.

The letter from Brand caught her unaware. For a moment all she could do was stare at it while her heart casually slipped into double time. Ripping open the envelope, her hands trembling, she slowly lowered herself into the cushioned chair and read.

Dearest Erin,

    I kept telling myself I wouldn't write. Frankly, I was hoping the two of us could start on fresh ground once I returned. I've discovered I can't wait. It was either write or go mad. Romano insists I give it one last shot. He's a friend of mine, and he knows your dad, too.

The last three months have been the longest of my life. I've always enjoyed sea duty, but not this time, not when matters between us have been left so unsettled.

All right, I'll admit it. I'm selfish and thoughtless, but damn it all, I love you. Believe me, I wish I didn't. I wish I could turn my back on you and walk away without a regret. I tried that, but it didn't work. Later, after you wrote, I reasoned I would give us both breathing room to settle matters in our own minds. That hasn't worked, either. And so what are we left with? Damned if I know.

I haven't a clue what's right anymore. I want another chance with you. If you're willing to give it a second shot, let me know. Only do it soon, would you? I'm about to go out of my mind.

                                                        Brand

Dearest Brand,

I don't know what's right anymore, either. All I do know is how wretched I feel ninety-nine percent of the time. I thought I could forget you, too, only it didn't work out that way. Believe me, I've tried. Nothing seems to work. I'll be so glad when we can sit down and talk face-to-face. I've never felt like this.

You might remind your friend Romano that we have met. Obviously he doesn't remember. I attended his wedding with my mom and dad. It must have been ten years or so ago.

Write me again soon. I need to hear from you.

Erin

"What do you mean you've tried to forget me?" The sharp question was followed by an eerie long-distance hum that echoed in Erin's ear.

"Brand? Is that you?" The phone had woken her, and Erin hadn't yet had time to clear her thoughts. She brushed the hair out of her face and focused her gaze on the illuminated dial of her clock radio. It was the wee hours of the morning.

"Yes, it's me."

"Where are you?"

"Standing in some pay phone in the Philippines." His voice softened somewhat. "How are you?"

"Fine." Especially now that she'd heard his voice. It had taken her several seconds to ascertain that he was real and not part of the wildly romantic dreams she shared with him. She'd fantasized a hundred times talking to Brand and woken hours later disillusioned by the knowledge that several thousand miles separated them. "How are you?"

"Fine. So you've tried to forget me."

"Yes... Oh, Brand, it's so good to talk to you." She scrambled to her knees, pressing the phone to her ear as if that would magically bring him closer. She felt like weeping, as nonsensical as it sounded. "I've been so miserable, and then you didn't write and didn't write and I swear I thought I was going crazy."

"Sweet heaven, Erin, I don't know what we're going to do. I wish to hell—" He was interrupted by someone in the background. Whoever it was seemed to be arguing with Brand.

"Brand?"

"Hold on, sweetheart. Romano's here, and he's giving me hell."

"Giving you hell! Why?"

Brand chuckled softly. "He seems to think it's important you know I've been behaving like a jealous idiot ever since I got your letter."

"You're jealous? Whatever for?" Erin found this piece of information nothing short of incredible. For all intents and purposes, she'd been living the life of a nun for three solid months.

Brand hesitated before explaining, "It all started when I heard from your dad. He told me Aimee and her husband had split up and that you two women had gone out on the prowl. Then your letter arrived, and you claimed you'd tried to forget me, and I put two and two together—"

"And came up with ten," Erin teased, having trouble hiding her delight. "Let me assure you, you don't have a thing to worry about."

"I can't help the way I feel," Brand admitted grudgingly. "No one's ever mattered to me as much as you. My mind got to wandering, and I couldn't help thinking… To make a long story short, I guess I've been a bit cross lately."

Once more the conversation was interrupted by Brand's friend. "All right, all right," Brand said. "According to half the men on the *Blue Ridge* I've been acting like a real bastard. Romano insisted I call you and find out exactly what's been going on before I jump to conclusions."

"Were you really jealous?" Erin still had a difficult time believing it.

"I already said I was," he snapped.

"If anyone should be worried, it's me. You're the one sailing to all those tropical islands. From what I remember, those native women are beautiful enough to turn any sailor's head."

"I swear to you, Erin, I haven't so much as spoken to a single woman since we left port. How can I when all I think about is you?"

"Two and a half more months," she reminded him.

"I know. I can't remember any tour taking so long."

"Me either. I've got a couple of letters off to you this week, and I baked some chocolate chip cookies. Dad always loved it when Mom mailed him cookies…. I thought maybe you would, too. Old habits die hard, I guess."

"I picked up something for you while we were in port, but I'd rather give it to you in person. Do you mind waiting?"

"No." But Erin noted that neither of them was willing to discuss how long it would be before they'd see each other again. Erin couldn't afford to fly off to Hawaii, especially after purchasing the piano. And Brand might not be able to get leave.

"Listen, Irish eyes, I've got to go."

"I know," she said, expelling a sigh of regret. "I'm so glad you phoned."

"I am, too. Write me."

"I will, I promise."

Yet both were reluctant to hang up the line until Erin heard Romano arguing with Brand in the background.

"Hey, Face, aren't you going to tell her you love her?"

Romano's question was followed by a short pause before Brand said, "She already knows."

Smiling to herself, Erin relaxed and grinned sheepishly. Yes, she did know, but it wouldn't have done any harm to have heard him tell her one more time.

Dearest Erin,
The cookies arrived today. You never told me you could bake like this. They're fabulous. I can't tell you how much it means to me that you'd send me cookies.

I don't know what the men think of me. For the first part of the cruise I was an ill-tempered bear, snapping at everyone. These days I walk around wearing a silly grin, passing out cookies like a first-grade teacher to her favorite pupils.

By the way, you haven't mentioned the piano lately. Did you know I play? My mother forced me to take lessons for five years. I hated it then but have had reason to be grateful since.

I'm sorry this is so short, but the mail's due to be picked up anytime and I wanted to get this off so you'd know how much I appreciate the cookies.

Miss you,
Brand

P.S. The next time you write, send me your picture.

"Well?" Erin asked for the third time as Aimee reviewed the stack of snapshots. Brand had been hounding her for weeks for a photo. She'd tried to put him off, explaining that she really didn't take a good picture, but he wouldn't listen, claiming that if she didn't send one he'd write and ask her family for a photo. It didn't take much thinking on her part to realize that her dad would take delight in sending off a whole series of pictures, no doubt starting with naked baby shots. "Which one is the best?"

Aimee shrugged laconically. "They're all about the same."

"I know, but which one makes me look sexy and glamorous and every lieutenant's dream?"

Aimee's questioning gaze rose steadily to meet Erin's. "He asked for your picture, you know, not one of Madonna in her brass-tipped bra."

"I realize that, but I wanted something special, something that made me look attractive."

"You are attractive."

"More than attractive," Erin added sheepishly. "Sexy."

"Erin, sweetheart, at the risk of offending you, I'd like to remind you we took these photos with my camera, which cost all of forty dollars. If you're looking for someone to airbrush the finish, you should have contacted a professional."

"It's just that—"

"Hey, sweetie, you don't need to explain anything to me."

Erin knew she didn't, but she couldn't help feeling a twinge of guilt. Aimee's divorce was progressing smoothly enough. Matters, however, were starting to heat up now that the attorneys were involved.

"So have you heard from the sailor boy lately?" Aimee asked with a hint of sarcasm. She sorted through the pictures again and selected three, setting them aside. Falling in love wasn't a subject that interested Aimee these days. The divorce was proving to be far more painful than she'd ever expected.

162   *Debbie Macomber*

"He writes often."

"And you?"

"I… I write often, too."

"How much longer before he's back in Hawaii?"

Erin had it figured out right down to the number of hours, although it would do her little good. "About six weeks."

Aimee nodded, but Erin wasn't completely sure her friend had even heard her.

"This one," Aimee said unexpectedly, handing her the snapshot. Erin was standing in front of a rosebush in her yard, where all of the photos had been taken.

She was wearing a dress in a soft shade of olive green, which nicely complemented her coloring. Her sleeves were rolled up past her elbow, and a narrow row of buttons ran down the length of the front. The outfit was complemented by a woven belt and a matching large-brimmed hat that shaded her face.

"This one. Really?" Erin questioned. It wasn't the one she would have chosen. Her eyes were lowered, unlike in the other photos, and her mouth was curved slightly upward in a subtle smile.

"He'll love it," Aimee insisted.

Dearest Erin,
The picture arrived in today's letter. I'd forgotten how beautiful you are. I couldn't take my eyes off you. It made me miss you so much more than I do already. An empty feeling came over me. One so big an earthmover couldn't fill it. I don't know how to explain it. I'm not sure I can.

   All I know is I love you so much it frightens me. Somehow, someway, we're going to come up

with a solution to all this. We have to. I can't bear
to think of not having you in my life.

I'm sorry to hear about Aimee and her husband
and hope they can patch things up.

And no, I haven't seen any women in grass
skirts lately. Haven't you figured it out yet, my
sweet Irish rose? I only have eyes for you.

Love,
Brand

Brand taped Erin's picture to the wall next to his
berth. He'd seen other guys do the same thing and had
never understood what led mature men to do something so juvenile. Now he understood. Love did. The
last person he saw when he went to sleep at night was
Erin, and she was the first one to greet him each morning. Sometimes he'd linger a few moments extra just
staring at her.

He loved the picture. Just the way she was standing
with her back to the sun, bright shreds of light folding
golden arms around her. Her eyes were downcast, and
she had the look of a woman longing to be kissed.

Brand ran his tongue around the outside of his lips.
It had been so long since he'd kissed Erin he'd almost
forgotten what it was like.

Almost forgotten.

What he did remember was enough to prompt a pronounced tightness in his pants. Although she was wearing a very proper olive-green dress in the snapshot, the
image of her standing in the sunlight reminded him of
the morning she'd wandered into the kitchen in her flannel gown. She'd smelled of lavender and musk, and the
yoke of her prim gown had been embroidered in satin
threads that emphasized her perky breasts. Erin had

beautiful breasts, and the sudden need Brand experienced to taste and feel them was enough to produce a harsh groan. His breath fled. It was time to take a cold shower, something he seemed to be doing a lot of lately. He pressed his fingers to his lips and then bounced them against Erin's pictures, doubting that she had a clue how crazy he was about her.

Dear Erin,
You don't know me. At least I don't think we've ever met. I'm Ginger Romano. My husband, Alex, and Brand Davis are both aboard the *Blue Ridge*. By now you've probably heard about Brand's promotion. He's been promoted to full-grade lieutenant.

Brand's real popular with the guys, and they wanted to do something special for him. That's why Alex wrote me about you. A few of Brand's friends decided to get together and throw a surprise party for him to celebrate his promotion.

Someone thought it might be fun if they hired a woman to jump out of a cake. That's when Alex came up with a much better idea. They're going to throw that party, and there's going to be a woman there all right, but we want to surprise him with you. Everyone went together and pitched in and we have enough for your airplane ticket. You're welcome to stay at the house here with Alex and me, if you don't mind kids. We have three, and they're a handful, but the welcome mat's out and we'd really be pleased if you could.

Let me know at your earliest opportunity if it's the least bit feasible for you to arrive the second week of October. We'll need to know soon,

though, so we can book your flight. Please remember this is a surprise.

    I'm looking forward to meeting you.

Sincerely,
Ginger Romano

"You're going?" Aimee asked again, as if she still
couldn't believe Erin had agreed to this crazy, spur-of-
the-moment plan. "You're honestly going?"

Maybe it was a crazy thing to do, but Erin couldn't
resist. She could never have afforded the airplane
ticket herself, and this seemed her golden opportunity
to spend time with Brand. They'd been apart so many
months, and they'd trudged over a mountain range of
emotions and doubts.

She had his picture, but she wasn't exactly sure she
remembered what he looked like. He'd contacted her
by phone only one time in the last six months. Was she
flying to him? In a heartbeat!

"I'm going," she assured Aimee, tucking her curling
iron in her suitcase.

"I don't suppose you need a friend to tag along for
moral support?"

"I do, but I can't afford you," Erin joked.

"Don't worry, I can't afford me, either. Apparently
no one can, not even Steve." She was trying to make
light of the facts with a joke, but it fell flat.

"Don't worry," Erin promised, "I'll be back in time
for the settlement hearing. I won't let you go through
this alone."

Aimee's eyes filled with appreciation. "Thanks. I'm
counting on you." She glanced around the bedroom one
last time. "Well, it looks like you've got everything
under control." Aimee made it sound like a sharp con-

trast to her own life, and Erin struggled with a sudden twinge of guilt.

"Hey," Aimee said with a short, pathetic laugh, "don't look so woebegone. It isn't every day you get an opportunity like this. Enjoy it while you can. Play in the sun, relax, stroll along the beach. I'll be fine… You don't need to worry about little ol' me."

"Aimee!"

"All right, all right, I'm being ridiculous. I do want you to have fun. It's just that I'm going to miss you something terrible."

"I'm going to miss you, too, but it's only a week."

Erin glanced around one last time to be sure she'd packed everything she needed. Aimee was driving her to the airport and dropping her off. In less than two hours she'd be boarding the flight. Several hours later, she'd step off the Boeing 747 in Honolulu, where Ginger would be waiting to pick her up. She'd be leaving the cold rain of Seattle behind and disembarking in balmy eighty-degree sunshine.

Not a bad trade.

The flight seemed to take an eternity. Several times Erin had to pinch herself to make sure all this was real. She felt like a game-show winner who hadn't expected anything more than the consolation prize. Yet here she was flying to Brand with seven uninterrupted days of heaven stretching out in front of her.

The *Blue Ridge* was due to sail into Pearl Harbor sometime late Wednesday afternoon. The party was scheduled for Thursday evening. Ginger had taken care of most of the details, along with a couple of other navy wives and Lieutenant Commander Catherine Fredrickson, another of Brand's friends. For the past month, Erin had been corresponding with Ginger, and she liked her immensely.

The hardest part was keeping the fact that Erin was in Hawaii a secret until Thursday evening.

"I don't know where the hell she could be," Brand told Romano Thursday morning. "I tried phoning every hour all night. She didn't mention she was going away."

"Maybe something came up."

"Obviously," he barked. Brand was in a sour mood. For days he'd been looking forward to phoning Erin. It was the first thing he'd done when he'd walked into his apartment. The anticipation of hearing her voice was the only thing that had gotten him through those last few weeks. Rarely had he ever been more restless or more ready for a tour to end.

Each night for three weeks he'd dreamed of listening to the soft catch in her voice when she realized it was him on the line. For the first time in six hellish months he could speak to her freely without someone standing over his shoulder the way Alex had in the Philippines. He hoped that when they spoke this time they might accomplish something.

At the very least they could discuss what they had to do to see each other again.

For several long months he'd thought of little else but being with Erin again. Yet, when the time arrived, she was gone. Vanished. No one seemed to know where she was.

Brand had gone so far as to contact her family. Casey didn't sound the least bit concerned, claiming Erin often had to travel out of town on business trips. But, now that Brand mentioned it, Casey did seem to remember Erin saying something about flying off to Spokane sometime soon.

If that was the case, she hadn't bothered to tell Brand.

"How about going out for a couple of beers?" Romano suggested late that same afternoon.

"Ginger's going to let you?" he asked disbelievingly.

"She won't care. Bobby's at soccer practice, and frankly, what she doesn't know won't hurt her."

Brand didn't know what had gotten into his friend. Usually Alex couldn't wait to get home to his family, and once he was back, he spent plenty of time with the youngsters. Brand had always admired the fact Romano was a good family man. He hoped when the time came he'd be as conscientious a husband and father.

Brand considered his options. It was either hang around his apartment all night, hoping Erin would contact him, or visit the Officers' Club and talk shop with a few old friends. The second option was by far the most appealing, yet something elemental tugged at his heart. He hated the thought he might miss Erin, if she should happen to call.

"Well?" Romano pressed impatiently. "What's your choice?"

"I don't suppose one beer would hurt."

A twinkling light flashed in Alex's sea-green eyes. "Nope, I don't think it will, either."

As soon as Brand had fastened his seat belt, Romano started the engine and drove past the Officers' Club and outside the navy compound. "Hey, where are we going?"

"For a beer," Alex reminded him, doing his best to hide a grin.

Something was up. Brand might not have a whole lot to do with navy intelligence, but he didn't need a master's degree in human nature to determine that something was awry.

"All right, Romano," Brand insisted, "tell me what's going on here."

"What makes you think anything is?"

"Let's start with the fact you're free the second night we're in port?"

"All right, all right, if you must know, the guys went together and planned a small party in your honor, Lieutenant Davis."

Amused, Brand chuckled. He should have known a long time before now that his friends wouldn't let that pass without making some kind of fuss. "Who's in on this?"

"Just about everyone. Only..."

"Only what?"

"There's one small problem, if you want to call it that." Romano hesitated. "It's a little bit embarrassing, but the guys wanted to make this special, so they hired a woman."

"They did what?" Brand demanded.

"Someone got the bright idea that it would be fun to see your face if they rolled in a cake and had a woman leap out of the top."

Brand slowly shook his head. "I certainly hope you're kidding."

"Sorry, I'm not. I couldn't talk them out of it."

Brand set his hand over his eyes and slowly shook his head. He should be amused by all this. "A woman?"

"You got it, buddy."

Brand mulled over the information and chuckled. There wasn't much he could do about it now, but he appreciated the warning. "Whatever happens, don't ever let Erin find out about it, understand?"

"You've got my word of honor."

The Cliff House was a restaurant with a reputation for excellent food and an extensive list of imported wine. Brand was mildly surprised that the establishment would sanction the type of entertainment his friends had planned.

The receptionist smiled warmly when Romano announced Brand's name, and she gingerly led them to a banquet room off the main dining room.

"Hey, you guys went all out," Brand muttered under his breath as they followed the petite Chinese woman.

"Nothing but the best," Romano assured him, still grinning.

Several shouts and cheers of welcome went out when the two men walked into the room. Brand was handed a bottle of imported German beer and a basket of thick pretzels and led to a table in the front of the room.

"Are you ready to be entertained?" Romano asked, claiming the empty chair beside him. He reached for a bowl of mixed nuts and leaned back, eager for the show.

Brand nodded. He might as well get this over with first thing and be done with it. He forced a smile and a relaxed pose while two of the crewmen from the *Blue Ridge* rolled out a six-foot-tall box tied up with a large red bow. It wasn't a cake, but close enough.

"You're supposed to untie the ribbon," Romano explained, urging him forward.

Reluctantly Brand stood and walked up to the front of the room. There must have been fifty men—and several women—all standing around, intently watching him. He tried to act nonchalant, as if he did this sort of thing every day.

He lifted one end of the broad red ribbon and tugged,

expecting it to fall open. It didn't, and he was offered loud bits of advice by the men on the floor.

Brand tried a second time, tugging harder. The ribbon fell away, and the four sides of the box lazily folded open. Brand wasn't exactly sure what he expected. His mind filled with several possibilities for which he was mentally prepared. But what did appear left him speechless with shock.

"Hello, Brand," Erin greeted with a warm smile as she stepped forward. She was wearing the same olive-green dress as in the picture she'd sent. For a wild moment, Brand was convinced she was a figment of his imagination. She had to be.

"Say something," Romano shouted. "Don't just stand there looking like a bump on a log."

"Erin?"

Her brown eyes had never been wider. "You're disappointed?"

"Sweet heaven, no," he groaned, reaching for her, dragging her into the shelter of his arms.

Ten

Brand blinked, unable to believe Erin was so soft against his body. Perhaps he was hallucinating. All the lonely months they'd spent apart might have dulled his senses. Was he so desperate for her that his mind had mystically forced her to materialize?

Brand didn't know, but he was about to find out. In a heartbeat, his mouth came crashing down on hers. She was real. More real than he dared remember. Soft. Sweet. And in his arms.

Low, guttural sounds made their way up his throat as he slanted his mouth over hers. The men behind him were hooting and cheering, but Brand barely heard them above Erin's small cry of welcome.

He felt the tears slide down her face, and he loved her so much that it was all he could do not to break down and weep himself. He kissed her again, sliding his tongue along hers, deep, deeper, into the honey-sweet depths of her mouth.

The boisterous shouts from behind him reminded Brand that, no matter how much he wanted to, he couldn't continue to make love to Erin. At least not in front of several dozen of his peers. Pulling away from her was the hardest thing he'd ever done.

"Are you surprised?" Romano teased, joining him in the front of the room and slapping him hard across the back.

Unable to speak, Brand nodded. His eyes, insatiable and greedy, locked with Erin's. He couldn't resist hugging her once more. Wrapping his arms around her, he closed his eyes and breathed in the scent of lavender and musk that was hers alone. He'd dreamed of this moment so often and now it was all coming to pass, and he couldn't believe it was happening.

He gazed into the sea of faces watching him, unable to express the gratitude in his heart.

"Come on, Lieutenant," Catherine Fredrickson instructed, "sit down before you make a fool of yourself. Dinner's about to be served." He and Catherine had worked together for nearly four years, and he was an admirer of hers. Their relationship was probably a little unusual, when he thought about it. Catherine was a friend, and he'd never thought of her as anything more. It worried him that Erin might feel threatened by the lieutenant commander.

"We brought out the dessert early," another friend teasingly called out to him.

Keeping Erin close to his side, Brand led the way to their table. Several friends came forward, eager to introduce themselves to Erin. Many had worked with her father at one time or another and were interested in news of the fun-loving Casey MacNamera.

No matter how many people spoke to him, or commanded his attention, Brand couldn't take his eyes off his beautiful Irish miss for more than a few seconds.

His gaze was magnetically drawn back to her again and again.

Erin's gaze seemed equally hungry. A myriad of emotions scored Brand, many of which he couldn't have identified. All he knew, all he wanted to know, was that Erin was sitting at his side. His heart swelled with a love so strong that it made him weak.

Men gathered around him. Friends asked him questions. Dinner was served. Brand laughed, talked, ate and did everything else that was required of him. But every now and again his eyes would slide to Erin's, and they'd nearly drown in each other's presence.

She was even more beautiful than he remembered. Not so strikingly attractive that her loveliness called attention to herself, but her rare inner quality of strength and gentleness shone through.

"How long have you known about this?" he whispered, twining their fingers.

"A month." She smiled shyly. "The longest month of my life."

"Mine, too." He braced his forehead against hers and breathed in the warm scent of her. It was in his mind, then and there, to tell her how much he loved and needed her. But emotion constricted the muscles of his throat, making speech difficult.

"Here," Romano said, slapping a set of keys on the tabletop.

Brand didn't understand.

"Take the car," he instructed.

"Your car? But how will you get home?" Brand realized his speech was too sporadic to make sense.

"Ginger," Romano answered with a chuckle. "Now get out of here before someone gives you a reason to stay."

Brand didn't need a second invitation. He stood, his fingers linked with Erin's. He took a long detour around the room, shaking hands with his comrades, wanting to thank his friends for the biggest—and by far the best—surprise of his life.

When he'd finished, he walked purposefully out of the restaurant.

"Oh, Brand…" Erin whispered once they were alone together. She seemed at a loss to continue.

Brand understood. For weeks he'd been planning what he wanted to say to her. His intention was to logically, intellectually lead her to the conclusion that they should do as he'd suggested months earlier and marry. He planned to tackle each one of her objections with sound reasoning and irrefutable logic. But every word he'd prepared sailed straight into the sunset without ever reaching his lips. All that mattered to Brand in that moment was holding her, loving her.

He gently brought her into his arms and buried his face in the delicate curve of her neck. Brand felt the series of quivers that racked her shoulders and moved down her spine. He pulled her flush against him in an effort to comfort her. Her tears dampened his neck, and her warm breath fanned his throat.

Holding her this close was torment of another kind. Her soft breasts caressed his hard chest, and her stomach was flattened against his. All torture should be this incredibly sweet, he reasoned.

He laid his hand on her hair, filled his fingers with it, savoring the silky smoothness of the thick auburn tresses.

"Let's get out of here," Brand whispered when he could endure the pleasure of holding her no longer.

"Where?"

If they went back to his place, there was no question in his mind that she'd spend the night in his bed. No doubt Romano and the others assumed that was exactly what would happen. Maybe Erin was thinking the same thing herself. He didn't know.

His heart and body were greedy for her. But his need wasn't so voracious that it blocked out sound judgment. He wanted Erin as his lover, but sharing a bed with her wasn't nearly enough to satisfy him. If he was looking for sexual gratification, he could find that with any number of women.

He yearned for much more from Erin. He wanted her for his wife, and he wasn't willing to settle for anything less.

Brand helped her into the car. He noted when he started the engine that Erin's hands were clenched together in her lap. She was nervous. A slow smile worked its way across his mouth. What the hell, he was as tense as she was. Only in his case he was too sophisticated to show it.

"Where are we going?" she asked in a voice so small he could scarcely make out the words.

"The beach."

She relaxed at that, tucking her hand under his arm and leaning her head on his shoulder as he steered the car out of the parking lot. The warm, soothing wind whipped past them as Brand drove the narrow, twisting road down the steep hillside. Palm trees swayed in the breeze, and the silver light of a full moon reflected against the crashing waves of the surf.

Walking hand in hand down the sandy embankment, Brand led the way toward the water. The night was warm and the beach empty.

Brand paused once they reached the ocean, faced her

and wrapped his arms around her trim waist, holding on to her. Her eyes met his, and he read the confusion and the doubts. Now wasn't the time for either.

"There's so much I planned to tell you," Erin murmured, seeming to search for the right words to say to him.

"Later," he whispered before his mouth met hers. "We have all the time in the world to straighten out our problems. For now, love me."

She moaned and slipped her arms up his chest, leaning into him as she gave him her mouth. Their kiss was like spontaneous combustion, their need for each other fierce and compelling. His tongue breached the barrier of her lips and plundered deep and long. All ten of his fingers sank into her hair as their kisses, tempered with tenderness, delved deeper and deeper. Sweeter than anything Brand had ever known. Slowly he ran his hands over her shoulders and the sides of her waist to her hips, finally cupping her buttocks. He drew her up slightly until her abdomen settled naturally over the hard imprint of his growing need. For an elongated second neither of them moved. Then Erin, his sweet, innocent Erin, started to rub against him, creating a hot friction, a burning need, that all but devoured him. Each sway of her hips, each rotation, eradicated every shred of reason Brand possessed.

"Ah, Erin," he rasped. Feverishly he tore his mouth from hers, hoping the cool air would clear his head. But it did little to help.

Her mouth. Her sweet, delectable mouth tasted even better than he'd fantasized. He couldn't seem to taste enough of her, and each kiss only quickened his appetite for more.

Even through the thick fabric of her dress he could

feel her nipples harden. Her breasts felt lush and full, pressed as they were against his chest. Ripe. He remembered how they felt in his hands, how they'd filled his palms, spilled over. Unable to resist, his thumbs skirted over her nipples.

She moaned softly as his fingers fumbled with the row of buttons until the first several were free. He slipped the top partway down her shoulders and was challenged by her teddy and bra.

"Are so many clothes necessary?" he moaned, then alternated his attention from one breast to the other, his mouth closing over the material, making wet circles in the satin.

"Yes, all these clothes are necessary," she whispered, and he could hear the laughter in her voice.

He wanted her. Then. There. His need was so great that a thin film of sweat broke out over his body. Brand closed his eyes and gnashed his teeth in an effort to rein in the desire that coursed through him like liquid fire, gathering inevitably in his loins.

Erin stepped away from him and slowly, purposefully, unfastened the buttons of her dress, letting it slip to the sand.

"W-what are you doing?" Dear sweet heaven, she was going to make this impossible.

She smiled boldly up at him. "Let's swim."

Brand was about to remind her that neither of them had a suit when she started running toward the water.

"Erin," he called after her, and at the same moment he sank to the sand and started unlacing his shoes. Five years in Hawaii and he'd never once done anything so crazy. She was out in the surf, splashing away like a dolphin, and he was struggling to remove his pants, which he sent flying into the night. Without bothering to unbutton his shirt, he slipped it over his head, balled it in his fist and impatiently hurled it down on the beach.

By the time he joined her, Erin was waist-deep in the surf, holding her arms out to him. "Come in, Lieutenant, the water's fine."

"If you'd wanted to swim, I'd have preferred to wait until I had on a suit, and not a double-breasted one."

"I'm double-breasted," she teased, leaping up and down in the water like a porpoise to give him a tantalizing view of her breasts. Brand was certain she had no idea how much she was revealing. When wet, the white satin material of her bra was as transparent as glass. She might as well be nude for all the cover her underthings afforded her.

With unhurried strides, Brand walked toward her. The tide slapped against his long legs, but he refused to pause, his pace uniform and steady.

"Besides," she added with a taunting grin. "We both needed to cool off, don't you agree?"

"I had everything under control."

"No, you didn't, and neither did I." She rubbed her hands up and down her arms as a tiny shiver went through her.

"This craziness is supposed to cool us off?" he muttered under his breath. If anything, Brand was hotter than ever. Her nipples had beaded, the dark aureoles pointing directly at him, commanding his attention. The ends of her hair were wet and dripping lazily onto her smooth shoulders. The salt water rolled down her creamy white neck and into the valley between her breasts. Everything seemed to point in that direction, including his gaze.

When she was a few yards away from him, Erin floated into his arms. Her body was warm and slippery as she locked her arms around his neck, and her long legs folded over his hips. The instant her weight settled against him, she felt the strength of him. Slowly she raised her soft gaze to his, and her eyes widened slightly.

"Brand?"

"As you can see, your plans have backfired, my dear."

"Now what?"

She shifted her weight slightly, scooting her derriere over the protrusion, and in the process nearly unmanned him. She was too innocent to understand what she was doing to him. If this continued much longer, they'd end up making love while standing waist-deep in the surf.

"Let me taste you," he pleaded, his voice low and guttural.

As though in a trance, Erin nodded. She reached back and unfastened her bra. Her breasts fell free of the restraining material and settled against the water-slicked planes of his chest. Her nipples, pouting prettily, felt so hot, so gloriously wonderful against his cool skin, that for a second he forgot to breathe.

She must have felt it, too, because her breath caught softly then. Clenching handfuls of his hair, she began to move, circling her breasts against him, creating a delicious, indescribable friction.

"Oh, baby," he groaned as he lifted her higher, sliding his open mouth across her breasts, creating a slick trail, sucking lightly from one breast and then the other, loving the taste of her. His mouth closed around her, and he gloried in the untamed eagerness of her response.

Her hands were in his hair, and she was making low whimpering sounds. He languidly paid attention to each breast, rolling his tongue around the passion-beaded nipple, sucking strongly, then gentling the action.

Between sighs and moans Erin encouraged him to take more and more of her into his mouth, her voice soft and trembling as she pleaded, rotating her hips against him, her feet digging into the small of his back.

Brand had reached the limit of his endurance. "Erin," he begged. "Oh, baby, hold still…please."

"No…oh, Brand, I…don't think I can… It feels so good."

"I know, baby, I know. Too good."

She gently thrashed against him. "Kiss me," she whispered.

Brand willingly complied. Her mouth opened under the force of his, and her tongue met his in joyous union. The slow, smooth gyration of her hips against him caused the blood to rush to his head until he feared he would lose his footing. He felt as powerless against Erin as he was against the flow of the tide.

His hand slipped inside the wide leg of her tap pants and over her bare derriere. Then, slowly, gradually, he slipped his fingers toward the warm, moist opening of her womanhood. She opened to him like a rosebud responding to the warming rays of the sun. Her pulsating warmth closed around him, and she started to whimper as he gently claimed possession of the innermost part of her body.

Making panting sounds, Erin squeezed her eyes closed and began to move against him, her actions countering his. Her nails dug deep into the thick muscles of his shoulders, but he felt no discomfort as her mouth hungrily latched on to his, her tongue boldly searching out his. He felt her climax and sensed the pulsating waves of undiluted pleasure as she relaxed heavily against him.

Gradually, her eyes opened, and their gazes held for a long moment. Brand loved her so much that he thought his pounding heart would explode in his chest. She smiled at him. Shyly. Almost apologetically. Her look was so tender that he could have drowned in it.

The sound of laughter coming from behind them on the shore brought Brand rudely back to reality.

"There are people coming," Erin whispered in a panic.

"I told you before this isn't such a good idea."

"But... Brand, I'm nearly naked."

"For all intents and purposes, you are indeed naked."

"Do something."

"You're joking."

"We can't just stand here."

"Why not? With any luck they'll stroll past and not notice two crazy people lolling around in the surf. Forget it, they'll notice."

Erin expelled a sharp breath and pressed her forehead against Brand's. "This is all my fault."

"I know," he whispered, kissing her soundly. "But I forgive you." He hugged her close, amused. Her face was beet red; even her breasts were rosy with embarrassment. He waited until the sound of voices had faded, and then he carried Erin effortlessly back onto the beach.

Erin was in the kitchen with Ginger Romano, slicing pineapple into a large stainless-steel bowl for a fresh fruit salad they were making for the evening meal. Ginger was shaping hamburger patties, pressing the meat firmly together between the palms of her hands.

"You're quiet this afternoon," Ginger said, smiling warmly in Erin's direction. The two had been standing side by side for the past ten minutes without a word passing between them. The silence, however, was a comfortable one. Erin and Ginger had become fast friends in the past few days.

For the first time that afternoon the house was relatively quiet. The two youngest Romano children were napping. Alex and Brand had taken six-year-old Bobby to the grocery store with them to buy charcoal briquettes for the barbecue.

Erin smiled lazily over at her friend. "I don't mean to be so uncommunicative. I was just thinking, I guess." She was due to leave Oahu in two short days. She didn't want to go. Seattle was her home, and she loved living in the Pacific Northwest, but she'd forgotten how beautiful Hawaii could be.

"Who are you trying to kid?" Erin muttered under her breath. It wasn't Hawaii she found so relaxing and stimulating. It was being with Brand.

"Did you say something?" Ginger asked.

"Not really... I sometimes talk to myself."

"I do that myself when I'm thinking. Usually I do it when something's worrying me."

"I was just wondering what's going to become of me and Brand." No one had said anything, but Erin couldn't shake the feeling that everyone was waiting for them to announce their wedding plans. The pressure was there; it was low-key and subtle, but nevertheless Erin could feel it as strongly as she'd felt the tide against her legs when in the ocean.

"I take it you've enjoyed yourself this week?" Ginger asked, setting the plate of hamburger patties aside.

"Everyone's been wonderful."

"You've been quite a hit yourself. We were all eager to meet you."

"In other words," Erin said with a teasing smile, "Brand's friends were more curious than generous when it came to sending me that airplane ticket."

"Exactly! I do hope you enjoyed this week in Hawaii."

"What's there not to enjoy?" Erin teased.

"Then you might consider moving here," she suggested boldly.

"No way." Erin was quick to discount the suggestion. "Seattle's home."

"Have you lived there long?"

"Two years. I graduated from the University of Texas, but spent the first two years in Florida before transferring."

"You did your graduate work in Texas, too?"

"No, I finished up in New York, so you can see why I'm happy to settle in Seattle at last. It's my first home, and I intend to stay put for a good long while."

"I can understand that," Ginger said thoughtfully. "You were certainly a hit. We're going to be sorry to see you go."

"I passed muster, then?"

"With flying colors. It does my heart good to see the mighty Brandon Davis fall in love. I was beginning to doubt it would ever happen. He's such a stubborn cuss. He'd date a woman for a few weeks, then lose interest and drop her. I knew from the moment he mentioned your name, you were different, and so did everyone else."

"Brand is special." She licked the juice from her fingers and set the paring knife in the sink. "Frankly, I can't help worrying that I'm simply more of a challenge to him than the other women he's dated. I'm not like the others. I refused to fall at his feet." Although she attempted to make light of the fact, she considered it the bona fide truth.

"I don't think that's it, exactly," Ginger countered quickly. She paused and leaned her hip against the counter. "In some ways, perhaps, but not completely. Now that I've gotten to know you, I can understand why Brand's so enthralled with you. You two complement each other. You seem to balance each other. Brand's outgoing, you're a little withdrawn. Not unsociable— don't misunderstand me. Brand's one hundred percent navy—"

"I'm one hundred percent not."

Ginger paused, and her smooth brow pleated in a frown. "It really troubles you, doesn't it?"

Erin nodded. "If I hadn't grown up around the military, I probably would naively accept this lifestyle as part of what it means to love Brand. But I've been there. The navy expects certain concessions from a wife and family, and frankly, I refuse to make those. I'm a navy brat, and I know what it means to marry a man in the military. It's one of life's cruel practical jokes that I'd meet Brand this way and fall for him."

"I don't look at it that way," Ginger said, scooting out a stool and sitting down. "Before I married Alex, I thought long and hard about accepting his proposal. I wasn't keen on marrying a navy man, knowing from the first that I would always place second in his life."

"Exactly," Erin agreed, but it was so much more than that. If she did marry Brand, her life would no longer be her own.

"I prefer to think of Alex and myself as a team. We're contributors to the defense and security of our country.

I'm proud of Alex and the role he plays, but I'm equally satisfied with my own contribution. If it weren't for my talents, my enthusiasm, my dedication, and that of the other wives and families, the navy would lose its effectiveness. I realize I sound like a propaganda machine, but frankly, it's the truth."

"I grew up hearing and believing all that." Erin straightened and ceremoniously squared her shoulders, keeping her eyes trained straight ahead. In a monotone, she recited what she could remember of the Navy Wifeline creed. "I believe that through better understanding of the navy, wives will enjoy and accept more enthusiastically the navy way of life, and we pledge our efforts... Blah, blah, blah."

"You do know it," Ginger said with a smile.

"For eighteen years I was part and parcel of the demanding tempo of navy life. I was uprooted more times than I can remember. I've lived on more bases than some admirals. It was one move after another, and frankly, I don't know if I'm willing to make that kind of sacrifice a second time."

Erin was being as honest as she knew how to be. Yes, she loved Brand, loved him with all her heart, but being in love didn't solve the problem.

"What are you going to do?"

"I don't know," she whispered, suddenly miserable.

Things had changed between Brand and Erin after their night on the beach. Never again had either of them allowed their lovemaking to progress to that level.

They spent every available moment together, but they did little more than kiss and hold hands. Although she'd seen the tourist attractions a number of times before, Brand escorted Erin all over the island. It was as though they both needed to see and appreciate the beauty and the splendor of Oahu through one another's eyes.

"I wish I knew what I could say that would help you," Ginger said, crossing her legs. She folded her arms around her middle and stared into space. "The thing that impresses me most about you and Brand is that it's like the two of you have been married for years and years. You seem to read one another's thoughts. It's uncanny. Forgive me for saying this, but it's almost as if you were meant to be together."

"It isn't as dramatic as you think," Erin argued. "I know the way a man in the navy thinks."

And behaves. Brand wasn't fooling her any. They hadn't talked once about the very subject that had driven them apart. Brand was biding his time, waiting until her defenses were lowered and she was weakest. His game plan was one Erin recognized well from her own father's school of strategy. Brand assumed that if he let matters follow a natural progression, things would work out his way. He seemed to believe that once she was head over heels in love with him, the fact he was navy wouldn't matter.

Wrong. It mattered a whole lot. Only she didn't want to spend their first time together in six months arguing. Apparently Brand didn't, either, and so the subject was one they'd both avoided. Brand by design. Erin…she didn't know. For selfish reasons, she guessed.

The front door opened, followed by the sound of running feet. "Mommy, we're home." Six-year-old Bobby burst into the kitchen like a pistol shot.

Brand and Alex followed closely behind. Alex carried a large bag of briquettes.

Slipping up behind Erin, Brand wrapped his arms

around her waist and kissed her cheek. "Did you miss me?"

"Dreadfully."

"That's what I hoped." He smiled wickedly and turned her around to reward her with a kiss. The intensity caught Erin off guard.

When Brand released her, his eyes held hers. "We need some time alone."

She nodded. The following afternoon she was scheduled to return to Seattle. The day of reckoning had arrived.

Erin was barely able to down her dinner. The four adults sat around the picnic table, lingering over their coffee, while the three youngsters ran wild in the backyard.

"Hawaii is beautiful this time of year," Erin remarked lazily, catching Brand's eye.

He slipped her hand into his and squeezed tightly. "It's beautiful any time of year." His look suggested they make their excuses, but Erin wasn't falling into his game plan quite so easily.

She stood and carried Brand's and her plate into the kitchen, rinsing them off and stacking them in the dishwasher.

"You've been quiet this afternoon," Brand commented, sticking their iced-tea glasses in the top rack. "Is something troubling you?"

She nodded sadly. "I don't want to leave you." It plagued her more than she dared admit. She couldn't stay. Seattle was her home, not Hawaii. Her house and her piano awaited her return. As did Aimee and her job.

Brand reached for her shoulders, turning her toward him. His eyes were hot and fervent as they stared into hers. "Then don't go back."

"It's not that simple," Erin protested.

"Why isn't it?"

Frantic for an excuse, Erin said the first thing that came to mind. "Because of Catherine Fredrickson."

"What the hell has she got to do with anything?" Brand demanded harshly.

Eleven

"Catherine's in love with you."

Brand stared at Erin stupidly, as if he weren't certain he'd heard her correctly. His expression was first astonished and then incredulous. "What the hell are you talking about? As I recall, the conversation went something along the lines that you didn't want to leave Hawaii, to which I had the simple solution. Don't go. As I recall, Catherine's name didn't once enter the conversation."

"She's in love with you."

"She's not, and even if she was, what has that got to do with anything?" Brand demanded, holding tight reins on his patience. He glanced over his shoulder as if he feared Alex or Ginger might make an appearance. Plainly the subject was one he didn't want them listening in on.

"It's...something a woman likes to know when she's interested in a man herself."

Brand made a harsh sound that was a groan of abject frustration.

"I... I think you should marry her." Erin thought nothing of the sort, but said so for shock value. It seemed to have the desired effect. Brand looked as if he wanted to take her by the shoulders and shake her until her teeth rattled.

Instead he marched to the other side of the kitchen and rammed his hand through his hair with enough force that if he did it a few more times he'd require a hair transplant. He turned, opened his mouth as though he wanted to say something, but quickly snapped it shut.

"She's perfect for you." Even as she spoke, Erin realized how true that was. It hurt to admit it, more than she dared concede. Almost from the beginning Brand had mentioned his two friends, Romano and Catherine, blending their names together as if the two were actually one. It was understandable. The three worked together. They were the very best of friends. Alex was married to Ginger, but that left Brand free for Catherine.

"Erin—"

"No," she interrupted. "I mean it. Catherine is the perfect woman for you. First of all, she's navy, and—"

"I don't happen to be in love with her," he barked. His long legs ate up the distance between them in three giant strides. "Hasn't the last week told you anything? The last week, nothing," he corrected sharply. "The last seven months!"

His anger did little to faze her. The more she dwelled on the subject of Brand and Catherine, the more sense it made to her. In fact, she didn't know why it hadn't occurred to her much sooner. It wasn't until she'd met the other woman that Erin had recognized the truth.

"I'm serious, Brand."

"I'm not," he snapped. "I've never so much as kissed Catherine. It would be like dating my own sister. I'm sure she feels the same way."

"Wrong." Breaking out of his hold, she reached for the coffeepot. As if she hadn't a care in the world, Erin ran water and measured the grounds, hoping the activity would hide the pain that was crowding her heart. The thought of Brand loving another woman nearly crippled her emotionally, yet she pressed the subject, driven by some unknown force.

"All right," Brand conceded, slowly, thoughtfully. "Let's say you're right, and Catherine does hold some romantic feelings for me—although I want you to know right now I think that's crazy. But for the sake of argument I'll accept that premise. We've been working together for nearly three years—"

"Make that four," Erin interrupted, continuing to busy herself by clearing away what remained of the dinner dishes.

"Okay, four years." His gaze narrowed, but apparently he wasn't willing to argue over minute details. "If I haven't fallen for Catherine in all that time, then what makes you assume I'd ever consider marrying her, especially now that I'm in love with you?"

"It's so obvious."

"What is?" he cried impatiently.

"That you and Catherine should be together. It all fits. I doubt you'd ever find anyone who suits you better." Gaining momentum, she continued, "It's true, you and I share a certain amount of physical attraction, but beyond that we seem to constantly be at odds."

Brand made the growling sound a second time, and then shocked her by stepping forward and gripping her hard by the shoulders. He squeezed so tightly that he half lifted her from the floor. "You know what you're doing, don't you?" he demanded.

She stared up at him mutely, stunned by this sudden show of force. It was so unlike Brand, which revealed how accomplished she was at getting a reaction from him.

"You're avoiding another confrontation," he told her, his voice firm and angry. "You don't want to leave Hawaii, or more appropriately, you don't want to leave me. Wonderful, because frankly, I don't want you to go, either. I love you. I have for so long I can't remember what it was like to not love you. I refuse to think of marrying anyone but you. To have you suggest I take Catherine as my wife makes damn little sense." His hold on her relaxed, and her feet were once again safely planted on the linoleum.

Erin lowered her gaze, realizing he was right but hating like hell to admit it. She was looking to avoid a showdown, and that was exactly what would have happened had their discussion followed the lead he'd taken. Admitting how badly she wanted to remain in the islands with him had left the door wide open for trouble. Brand wanted her to stay, too.

She remained stiff in his arms for a moment. Then a sigh raked her shoulders and she relaxed against him, wrapping her arms around his middle.

"You're right," she whispered. "I'm sorry...so sorry."

Brand froze briefly and muttered something under his breath that Erin couldn't detect. As though he couldn't bear the tension another moment, he buried his hands in her hair and drew her firmly into contact with his muscular, trim body. She tilted her head to smile up at him, and Brand took advantage of the movement by placing his mouth over hers.

His kiss revealed a storehouse of need. His tongue probed her mouth, and she opened to him as naturally as a castle gate opens to an arriving king. A wide host of familiar sensations warmed her, a heat so intense it

frightened her. It had always been this way between
them. He touched her, and it was like fire licking at dry
kindling. Her response to Brand continued to amaze
Erin. He'd kiss her, and the excitement seemed to explode throughout her body. In the beginning, his kisses
had produced a warm sort of pleasure, but since their
six-month separation, every time he held her in his arms
her response was one of hungry need.

She nestled into his embrace the way a robin settles
into her nest, spreading its wings, securing itself against
the storm. It felt so incredibly good to have him hold
her. Nothing she had ever known compared to the feelings of security he supplied.

She dragged in a deep breath, savoring the scent
of warm musk that was uniquely his. Brand groaned
and deepened the kiss, and Erin welcomed the intimacy of his tongue stroking hers. Unable to remain
still, she started to move against him. Her nipples had
hardened and were tingling, and the only way to relieve
that shocking pleasure was to rotate the upper half of
her body against him.

A low, rough sound rumbled through his throat as he
gripped her by the hips and pressed her flush against
him, adjusting her stance to graphically demonstrate
his powerful need for her.

It felt familiar and so very good. Erin locked her
arms around his neck and moved with him, her grinding hips contrasting the action of his own, enhancing
the pleasure a hundredfold. Erin felt as though she were
on fire, hot and aching, wanting everything at once.

"Oh, baby," he whispered in a voice that was guttural.

The noise from behind was as unexpected as it was

unwelcome. Brand jerked his head back and ground his teeth in wretched frustration.

"Hello," Bobby greeted enthusiastically, closing the sliding glass door as he casually strolled into the kitchen. "Dad sent me in here to ask what was taking you two so long."

Brand's gaze narrowed menacingly. "Tell your dad…"

"We'll be right out," Erin completed for him.

"When are we going to have the ice cream?" the youngster wanted to know, walking over to the freezer, opening the door and staring inside. "It's time we had dessert, don't you think?"

Erin nodded. "If you want, I'll dish it up now and you can help me carry it out to everyone."

The boy eagerly nodded his head. Then, glancing at Brand, he seemed to change his mind. "Only don't let Uncle Brand help you. He might kiss you again and then you'd both forget."

"I won't let him kiss me," Erin promised.

"Wanna bet?" Brand teased under his breath.

Bobby studied the two of them quizzically. "Uncle Brand?"

"Yes, Bob."

"Are you going to marry Erin?"

"Ah…"

"I think you should, and so does my dad."

A moment of tense silence filled the room. Erin swallowed the lump that threatened to choke her. Her eyes were locked with Brand's, and she struggled to look away, but his gaze refused to release her.

"I… Let's get that ice cream," Erin suggested, hoping she sounded carefree and enthusiastic when she felt neither.

* * *

Erin's suitcases were packed and ready for her flight as she walked through Alex and Ginger's home one last time before Brand arrived to drive her to the airport. She'd woken that morning with a heavy feeling in her chest that had only grown worse as the day progressed. She dared not question its origin or what she needed to do to relieve it.

She knew the answer as clearly as if a doctor had given her a written diagnosis. Leaving Brand was far more difficult than she'd ever dreamed it would be.

He hadn't pressured her to marry him. Not once. In fact, she was the one who'd brought up the subject, when she'd suggested he consider Catherine for his wife. That idea had all too quickly backfired in her face. And rightly so. She'd been an utter fool to suggest Brand romantically involve himself with another woman. Even now, just musing over the thought brought with it an instant flash of regret and pain.

Erin liked Catherine, enjoyed her company and wished her well, but when it came to Brand, Erin had discovered she was far more territorial than she ever realized. The awareness came as something of a shock.

Brand arrived and loaded Erin's suitcases into the trunk of his car. If he was unusually quiet on the drive to Honolulu International, she didn't notice, since she didn't seem to have much she wanted to say, either.

They sat next to each other in the crowded gate area, tightly holding hands while waiting for her flight number to be called. Erin's throat was so tight, she couldn't have carried on a conversation had the fate of world peace depended on it.

Each second that ticked away seemed to suck the

energy right out of the room. Apparently no one else noticed except Brand.

When her flight was called, those gathered around her stood and reached for their personal items and brought out their tickets.

The first few rows had boarded when Brand stood. "You'll need to go on board now." He stated it matter-of-factly, as if her going was of little importance to him.

She nodded and reluctantly came to her feet.

"You'll call once you arrive back in Seattle?"

Once again she nodded.

Brand smoothed his hands over her shoulders, and his gaze just managed to avoid hers. "I'm pulling as many strings as I can to transfer to one of the bases in Washington state."

He hadn't mentioned that earlier, and Erin's hopes soared. If Brand lived on any of the navy bases near Seattle, even if it was one across Puget Sound, it would help ease the impossible situation between them. Then they would have the luxury of allowing their relationship to develop naturally without thousands of miles stretching between them like a giant, unyielding void.

"You didn't say anything about that earlier," she said, hating the way the eagerness crept into her voice. That he was prepared to leave the admiral's staff to be closer to her spoke volumes about his commitment to her.

"I didn't mention it before because it isn't the least bit probable."

"Oh." Her hope and excitement quickly diminished.

The final boarding call for her flight was announced. Erin glanced over her shoulder, wanting more than she'd ever wanted anything to remain with Brand. Yet she knew she had to leave.

"I don't suppose…" Brand began enthusiastically, then stopped abruptly.

"You don't suppose what?"

"Never mind."

"Never mind? Obviously you had something you wanted to say."

"That won't work, either."

"What won't work?" she demanded impatiently.

"Have you ever considered moving to Hawaii?" he asked, without revealing the least bit of emotion either way.

She was so stunned by the suggestion that it left her breathless. "Moving to Hawaii?" she gasped.

As crazy as it seemed, the first thought that filtered into her brain was that she'd be forced to sell her grand piano with the house, and frankly, not that many folks would be interested in something that large, especially when it dominated a good portion of the living room.

"Never mind," Brand said irritably. "I already said that wouldn't work."

She stared up at him, wondering why he was so quick to downplay his own suggestion until she realized how unfeasible the idea actually was. She had her job and her home and her sturdy, hard-to-move furniture. What about the roots she was so carefully planting in the Seattle area? Her friends? The Women in Transition classes she taught evenings?

"I can't move."

Brand frowned and nodded. "I know. It was a stupid idea. Forget I suggested it."

The way their courtship was progressing, she'd leave behind everything that was important to her for Brand and move to Hawaii just in time for him to be transferred to Alaska. Knowing the way the navy worked, she could count on something like that happening.

The attendant's voice announcing the last call for her flight was an intrusion Erin didn't want or need.

"Why didn't you say something sooner?" she demanded. At least they could have discussed it without the pressure of her being forced to board the plane. As it was, they'd sat, holding hands, for an hour without uttering more than a few words.

"I shouldn't have said anything now." His gaze gentled, and he brushed the tips of his fingers across her cheek, his touch light and unbelievably tender. His eyes momentarily left hers. "You have to go," he told her in a voice that was low and gravelly.

"Yes... I know." But now that the time had arrived, Erin wasn't sure she could turn and walk away from Brand and manage to keep her dignity intact. Oh, hell, she didn't know what she was going to do. He was everything she ever dreamed she'd find in a man, and, at the same moment, her greatest fear.

He hugged her all too briefly, then dropped his arms and stepped away from her. Wanting more than anything to wear a smile when she left him, she beamed him one broad enough to challenge Miss America. Then, with a dignified turn, she headed for the jetway.

"Erin." Her name was issued in a low growl. He was at her side so fast it made her dizzy. He hauled her into his arms and kissed her with a hunger that left her weak and clinging.

"I'm sorry," the flight attendant said, standing at the gate. "You'll have to board now. The flight's ready to depart."

"Go ahead," Brand whispered, stepping away from her.

"Oh, Brand." Erin hated the way her eyes filled with

ready tears. Mascara running down her cheeks ruined
the image she was working so hard to leave in his mind.

"Go back to Seattle," Brand said harshly, "go ahead
and go, before I end up pleading with you to stay."

"Where have you been all weekend?" Aimee demanded, walking directly past Erin and into her living
room, carting a large paper sack in one hand and a cigarette in the other. "I must have called twenty times."

"I took a ride up to Vancouver."

"All by yourself?" She sounded incredulous. "Good
grief, you just got back from a week's vacation in
Hawaii. Don't tell me you needed to get away." She
whirled around her, searching for some unknown object. "Where do you keep your ashtrays?"

Erin followed her friend into the kitchen while
Aimee searched through a row of four drawers. She
dragged the first one open, briefly scanning the contents, only to slam it closed.

Removing a small glass ashtray from the cupboard,
Erin held it out in the palm of her hand to her co-worker.
"When did you start smoking?" She couldn't remember
seeing Aimee with a cigarette before.

"I smoked years ago, when I was young and stupid.
It's really a filthy habit. Trust me, whatever you do,
don't start." Even as she was speaking, she opened her
purse and brought out a pack. It was a brand designed
especially for women, and the smokes were thin and
long.

"Aimee!" Erin cried. "What's happened to you?"

As if she suddenly needed to talk, Aimee pulled out
a chair and collapsed into it, automatically crossing her
legs. Her foot started to swing like a precision time-
piece, moving so fast she was creating a brisk breeze.

"I stopped off to show you my new outfit," Aimee announced. "I bought it to wear for the settlement hearing. If Steve's going to divorce me, I want to look my absolute best."

"In other words, you want him to regret it."

"Exactly." For the first time, a smile cracked the tight line of her mouth.

"Why don't you just come right out and tell him that?"

"You're joking!"

"I'm not," Erin assured her. She'd been away seven days, and upon her return she'd barely recognized her best friend. Aimee had lost a noticeable amount of weight and was so uptight she should be on tranquilizers. The fact she'd taken up smoking was a symptom of a much deeper problem.

"Steve and I are no longer on speaking terms."

"But I thought the two of you had never gotten along better."

"That was before," Aimee explained, grinding the cigarette butt in the ashtray.

"Before what?"

"Before...everything."

"Are you sure you're not misinterpreting the situation?" Erin didn't know Steve well, but she would have thought he was more fair-minded than that.

"That's not the half of it." The more Aimee talked, the faster her leg swung. Erin didn't dare focus her attention on the moving foot, lest it hypnotize her.

"You mean there's more?"

"Someone's moved into the duplex with him."

The pain was alive in Aimee's eyes. "A woman?" Erin asked softly.

"I... I don't know, but I imagine it must be. I know my husband—he enjoys regular bouts of sex."

"How'd you know someone moved in with him?" Erin couldn't help being curious. She strongly suspected that her friend was doing a bit of amateur detective work and coming up with all the wrong conclusions.

"I happened to be in the neighborhood and decided it wouldn't do any harm to drive by his place and see what Steve was up to. I'm glad I did, too, because there was a white convertible parked in his driveway." She blew a cloud of smoke at the ceiling, and when she set the cigarette down Erin noted that her hands were trembling.

"A white convertible?"

"Come on, Erin," Aimee said with a heavy note of sarcasm. "I'm not stupid. It was after midnight."

"That explains everything?"

"You and I both know a woman's more likely to drive a white car. Men like theirs black or red. The way I figure it, either Steve's got some cupcake shacked up with him or else he's having himself a little fun on the side. My guess is he's been into side dishes for a good long time."

"Aimee, that's ridiculous."

"Not according to my attorney."

"What makes him suggest anything like that? Honestly, I think this whole thing's gotten out of hand. Not so long ago you claimed Steve wasn't the type to mess around." The picture of the man who'd come to their table to correct a wrong impression the night they were in the Mexican restaurant played in Erin's mind.

"I called my lawyer first thing the following morning and gave him the license plate number. If Steve's fooling around, and I'm confident he is, then he's going to hear about it in court. If he wants another relationship, then the least he could do was wait for the ink to dry on the divorce decree."

Erin couldn't believe what she was hearing. Then again, it shouldn't shock her. Through the class she taught at the community college, she'd seen the emotional trauma, the bitterness and the pain of divorce cripple even the strongest women.

What surprised Erin was that this was Aimee. Calm, unruffled Aimee. In the time they'd worked together, Erin had seen her friend handle one explosive situation after another, competently, without accusation or blame.

"Anyway," Aimee said, reaching for the Nordstrom bag at her side, "I wanted you to see the new dress I got for the court date. God knows I can't afford it, but I bought it anyway." She carefully unwrapped the tissue from around the silk blouse and skirt that was a bright shade of turquoise.

"Oh, Aimee, it's gorgeous."

"I thought so, too. I'll look stunning, won't I?"

Erin nodded. She wouldn't be able to go inside the judge's chambers with her friend. According to court rules, Erin would have to wait in the hallway, but then, all Aimee really needed was emotional support before and after.

"By the way, what were you doing in Canada this weekend?" Aimee asked, waving the cigarette smoke away from Erin's face. She glanced at the tip and extinguished it with a force that nearly pushed the ashtray from the table.

Erin hesitated, then decided that the truth was the best policy. "I needed to get away."

"I might remind you, you just spent the last week away."

"I know." In the five days since her return, Erin had

spoken to Brand twice. Once, briefly, shortly after she'd arrived home. Then, later in the week, he'd contacted her again. He'd sounded tired and out of sorts. Although they'd spoken for several minutes, Erin had come away from the conversation feeling lonely and depressed.

As much as she tried to avoid doing so, Erin dwelt a good deal on what she'd suggested to Brand about him and Catherine. It hurt to think of Brand with another woman. Hurt, she decided, was too mild a word to describe the fiery pain that cut a wide path through her heart when she considered the situation. It would solve everything if the two of them were to fall in love. They had so much in common, including an appreciation of the many exciting aspects of navy life. Exciting to everyone, that is, who could accept the policies and the programs of a military lifestyle.

Someone who wasn't a navy brat. Someone who didn't know any better.

"Erin?" Aimee said softly. "Are you all right?"

"Oh, sure. I'm sorry," she said, forcefully bringing herself back to the present. "Were you saying something I missed?"

"No." But the other woman regarded her closely. "You never did tell me much about Hawaii. How was your time with Brand?"

"Wonderful." If anything, it had been too wonderful. She'd cherished each minute, greedy for time alone with him. They'd both been selfish, not wanting to share their precious days with others.

No one had seemed to mind. In fact, it had been as if Brand's friends were going out of their way to arrange it so.

"I hear Hawaii is really beautiful," Aimee continued.

"At one time, Steve and I were planning a trip there for our tenth wedding anniversary."

"It is beautiful."

"But you wouldn't want to live there?"

The question took her by surprise. Erin blinked, not knowing how to answer. Could she live in Hawaii? Of course. The question didn't even need consideration. Anyone would enjoy paradise. If Brand were to own a business there, she'd marry him in a minute and plan on settling down and building an empire with him. But Brand was part of the military, and if she were to link her life with his, then she'd have to be willing to whole-heartedly embrace that lifestyle, and she didn't know if she could.

"Well?" Aimee pressed.

"No," Erin said automatically. "I don't think I could live in Hawaii."

"Me either," her friend muttered, and reached for a cigarette. "At least not now. Someplace cold and isolated interests me more at the minute."

"Greenland?"

"Greenland," Aimee echoed. "That would be perfect." She averted her eyes and pretended to remove a piece of lint from the leg of her slacks. "So," she said, expelling a breath sharply. "You'll meet me at the courthouse Monday morning?"

"I'll be there."

"Thanks. I knew I could count on you."

The phone rang just then, and Erin leaned toward the wall to reach for it.

"Hello," she said automatically.

There was no response for a couple of seconds, long enough for Erin to believe it was a crank call.

"Erin MacNamera?" Her name sounded as though it

came from a long way off, but not long-distance. The telltale hum was decidedly missing.

"Yes, this is Erin MacNamera." The female voice was vaguely familiar, but Erin couldn't place it.

"This is Marilyn…from class. I'm really sorry to trouble you," she said, clearly trying to disguise the fact that she was weeping.

"It's no trouble, Marilyn. It's good to hear from you. How are you? I haven't talked to you in weeks."

"I'm fine." She paused and then gave a short, abrupt laugh. "No, I'm not…all right. In fact, I thought I should call someone. Do you have time to talk right now?"

Twelve

That night, after Aimee's settlement hearing, Erin woke from a sound sleep with tears in her eyes. She lay for several moments, trying to remember what she'd been dreaming that had been so bitterly sad. Whatever it was had escaped her. She rolled over and glanced at her clock, then sighed. It would be several hours yet before the alarm sounded.

Snuggling up with her pillow, she intended to go back to sleep, and was somewhat surprised to discover she couldn't. The tears returned, rolling down her cheek at an alarming pace.

Sitting up, she reached for a tissue, blowing her nose hard. She couldn't understand what was happening to her or why she would find it so necessary to weep. A parade of possible reasons marched through her mind. Hormones. She was missing Brand. Her experience with Aimee that morning. Marilyn. There were any number of excuses why she would wake up weeping. But none that she could readily understand.

She drew the covers over her shoulders and lay staring into space. How she wished Brand were with her then. He'd take her in his arms and comfort her in a soft and reassuring way. He'd kiss away her doubts and her fears. Then he'd touch her in all the ways he knew would please her and gently coax the tears away with his warmth and his wit.

Erin missed him more in that moment than she had in the six months he'd been away at sea.

She closed her eyes, and faces and tension crowded her mind. They were the faces of the men and women she'd seen in court that morning. The eerie silence that had nearly stifled her as she'd waited for Aimee and Steve to come out of the judge's chambers.

The silence had been like nothing she'd ever experienced. Long rows of mahogany benches had lined the hallway. It was ironic that they should resemble church pews. Lawyers conferred with their clients while waiting their turn with the judge. Aimee must have crossed and uncrossed her legs a hundred times, she'd been so nervous. Then she'd started swinging her foot fast enough to cause a draft.

Later, when she and Steve had gone before the judge, Erin had been surrounded by the silence. The wounded, eerie silence of pain.

Erin was worried about Marilyn, too. The older woman had phoned needing to talk. The pain and the anger of her circumstances had gotten so oppressive she couldn't tolerate it another minute. Reaching out for help was something they'd discussed in class. Erin had spent almost an hour on the phone with Marilyn, listening while she talked out her pain.

Marilyn was just beginning to draw upon that well of inner strength. Erin had every confidence that the older woman would come away strong and secure. She wasn't so sure about the young woman she'd seen in the courthouse earlier that day, however.

The desperate look on the woman's face returned to haunt her now. She'd been weeping softly and trying to disguise her tears. Trembling. Shaken. She looked as if she'd been knocked off balance.

Erin's heart throbbed anew at the anguish she'd viewed in the young mother's eyes. She knew nothing of her circumstances, only what she'd overheard while waiting for Aimee. Yet the woman's red eyes and haunting look returned to torment Erin hours later.

After the hearing before the judge, Aimee had been shaken to the core, and Erin had suggested they go out for lunch instead of rushing back to the office. Aimee hadn't said much, and the two had eaten in silence. It was the same throbbing silence Erin had experienced earlier in the courtroom.

Now, hours later, in the wee hours of the morning, it was back again, nearly suffocating her with its intensity, and she hadn't a clue why.

Sitting at his desk, Brand had a vague uneasy feeling he couldn't quite place. He'd heard regularly from Erin since her return to the mainland.

When it came to dealing with his sweet Irish rose, he was playing his hand close to his chest. Being patient and not pressing her for a commitment was damned difficult.

He loved her, there was no question in his mind about that. He also knew it was asking a good deal of her to love him back. It would be a whole lot easier if he wasn't navy. Erin wanted stability, permanence, roots. All Brand had to do was prove to her she could have all that and still be his wife. The military had provided more security than he'd ever known as a civilian.

The navy was his life, and Brand believed that, in

time, Erin would come around to his way of thinking. She loved him. A smile courted the edges of his mouth as he recalled their time together in the surf and Erin's eager response to his touch. They'd never come closer to making love than they had that night. It was something of a miracle that they hadn't.

When they'd first met and dated, the physical attraction between them had been nearly overpowering. He'd never experienced anything like it. If they were together for any length of time, he could be assured that the magnetism between them would reach explosive levels. That hadn't changed, but another dimension had been added in the months they'd known each other. They'd bonded emotionally. Erin had become a large part of Brand's life. She'd helped define who he was, how he thought and the way he governed his actions. She was the first person he thought of when he rolled out of bed in the morning. Generally, he woke regretting that she wasn't at his side, and mused how long it would take for her to come to her senses and marry him.

Thoughts of her followed him through most of the day. He lived for the mail. If there was a letter from her, he read it two and three times straight through, savoring each word. Often right then and there, with his concerns fresh in his mind, he sat down and wrote her back. Brand had never been much of a writer. Letters were time-consuming, and he sometimes had trouble expressing himself with the written word. Not wanting to be misinterpreted, he'd opt for a quick phone call instead. Sea duty this last time around had been a challenge for him in more ways than one, but he'd learned some valuable lessons. He needed to hear from Erin.

Not wanted. Needed.

While on duty aboard the *Blue Ridge*, he'd been

forced to admit for the first time how much he did need her. He'd tried not to love her, he'd attempted to put her out of his mind and his life, but he'd discovered to his chagrin that he was unable to do so.

Erin MacNamera was the most important person in his world. Since he couldn't give her up, he had no other option but to be patient and bide his time.

The vague uneasy feeling persisted most of the afternoon.

Catherine's news was equally unsettling.

"What do you mean you're being transferred to Bangor?" Brand demanded. He didn't use profanity often, but he couldn't hold back a couple of choice words when he learned Catherine was being stationed in Washington state.

"Hey," she argued, "I didn't ask for this. Personally, I'm not all that thrilled about it."

"You didn't ask for it, I did." Brand would have been willing to surrender his commission for the opportunity to move closer to Erin. It seemed he was thwarted at every turn when it came to loving her.

A letter from Erin was waiting for him when he arrived home that evening. He stared at the envelope, grateful that something good had come of this day. He'd been beginning to have his doubts.

Standing in the middle of his compact living room, he tore open the letter with his index finger and read:

Dearest Brand,
This is the most difficult letter I've ever written in my life. I've started it so many times, tried to make sense of my feelings, praying all the while that you'll understand and forgive me.
    I woke up early the other morning, weeping.

Aimee had needed me to go to the courthouse
with her for her settlement hearing. I had waited
outside in the hallway for her, and while I was
there I saw a woman in her early twenties crying. Never have I had any experience affect me
more profoundly. There was so much pain in that
hallway. It seemed to reach out and grab hold of
me. Perhaps it was because Aimee's settlement
hearing followed on the heels of an episode with
Margo. She's had her ups and downs over the last
nine months, small triumphs followed by minor
setbacks. I've worked with so many divorcing
women since I started my job. I'm beginning to
wonder if anyone stays married anymore. How
can Margo's husband walk away after thirty years
of marriage? How could he possibly abandon her
now? It doesn't make sense to me.

Even Aimee surprises me. I knew she and
Steve were having problems, but I never dreamed
matters would go this far.

I suppose you're wondering what Aimee's settlement hearing and Margo's problems have to do
with the fact I woke up crying. Trust me, it took a
long time for me to make the connection myself.

Deep down, in the innermost part of my being,
the trauma involving Aimee and Margo forced me
to face up to my true feelings regarding our relationship. I do love you, Brand. So much so that it
sometimes frightens me, but we can't continue,
we can't go on pretending our differences are all
going to magically disappear someday. Falling
in love caught us both unaware. You certainly
didn't intend to leave Seattle caring about me, and
I never intended to love you. It happened, and we

both let it. Now we're left to deal with the way we've tangled our two lives.

I realize my thoughts are all so scrambled yet, and you don't have a clue of what I'm trying to say. I'm not even sure I can explain it myself. I suppose I recognized it first when I talked to Margo late one evening when she was suffering from a bout of deep emotional pain. Following on the heels of that was Aimee's settlement hearing.

I know you're hoping we'll soon be married. You've been so patient and understanding. I knew how much you truly loved me when you stopped pressuring me to become your wife.

In the last few weeks, I've given a good deal of thought to your proposal, and to be honest was leaning in that direction.

I've made my decision, and it was the most heart-wrenching one of my life. I can't marry you, Brand. It came to me recently why. It isn't because I don't love you enough. Please believe that. Learning not to love you will likely take me a lifetime.

If we do marry, someday down the road we're going to divorce. Our differences are fundamental ones. You're a part of the navy. I honestly believe that what attracted me to you so strongly was your likeness to my father. You certainly don't resemble him physically, but on the inside you two could be mistaken for blood relatives. You think so much alike. Your lives don't belong to yourselves, or your family. They belong to good ol' Uncle Sam.

I had eighteen years of that, and I can't and

won't accept that crazy lifestyle a second time. I hated it then, and I'll hate it now.

This isn't a new issue. It's the same one we've been pounding out almost from the moment we met. The problem is, I grew to love you so much I was willing to give in on this, thinking that if we married everything would work out all right. I was burying my head in the sand and pretending. But someday in the future, we'd both have paid dearly for my refusal to accept the truth. By then there'd probably be children, too. I couldn't bear for our children to suffer through a divorce.

It's ironic that I work almost exclusively with divorced women. Month after month, class after class, and it still didn't hit me how ugly and painful it is to dissolve a marriage until I saw what's happened to Aimee. She and Steve are in so much pain. It hurts me to see her suffer. I barely know Steve, and I hurt for him, too. My attitude toward marriage has gotten so sarcastic lately. I'm beginning to question if anyone should willingly commit their lives to another.

Aimee's so bitter now. I think she's convinced herself she hates Steve. The woman in the hallway at the courthouse, too. I felt something so strongly when I saw her. That sounds crazy, doesn't it? Everyone there was in such deep emotional pain. When I thought about it, I realized that so many of those men and women started out just the way we are. At one time they'd been as deeply in love as we are now. Only we'd be starting off with a mark against us, feeling the way I do about the navy.

Please accept my decision, Brand. Don't write me back. Don't call me. Please let this be the end.

It's been the most painful and difficult decision of my life. Yet deep in my heart I know it's the right one. You may disagree with me now, but someday, when you look back over this time, I believe you'll realize I'm doing the right thing for us both, although God help me, it's the most painful decision I've ever made.

Thank you for loving me. Thank you for teaching me about myself. And please, oh, please, be happy.

Erin

Brand closed his eyes. He felt as though a two-by-four had been slammed into his stomach. For one frenzied moment he thought he might be sick. It was the oddest sensation, as though he'd been physically attacked, badly injured, and was experiencing the first stages of shock.

It took him a couple of minutes to compose himself. His heart was pounding inside his chest like a huge Chinese gong. He paced back and forth in fruitless frustration, sorting through his limited options.

Before he leaped to conclusions, he needed to reread Erin's letter and determine how serious she actually was. He did so, sitting himself down at his desk and digested each word, seeking…hell, he didn't know what he was looking for. Loopholes? An indication, any evidence he might find, that she didn't mean what she wrote. A glimmer of hope.

The second reading, and later a third, told him otherwise. Erin meant every single word. She wanted out of the relationship, and for both their sakes, she didn't want to hear from him again.

* * *

A week had passed since Erin had mailed Brand the final letter.

"Coward," she muttered under her breath. This was what she got for not confronting him over the phone. She'd known from the first that she was taking the easy way out. Originally she'd told herself she was looking to avoid any arguments or lengthy discussions. Only later was she willing to admit that she was a wimp.

"Are you back to talking to yourself again?" Aimee muttered from her desk across the aisle from Erin's.

"What did I say this time?"

"Something about being a coward."

"Oh... I guess maybe I did." It was funny, really. Ironic, too, that she'd made the most courageous, and by far the most difficult, decision of her life, and a week later she was calling herself a coward.

"I would do the same thing all over again," she whispered, and her voice caught slightly. Caught on the pain. Caught on the regret.

"Are you still carrying on about Brand?" Aimee demanded unsympathetically.

Erin nodded.

"Trust me, all of womankind is better off without men. They use and abuse, in that order," Aimee said, and snickered softly. "I'm beginning to sound a bit jaded, aren't I? Sorry about that. You've been in the dumps all week, and I haven't been much help."

"Don't worry about it. You're having problems of your own."

"Not so much anymore. Steve and I have come to terms. The final papers are being drawn up, and the whole messy affair is going to be over. At last. I didn't think this was ever going to end."

"Are you doing anything after work?" Going home to an empty, dark house, even with a grand piano to greet her, had long since lost its appeal. Before she'd written the final letter to Brand, she'd hurried home, praying there'd be a letter waiting there for her. But there wouldn't be any more letters. At least not from Brand. Once she realized that, she'd suddenly started looking for excuses not to go home after work.

"What do you have in mind?" Aimee asked.

"James Bradshaw, the famous divorce attorney, is giving a workshop on prenuptial agreements. I recommended it to the women in my class. I thought you might like to join us."

"Hey, sorry, I can't do anything tonight," Aimee answered in a preoccupied voice. She shuffled a couple of files before she continued. "Prenuptial agreement? Good grief, Erin, you're not even married and you're planning for a divorce."

"Not me," Erin replied. "It's for the women in my class. After seeing what's happened to Marilyn and women like her, and now you, I think it's smart to have everything down in black and white."

Aimee busied herself at her desk. "Personally, I don't think it's a good idea to start out a marriage by planning for a divorce."

Erin stared at her friend, not knowing what to think. Aimee was at the tail end of a divorce that had cut her to the quick. If anyone understood the advisability of prenuptial agreements, Erin thought, it should be her friend.

"Listen—" Aimee rolled back her chair and sighed. "Forget I said that. I'm the last person in the world who should be giving romantic advice. My marriage is in shambles and... I feel like one of the walking wounded myself. Maybe the lecture isn't such a bad idea after all."

"Go on," Erin urged. "I'd be interested in hearing your opinion."

Aimee didn't look as if she trusted her own thoughts. "As I said, I don't think it's a good idea to start off a marriage by planning for divorce. I know that's an unpopular point of view, especially in this day and age, but it just doesn't feel right to me."

"How can you say that?" Erin cried. "You're going through a divorce yourself. Good grief, you've been through hell the last few months, and now all of a sudden you're making marriage sound like this glorious, wonderful state of being. As I recall, you and Steve can't carry on a civil conversation. What's changed?"

"A lot," Aimee announced solemnly. "And you, my friend, have the opportunity to gain from my experience."

Feeling uncomfortable, Erin looked away.

"We're both here day in and day out, working with women who are making new lives for themselves," Aimee continued. "But finding them a decent job is only the beginning. They've been traumatized, abandoned and left to deal with life on their own. If you want the truth, I'm beginning to believe our thinking's becoming jaded. Not everyone ends up divorced. Not everyone will have to go through what these women have. It's just that we deal with it each and every day until our own perception of married life has been warped."

"But you and Steve—"

"I know," Aimee argued. "Trust me, I know. I pray every day I'm doing the right thing by divorcing Steve."

Erin was praying the same thing herself for the

both of them. "But if you're having second thoughts, shouldn't you be doing something?"

"Like what?" Aimee suggested, her voice flippant. "Steve's already involved with another woman."

"You don't know that."

"Deep down I do. You saw him the day we went to court. He wore that stupid green tie just to irritate me, and the looks he gave me... I can't begin to describe to you the way he glanced at me, as if...as if he couldn't believe he'd ever been married to me in the first place. He couldn't wait for the divorce to be final."

"But I thought this was a friendly divorce."

Aimee's gaze fell to her hands. "There's no such thing as a friendly divorce. It's too damn painful for everyone involved."

"Oh, Aimee, I feel so bad for you and Steve."

"Why should you?" she asked, the sarcastic edge back in her voice. "We're both getting exactly what we want."

Erin knew nothing more that she could say. She didn't have any excuse to linger around the office. The lecture wasn't until seven, and it was optional as far as her class was concerned. She didn't have to be there herself, but she thought it would help kill time, which was something that was weighing heavily on her these days.

Erin's thoughts were heavy as she walked outside the double glass doors of the fifteen-story office complex. The wind had picked up and was biting-cold. She hunched her shoulders and tucked her hands inside her coat pockets as she headed for the parking lot on Yesler.

With her head down, it was little wonder she didn't notice the tall, dark figure standing next to her car. It wasn't until she was directly in front of him that she realized someone was blocking her path.

When she looked up, her heart, in a frenzy, flew into her throat.

Brand stood there, his eyes as cold and biting as the north wind.

"Brand," she whispered, hardly able to speak, "what are you doing here?"

"You didn't want me to write you or contact you by phone. But you didn't say anything about not seeing you in person. If you want to break everything off, fine, I can accept that. Only you're going to have to do it to my face."

Thirteen

"You couldn't let it go, could you?" Erin cried, battling with an anger that threatened to consume her. Tears blurred Brand's image before her, and for a second she couldn't make out his features. When she did, her heart ached at the sight of him.

"No, I couldn't leave it," Brand returned harshly. "You want to end it, then fine, have it your way. But I'm not going to make it easy for you."

"Oh, Brand," she whispered, her anger vanishing as quickly as it had come, "do you honestly believe it was easy?"

"Say it, Erin. Tell me you want me out of your life."

He towered over her like a thundercloud, dark and menacing. Erin's feet felt as if they were planted ankle-deep in concrete. She needed to put a few inches of distance between them, grant them both necessary breathing room. As it was, she was having a difficult time getting oxygen into her lungs.

"Could we go someplace else and discuss this?" She barely managed the tightly worded request. The urge to break down was nearly overwhelming. It hurt as much to talk as to breathe.

Of his own accord, Brand stepped away from her. "Where?"

"There's an… Italian restaurant not far from here." The suggestion came off the top of her head, and the minute she said it, Erin realized attempting to talk would be impossible there.

"I'm not discussing this with a roomful of people listening in on the conversation."

"All right, you choose." A restaurant hadn't been a brilliant idea, but Erin couldn't think of anyplace else they could go.

She wished with everything in her heart that Brand had accepted her letter and left it at that. Having him confront her unexpectedly like this made everything so much more difficult.

"If we're going to talk, it has to be someplace private," he insisted.

"Ah…" Erin hesitated.

"My hotel room," Brand suggested next, but he said it as though he expected her to argue with him.

"Okay," she agreed, not questioning the wisdom of his idea. Her primary thought was to get this over with as quickly as possible. It didn't matter where they spoke, because in her heart she knew it wouldn't take more than a few minutes. "I don't have a lot of time."

"You've got a date?" He bit out the question.

"No… I'm suppose to be at a lecture."

"When?"

"By seven."

"You'll be there." Brand took off walking, expecting her to follow behind. She did so reluctantly, wishing she could avoid this confrontation and knowing she couldn't.

His pace was brisk, and Erin practically had to trot

in order to keep up with his long-legged strides. They'd gone four or five blocks when he entered the revolving glass door that led to the tastefully decorated hotel lobby.

He paused outside the elevator for Erin to catch up to him. She was breathless by the time she traipsed across the plush red-and-white carpet.

In all the time she'd known Brand, she'd never seen him quite like this. He was so unemotional, so unfeeling. Aloof, as if nothing she could say or do would disconcert him.

His room was on the tenth floor. He unlocked and held open the door for her, and she walked inside. It was a standard room with a double bed, a nightstand and a dresser. In the corner, next to the window, were a table and two olive-green upholstered chairs.

"Go ahead and sit down," he instructed brusquely. "I'll have room service send up some coffee."

Erin nodded, walked across the room and settled in the crescent-shaped chair.

Brand picked up the phone, pushed a button and requested the coffee. When he'd finished, he surprised her by sauntering to the other side of the compact room and sitting on the edge of the mattress.

Erin's gaze fell to her hands. "I wish it didn't have to be this way. I'm so sorry, Brand," she said in a small voice.

"I didn't come all this way for an apology."

He seemed to be waiting for something more, but Erin didn't know what it was, and even if she had, she wasn't sure she could have supplied it. The strained silence was so loud, it was all Erin could do not to press her hands over her ears.

"Say something," she pleaded. "Don't just sit there looking so angry you could bite my head off."

"I'm not angry," he corrected, clenching his fists, "I'm downright furious." He bounded to his feet and stalked across the compact room. "A letter," he said bitingly, and turned to glare down at her. "You didn't have the decency to talk this out with me. Instead, you did it in a letter."

"I...was afraid..."

She wasn't allowed to finish. Brand advanced two steps toward her, then stopped. "Have I ever given you a reason to fear me? Ever? Am I so damn difficult to talk to? Is that it?"

"I wasn't afraid of you."

"A letter doesn't make a whole lot of sense."

"I know," she whispered woefully. "It seemed the best way at the time. I didn't mean to hurt you. Trust me, it hasn't exactly been a piece of cake for me, either."

"Explain it to me, Erin, because I'm telling you right now, I can't make heads or tails out of that letter. You love me, but you can't marry me because you're afraid we'll end up divorcing someday and you don't want to put our children through the trauma. Do you realize how crazy that sounds?"

"It isn't crazy," she cried, vaulting to her feet. "Okay, so maybe I didn't explain myself very well, but you weren't there. You don't know."

"I wasn't where?"

"In the courthouse that day with Aimee." She covered her face with her hands and shook her head, trying to dispel the ready images that popped into her head. The same ones that had returned to haunt her so often. The young mother, who was consulting with her attorney and trying so hard to disguise the fact that she was crying. Aimee, her legs swinging like a pendulum gone berserk while she smoked like a chimney the whole time, pretending she was as cool as a milkshake. The heartache. The pain that was all so tangible. And the silence. That horrible, wounded silence.

"What makes you so certain we'll divorce?" Brand demanded.

Lowering her hands, she sadly shook her head. "Because you're navy."

"I'm getting damn tired of that argument."

"That's because you've ignored my feelings about the military from the first. I told you the night we met how I felt about dating anyone in the military. I warned you...but you insisted. You refused to leave well enough alone—"

"Come on, Erin," he argued bitterly, "I didn't exactly kidnap you and force you to date me. You were as eager to get to know me as I was you."

"But I—"

"You don't have a single quarrel. You wanted this. You can argue until you're blue in the face, but it won't make a damn bit of difference."

"I can't marry you."

"Fine, then we'll be lovers." He jerked off his blue uniform jacket and started on the buttons of his military-issue shirt.

Stunned, Erin didn't move. She couldn't believe what she was seeing. "I... I...what about the coffee?"

"Right. I'll cancel it." He walked over to the phone and dialed room service. When he turned back to her, he seemed surprised that she was still wearing her coat. "Go on," he urged. "Get undressed."

Erin's mind raced for an excuse. "You're not serious," she said, crowding the words together.

"The hell I'm not. I don't suppose you're protected," he said, pausing momentarily. "Well, don't worry about it. I'll take care of it." He sat on the end of the bed and removed his shoes, then stood and methodically undid his belt. While she stood stunned, barely able to believe what she was viewing, he unzipped his pants and calmly stepped out of them.

Erin sucked in a sharp breath and backed up two or three paces. Brand must have sensed her movement, because he glanced up, seemingly surprised to find her standing so far away from him.

"Take off your clothes," he ordered. He stood before her in his boxer shorts and T-shirt, seemingly impatient for her to remove her own things.

"Brand, I…can't do this."

"Why not?" he demanded. "You were plenty eager before. As I recall, you once told me you'd rather we were lovers. I was the one fool enough to insist we marry."

"Not like this," she pleaded. "Not when you're so… cold."

"Trust me, Erin, a few kisses will warm us both right up." He walked over to her and systematically unbuttoned her coat. She stood, numb with disbelief. This couldn't actually be happening, could it? In answer to her silent question, her coat fell to the floor.

Brand's eyes were on hers, and she noted that the anger was gone, replaced with some emotion she couldn't name. With his gaze continuing to hold hers, Brand reached behind her for the zipper at the back of her dress. The hissing sound of it gliding open filled the room as though a swarm of bees were directly behind them. She raised her hands in a weak protest, but Brand ignored her.

Easing the material over her smooth shoulders, he paused midway in his journey to press his moist, hot mouth to the hollow of her throat. Tense and frightened, Erin jerked slightly, then reached out and gripped the edge of the table to steady herself.

"Brand," she pleaded once more. "Please don't... not like this."

"You'll be saying a lot more than please before we're finished," he assured her.

His mouth traveled at a leisurely pace up the side of her neck, across the sensitized skin at the underside of her jaw. Despite everything, his nearness warmed her blood.

Everything was different now. He was loving and gentle and so incredibly male. He smelled of musk. Erin had forgotten how much she enjoyed the manly fragrance that was Brand. He turned his head and nuzzled her ear with his nose, and unable to resist him any longer, Erin slipped her arms around his middle and tentatively held on to his waist.

He rewarded her with a soft kiss and braced his feet slightly apart. Then, dragging her by the hips, he urged her forward until she was tucked snugly between his parted thighs. Once she was secure, he slipped her arms free of the restricting material of her dress and slowly eased it over her hips.

Erin wasn't ready for this new intimacy and resisted. Brand reacted by kissing her several times until she willingly parted her mouth to eagerly receive his kisses. The gathered silk material of her dress pooled at her feet.

His hands were at the waistband of her tap pants when he paused as though he expected her to resist him anew. "I think we should stop now," she whispered, knowing that if the loving continued much longer they'd both be lost.

"That's the problem," he whispered, his mouth scant inches from her own. "We both think too much. This time we're going to feel."

"Oh, Brand…" She was confused and uncertain but too needy to care.

"I want you, Erin, and by heaven, I fully intend to have you."

If she pushed him away or made the slightest protest, Erin was convinced, Brand would immediately cease their lovemaking. But she seemed incapable of doing either. All she could seem to manage was a weak mewling sound deep in her throat that encouraged Brand to take further liberties with her. She felt torn between the dictates of her body and the decree of her pride. She couldn't allow this to happen, and yet she was powerless to stop him.

He kissed her again and again. A trembling started in her knees, spreading to her thighs until she could barely support herself. She sagged against Brand. He accepted her weight, and without her quite figuring out how he managed it, Erin found herself sprawled across the mattress with Brand lying alongside her.

"My sweet Erin, oh, my love," he whispered, his eyes tender. "Tell me you want me. I need you to say it… just this once. Give me that to remember you by." The words were issued in sweet challenge between wild, carnal kisses.

"Oh, Brand." She breathed his name when she could, but talking, indeed breathing, had become less and less important.

"Say it," he demanded again, easing his hands over

her flat, smooth stomach to caress the womanly part
of her.

"Do you want me?" he whispered.

"Yes...oh, yes."

Erin had never felt as she did at that moment. Never
so needy or so feminine. He kissed her and moved over
her, his hands in her hair, lifting her mouth upward to
meet his. Brand made her feel as if she were exploding
from the inside out. This feeling, so beautiful, so brilliant and warm, filled her eyes with tears that splashed
onto her cheeks.

He straddled her, eager now, his hands gripping the
waistband of her tap pants. He paused when he noticed
her tears.

Slowly he eased himself off her and sat on the edge
of the mattress, his eyes closed. "I can't do it. Dear God
in heaven, I can't do it."

Erin couldn't move. Her breasts were heaving, and
tears rained down the side of her face and leaked onto
the bedspread. "It would never work between us, Brand.
I couldn't bear to go through a divorce." She paused
and twisted her head away so that she wouldn't have
to look at him.

"You honestly believe that, don't you?" He slowly
shook his head.

"I do mean it. Would I put us through this torture
if I didn't?"

"Honest to God, I don't know." Before she fully realized his intention, Brand moved off the bed and reached
for his clothes.

Erin sat up, distributing her weight on the palms of
her hands. He was actually dressing. A few moments
earlier he'd been preparing to make love to her, and now
he was dressing. "I want you, Erin," he said when he'd

finished. "I'll probably regret not making love to you to the day they lower me into my grave."

"But why…aren't you?"

"Damned if I know. Maybe it's because I count your father as a friend." He paused and rubbed his hand across his face. "More likely I'm afraid if we make love, once would never be enough, and we'd spend the rest of our lives the way we have the last eight months. Personally, I can't deal with that. I don't think you could, either."

He was right; she'd never been so miserable.

"Go ahead and get dressed."

"First you demand that I undress, now you want me to dress. I wish you'd kindly make up your mind," she muttered peevishly. She scooted off the mattress and reached for her clothes, jerking them on impatiently.

"You claimed you wanted to talk," she reminded him once she'd finished.

He nodded. "Coming here wasn't a brilliant idea." His smile was decidedly off center. He hesitated, his eyes sad. "My anger frightened you?"

"Only at first, when you seemed so indifferent."

He nodded and leaned against the wall, as if standing upright were becoming too much of a burden for him. "You meant what you said in that letter?"

Erin closed her eyes and nodded.

"I was afraid of that."

"Brand, I'd give anything if I could be different. Anything, but—"

"Don't," he said, cutting her off. "It isn't necessary."

"Please try to understand," she pleaded softly. "I went through hell. For nights on end I'd wake up weeping and not know why, and then I realized it all boiled down to what was happening to you and me. Deep down I knew it would be that way."

Brand said nothing. She'd pleaded with him not to argue with her, begged him to accept the inevitable, but his silence now was like having a knife plunged directly into her soul.

"There isn't anything more to say then, is there?" he said, his back as stiff as a flagpole as he walked over to the closet and removed his suitcase.

"You're leaving?" It wasn't her most brilliant deduction in the past year.

"There isn't any reason to stay."

No, she admitted miserably to herself. There wasn't. Reluctantly, she stood, her heart aching as it never had. Before she left him, before she walked out of his life, she had to say one last thing. When she spoke, her voice wavered slightly, then leveled out. "You probably hate me now.... I wouldn't blame you if you did. But please, in the future, when you can, try to think kindly of me. Please know that more than anything I want you to be happy."

"I will be happy," he said forcefully. "Damn happy."

She nodded, although she didn't believe it would be true for a good long while for either of them.

"Go ahead and marry your stockbroker, or attorney, or whoever it is who interests you," he continued. "Settle down in your four-bedroom colonial with your two point five children and live the good life." Brand's words were biting and sharp. Forcefully he shoved his clothes inside the suitcase, not taking the time to fold them properly. "Plant those roots so deep they'll reach all the way to China."

Erin blinked back tears. He was so bitter, and there was nothing she could say to make it better. She stiffened, knowing he needed to vent his frustration and his pain.

"By all means, marry your stockbroker," he repeated forcefully. "Security is everything. Tell yourself that often, because I have the feeling you're going to need to remember it."

Erin knotted her fists at her side. The lump in her throat had grown to gargantuan proportions.

"Goodbye, Erin," he whispered as he eased the lid of the suitcase closed. He looked toward the door, silently asking that she walk out of his room as willingly as she was walking out of his life.

"I know it hurts, but it's better this way," she whispered, her voice low and choppy.

He paused and grudgingly smiled at her. "Far better," he agreed.

Fourteen

"Come on, Erin," Aimee urged. "It's December. Liven up a little, would you?"

"I'm alive." Which was stretching the truth. Oh, she functioned day to day and had for the past several weeks, since she'd last seen Brand. The emotional pain had been intolerable in the beginning, but, as expected, the intensity had lessened. She'd counted on being much better by now, however.

Severing the relationship with Brand was what she wanted, she reminded herself. Marrying Brand would have been the biggest mistake of her life. It was amazing how many times a day she was forced to remind herself of that.

"How about doing some Christmas shopping after work?" Aimee suggested.

"Thanks anyway, but I finished mine last week." Erin appreciated the offer, but try as she would, she couldn't muster much enthusiasm for the holidays. The crowds irritated her, and she hated being impatient and grumpy when everyone around her was filled with good cheer.

Bah, humbug! Erin had always loved the holidays.

As hard as she tried not to, she couldn't help wondering about Brand. Was he still in Hawaii? Had he started dating? Was he happy?

By force of will, Erin managed to avoid thoughts of him during the day. Every time her mind turned to the Hawaii-based lieutenant, she immediately focussed on another subject. World peace. Jalapeño jelly. Scissors. Anything and everything but Brand.

It was later, when she was about to slip into the welcome void of sleep, that she found herself most vulnerable. She'd be wandering between the two worlds when Brand would casually stroll into her mind.

He didn't speak; not once had he uttered a word. He just stood there, straight and tall, dressed in his uniform. Proud. Strong. Earnest.

Erin tried to make his image disappear. More than once she'd sat bolt upright in bed and demanded that he clear out of her mind. He always did, without question, but when she lay back down, she always regretted that he was gone.

There had been one improvement, if she could call it that. The episodes when she woke in the middle of the night weeping for no apparent reason had passed. But it was damn little comfort for all the lonely days and nights those unexplained bouts had spawned.

Erin and Aimee walked out of the office together. The air was filled with a joyous holiday flavor. Bells chimed at every street corner. Storefronts were decorated with large swags of evergreen draped above doorways, stretching from one business to the other. Huge red plastic bells adorned streetlights. Erin walked past it all, barely noticing.

"Call me if you change your mind," Aimee said before heading in the opposite direction.

"I will, thanks." But Erin already had her plans for the evening. She was going home, cuddling up in front of the television and mindlessly viewing situation comedies until it was bedtime. It wasn't exciting, nor was it inspiring, but a quiet dinner and television were the only things she could effectively deal with that night. After months of teaching sessions on self-acceptance and being kind to oneself, Erin was determined to follow her own advice.

Erin's mail contained three Christmas cards. The first was from Terry, an old college friend. Terry had married the previous year, and her printed Christmas letter shared the happy news of her pregnancy.

"Terry with a baby," Erin mused aloud, remembering distinctly how they'd both been certain they were destined to remain single the rest of their natural lives.

The second card was from Marilyn. Erin read her brief note with interest. The older woman was forming friendships and had attended a dance with a woman friend who had been widowed several years earlier. Marilyn's note ended with the happy news that she'd danced three times. She claimed she felt more like a wallflower than like Cinderella, but she was ready to attend another dance the following week.

The third Christmas card was from her parents. Erin read over the greeting and was pleased to note that her father had included a short typed sheet along with her mother's much thicker letter. She read her father's letter first.

Dear Erin,
Happy holidays. Your mother and I mailed off a package to you this afternoon, which should arrive in plenty of time for Christmas. I wish we

could be together, but that's what happens when kids grow up and leave home. Your mother and I are going to miss being with you this year.

I don't have much news. Your mother will tell you everything that's up with your brother and sister. They're well and happy, and that's all that counts.

Now what's this I hear about you putting your house up for sale? I remember when you bought it you claimed you were going to live there for the next thirty years. You've only been there two years. I'm afraid you've got more navy blood in you than you realize.

The last bit of information may come as something of a shock. I thought about letting you hear it from someone else but decided that would be cruel. I heard through the grapevine Brand Davis is engaged to Catherine Fredrickson. Apparently they've been friends for a long time. I'm sorry if this news hurts you, baby, but I thought you'd want to know.

Have a good time opening up that box of goodies your mother and I mailed.
Love,
Dad

Erin didn't feel anything. Nothing whatsoever. So Brand was marrying Catherine. It was what Erin herself had suggested months earlier. He certainly hadn't allowed any grass to grow under his feet, she mused somewhat bitterly.

A numbing pain took hold and, deciding to ignore it, Erin set aside the mail and fixed herself a dinner consisting of soup and a turkey sandwich. When she finished, she stared at the bowl and plate and decided she couldn't force herself to eat it. Watching television had lost its appeal, too.

Being alone felt intolerable, and she decided to go for a drive. Mingling with other people seemed important all of a sudden. She wandered through a small shopping complex close to her house, bought a couple of cards at the Hallmark store and strolled back to the parking lot.

"Brand is marrying Catherine," she said aloud in the confines of her car as she drove home. "More than anything, I want him to be happy." She had to say it aloud to remind herself that it was true.

Erin drove past the street where she should have turned off, but for some unknown reason she continued driving, her destination unclear.

An hour passed, and when she found herself close to Aimee's she decided her subconscious was telling her she needed to talk over Brand's engagement with her best friend.

Although Aimee's car was parked in front of her house, she didn't answer the doorbell for several minutes. When she did appear, she was dressed in her housecoat and slippers.

"Erin?" she cried after opening the door. "What are you doing here? Good grief, you look like you've seen a ghost. Come on in." She skillfully steered her through the living room and into the kitchen.

It seemed to Erin that Aimee didn't want her in the living room, which was preposterous, but in case she was arriving at a bad time she asked, "Should I come back later?"

"Of course not," Aimee returned quickly.

A little too quickly, Erin thought. "You look like you were taking a bath."

"No…no."

Erin's gaze narrowed suspiciously. "Then why are you wearing a robe?" It wasn't anywhere near time for bed.

Aimee glanced down at the purple velvet as if she'd never seen it before. "Ah…"

"Aimee," Erin whispered heatedly. A sinking feeling attacked the pit of her stomach, and she looked around. "Have you got a man in your bedroom?"

The dedicated social worker squeezed her eyes closed and nodded several times.

"Why didn't you say something?" Erin felt like a complete idiot. She wanted to crawl under the carpet and hide.

"I couldn't say anything," Aimee protested at length. "You wouldn't drop by unexpectedly like this unless it was something important. One look at you, and I knew you were upset."

"I'm more upset now than I was before I arrived. It would have been better if you hadn't answered the door."

"May I remind you that you're my best friend," Aimee countered heatedly, although they both continued to whisper in an effort not to be overheard by the mystery man in Aimee's bedroom.

Erin couldn't be more surprised by her friend's actions had she announced she was considering entering a convent. To the best of Erin's knowledge, Aimee had never fooled around. She'd been asked out on a date once or twice but had always declined, claiming she wasn't ready for the singles scene just yet.

It wouldn't be the first time Aimee had surprised her, but until now the surprises had all been pleasant ones. Her friend's divorce was only days from being final-ized. Perhaps the pain of what was happening between her and Steve had led her friend into an act completely out of character.

For some time now, Erin had sensed that something was developing in Aimee's life, but she wouldn't have suspected for the world that it was another man. Aimee had given up smoking and was calmer than she had been a few months earlier. Erin had attributed the changes to part of the healing process.

"It's not what you're thinking," Aimee muttered, chastising Erin with a single look. She glanced over her shoulder. "Steve, kindly come out here and save my reputation."

"Steve?" Erin repeated, stunned. "You and Steve? You're divorcing him, remember?"

"Yes, me and Steve," Aimee confirmed. "Steve," she called a second time.

"Honey, if I come out now, I may save your reputation, but it sure as hell will ruin mine."

Aimee actually blushed. Erin couldn't believe it. Her best friend's cheeks went a bright shade of pink.

"Steve?" Erin repeated Aimee's husband's name, still unable to believe what she was hearing.

Aimee nodded, then walked over to the kitchen counter and assembled a pot of coffee.

"You and Steve are…" Erin motioned with her hand, as if that would complete the sentence for her. A tardy smile quivered at the corners of her mouth. "When did all this get started?"

"Will you kindly quit looking at me like you're going to burst out laughing?"

"I can't help it. The last time you mentioned Steve's name it was to claim he was involved with another woman. What about the white car parked outside his apartment? You were convinced he wore that ugly green tie to the settlement hearing to irritate you, and—"

"That was before," Aimee reminded her. "That car belonged to his brother, and hell, I should have known better. I was eager to leap to all the wrong conclusions."

"As I recall, you two were finished, and you couldn't wait to sign the final papers."

"We still might."

"What?" Aimee was certainly full of shocking surprises this evening.

"We were talking about it earlier. It might be wise to start on fresh ground—bury the past, so to speak. We haven't decided yet, but we're leaning toward staying married for…for a couple of reasons."

"But what happened to change everything?"

A slow, almost silly smile lit up Aimee's eyes. "About a month ago—"

"A month?" Erin echoed in strained disbelief. It was hard to imagine that she hadn't suspected something earlier. The two were best friends, and Erin felt she really knew Aimee. "You two have been chummy for a month?"

"Longer, actually," Aimee admitted, keeping her voice low. "Steve called about six weeks ago, needing to come over to the house and pick up some things. The atmosphere was cool between us then, to say the least. We arranged a time suitable to us both. I wasn't keen on being here alone with him, but someone had to be here. I didn't trust him not to take more than what he'd come for, and so I gritted my teeth and met him myself."

"You should have asked me." As matters had turned out, Erin was grateful her friend hadn't.

"I know," Aimee agreed, "but it was shortly after

Brand left, and you were still so raw. I didn't want to burden you with my problems."

"We've been burdening each other for a good long time. But go on. I'm dying to find out what happened."

Aimee smiled. It was the same silly smile as before. "It got worse before it got better. Actually, it got a whole lot worse. Steve arrived, and we got in this huge fight about a light fixture, of all things. I told him he could have the stupid thing. He claimed he didn't want it, but I refused to let that pass. He was still arguing with me when I dragged out the chair and started to remove it from the wall."

"Aimee!"

"I know, I know. My expertise doesn't involve anything electrical, which Steve took delight in reminding me. At the moment, I think, he was hoping I'd electrocute myself. Fortunately, I fell before that happened."

"You fell?"

"Conveniently into Steve's arms, and we both went crashing to the floor. I was furious and outraged and blamed him. I started listing his legion of faults, and he kissed me just to shut me up so he could see if I'd been hurt."

The picture that formed in Erin's mind was a wildly romantic one. Aimee hopping mad, and Steve more interested in making sure she hadn't been hurt in the fall than in listening to her tirade.

"One thing led to another, and before we knew it we were in bed together."

"Oh, Aimee that's so romantic."

"Romantic, nothing. I was furious, claiming he'd seduced me. Steve adamantly denied it and said I was the one who'd seduced him. Before the night was over, we'd seduced each other a second time. Both of us were more than a little chagrined over what happened. Steve left the following morning without taking any of the things he claimed he needed so badly. I called him the next day, and he returned for the items…only he ended up spending the night again."

"But what about everything that led up to the divorce? You were miserable together. Remember?"

"Nothing's really changed," Aimee explained. "Only our attitude has. We're committed to working out our problems. Steve's willing to see a counselor. In fact, he's the one who suggested it."

"So you've talked everything out?"

"We talked, among other things," Steve inserted as he walked into the kitchen. Standing behind Aimee, he slipped his arms around her waist and cuddled her close. "Should we tell her?" he asked his wife.

"Nothing's for sure yet," Aimee said, twisting her head around to look up at him.

"I'm sure of it."

Erin hadn't a clue what the two were discussing. "Tell me what?"

"Aimee's pregnant. At least we think she is."

"Steve, I haven't been to the doctor yet. You can't go around announcing it until I've been in to see Dr. Larson."

"All those pregnancy test kits you bought claim you are. That's good enough for me." He broke away from his wife and strutted around the kitchen in a walk that would have done a rooster proud.

Delight brightened Aimee's eyes as she held out her hands to Erin. "After ten years. I can't believe it. We tried so hard and for so long." Her face broke into an eager smile. "Oh, Erin, I'm going to have a baby."

The two gripped hands, and Erin felt tears of shared happiness fill her eyes.

"Hey, you two, kindly give credit where credit is due." A light shone in Steven's eyes, one that had been decidedly missing the other times Erin had seen him.

"I couldn't be happier for the two of you," Erin said, sincerely meaning every word, but at the same time the pain she felt knowing Brand was marrying Catherine felt like a heavy chain tightening around her heart. First Terry, and now Aimee.

"You didn't come over here because you suspected anything was developing between Steve and me," Aimee reminded her, scooting out a chair at the table. By now the coffee had brewed, and Aimee automatically brought down mugs.

Steve kissed his wife's cheek. "I'll leave you two to talk," he said, and smiled warmly at Erin before returning to the living room.

"Brand's engaged," Erin announced, her voice trembling slightly. "My dad wrote and told me. He claimed it was better I hear the news from him than someone else."

"Oh, Erin, I'm so sorry."

"What's to be sorry about?" she asked with a shaky laugh. "If marrying Catherine is what it takes to make Brand happy, then why should I feel bad?"

"You love him."

"I know."

Aimee was quiet for a moment. "Have you given any more thought to what I said all those weeks ago about having our jobs taint our views on marriage?"

Erin hadn't. She'd been sifting through so much emotion and pain that she'd filed her friend's thoughts away in the farthest corner of her mind. "Not really."

"Then do. Not all marriages end in misery and heart-ache."

"It sometimes seems that way."

"I know," Aimee was quick to agree. "Think about it, Erin. You haven't been at this job long enough to gain perspective yet. That comes with time. I fell into that same trap myself.

"There are plenty of good marriages out there that work because the two people involved are prepared to do whatever they have to to see that it does."

Erin drew in a deep breath. "It's too late now for Brand and me."

"That's what I thought," Aimee reminded her.

"I want Brand to marry Catherine," Erin murmured, telling the biggest lie of her life. "They're perfect together... I said so from the first."

A Christmas card to Brand wouldn't hurt, Erin decided later. One with a brief note of congratulations. It took her nearly three days to compose the few lines.

Dear Brand,
Merry Christmas. I always claimed you and Catherine were perfect together. Now Dad tells me he heard through the grapevine that the two of you have set the big date. Congratulations.
    I honestly mean that. I wish you only the best. You deserve it.
Erin
P.S. Neal and I are getting along famously.

Neal, Brand mused, reading over the short message a second time. He didn't know what tricks Erin was up to now, but he wasn't in the mood for it. He'd put her out of his life, and he was managing nicely.

"Who the hell are you kidding?" he asked out loud.

"You say something?" Romano asked.

"Nothing that concerns you," Brand barked. "Who the hell leaked out information about me and Catherine?"

"What kind of information?"

"That we're marrying."

"Hell, I don't know who'd say anything. Is it true?"

Brand answered that with a single intense look.

"Hey, don't get mad at me. I was just asking." Alex scooted away from his desk. "What's with you today, anyway?"

Brand debated on whether he'd let his friend know or not, then decided he owed everyone around him an explanation. He hadn't been the best company the past few weeks. "I got a Christmas card from Erin."

Romano responded with a low whistle. "No wonder you've been acting like a wounded bear all day. What'd she have to say?"

"Congratulations to me and Cath," he answered with a low snicker.

"You going to write and let her know the truth?"

"No," Brand answered without hesitating. If Erin wanted to believe he was marrying Catherine, he'd let her.

"I take it you don't plan on looking her up next week, either?"

"Hell, no." Brand had cursed the assignment that was taking him into Seattle. The timing couldn't have been worse. Two months, and he was only now getting to the point that he could go a small portion of the day without dwelling on the situation between him and Erin.

He wasn't about to set himself up for more pain. He'd had all he could take.

Brand altered that decision, however, shortly after he checked into the Seattle hotel. He had a rental car, and with time to kill he decided it wouldn't hurt to swing past Erin's house. If luck was with him, he might catch a glimpse of her.

Luck, however, hadn't exactly been tossing charms his way lately, he was quick to note.

"You're acting like a lovesick fool," he told himself as he exited from the freeway and climbed the twisting roadway that led to West Seattle. "Why the hell shouldn't you?" he asked himself next. "You've been a lovesick fool from the moment you met Erin Mac-Namera."

By the time he was on the side street that led to her house, Brand was having third and fourth thoughts. They vanished the minute he saw the For Sale sign.

He waited until the blazing anger that raged through him had dissipated enough for him to think clearly. When it had, he stepped out of the car and marched to her front door and rapped hard against the wooden structure.

She took her sweet time answering. Her complexion went pale when she saw him, and his name was only a voiceless movement of her lips.

"What's that For Sale sign doing on the front lawn?" he demanded.

Erin looked up at him as if she were sorely tempted to reach out and touch him to be sure he wasn't a figment of her imagination.

"The For Sale sign," he repeated harshly, pointing to it in case she wasn't aware it was there.

"I'm selling the house," she whispered, then blinked twice. "What are you doing here?"

"I'm on assignment. I want to know why the hell you're moving."

"It's…well, it's not easy to explain."

She stepped aside for him to come into the house. Brand had no intention of doing so. He was walking a fine line as it was. His anger had carried him all the way to her front door, but being this close to Erin, loving her as much as he did and loathing her for the hell she'd put him through, wasn't exactly conducive to them being alone together. He'd forgotten how beautiful she was, with her rich auburn hair and her expressive dark eyes. They registered a multitude of emotions.

"I can't…explain it out here," she said when he doggedly remained where he was. "Come inside. There's coffee."

"If you don't mind, I'd prefer not to. Just kindly tell me why you're moving?"

"You don't want to come inside?" Erin sounded hurt and incredulous.

"No." Once again he pointed to the sign.

"I have to sell," she explained haltingly. "Well, I don't exactly have to… Actually, if you want the truth, I'm sick of the grand piano. It takes up the entire living room, I don't have the time for lessons and I lack talent."

"That isn't any reason to sell. A few months ago a bulldozer was the only thing that would get you out of this house."

"It isn't the house that was so important to me."

"Then what the hell was it?"

"Roots," she shouted back, just as angry and impatient with him as he was with her.

Brand wasn't buying that for one minute. "Now we

both know, don't we, Erin? All this business about need-ing security was bull. You don't have any more roots in Seattle than you did anyplace else. You can pretend all you want after today, sweetheart, but for right now, you're going to admit the truth."

She frowned as if she hadn't a clue what he was saying.

"You're bored and restless," he elaborated.

She denied that with a hard shake of her head. "That's not true."

"Sorry, sweetheart, I should have recognized the symptoms, but I was so damn much in love with you, a battleship would have escaped me."

A lone tear ran down the side of her face, but Brand was in no mood to react to her anguish. Perhaps deep down he was pleased to see her crying, although he didn't like to think that was true. She'd put him through hell, and if she was suffering a little, then so much the better.

"You thrive on change, you always have, only you refused to admit it. You're looking for a challenge, be-cause it's the only thing you've ever known. You grew up learning how to adjust to situations, and now all of a sudden there's nothing new. Everything is the same, one day after the next, and you're looking for a way out, only you're sugarcoating it with the idea that you don't have enough room in your living room. Did it ever occur to you that you might sell the piano?"

"No," she whispered in a tight, strained voice.

"I didn't think it would." She thought more like a navy wife than Brand had ever realized.

Neither of them spoke for several tense moments. Brand knew he should turn and walk away from her. He'd said everything he wanted to and more. Erin stood before him as pale as a canvas sail bleached by the sun, holding herself proud, her head high and regal.

He started to move, but every step felt as if he were dragging an anchor with him. Part of him yearned to shout back at her, tell her she'd never find a man who loved her as much as he did, but she'd rejected his love once, and he was too damn proud to hand her the power to injure him again.

He was halfway to his car when she called out to him. "Brand..."

He twisted around and discovered that she'd walked down the steps toward him. "What?" he demanded brusquely.

She shook her head. Then, using the back of her hands, she wiped the moisture from her face. "I'm so—"

"Don't apologize," he said, in as cutting a voice as he could manage. He could take anything but that. She didn't want him, didn't love him enough. By God, he wasn't about to let her water down her regrets by telling him how sorry she was.

"I wasn't," she whispered brokenly. "Just be happy."

Something broke within Brand, something deep and fundamental that had been wounded that afternoon in the Seattle hotel. "Be happy," he shouted, marching up to her. He gripped her hard by the shoulders. The power of the emotion had a stranglehold on all his good intentions to turn and aloofly walk away from her. He had damn little pride left when it came to Erin, but for once he was determined to close himself off from her. After all the times she'd hurt him, it felt good to be the one in control. He struggled to remain indifferent and detached.

He ruined everything by announcing the truth. "Do

you honestly believe I can be happy without you in my life?" he demanded. "Fat chance, sweetheart."

She blinked up at him, her eyes stricken and wide. "But you're marrying Catherine."

He snickered loudly. "Your father should know by now not to trust everything he hears."

"You mean you're not?"

"Not anytime soon," he bit out caustically.

Indescribable joy crowded Erin's face before she gave a hoarse shriek. She tossed her arms around his neck and shocked him by spreading madcap kisses all over his face. Her hands were splayed over his ears as her sweet mouth bestowed a fleeting succession of kisses wherever her lips happened to land. Tears mingled with those first kisses and mumbled, unintelligible words.

"Erin, stop," he demanded. At the first touch of her mouth, the hard protective shell he'd erected around his heart cracked. He'd worked like a madman to fortify it from the moment he'd knocked on her front door. He didn't know how much longer he could hold out with her touching him like this.

Her lips found his, and he opened to her, hungry and eager and too battle-weary to fight her any longer. He took control of the kiss, plowing his hands into her hair and slanting his mouth over hers. She sighed and locked her arms around his neck and kissed him back with a need that made Brand bitterly regret the fact they were outside her house.

"You're going to marry me," he told her forcefully.

"Yes...yes," she answered, as if there had never been any question about it. "Only let's make the wedding soon."

Brand frowned. He couldn't believe what he was hearing. "I'm probably going to get transferred."

"I know."

"In the next twenty years I may be stationed from here to kingdom come. We'll move any number of times."

"No doubt we will, but I'm used to that."

The rigid control he'd maintained early on had melted and puddled at his feet, but Brand wasn't completely convinced this was for real. He wasn't leaving anything to speculation. "There are going to be children."

"I certainly hope so."

"You wanted roots, remember?"

"I've got them, only they're wound around you."

Brand felt dizzy with relief and a profound sense of completeness. "Why?"

She laughed softly, and he heard the pain mingled with the joy. "You're right...you were right all along, only I was too blind to realize it. For months I've been restless and bored, just like you said. I wanted to blame that feeling on you, but it started long before we met. Nearly every weekend I was taking long drives. Last month I put the house on the market, thinking once it sold I'd put in my notice at the office and move to Oregon.

"I was wrong about so many things. Aimee was right—I hadn't been with the Community Action Program long enough to realize some marriages do work. People can stay in love forever. I'd forgotten that and so many other things. Did you know I attended four different universities? Can you believe that? All along I kept claiming I wanted roots, but I was too blind to see how bored I get in one place. When I did realize that, it was too late—I'd heard about you and Catherine. Oh, Brand, I'm so ready to be your wife. So ready to settle down."

"The only place you're going to settle is with me."

"Aye, aye, Lieutenant," she whispered. Her mouth claimed his for a lengthy series of delicate, nibbling kisses.

Epilogue

"Here we are again," a smiling Ginger Romano commented to Erin as they stood on the crowded pier. The two were part of a large gathering of family members waiting for the crew of the *Blue Ridge* to disembark after a lengthy cruise. The ship was returning from monitoring sea trials and had been gone nearly five months.

Erin was eager for Brand's return for more than the usual reasons. She'd missed her husband the way she always missed him when he was away for any length of time. They'd been blissfully happy in the two years since their marriage. Becoming Brand's wife had taught Erin several valuable lessons about herself. She loved navy life. Thrived on it, just the way he'd claimed she would. She was home, where she'd always meant to be. The navy was in her blood, the same way it was in her father's and in Brand's. She might not have a whole lot to do with national defense, but she, and the other wives like her, were as important to the navy as the entire Pacific fleet.

"There's Daddy," Ginger shrieked, pointing to Alex

as he walked down the gangplank. Bobby and the two little ones went racing toward their father.

Brand was directly behind Alex. He paused and searched the crowd for Erin. Her heart sped as she started toward him at a dignified gait. Soon, however, she broke into a run as Brand started rushing toward her. He caught her by the waist and lifted her high above his head; their mouths found and clung to each other in a love feast of longing and need.

"Welcome home, Lieutenant," she said when she could, wiping the moisture from her face. Generally she wasn't emotional at these reunions, and she didn't want to give away her secret too quickly.

Slowly Brand lowered her to the ground, but he didn't release her. "You missed me?"

"Like crazy."

"You're pale." His hand tenderly caressed her cheek. "You haven't been overdoing this volunteer work, have you?"

"I love working with the Chaplain's Office."

"That didn't answer my question."

"Quit arguing and kindly kiss me."

Brand was all too eager to comply, pulling her flush against him, his mouth greedy over hers. When he raised his head, his eyes were narrowed and questioning.

"Erin?"

"Yes." She smiled saucily up at him.

"You've gained weight?"

"Is that a question or a statement?"

He stepped back from her, and Erin watched as his gaze shifted from her swollen breasts to the slight swell of her smoothly rounded stomach. He splayed his fingers over the mound and stared at her as if he'd never seen a pregnant woman in his entire life.

"Yes, my darling, we're pregnant."

"A baby," he whispered haltingly. "But…you never said a word."

"I didn't find out until after you'd left, and then I thought a pregnant wife would make a delightful surprise for your homecoming."

"A baby," he whispered a second time, and seemed to be struggling for words. He gently cupped her face in his hands and brushed the pads of his thumbs across the slick tears that streamed down her cheeks. "I love you, Erin MacNamera Davis, more and more each day. Thank God you came to your senses and married me."

Erin thanked God, too. Her husband's large hand flattened across her abdomen as he brought her protectively into the circle of his arms. "A baby," he whispered, as if he still couldn't believe it was true.

"Our own navy brat," Erin added, just before their mouths merged.

* * * * *

NAVY WOMAN

Dedicated to

Betty Zimmerman

A remarkable woman and a very special aunt

Special thanks to

Cheryl K. Rife, LCDR, JAGC, USN

One

Rain. That's all it had done from the moment Lieutenant Commander Catherine Fredrickson, Judge Advocate General Corps—JA6C—arrived at the Naval Submarine Base Bangor in Silverdale, Washington. October in Hawaii meant balmy ocean breezes, *mai tais* by the pool and eighty-degree sunshine.

In other words she'd left paradise and had been transferred to purgatory.

If the weather wasn't enough to discourage her, the executive officer, Commander Royce Nyland was. Catherine had never met anyone who irritated her more. The legal staff stationed in Hawaii had shared a camaraderie that made working together a pleasant experience.

Bangor was a different story, but the contrast was most telling in the differences between Catherine's two superiors. She simply didn't like the man, and from all outward appearances the feeling was mutual.

From the first, Catherine knew something wasn't right. In no other station had she been required to stand duty so often. For four weeks straight she'd been assigned the twenty-four-hour watch on a Friday night. It was as if Commander Nyland had made it his personal goal to disrupt her entire life.

After a month, Catherine was getting downright testy about it.

"Fredrickson, do you have the files on the Miller case?"

"Yes, sir." She stood, reached for the requested file and handed it to the man who'd been dominating her thoughts for the majority of the day.

Commander Nyland opened the file and started reading as he walked away from her. Catherine's gaze followed him as she tried to analyze what it was about her he disliked so much. Perhaps he had something against brunettes. Although that sounded crazy, Catherine couldn't help wondering. Maybe it was because she was petite and small-boned. More than likely, she reminded him of someone he once knew and disliked intensely. Well that was just too damn bad. As far as Catherine could see, she'd done nothing to deserve his disdain, and frankly, she wasn't about to put up with any more of it.

Scuttlebutt had it that he was single. Catherine had no trouble believing it. If his behavior toward her was any indication of how he treated women, then this guy needed a major attitude adjustment.

His apparent dislike of her solved one problem. Catherine needn't worry about anything romantic developing between them. If she were looking for an effective way to end her Navy career, all she had to do was start fraternizing with a superior officer within the same command. It was the quickest way Catherine knew to be court-martialed. The Navy refused to tolerate such behavior.

Besides his rotten attitude, Commander Nyland

wasn't her type. Catherine liked her men less rough around the edges and a whole lot more agreeable.

In eleven years of Navy life, Catherine had worked with her share of officers, but no one had ever struck such a strong, discordant note with her.

Nothing she did pleased him. Nothing. The closest she'd ever gotten to praise from her XO had been a hard nod, as if that were sufficient compliment. A nod!

The crazy part of it was, Catherine had actually gotten excited over it. All day she'd gone around wearing a silly grin.

She needed to get back to Hawaii, and fast.

"Come into my office, Lieutenant Commander."

Catherine glanced up, startled to discover Commander Nyland standing directly in front of her desk.

"Yes, sir," she answered briskly. She stood and reached for a notepad before following him into his office.

Commander Nyland took his seat and motioned for Catherine to sit in the cushioned chair located on the opposite side of his desk.

Catherine glanced around and swallowed nervously. She didn't like the looks of this. The great and almighty commander was frowning. Not that it was the least bit unusual. To the best of her memory, she couldn't remember him ever smiling.

She quickly reviewed the cases she'd been working on for the past few days, and could think of nothing that would warrant a tongue-lashing. Not that he needed an excuse, of course.

The silence stretched to uncomfortable lengths as she waited for him to acknowledge her. It was on the tip of her tongue to remind him he was the one who'd called her into his office, but she'd be a fool to allow a hint of sarcasm into her voice.

"I've been following your progress for the past several weeks." His indifferent blue gaze raked her features. Catherine had never been more aware of her appearance. Her thick, dark hair was coiled in a businesslike knot at her nape, and her uniform jacket and skirt were crisp and freshly pressed. She had the impression if he found one crease, she'd be ordered to stand in front of a firing squad. No man had ever made her feel more self-conscious. He continued to stare at her as if seeing her for the first time. There was no hint of appreciation for her good looks. Catherine wasn't conceited, but she was reasonably attractive, and the fact the man looked at her as if she were little more than a mannequin was vaguely insulting. Okay, she was being unreasonable, Catherine mused. If she had recognized a flicker of interest in those cobalt-blue eyes of his, that would have been worse.

"Yes, sir."

"As I was saying," he continued, "I've had my eye on your work."

She noted that he made a simple statement of fact without elaborating. If he'd been watching her, then she'd admit, not openly of course, that she'd been studying him, too. He may be disagreeable, and to her way of thinking, ill-tempered, but he was respected and generally well liked. Personally, Catherine found him to be a real pain, but her thinking was tainted by a four-week stint at standing duty on Friday nights.

Politics existed in every office, but there seemed to be more in Bangor than the other duty stations Catherine had been assigned. As the executive officer directly below Captain Stewart, Commander Royce Nyland was empowered to run her legal office. He did so with a detached, emotionless ability that Catherine had rarely seen. In many ways he was the best officer she'd ever worked with and, in others, the worst.

It was apparent the man was a born leader. His lean, muscular good looks commanded attention. His office demanded it.

Actually, now that she had an uninterrupted minute to analyze the commander, she was willing to admit he was fairly attractive. Not handsome in the classic sense. Appealing, she decided. Not ordinary.

His features weren't anything that would cause a woman to swoon. His hair was nearly black. Its darkness coupled with his deep blue eyes was a contrast not easily ignored. He was broad-shouldered, and although she knew him to be of medium height, an inch or so under six feet, he gave the impression of power and strength in everything he did.

Her scrutiny didn't seem to bother him. He leaned back in his chair, expelled his breath and announced, "I'm pleased to tell you I've chosen you as a substitute coordinator of the physical fitness program for the base."

"Substitute coordinator," Catherine repeated slowly. Her heart beat dull and heavy before it dropped like a lead weight to her stomach. It took a second to right itself before she could respond. If there was one after-hours duty she would have done anything to avoid it was that of coordinator of the physical fitness program. It was by far one of the least envied jobs on base.

The Navy was serious about keeping men and women in top physical condition. Those who were overweight were placed on a strict dietary schedule and exercise regime. As coordinator, Catherine would be subjected to endless meetings to chart the individuals' progress. She'd also be expected to formulate an exercise program designed specifically to meet each person's needs. In addition, she would be given the painful task of having someone discharged from the Navy if they failed to meet the requirements in regard to weight and fitness.

"I believe you're qualified to handle this job effectively."

"Yes, sir," she said, biting her tongue to keep from saying more. Tackling this duty, even on a substitute basis, meant she wouldn't have time to breathe. It was a time-consuming, distasteful assignment. If the executive officer had been actively seeking to destroy any chance she had of developing a social life, he'd done so in one fell swoop.

"Lieutenant Osborne will meet with you and give you the necessary paperwork at 1500 hours. If you have any questions, you should gear them to him." Already he was looking away from her, dismissing her.

"Thank you, sir," she said, struggling with everything in her not to let her irritation show. She left his office and closed the door with a decided click, hoping he'd believe the wind had caught it. Hell, he was fortunate she didn't tear the damn thing right off its hinges.

With as dignified a walk as possible, she returned to her office. She set the pad down a little too hard, attracting the attention of Elaine Perkins, her secretary, who occupied the scarred desk outside Catherine's office.

"Problems?" she asked. As a Navy wife, Elaine was well acquainted with the difficulties of military life.

"Problems?" Catherine echoed sarcastically. "What could possibly be wrong? Listen, do I have something repugnantly wrong with me?"

"Not that I've noticed," Elaine was quick to tell her.

"I don't have bad breath?"

"No."

"Does my slip hang out from under my skirt?" She twisted around and tried to determine that much for herself.

"Not that I can see," Elaine assured her. "What makes you ask?"

"No reason." With that, Catherine stalked out of the office and down the hall to the drinking fountain. Her hand trembled slightly as she leaned forward and scooped up a generous mouthful, letting the cold water soothe her injured pride.

Catherine wished she could talk to Sally. The two were the only women officers in a command of several hundred men, but that wasn't possible now. Once she'd composed herself sufficiently to return, Catherine did so, forcing a smile.

"I'm *pleased* to inform you you've been chosen as the substitute coordinator of the physical fitness program," Catherine mumbled under her breath as she traipsed toward the running track several hours later. Dusk was settling over the compound, but there was enough time to get in a three-mile run before dark.

Pleased was right. Commander Nyland had looked downright gleeful to assign her the task. The more Catherine thought about it, the more furious she got.

Venting some of this discontent seemed like a good idea. Clouds threatened a downpour, but Catherine didn't care. She'd just received the worst collateral duty assignment of her career, and she needed to vent the frustration and confusion before she headed home to the apartment she rented in Silverdale. Taking giant strides, she crested the hill that led to the track, then stopped abruptly. Several runners circled the course, but one runner in particular stood out from the rest.

Commander Nyland.

For a long moment Catherine couldn't keep her eyes off him. There was a natural, fluid grace to his movements. His stride was long and even, and he ran as if the wind were beneath his feet. What struck her most was his quiet strength. She didn't want to acknowledge it. Nor did she wish to find a single positive attribute about this man.

If there was any justice in the world, lightning would strike him dead. Glancing to the sky, she was depressed to note a touch of blue in the far horizon. Typical. Just when she was looking for rain, the sun had decided to play a game of hide-and-seek with her. If lightning wasn't going to do the good commander in, then all she could hope for was a bad case of athlete's foot.

Once again she grumbled under her breath, seriously considering leaving the base without running. If she did go down to the track, it was likely she'd say or do something that would get her into trouble with the commander.

Evidently she'd done something horrible to warrant his dislike. After he'd ruined four weekends straight for her, he'd topped himself by giving her the least desirable assignment on base. What next? KP?

Catherine started to turn away, then abruptly changed her mind. She wasn't going to allow this man to dictate her entire life! She had as much right to run on this track as anyone. If he didn't like it, he could be the one to leave.

With that thought in mind, she stepped alongside the court and went through a series of warm-up exercises. Actually, the more she thought about it, she was downright eager to get onto the track. She was petite, but she was a fine runner. She'd been on the varsity cross-country teams in both high school and college and did a consistent seven-minute mile. If there was an area in which she excelled, it was running.

She did the first lap at a relaxed pace, easily lapping a couple of the overweight men. Commander Nyland didn't acknowledge her one way or the other, which was perfectly fine with Catherine. She'd hadn't come out here to exchange pleasantries with him.

The second and third laps, Catherine stepped up her pace. It normally took her a mile or so to fully warm up. As she increased her stride, she noticed that she was never quite able to catch her XO.

The one time she did manage to pass him, he scooted past her seconds later, leaving her to eat his dust. Frustrated, Catherine decided she might not be able to outrun him, but by heaven she'd outlast him. He was fast, but she'd easily outdistance him.

She continued her killing pace until she was sure she'd gone six miles or farther. Her lungs ached, and her calf muscles strenuously protested the abuse. Yet she continued, more determined than ever not to surrender her pride to this disagreeable commander. If she was hurting, then so was he.

She would rather keel over from exhaustion than quit now! It was more than a matter of pride.

Soon fat raindrops fell from the darkening sky and splashed against the dry, gritty surface. Still Catherine and the commander ran. What few runners remained quickly dropped out until it was the two of them alone against the forces of nature. Against each other, in a silent battle of wills.

They didn't speak. Not once. Catherine ran until she

thought she was going to be sick, yet she dared not stop. Night fell like a curtain of black satin around the grounds. Catherine barely managed to see her own feet, let alone the distant silhouette of the commander. Soon he disappeared from her range of view entirely. It wasn't until she heard his footsteps coming up behind her that she realized he'd been able to come all the way around to lap her. He slowed his pace until his steps matched her own without breaking his stride.

"How much longer are we going to keep this up, Fredrickson?" he demanded.

Damn, he didn't even sound out of breath, Catherine noted.

"I don't know," she returned, sounding very much as though she should have yielded several miles back.

"You're tiring."

How kind of him to tell her so. "You are, too," she insisted.

"I have to admit you're a hell of a runner."

"A compliment, Commander?"

She sensed his smile. It made absolutely no sense the way her heart reacted knowing that. It was as if she'd been blessed by an unexpected second wind. By some odd twist of fate, she'd actually managed to amuse ol' stone face.

"Don't let it go to your head."

"No chance of that," she quipped, wondering if she'd heard a hint of amusement in his tone. "I don't suppose you happened to notice it's raining." Although she attempted to make light of it, she was drenched to the bone.

"Is that what all this wet stuff is?"

"I'll tell you what," she said between breaths, "I'll stop running if you do. We'll call it a draw."

"Agreed." Royce slowed his pace to a trot, and Catherine reluctantly did the same, not sure even now that she could trust him. After several steps, she stopped and leaned over, bracing her hands on her knees while she struggled to capture her breath.

The rain continued to pound down with a vengeance. While they were jogging, it was a simple enough matter to ignore the downpour. Now it wasn't so easy. Her hair, which had once been neatly secured at her nape, was plastered to her cheeks like wet strings. A small river of rainwater was navigating over her neck and down to the small of her back.

"Go home, Fredrickson," Royce said after a moment.

Catherine bristled. "Is that an order?"

He paused. "No."

He started to walk away from her, then unexpectedly turned back. "Before you leave, satisfy a curiosity. You requested a transfer from San Diego several years back. Why?"

Catherine knew it was all part of her personnel file, but his question caught her off guard. Her response was quick, light-hearted, almost flippant. "Who wouldn't want to live in Hawaii?"

"That wasn't the reason you wanted out of San Diego." His voice was deceptively unconcerned, as if he knew far more than he was letting on. "You wanted that transfer and you didn't care if you got Hawaii or Iran."

"There were personal reasons," she admitted reluctantly. Catherine couldn't understand why he'd chosen to ask her these questions now. The man continued to baffle her.

"Tell me the truth."

Catherine tensed, disliking his casual tone. Nor was she pleased with the way he implied she was lying. By mentally counting to ten, she willed herself to remain calm.

"That is the truth. I've always wanted to live in Hawaii."

"My guess is that a man was involved."

Catherine's stomach knotted. She didn't often think about Aaron. For the past three years she'd done a superb job of pretending they'd never met. Leave it to Royce Nyland to harass her battered heart with memories of her former fiancé. All right, that was a bit strong. He wasn't exactly tormenting her, and her heart wasn't all that scarred.

"What makes you think my request had anything to do with a man?" she asked, making light of his comment. She increased her strides, wanting to get this interrogation over with as soon as possible.

"Because it generally is."

That wasn't the least bit true, but Catherine wasn't going to stand in the rain and argue with him.

"A change of scenery appealed to me at the time." She needed to get away from San Diego for fear she'd run into Aaron. She wouldn't have been able to bear seeing him again. At least that was what she told herself. Over time, she wasn't nearly convinced that was true. She'd fallen head over heels in love with him much too quickly. Then she'd flown out as a defense attorney for trials aboard the *Nimitz* and returned several weeks later to learn Aaron hadn't exactly been holding his breath waiting for her.

The first minute she was back, Catherine had rushed to her fiancé's apartment to find him lying on the sofa with the young blond divorcée who lived next door. Aaron had scrambled off the davenport in a rush to explain while the red-faced divorcée hastily rebuttoned her blouse. It had all been innocent fun, Aaron claimed. Hell, how was he supposed to amuse himself while she was away for weeks on end? He advised Catherine to be a sport since he and the blonde had only indulged in a little entertainment.

In thinking back over the episode, Catherine was surprised by how completely emotionless she'd remained. The solitary diamond on her finger suddenly weighted down her hand. That much she remembered with ease. She'd stared down on it and then wordlessly slipped it from her finger and returned it to Aaron. For several moments he was paralyzed with shock. Then he'd followed her to the parking lot and pleaded with her to be more understanding. If it offended her so much, he'd make sure it didn't happen again. There was no need to overreact this way. None whatsoever.

In retrospect Catherine had come to realize that her pride had taken far more of a beating than her heart. She was almost relieved to have Aaron out of her life, only she hadn't realized that until much later.

"Catherine?"

Royce's deep, masculine voice pulled her back into the present. To the best of her knowledge it was the first time he'd ever used her name. Until then it had been Lieutenant Commander or Fredrickson, but never Catherine. This, too, had a curious effect upon her heart.

"There was a man involved," she announced stiffly, "but that was several years ago now. You needn't worry my former engagement will affect my work for you. Now or in the future."

"I'm pleased to hear it."

"Good night, Commander." They crested the hill where Catherine's bright red GEO Storm was waiting for her.

"Good night."

Trotting, Catherine was halfway down the hill when Royce stopped her.

"Catherine."

"Yes?" She turned around to face him, brushing the wet curls from her cheeks.

"Are you living with someone?"

The question took her by complete surprise. "That's none of your business."

Royce said nothing. He stood several feet away from her, his harsh features illuminated by the streetlight. His face was tight, as if he were holding himself in check. "Trust me, I have no interest in your love life. You can live with whomever you please or be engaged to five men at once for all I care. What does concern me is the legal department. The work is demanding and the schedule grueling. I like to know where I stand with my staff and try to avoid causing unnecessary complications in their lives."

Catherine didn't respond right away. "Since you find it so important, then I might as well confess I am shacked up with someone." From the distance Catherine couldn't tell if she got a reaction or not. Most likely he was telling the truth and he didn't care one way or the other. "Sambo."

"Sambo?" he repeated frowning.

"You heard me correctly, Commander. I live with a cat named Sambo." With that, she gave a cheerful laugh and was gone.

Royce found himself smiling in the dark, the rain pelting down around him in a great torrent. His amusement, however, vanished quickly. He didn't like Catherine Fredrickson.

"No," he muttered aloud, retracting the thought. That wasn't true. He did like her. There were any number of admirable traits about the Lieutenant Commander he couldn't help but respect.

She was dedicated and hardworking, and she'd fit in easily with the rest of his staff. She wasn't a complainer, either. Before he'd left the office that evening, he'd checked over the duty roster and was surprised to note that he'd assigned Catherine duty every Friday for four weeks running. He hadn't realized his mistake. Anyone else would have pointed it out to him, and rightly so. Her name had drifted easily into his mind when he learned Lieutenant Osborne was going on sea trials and a substitute coordinator was needed to take over the physical fitness program.

He knew Catherine wasn't overly pleased by the assignment. Her eyes had flashed briefly with rebellion, but that was the only outward sign she'd given that she wasn't thrilled with the added responsibility.

That woman had eyes that would mark a man's soul. Normally Royce didn't pay much attention to that sort of thing, but her eyes had garnered his attention from the first moment they'd met. They shimmered, and seemed to trap pieces of light. But more than that, they seemed warm and caring.

He liked her voice, too. It was rich and sweetly feminine. Female. Hell, Royce mused, he was beginning to sound like a romantic poet.

Now that thought was enough to produce a hearty laugh. There wasn't a romantic bone left in his body. His wife had squeezed every ounce of love and joy out of him long before she went to the grave.

Royce didn't want to think about Sandy. Abruptly he

turned and walked toward his car, his strides hurried, as if he could outdistance the memory of his dead wife.

He climbed inside his Porsche and started the engine. His house was on the base, and he'd be home within five minutes.

Before long, however, it was Catherine who dominated his thoughts again. He wasn't overly thrilled with the subject matter, but he was too damn tired to fight himself over it. When he arrived home, his ten-year-old daughter, Kelly, would keep him occupied. For once he was going to indulge himself and let his thoughts wander where they would. Besides, he was curious to analyze his complex reaction to Catherine Fredrickson.

Not that it was important. Not that he needed to know anything more about her than he already did. He was simply inquisitive. He supposed when it came right down to it, he didn't feel one way or the other about her.

No, that wasn't true, either. She intrigued him. He didn't like it. He didn't understand it. He wished he could put his finger on exactly what it was about her that fascinated him so much. Until that afternoon, he hadn't even been aware of it.

She wasn't that much different than the other Navy women he'd worked with over the years. Not true, he contradicted himself. She had a scrubbed-clean look about her, a gentleness, a gracefulness of heart and manner that piqued him.

Another thing he'd learned about her this evening. By heaven that woman was bullheaded. He'd never seen anyone run with cursed stubbornness the way she had. It wasn't until it had started to rain that Royce recognized the unspoken challenge she'd issued. Absorbed in his thoughts, he hadn't noticed she was on the track until she'd zoomed past him and then smugly tossed a look over her shoulder as if to announce she'd won. Hell, he hadn't even realized they were in a race.

As if that wasn't enough, she wouldn't stop. They both had reached their physical limits, and still that little spitfire continued and would have, Royce was convinced, until she dropped.

He pulled into the driveway and cut the engine. His hands remained on the steering wheel as a slow smile spread across his features. *Woman*, he mused, *thy name is pride*.

The drape parted in the living room, Kelly's head peeked out. Just the way the drape was tossed back into place told him the ten-year-old was angry. Damn, Royce wondered, what the hell had he done this time?

Kelly usually ran outside to greet him. Not tonight. Whatever it was must have been a doozy. His daughter could be more stubborn than a Tennessee mule. This must be his day for clashing with obstinate women.

Two

Fresh from the shower, Catherine dressed in a warm robe, and wrapped her hair in a thick towel. She sat in the living room, her feet propped against the coffee table with Sambo nestled contentedly in her lap.

Sipping from a cup of herbal tea, Catherine mulled over the events of the day. A reluctant smile slowly eased its way across her face. Her dislike for Royce Nyland didn't go quite as deep as it had before their small confrontation on the racetrack. The man wasn't ever going to win any personality awards, that was for sure, but she felt a grudging respect for him.

Sambo purred and stretched his furry legs, his claws digging deep into the thick robe. Catherine stroked her pet, letting the long black tail slip through her fingers as she continued to mull over the time she and Royce had shared the track. The realization that she actually enjoyed their silent battle of wills warmed her from the inside out. For some unknown reason, she'd managed to amuse him. Because of the dark, Catherine hadn't been able to witness his stern features relax into a smile. She would have liked to have seen that, taken a picture to remind her that the man *could* smile.

Her stomach growled, and Catherine briefly wondered what was stashed in her freezer. Hopefully something would magically appear that she could toss in the microwave. She definitely wasn't in the mood to cook.

On her way into the kitchen, she paused in front of the photograph that rested on the fireplace mantel. The man staring back at her had deep brown eyes that were alive with warmth, wit and character.

Catherine's eyes.

He was handsome, so handsome that she often stared at the picture, regretting the fact she had never been given the chance to know him. She'd been only three when her father had been shipped to Vietnam, five when he'd been listed as Missing in Action. Often she'd reached back as far as her memory would take her to snatch hold of something that would help her remember him, but each time she was left to deal with frustration and disappointment.

The man in the photo was young, far too young to have his life snuffed out. No one would ever know how he'd died or even when. All Catherine's family had been told was that his Navy jet had gone down over a Vietcong infested jungle. They never were to know if he survived the crash or had been taken prisoner. Those, like so many other details of his life and death, had been left to her imagination.

Catherine's mother, a corporate attorney, had never remarried. Marilyn Fredrickson wasn't bitter, nor was she angry. She was far too practical to allow such negative emotions to taint her life.

Like a true Navy wife, she'd silently endured the long years of the cruel unknowns, refusing to be defeated by the helplessness of frustration. When her husband's remains had been returned to the States, she'd

stood proud and strong as he was laid to rest with full
military honors.

The only time Catherine could ever remember her
mother weeping had been the day her father's casket had
arrived at the airport. With a gentleness and a sweetness
that impressed Catherine still, her mother had walked
over to the flag-draped casket, rested her gloved hand
at the head and brokenly whispered, "Welcome home,
my love." Then she'd slumped to her knees and sobbed
until she'd released a ten-year reservoir of submerged
emotions.

Catherine had cried with her mother that day. But
in death, as he had been in life, Andrew Warren Fredrickson remained a stranger.

In choosing to become a Navy attorney, Catherine
had followed both her parents' footsteps. Being a part of
the military had brought her as close as she was likely
to get to understanding the man who had given her life.

Lulled by her thoughts, Catherine ran the tip of her
finger along the top of the gold frame. "I wonder if you
ever had to work with someone like Royce Nyland,"
she said softly.

She did that sometimes. Talked to the photograph
as though she honestly expected her father to answer.
She didn't, of course, but carrying on a one-sided conversation with the man in the picture eased the ache in
her heart at never having known him.

Sambo meowed loudly, announcing it was well
past dinnertime, and Catherine had best do something
quickly. The black feline waited impatiently in front
of his bowl while Catherine brought out the pouch of
soft cat food.

"Enjoy," she muttered, wincing as she bent over to
fill the food dish. Holding her hand at the small of her

back, Catherine cautiously straightened. Her pride had cost her more than she'd first realized.

"But, Dad, I've just got to have that jacket," Kelly announced as she carried her dinner plate over to the sink. She rinsed it off and set it in the dishwasher, a chore that went above and beyond her normal duties. As far as Royce was concerned, she was going to have to do a whole lot more than stack a few dishes to change his mind.

"You have a very nice jacket now," he reminded her, standing to pour himself a cup of coffee. He supposed he should be grateful she'd chosen to overlook the fact he was forty minutes later than he'd told her he would be. After her initial protest she'd been suspiciously forgiving. Now he knew why.

"But my jacket's from last year and it's really old and the sleeve has a little tear in it and no one is wearing fluorescent green anymore. I'll be the laughingstock of the entire school if I wear that old thing."

"That 'old thing' as you put it, will do nicely. The subject is closed, Kelly Lynn." Royce was determined not to give in this time. He was walking a fine line with his daughter as it was, and loomed dangerously close to overindulging her. It was easy to do. She was a sweet child, unselfish and gentle. Actually it was something of a wonder that Kelly should turn out to be such a considerate child. The ten-year-old had been raised by a succession of babysitters. From the time she was only a few weeks old, Kelly had been lackadaisically palmed off on others.

Sandy had only agreed to have one child, and she'd done so reluctantly six years into their marriage. Her career as a fashion buyer had dominated her life, so much so that Royce doubted that his wife had possessed a single mothering instinct. When she'd been killed in a freak auto accident, Royce had grieved for her loss, but their relationship had been dead for several years.

If Kelly had been shortchanged in the mother department, Royce wasn't convinced she'd done much better with him as a father. Heaven knew Royce's reputation was that of a hard-nosed bastard. But he was fair and everyone knew it. He did the best he could, but often wondered if that was good enough. He loved Kelly and he wanted to do right by her.

"All the other girls in school have new jackets," she mumbled under her breath.

Royce ignored the comment and between sips of coffee placed the leftovers inside the refrigerator.

"I've already saved $6.53 from my allowance?" She made the statement into a question, seeking a response.

Royce returned the carton of milk to the shelf.

"Missy Gilbert said the jackets were going to be on sale at JCPenney and with next week's allowance I'd have almost one fourth of the total cost. I'm trying real hard on my arithmetic this year, you know."

"Good girl." The two of them had suffered through more than one go-round with fractions.

Kelly turned her big baby blues full force on him. "What about the jacket, Dad?"

Royce could feel himself giving in. This wasn't good. He should be a pillar of strength, a wall of granite. He'd already told her once the subject was closed. The jacket she had now was good enough. He remembered when they'd bought it last year. Royce had been appalled at the outrageous shade of putrid green, but Kelly had assured him it was perfect and she would wear it two or three years.

"Dad?" she asked ever so sweetly, the way she always did when she sensed he was weakening.

"I'll think about it."

"Thanks, Dad," she cried, rushing across the room and hugging his waist. "You're the greatest."

An odd sense of self-consciousness attacked Catherine when she went down to the track the following evening. As she suspected, Royce was there ahead of her, running laps, as were several other men.

Royce hadn't said more than a handful of words to her all day, which wasn't unusual. He was as polite and as cool as always. When he came into the office that morning, he'd glanced her way, and Catherine could have sworn he was looking straight through her. His hard blue eyes had passed over her without so much as a flicker of friendliness. If she were to take the time to analyze his look, she suspected it had been one of cool indifference. It wasn't that Catherine expected him to throw his arms around her and greet her like a long-lost friend. On second thought, maybe that was the problem.

They'd shared something on that running track, a camaraderie, an understanding and appreciation for each other. Catherine didn't expect warm embraces, but she hadn't expected him to regard her so impersonally. Apparently she'd read more into their talk than he intended.

That was her first mistake, and Catherine feared she was ready to commit mistake number two.

Squaring her shoulders, she traipsed down the hillside to the running track. She was later this evening than she had been the night before. No thanks to Commander Nyland. For the past two hours she'd been reviewing files and charting progress as the substitute coordinator for the physical fitness program. Her eyes hurt, her shoulders ached and she was in no mood to lock horns with the executive officer, unless, of course, he started something first.

Catherine completed her warming-up exercises and joined the others circling the quarter-mile track. She needed to unwind, vent the frustration she felt over being assigned this extra duty, which was an imposition she didn't need. It seemed that the commander had seen fit to delegate CDO duty that Friday night to someone else. Lucky for that someone.

Her first lap was relaxed. Catherine liked to ease herself into running, starting off slow and gradually gaining her momentum, peaking at about the second mile and finishing off the third in a relaxed stride.

Royce passed her easily on the first go-round. Catherine fully expected that he would. Once again she was impressed with the power and strength she felt as he shot past her. His skin was tan and his muscles bronzed. It was as if he were a living, moving work of art, perfect, strong and male. Her heart raced much faster than it should. A rush of sensation so powerful it nearly knocked her off her feet took her by surprise. On the heels of that emotion came another, one more potent than the first. Anger. He zoomed past her again and it was all she could do to hold herself back from charging ahead.

On the third lap she couldn't help herself, and she let loose, running as though she were in the Olympic time trial and this was her one and only chance to make the team.

The sense of satisfaction she gained leaping past Royce was enough to make her forget how hard she was pushing herself to maintain this stride.

The feeling of triumph was short-lived, as she knew

it would be. Royce stepped up his pace and quickly charged around her. Then he slowed down and waited for her steps to join his.

"Good evening, Lieutenant Commander," he greeted, cordially enough.

"Commander." She wasn't in any mood to wish him a pleasant anything. Once again he'd managed to irritate her. No man had evoked such heated feelings from her, whether they be reasonable or unreasonable. It was all because of Royce Nyland that she'd been the one poring over a carload of files late into the afternoon.

Royce increased his stride, and Catherine struggled to keep even with him. She had the feeling that he could have left her to eat his dust at any time, and was simply toying with her the way a cat enjoys playing with a cornered mouse. None of that seemed to matter as she pushed herself harder than ever.

After a couple of laps, Catherine sensed his amusement. No doubt she and her damnable pride were a keen source of entertainment to the obstinate executive officer.

Somehow Catherine managed to keep up with Royce for three complete laps, but she knew she couldn't continue the killing pace any longer. It was either drop out now or collapse. Catherine chose the former.

When she pulled back, slowed her pace to a fast walk, Royce raced ahead, then he surprised her by turning around and coming back. He kept his arms and feet in motion as he matched her speed.

"You all right?"

"Just ducky." She barely managed to breathe evenly, and prayed a sufficient amount of sarcasm leaked through to convey her mood.

A crooked smile slanted his mouth, his look cool and

mocking. "Do you have a problem, Lieutenant Commander?"

"Off the record?" she asked, without hesitating. A month of frustration could no longer be contained, and she was bursting to let him know exactly what she thought of him.

"By all means."

Catherine might be digging herself in deeper than she dare, but her patience was shot. "Is there something about me that troubles you, Commander?" She didn't give him time to respond, but rushed ahead, "Because something's rotten in Denmark, and frankly, it isn't my problem.... It's yours."

"I don't treat you any differently than anyone else," Royce inserted smoothly.

"Like hell you don't," she shot back heatedly. Thankfully the others had left the track, which might or might not be a blessing.

"I don't see you assigning anyone else to stand duty four weeks straight. For some unknown reason you've chosen to destroy my weekends. I've spent eleven years in this man's Navy and I've never stood duty more than once a month. Until you were assigned my XO. Apparently you don't like me, Commander, and I demand to know why."

A nerve twitched in his lean, hard jaw. "On the contrary, I find your dedication to duty to be highly commendable."

Catherine didn't actually expect him to admit his dislike of her, but she wasn't willing to listen to his military rhetoric, either. "I suppose my dedication to duty is what made you decide to bless me with this plush job of coordinating the physical fitness program? Was that supposed to be a bonus for all the extra hours I put in on the Miller case? If so, find another way to thank me, would you?" She was trying to talk and draw in deep breaths at the same time and doubted that Royce could make out more than a few words.

Royce stiffened. "Is that all?"

"Not quite." She was only beginning to gain her momentum. "Off the record, Commander, I think you're a real jerk."

When she finished, Catherine was overwhelmed with a feeling of release. She started to tremble, but she wasn't sure if the shaking could be attributed to the fact she'd pushed herself physically to the point of collapse or that she'd stood on a military compound and shouted insults at her executive officer at the top of her lungs.

His look was impossible to read. The feeling in the pit of her stomach was decidedly uncomfortable.

"Is that a fact?" he demanded.

"Yes." Her voice wobbled with uncertainty, sounding as though it were coming from the bottom of a well. She drew in a deep breath, knowing she'd stepped over the boundaries of what should and shouldn't be said to a superior officer. The blood that seemed to have been pounding in her ears like ringing church bells suddenly went silent.

With her hands knotted into tight fists at her sides, she braced herself for the backlash. If she thought to clear the air, she was sadly mistaken. If she'd accomplished anything it was to sabotage her own career.

Royce didn't say anything for several moments, but the nerve in his jaw continued twitching. Then he nodded as though they'd casually been discussing the weather, turned and resumed running. Catherine was left standing alone to stare after him.

* * *

Catherine spent an uncomfortable night, tossing and turning and finally talking over her troubles with Sambo. To her way of thinking, Royce would either ignore her outburst or see to it that she was transferred to a Third World country. However he reacted, she would be getting exactly what she deserved. No one spoke to their XO the way she had. No one.

For hours she lay awake analyzing what had happened. After several soul-searching sessions, she still didn't know what had caused her to get loose enough to say the things she did.

The following morning, Royce was already at his desk, behind closed doors when she arrived. She glanced cautiously toward his office. If there was a merciful God, then Commander Nyland would be willing to forget and forgive her outburst from the day before. She would apologize, grovel if need be, but leaving matters as they were was clearly unacceptable.

"Morning," she said gingerly to Elaine Perkins. "How's the great white hunter today?" she asked, hoping her secretary had had a chance to judge Royce's mood.

"Same as usual," Elaine told her, sipping coffee from a thick ceramic mug. Her voice drawled with a thick southern accent. "He asked me to send you into his office when you arrived."

Catherine felt the starch go out of her knees. "He asked to see me?"

"You heard me right. What are you looking so worried about? You haven't done anything, have you?"

"Nothing," Catherine whispered in reply. Nothing except stick her head in a noose and sling the other end of the rope over the highest branch in the tree.

Squaring her shoulders in her best military form, she walked across the office and knocked politely on the commander's door. When she was ordered to enter the room, she did so with her eyes focused straight ahead.

"Good morning, Lieutenant Commander."

"Sir."

"Relax, Catherine." He leaned back in his chair, his chin resting on folded hands as though he were still weighing his decision.

Relax, he'd told her to relax, only Catherine hadn't figured out how she was supposed to be at ease when her career was on the line. She hadn't joined the Navy like so many other women with her head in the clouds, seeking adventure, travel and a paid education. She knew from the beginning about the rigorous routine, the political infighting and the fact she'd be dealing with world-class chauvinists.

Nevertheless she loved being part of the Navy. She'd worked hard, and her efforts had been rewarded. Now this.

"Since our recent discussion I've been having second thoughts," Royce said flatly.

Catherine swallowed against the heaviness in her throat. She doubted if she could have spoken if she tried.

"From everything I've read about you, you have an excellent record." He leaned forward and closed her file. "Effective immediately, I'm removing you as the substitute coordinator of the physical fitness program, and assigning Lieutenant Johnson the duty."

Catherine was sure she hadn't heard him correctly. Her eyes, which had been trained on the opposite wall, skirted to his. A breathless moment passed before she could speak, "You're removing me from the physical

fitness program?" She couldn't have been more surprised had he announced he was working for the KGB.

"That's what I just said."

Catherine blinked, not knowing what to say. "Thank
you, sir," she finally managed.

"That will be all," he said, dismissing her.

She hesitated. She'd wanted to apologize for her outburst from the day before, but one look told her Royce
wasn't interested in listening to her list her excuses.

As it was, her knees were knocking so badly that she
walked over to her desk, slumped into the chair and held
on to the edge as though it were a lifeline.

Catherine didn't see Royce for the remainder of the
day, for which she was grateful. It gave her time to sort
through her emotions, which were as confused and tangled as thin gold chains. She didn't know what to make
of the executive commander. Every time she had him
figured out, he'd do something more to confuse her.
Complicating the matter even further were her muddled
feelings toward him. He was by far the most virile man
she'd ever met. She couldn't be in the same room with
him and not experience that magnetism. Yet, she found
herself intensely disliking him.

An early October drizzle moistened the air when
Catherine walked out to the parking lot later that same
afternoon. Rain, rain and more rain.

It was already dark, and her calf muscles were so
sore she'd decided to skip running at the track. At least
that was the excuse she'd given herself. How much truth
there was to her rationale was something she'd prefer
not to question.

Her GEO Storm was parked in the far end of the lot,
and Catherine walked briskly toward it, hunching her

shoulders against the chilly air. She opened her door, gratefully climbed inside and turned the ignition. Nothing. She tried again with the same results. The battery was completely dead.

With her hands braced against the steering wheel, Catherine groaned. She knew as much about the internal workings of a car as she did about performing brain surgery. Her automobile was only a few months old; surely there wasn't anything wrong with the engine.

Climbing out, she decided to check under the hood. How much good that would do was highly debatable, especially in the dark. It took her several minutes to find the clasp that would release the lock. In the dim light from the street lamp, she couldn't see much of anything.

The only thing she could think to do was call a towing service. She was walking back to her building when a low black sports car rolled past her, then circled around.

"Problems?" It was Royce Nyland.

Catherine froze, her first instinct was to claim she had everything under control and send him on his way. Lie, fib, anything that would postpone another encounter. She hadn't had the time to filter through her emotions from the one earlier in the day. Royce Nyland flustered her, and clouded her judgment. She wanted to dislike him, categorize him and wrap him up in one neat package. But every time she'd attempted to gain perspective, he did something to alter her opinion of him. He brought out the worst in her and yet she'd never worked harder to impress an officer. Then it came to her with driving force. She was sexually attracted to Royce Nyland.

Attracted in a way that spelled trouble for them both. As long as she was under his command, anything romantic between them was strictly prohibited. The Navy didn't pull any punches when it came to emotional involvement between men and women, one a supervisor to the other. Not even a hint of impropriety would be tolerated.

For her sake as well as his, she must ignore the fact her heart raced every time she saw him. She had to ignore the way her eyes sought him out whenever he walked into the room. When they were on the track together, she had to disregard the strength and power that radiated from him like warmth from a roaring fire. Royce Nyland was as off-limits to her as a married man.

"Is that your car?" he asked, obviously impatient with her lack of response.

"Yes...it won't start."

"I'll take a look at it for you."

Before she could tell him she was about to call for a tow truck, he switched gears and drove over to where her Storm was parked with its hood raised. By the time she walked back, he was sitting in the driver's seat.

"It looks like you left your lights on this morning. The battery's dead."

"Oh... I must have." She wasn't usually this slow-witted. Running around the track with Royce was one thing, but standing in the far end of the parking lot in the shadows was another. Instinctively she backed away.

"I have a battery cable in my car. I'll give you a start." It took only a matter of minutes for him to arrange the clamps linking the cables between the batteries of the two cars. They worked together and within a matter of minutes, her engine was purring contentedly.

She climbed out of the car while Royce disconnected the cable. Although it wasn't all that cold, she rubbed her hands together several times.

"Thank you."

He nodded, tossed the cable into the trunk of his car and was prepared to leave when she stopped him.

"Royce."

She hadn't meant to say his name, it had slipped out naturally. Apologizing had never come easy to her, but she owed him one—for the heat of her anger, the unreasonableness of her attack. "I shouldn't have said what I did the other night. If there's any excuse, it's that I was tired and short-tempered. It won't happen again."

"It was off the record, Fredrickson, don't worry about it." His mouth slowly curved into a smile. Their eyes met, solidly, hungrily and God help her, Catherine felt herself step toward him.

"I'm worried." But it wasn't what she'd said or done that she was talking about and she knew they both knew it. His eyes continued to detain hers. She'd never seen eyes so dark. They told her things she'd only suspected. Things she didn't want to know and had no business knowing.

He was lonely. So was she.

He was alone. So was she.

So alone she lay in bed at night and ached. The need to be touched and held and kissed sometimes filled her with desperation.

She sensed the same desperation in Royce. It was what had drawn them together; it was what was keeping them apart.

The seconds throbbed between them like a giant time clock. Neither moved. Catherine dared not breathe. She was one step from walking directly into his arms, one word from spilling out everything she was feeling. The tension between them was as threatening as a thundercloud in a sky of blue. As strong as a prize fighter.

It was Royce who moved first. Away from her. Catherine sighed, her relief was so great.

"There won't be any problems," he whispered, turned and walked away.

She knew he wasn't speaking about her car.

Catherine wished she could believe it, but something told her it was far from the truth.

Royce was shaking. His hands were actually trembling as he sat in his own driveway, composing himself before he walked inside the house. He'd come so close to kissing Catherine that even now the thought of her filling his arms was enough to produce an ache so powerful, so sharp, it took his breath away. Royce was a man who thrived on discipline. He prided himself on his self-control, and yet he'd come a hair's space from tossing away everything he knew was right. And for what reason? Catherine Fredrickson turned him on.

For three years, Royce had shut off the valve that controlled his carnal appetites. He didn't need love, didn't need tenderness or require a woman's touch. Those were base emotions, best ignored. And neglect them he had until he'd met Catherine.

From the moment she'd walked into his office, he'd been confronted with a surge of unexpected, and unwanted feelings. He hadn't recognized what he was dealing with in the beginning. Subconsciously he had, otherwise he would never have gone out of his way to ruin her weekends by assigning her duty four Friday nights running. It didn't take a psychiatrist's couch to figure that one. He'd been batting a thousand when her name was the first one that drifted into his mind when he learned a substitute coordinator was going to be needed for the physical fitness program.

In analyzing his deeds, Royce realized he was punishing Catherine. With just cause. The lieutenant commander was a constant thorn in his flesh, a reminder that he was a man with needs that refused to be denied any longer.

Unfortunately there was a good deal more at stake than satisfying a deep physical hunger. Catherine was under his command, which put pressure on them both. She was strictly off-limits. Neither of them could afford to indulge in this attraction. It would only end up hurting them both. Their careers would suffer, and they'd both worked too damn hard to screw it up now over a few undisciplined hormones.

Dragging a fresh breath through his lungs, Royce closed his eyes and tried to push the picture of Catherine from his mind. He'd seen the emotions tearing at her in the parking lot, witnessed the pride-filled way in which she'd tilted her chin. Damn but the woman was proud. She apologized, accepting all the blame herself, although heaven knew everything she'd said was right. In that moment, he never respected a woman more. For her honesty, for her directness, for the fact she was willing to deal with whatever it was between them, lay it on the ground and call it what it was.

In those few words, heavy with meaning, Catherine had told him something he'd long suspected. Lieutenant Commander Catherine Fredrickson was a woman of substance. One so rare, one so beautiful, he didn't know what the hell he was going to do to get her out of his mind. All he knew was that he must succeed even if it meant requesting a transfer and uprooting Kelly from the only home she'd ever known.

Three

"Can we go to a movie, too?" Kelly asked, snapping her seat belt into place. They were on their way to the Kitsap Mall, where the all-important jacket was on sale. It was either buy his daughter the coat or ruin her life before the eyes of her peers. Royce couldn't remember clothes and shoes being so vital when he was in grade school, but the world was a hell of a lot different place when he was ten.

"Dad," Kelly pressed, "what about a movie?"

"Sure," he agreed easily enough. Why not? He'd been short-tempered all week, due mainly to the fact he was dealing with his feelings for Catherine. Kelly deserved a reward for putting up with his sour mood.

As for what was happening—or better said, what was *not* happening—between him and Catherine, Royce had rarely spent a more uncomfortable week. He couldn't walk into the office without being aware of her. Her presence was like a time bomb silently ticking in the corner of the room. Every now and again their eyes would meet and he'd be left to watch the emotions race across the landscape of her dark brown eyes. With everyone around them in the office, there hadn't been a problem. It was the evening run that tested his soul.

Every afternoon Royce told himself he wouldn't run. Every afternoon, like precision clockwork, he was at the track, waiting for Catherine to arrive. They ran together, without speaking, without sharing, without looking at each other.

It was uncanny the comfort he found circling the track with the petite lieutenant commander at his side. The track was neutral ground, safe territory for them both. Those all-too-short minutes with Catherine were the reason he got out of bed in the morning, the reason he made it through the day.

When she smiled at him, Royce swore her eyes scored his heart. In the evenings when they'd finished jogging, Catherine would thank him for the workout and then silently return to her car. The moment she was out of sight, Royce was left feeling bereft. He hadn't realized what poor company a disciplined lifestyle could make, and what poorer company the long, lonely nights in an empty bed could be. The desolation was as powerful as a blow to his gut.

The evenings were another matter. He almost feared sleep because the moment he slipped into unconsciousness, Catherine filled his mind. She was soft and warm, and so real that all he had to do was reach out and draw her to his side. Royce would never have guessed his mind would play such cruel tricks on him. He was having trouble enough keeping Catherine at a distance, emotionally and physically. In sleep, his mind welcomed her, tormenting him with dreams he couldn't control. Dreams of Catherine running toward him on the beach, holding her arms out to him. Catherine feminine and soft in his embrace. Catherine laughing. Royce swore he never heard a sound more beautiful in all his life.

If there was anything to be grateful for, and it was damn little, it was the fact the dreams had never developed into anything even remotely physical between them.

In the mornings, Royce woke annoyed with himself, annoyed at Catherine for refusing to leave him alone and irritated with the world. With all the strength of his will, which was admittedly formidable, Royce pushed all thoughts of the lieutenant commander from his mind.

For as long as Catherine was under his command, all Royce could indulge himself in were involuntary dreams. He refused to allow himself the pleasure of recapturing the fantasy of him and Catherine alone together in quiet moments. Unhurried moments. With no demands. No deadlines. Moments when his heart and his soul were at rest.

Life could be a cruel hoax, Royce sharply reminded himself. He'd been taught that time and time again. He wasn't about to lose everything that was important to him over a woman, even if she did have eyes that looked straight through him.

The mall was crowded, but then it generally was on weekends, especially now that folks were gearing up for Christmas. Royce allowed Kelly to drag him into the JCPenney store. But that was only the beginning of the ordeal. The jacket she was so keen on had sold out in her size. The helpful salesclerk had phoned three other stores and there wasn't a single one available. Even the catalog had sold out.

"I'm sorry, sweetheart," Royce told her. She was bitterly disappointed and trying hard not to show it.

"Do you want to look around for a different coat?"

Surely there was a father-of-the-year award for him in this offer. They'd spent nearly an hour on this wild-goose chase already, and Royce's patience had worn paper thin.

Kelly sat on the wooden bench outside the department store, her head bent low. Royce was about to repeat the question when she shrugged.

"How about something to drink?" Royce was half an hour overdue for a cup of coffee.

Kelly nodded eagerly. She stood and slipped her small hand into his. She didn't do that often, and Royce guessed she did so now needing his reassurance.

Royce bought her a Pepsi and himself a cup of fresh, hot coffee while Kelly scouted out a place for them to sit. Since it was close to noon, the tables were mostly occupied. They found one and sat down in the white wire chairs.

"Dad," Kelly whispered excitedly, "look at that pretty lady over there."

Hell, as far as Royce could see, the entire mall was filled with pretty ladies. "Where?"

"The one in the pink-and-green-and-blue jacket. Over there." Knowing it was impolite to point, Kelly wiggled her index finger back and forth in the general direction of where she wanted him to look. "Look, she's sorta walking toward us. Hurry and look before she turns away."

As he'd mused earlier, life could be filled with cruel hoaxes, and it was about to play another one on him now. Before he even realized what he was doing, Royce was on his feet. "Hello, Catherine."

"Royce." Her dark eyes were bright with surprise as well, and frankly, she didn't look any more pleased than he felt.

"How are you?" he heard himself ask stiffly.

"Fine."

"Dad." Impatiently, Kelly tugged on the hem of his leather jacket. "I like her coat...a whole lot."

Royce watched as Catherine's eyes momentarily left his and landed on Kelly. Once again surprise registered in the dark depths, but was quickly replaced by a gentleness and warmth that tightened strong cords around his heart. He'd never mentioned his daughter, and it was apparent she hadn't known he'd been married. Maybe she thought he was married still.

"This is my daughter, Kelly," Royce said, his voice low and throaty.

"Hello, Kelly. I'm Catherine." She dragged her eyes away from him and held out her hand to his daughter. "Your dad and I work together." She said this, Royce was convinced, as a reminder to them both. Hell, he didn't need it.

"Your jacket is real pretty," Kelly said quietly. She continued to tug on Royce's sleeve until he was convinced she'd pulled the armhole down to his elbow.

"What Kelly would like to know is where you bought it," Royce inserted dryly.

"And if they have kid sizes?" the ten-year-old asked excitedly.

"I got it right here in the mall, in Jacobson's."

"Dad," Kelly said, pushing aside her drink, "let's go look, okay?"

Royce glanced longingly at his coffee. He'd barely had time to take a single sip. Kelly was looking at him as if to say Jacobson's was sure to sell out in the next ten minutes if they didn't get there.

"I don't know if they have kid sizes," Kelly stated urgently, as though another five or ten minutes was sure to make the difference. "I know it's a ladies' store and everything, but you can wait outside if you want and I'll go in by myself."

"Why don't I take you down," Catherine suggested.

It took a fair amount of self-control not to leap up and kiss her. "You don't mind?" He had to ask. Pride demanded that much, at least.

"Not a bit. Go ahead and enjoy your coffee," Catherine suggested, her gaze returning to him. "We won't be more than a few minutes."

He should refuse. Royce knew it the minute she made the offer, but Kelly was looking up at him, her eyes alive with excitement, and before he could argue with himself, he nodded.

A daughter, Catherine mused. Royce had a daughter. Catherine had worked with him for five weeks, and no one had bothered to mention the fact he'd been married or that he was raising Kelly. The child was incredibly sweet, with long dark hair and eyes so blue they reminded Catherine of wild bluebonnets. Kelly was as gentle and cute as Royce was remote and indifferent.

Catherine had noted how closely Royce had watched her when he introduced Kelly. His eyes had darkened into a brittle defiance as though he expected her to do or say something about the fact she hadn't known about the child. She found herself staring at him and the proud lines of his chiseled features. Catherine's gaze had moved smoothly from father to daughter. There was no doubt in her mind the two were related. Kelly possessed the same beautiful blue eyes, and although her face was heart-shaped and feminine, she was clearly a Nyland.

Until she'd walked into the shopping complex, Catherine hadn't realized how hungry she was for the sight of Royce. From clear across the other side of the mall, she'd walked directly to his side, guided by instinct to the man who'd dominated her thoughts for days on end.

"We went to the JCPenney store," Kelly explained as they walked side by side down the wide concourse, "but all the jackets in my size were sold. We looked and looked and I was feeling really low so Dad bought me a Pepsi and then we saw you," Kelly explained in one giant breath. "Your jacket is just perfect."

Catherine had bought it a couple of weeks earlier. Being new to the Pacific Northwest, she needed something heavier than a raincoat. The jacket had caught her eye in a ski shop, and although Catherine didn't ski, she'd been attracted to the colors, just the way Kelly had.

"I like it, too. And as I recall, they did have children's sizes."

"Dad doesn't like to shop much," Kelly explained as they wove their way between the moving crowd. "He does it for me, but I know he'd rather be watching a silly football game. Men are like that, you know?"

"So I've heard." As far as understanding the male of the species, Royce's daughter knew a whole lot more than Catherine did. For as long as she could remember, it had always been her and her mother. In college she'd lived in a girls' dormitory.

"Dad tries real hard, but he doesn't understand a lot of things about girls."

Catherine couldn't help grinning at that. Evidently she wasn't the only one at a loss when it came to understanding the opposite sex. Apparently what she and Royce needed was a ten-year-old to straighten out their lives.

They found the store, and indeed there was a jacket almost identical to the one Catherine had that was in Kelly's size. After Royce's daughter tried it on and modeled it in front of a mirror, Catherine had the salesclerk put it on hold.

Kelly raced back to the large open eating area to tell Royce about the rare find. Catherine followed close behind.

"It's got pink and green and blue. Not the same shade of blue as Catherine's, but almost. I can have it, can't I?" She dug into her small pocket at the top of her jeans and dragged out the five single dollar bills one at a time and then several coins from a different pocket. "I'll pay for part of it."

Royce stood and tossed the empty coffee cup into the garbage. "All right, all right. I know when I'm defeated." He glanced over at Catherine and winked.

Catherine couldn't believe it. The iceman winked as if he were a regular human being. Royce Nyland was one man in the office, another on the running track and someone else entirely different when he was with his daughter.

"I…can see you've got everything under control here," Catherine said, thinking she should probably leave. She felt awkward with Royce.

"Don't go," Kelly cried, reaching for Catherine's hand with both of her own. "Dad said he'd buy me pizza for lunch, and I want you to come, too."

"I'm sure Catherine has other plans," Royce said matter-of-factly.

Catherine noted that he didn't repeat the invitation, which was just as well. Yet, she couldn't hold back the sense of disappointment. "Yes, I do have some things to do. I was just going into the pet store to buy my cat a new litter box."

"I love the pet store," Kelly piped in eagerly. "Once they even let me hold a new puppy. I wanted to buy it real bad, but Dad said we couldn't because there wouldn't be anyone home during the day to take care of him."

Catherine's heart melted as she gazed down on Royce's daughter. So young and tender. Catherine remembered herself at that age and how life had been such a wonderful adventure then.

"Oh, do come, Catherine. Please."

Catherine's gaze moved to Royce. She expected his eyes to be cool and unreadable as they were so much of the time. Instead she found them troubled and unsure, yet inviting. Catherine felt as if the air had been sucked from her lungs.

"I…are you sure I wouldn't be intruding?" By everything that was right, she knew she should refuse. They were standing so close to the fire, close enough to get burned, and yet they each seemed to be taking turns tossing kindling into the flames.

"I'm sure," Royce answered.

"Oh, good," Kelly cried, seemingly unaware of the tension between Catherine and her father. "I certainly hope you don't like anchovies. Dad gets them on his half whenever we order pizza. Those things are disgusting."

A half hour later, they were sitting in a pizza parlor. Catherine and Kelly shared an Italian sausage and olive pizza pie while Royce ate his own, covered with the tiny fish both women found so offensive.

Although it was comfortably warm inside the restaurant, Kelly insisted upon wearing her new coat.

"Are those fingernails actually yours?" Kelly asked halfway through the meal.

Catherine nodded, her mouth full of pizza.

"You mean you don't have a single acrylic tip?"

It was incredible to Catherine that a ten-year-old knew about such things. "Not even one," she assured the girl.

Kelly's eyes widened with renewed respect. She held up her hand for Catherine to examine, showing the short, stubby ends of her own nails. Catherine reached for her purse and brought out her fingernail kit for Kelly to examine, explaining each instrument.

"What are you two talking about?" Royce demanded in mock exasperation. "As near as I can figure, you women have your own language."

Kelly reverently closed the case and returned it to Catherine. Her eyes drifted from Royce to her and then back again. Catherine could almost see the tiny wheels churning in the little girl's head.

"Are you married, Catherine?" the girl asked innocently enough.

"Ah...no." Catherine's throat felt tight and dry all of a sudden.

"Neither is my dad," the ten-year-old added, her words fraught with meaning. "My mom died, you know?" Kelly said it with complete lack of emotion, as though losing a mother was simply part of growing up.

"No... I wasn't aware of that." Catherine avoided looking at Royce.

Kelly took another couple of moments to assess the situation. "So you and my dad work together?"

"Kelly Lynn." Royce used a tone Catherine had heard often in the office. It brought trained sailors to attention, and it worked just as well with his daughter.

"I was only asking."

"Then don't."

"All right, all right, but I didn't mean anything by it." Royce's daughter returned to her pizza, took a bite and chewed two or three times before adding. "Catherine's coming to the movie with us, isn't she?" The question was directed to Royce, who once more narrowed his eyes at his daughter.

"I'll let you choose the movie if you want," Kelly offered. Evidently the choice of which film they'd see was a long-standing battle between them, and that she'd offer to let him pick was a major concession.

Catherine didn't know what Royce was waiting for. He shouldn't even be entertaining his daughter's suggestion. The fact they were having lunch together was one thing, but sitting in a movie theater together would be…should be out of the question.

"Dad?" Kelly probed.

Royce looked to Catherine, and his hard blue eyes held hers for the long, drawn-out moment. Tension thickened the air until she was convinced neither of them was breathing.

"Catherine has other things to do," Royce informed his daughter.

Catherine was quick to reassure Kelly. "I really do, sweetheart. Perhaps we can all go another time."

Royce's young daughter accepted Catherine's decision with a quick nod, but it was apparent the girl was disappointed. She wasn't the only one. Catherine's heart felt as heavy as concrete. She'd never felt closer to Royce than this time with his daughter. He'd lowered his guard enough for her to glimpse the nurturing, caring man shielded behind the thick wall of pride and tradition.

After wiping her hands clean with a napkin, Catherine reached for her purse and slid from the booth. "Thank you both for lunch, but I really should be going."

Kelly slid out of the booth, too. "I wish you were going to the movie with us."

Her eyes found Royce's as she whispered, "So do I."

Catherine was halfway to the door when Royce stopped her. For a moment he didn't say anything, but stared down at her. His face revealed none of his thoughts, and briefly Catherine was aware of what a talent he possessed to hide his emotions so well.

His eyes continued to hold hers and seemed to scorch her with their intensity before he spoke, listing the movie and the time. "In case you change your mind," he said, before turning back to his daughter.

By the time Catherine was inside her car, she'd started to tremble. What was the matter with Royce? Had he gone mad? Had she?

Royce, her XO, knowing what they were both risking, seemed to be telling her he wanted her to come to the movie. But he was leaving the decision in her hands. God help them both, she wanted it, too.

A movie wasn't an affair, she reminded herself. If they both happened to show up at the same movie at the same time, no one would put the wrong connotation on that. The rule book didn't say they couldn't be friends. If friends just happened to meet at a movie, it wouldn't be unheard of for them to sit together. Would it?

Catherine didn't know what to do. Her head was telling her one thing, and her heart another. Both their careers could be jeopardized. It was far too much to risk for the pleasure of sitting next to each other in a matinee.

Yet when the time approached, Catherine was behind

a line of preteens. Her heart was hammering so loudly, she was convinced everyone around her must be able to hear it, too. Once she glanced over her shoulder, thinking the shore patrol was on her tail. The thought was ludicrous, which only went to prove the state of her mind.

Royce was sitting in the last row, with Kelly in the seat next to him. The girl noticed Catherine immediately and leaped up from her chair as though she'd been sitting on a giant coiled spring. She hurriedly scooted down the aisle and enthusiastically hugged Catherine.

"I was hoping you'd come." She grabbed Catherine's hand and energetically led her to the seats.

Catherine didn't look at Royce. She feared what she'd read in his eyes.

"Missy's here," Kelly cried, and waved madly, as though the fate of the free world depended on how quickly her friend recognized her. "Can I go show her my new coat?"

Royce's hesitation was noticeable before he agreed, and Kelly raced away.

Catherine sat down, leaving an empty seat between them.

Royce continued to look straight ahead as though he'd never seen her in his life. "Are you crazy?" he hissed under his breath after an exaggerated moment. But it was the kind of anger that comes from caring too much, directed at himself as much as at her.

"Are you?" she came back just as heatedly. She was equally furious and for all the same reasons. She wasn't going to take the blame for this. She'd made her decision and her excuses at the restaurant. They both had. He was the one who'd dropped the anchor in her lap by making a point of letting her know which movie and what showing. He'd blatantly asked her to come, and now he seemed to regret she was there.

"Yes, I think I am crazy," Royce admitted reluctantly.

"I wasn't going to come," she told him softly. Even after he'd let it be known he wanted her with him and Kelly.

"Then why did you?"

Catherine didn't know. Maybe it was because she liked to live dangerously, walk as close to the edge of the cliff as possible without falling off. "I don't know. Why did you?"

Royce chuckled, but there was no amusement in his laugh. "Hell, I don't know. I guess I like tampering with the fates."

"Dad." Kelly was scooting down the narrow row sideways in a rush to return to her father. "Missy wants me to sit with her. You don't care, do you?"

Once again Royce hesitated before answering. "Go ahead."

"Thanks, Dad." Kelly scooted past Catherine, paused and winked. Winked! The same way Royce had winked at her earlier. Only she didn't know what Kelly meant any more than she'd understood the gesture from Royce.

Kelly left to join her friend, and the tension between her and Royce was so strong, Catherine didn't know if she could endure it any longer.

"I'll move." She started to stand, when he stopped her.

"No," Royce said automatically, his hand grasping her arm. "Stay." The word was soft and pleading.

Catherine couldn't refuse him, and when she sat down, he moved one seat over, sitting next to her. Almost immediately the theater darkened and music filled the room. Royce stretched out his long legs, and his thigh inadvertently brushed hers. Catherine's breath caught in her throat at the sudden rush of sensation that raced up and down her limb. Royce, too, gave a small gasp. The firm pressure of his leg felt muscular and hard. It was funny how easy it was for her to forget how good a man can feel. Catherine glanced up to find Royce openly studying her. His eyes were bright with a heat that warmed her from the top of her head to the soles of her feet. With a determined effort she dragged her gaze away from his.

Royce shifted his weight and with a good deal of reluctance moved his leg. They both breathed a little easier. This was difficult enough without adding more temptation, more fuel to the fire.

Catherine doubted that either one of them was able to follow the plot of the movie. If anyone had asked her, Catherine wouldn't have been able to discuss a single detail. Her concentration was centered on the man sitting next to her.

At some point, Royce thrust a bucket of popcorn between them. In an effort to fix her attention on the screen, Catherine reached for a handful of the kernels and ate them one by one. About the third or fourth dip into the bucket, Catherine's hand inadvertently bumped Royce's. She quickly withdrew her fingers, only Royce wouldn't allow it. He reached out and grasped her hand, then slowly, as if damning himself for his weakness, laced his fingers one by one with hers. His grip was tight, his nails cutting into her smooth flesh. It was as though he never intended on letting her go. The bucket of popcorn disappeared, and still Royce held her hand.

There was no way Catherine could explain the tumult of emotion that overtook her at the gesture. A host of unexplainable sensations assailed her, hidden, unrecognized emotions were so prominent that her head started to spin. If he was kissing her or touching her breasts or making love to her, Catherine could have understood, could have accepted her reaction.

But all he was doing was holding her hand.

She'd never felt more vulnerable or more exposed. She was risking everything that was important to her. Royce was taking a chance with his career, and for what?

The question was a harsh one, and the answer...the answer was even harsher. She knew next to nothing about Royce. He'd been married, his wife had died and there was a child. He was Navy, a man born to lead others. He was respected. Admired. But they'd never sat down and talked about their lives, never shared anything beyond the basic everyday-working-together kind of conversation. That they should experience this powerful pull toward each other, this forceful attraction, was a quirk of nature. There was no rhyme. No reason. Yet it would have taken an act of congress to move Catherine out of that movie theater.

The film ended. Catherine was hardly aware of the fact until he released her hand. She wanted to protest, longing to maintain the contact, as innocent as it was, until the last possible moment.

"Catherine," he whispered, leaning close. "Go now."

"But..."

"For the love of God, don't argue with me. Just leave."

Something in his voice, a warning, a threat, Catherine didn't know which, prompted her to move quickly. "I'll see you Monday," she said, standing.

But she'd be thinking about him every minute in between.

* * *

"Is there something going on between you and Commander Nyland?" Elaine Perkins asked Monday morning when Catherine arrived for work.

Her heart sank to her knees before quickly rebounding. "What makes you ask that?" she asked, forcing her voice to remain light and breezy.

"He wants to see you first thing. Again."

"He wants to see me first thing?" Catherine was beginning to sound like an echo.

"And when the almighty commander speaks, we obey," Elaine said as a means of reminding them both. "All I want to know is what you've done this time?"

"What makes you think I did anything?" Catherine asked as she hung up her coat.

"Because he looks like he's in a mood to wrestle crocodiles. That man is as mean as a shark with a toothache, and if I were you, I wouldn't tangle with him."

"Don't worry." Squaring her shoulders, she approached Royce's office and knocked politely.

"Come in." His frown deepened when he saw her. Perkins was right; Royce didn't look any too cheerful. The iceman had returned. Gone was the indulgent father, replaced by the man so ingrained in military procedure Catherine was convinced she had been imagining someone else on Saturday.

"Sit down, Lieutenant Commander." She wasn't Catherine any longer, but a rank.

She did as he requested, not knowing what to expect.

Royce rolled a pencil between his palms. "I don't think it's a good idea for us to continue exercising together in the afternoons."

Catherine's eyes flew to his. It was the only thing

they shared, that time together, and although it was entirely selfish of her, she didn't want to give it up.

"I realize you have as much right to use the track as I do, so I'd like to suggest a schedule. Unfortunately the afternoons are the only time I'm free...."

"My schedule if far less restrictive, *sir*," she said, bolting to her feet. "Don't worry. I'll make an effort to avoid any possibility of us meeting. Would you like me to stop frequenting the Kitsap Mall while I'm at it?"

The telltale muscle leaped in his jaw. Catherine didn't know why she was taking the offensive so strongly. He was only saying and doing what needed to be done, what should have been said long before now. But she felt as if the rug had been pulled from beneath her feet and she was teetering for her balance.

"You may shop wherever you choose."

"Thank you," she returned crisply. "Is that all?"

"Yes."

Catherine turned to leave.

"Catherine..." He stopped her as she reached his door. She turned back, but he shook his head. "Nothing, you may go."

Four

Catherine understood. Conclusively. Decisively.

Commander Royce Nyland, her executive officer, she reminded herself, was shutting her out. Apparently it was easy enough to do. He'd rerouted his emotions so often that barricading any and all feelings for her was a simple matter.

She, unfortunately, wasn't achieving the same level of success. Royce Nyland had invaded her life. As hard as she tried, her efforts to adjust her own attitude had done little, if any, good.

She didn't want to feel the things she did for him, and frankly she didn't know how to deal with them. This was a new experience for her. How was she supposed to block him from her mind when thoughts of him filled every minute of every day?

He'd ordered her to stop, she reminded herself. When a superior officer spoke, Catherine, ever loyal, ever Navy, obeyed. No one had told her it was going to be easy. But then again, no one had bothered to explain how damn difficult it would be, either.

Nothing like this had ever happened to Catherine

before, and frankly… Frankly, she didn't want it happening to her now.

Royce didn't want to jeopardize his career. She didn't want to jeopardize hers, either. He had little use for love in his life; she'd lived without it so long she didn't know what she was missing. If he could ignore the empty hole that grew deeper and wider with each passing day, then, she determined, so could she.

Maintaining her daily exercise program became of primary importance to Catherine. Never having liked running in the streets, she ran on the base track at odd hours of the day. She was careful not to infringe on Royce's time, holding on to this small link with him because it was all she had.

Early Friday morning, two weeks after Royce had called her into his office for their latest discussion, Catherine parked her car close to the jogging track.

She'd just finished her second lap when another runner joined her, coming up from behind her, gaining on her easily.

"Good morning."

Catherine's throat constricted. She'd worked so hard not to intrude on his exercise time, running in the early morning hours in order to avoid the possibility of them stumbling into each other.

The immediate sense of unfairness and outrage was nearly overwhelming. Instantly she wanted to confront Royce, shout at him, demand that he leave her alone, but he spoke first. "You're angry."

"You're damn right I am. What are you doing here?" Her voice was low and accusing. Suddenly she felt tired. Tired of pretending. Tired of ignoring emotions so strong she was choking on them. Tired of hiding.

"I need to talk to you."

"So talk." Her nerves were raw, stretched to the breaking point. They had been for weeks.

They jogged half a lap before he spoke. For someone who was so eager to communicate, for someone who'd broken the very rules he'd initiated, he seemed to be having a hard time getting started.

"I had to do it, Catherine," he said with enough force to shake the ground. The words weren't loud, but packed with emotion. "We've both been in the Navy too long, and love it too much to risk everything now."

"I know." Her anger vanished as quickly as it had risen and her voice trembled slightly despite her best efforts to keep it even and unaffected. She wasn't nearly as good as Royce when it came to disguising her emotions.

"What I didn't realize was how damn difficult it was going to be." He said this softly, as though admitting to a wrongdoing, as though it were important she know.

Catherine knotted her hands tightly at her sides. She never expected him to admit it, never dreamed he would. He'd given every indication that pushing her from his thoughts, from his heart, hadn't caused him a moment's concern. Surely he must have known how difficult it was for her. She'd buried herself in her work, repainted her entire apartment, stayed up late listening to Johnny Mathis records in a futile effort to forget Royce. But nothing worked. Nothing.

"Kelly asks about you every night," Royce confessed next.

"I'm sorry," she whispered, knowing that involving his daughter in this had made everything more difficult. "I didn't purposely run into you that day."

"I know. I'm not blaming you, I just wish to hell it

hadn't happened. No," he altered quickly, regretfully, "that isn't true. I'm thankful Kelly met you."

"It would have been better for us both if it hadn't happened." Yet Catherine would always be grateful for that one day with Royce and his daughter. It gave her something to hold on to for all the long, lonely nights.

"There's a rumor going around," Royce said after a moment. Catherine's heart tripped. The fear must have shown in her eyes because Royce added, "It's not about us, don't worry."

The military abounded with rumors. That Royce thought it important enough to repeat one to her meant something was deeply troubling him.

"I heard by means of the grapevine that I may be sent over to Turkey to work at NATO."

His words fell like heavy stones upon Catherine's heart, each one inflicting a sharper, more profound pain. "Oh, Royce." Her tone was low and hesitant, filled with concern.

"If I am, I'll need someone to take Kelly for me."

Catherine would do it in a heartbeat, but surely there was someone else. A relative or a long-standing family friend. As a single parent, Royce must have completed a parenting plan so there would be someone to take Kelly with as little as twenty-four-hours' notice.

"I spoke to Kelly about the possibility of us being separated last night. I didn't want to alarm her, but at the same time I didn't think it was fair to hide it from her, either."

Catherine nodded, impressed with his wisdom in dealing honestly with his daughter.

"Kelly's lived in Bangor all her life, and I'd hate to uproot her."

"I understand." The ten-year-old had already lost

her mother, and if her father were to be given shipping orders to the Middle East, everything that was familiar to Kelly would be stripped from her. The fact he'd been stationed at Bangor this long was something of an oddity.

"Sandy's family lives in the Midwest. She was never close to her mother and had lost contact with her father several years before. She has a couple of stepbrothers, but I've never bothered to keep in touch with them. To be honest, I haven't heard from her side of the family since the funeral."

"Kelly can stay with me," Catherine offered.

They had stopped running by this time and were walking the track, their pace invigorating. The air was cold and clean, and when Royce spoke, his breath created a thin fog in the autumn morning.

"If you can't, my parents will be happy to have her, but they're living in a retirement community in Arizona, and frankly, I hate to complicate their lives at this point."

"I mean it, Royce. I'd love to have Kelly stay with me."

"Thank you," he whispered. His voice was hoarse, and intuitively Catherine knew how difficult it was for Royce Nyland to admit he needed someone for something. Knowing he needed her, even if it was for his daughter's sake, did something to her heart. Her vulnerable heart. Susceptible only to him.

Royce picked up the pace, and they resumed jogging at a leisurely pace.

"How's Kelly taking the news?" Catherine asked, concerned about the grade schooler.

"Like a real trooper. I think she's more excited about the possibility of living with you, something she suggested by the way, than she's concerned about me leaving."

"Typical kid reaction."

"She really took to you."

Catherine smiled, her heart warming. "I took to her, too."

Royce laughed. It was the first time Catherine could remember ever hearing Royce amused.

"What's so funny?"

Royce sobered almost immediately. "Something Kelly said. Hell, I didn't even know she wanted a sister."

"A sister?"

Royce looked away abruptly. "Never mind," he said curtly.

They circled the track once more, their time slipping away like sand between splayed fingers. It felt so good to be with Royce, these moments together were like a rare, unexpected gift meant to be savored and enjoyed. Catherine had trouble keeping her eyes off him. He was tall and lean, his muscular shoulders broad. The sunlight was breaking over the hill, glinting on his thick, dark hair.

They parted at the last possible minute. Royce left first, heading toward the office. Catherine took a hurried shower. She stood under the spray, letting it pelt against her face and tried not to think of Royce being transferred all the way to Turkey.

It would solve one problem; she wouldn't be under Royce's command and if they chose to become romantically involved the Navy would not care. Of course they'd be separated by thousands of miles, but the Navy generally went out of its way to make falling in love difficult.

Catherine arrived at the office, feeling refreshed.

She greeted her secretary, poured herself a cup of coffee and sat down at her desk. She didn't look for Royce, but lately she'd made a habit of not seeking him out, even if it was only with her eyes.

She was absorbed in her own work for an hour or more when Commander Parker strolled into her office. Catherine had briefly met Commander Parker when she was first assigned to the Bangor station. He was in his mid-thirties, single and something of a flirt. He'd asked Catherine out to dinner one of the Friday nights Royce had seen fit to assign her duty, and she'd been forced to refuse. Apparently he'd taken her rejection personally, and hadn't asked her out since.

"Have you seen Commander Nyland?" Elaine Perkins asked a minute or so later.

"He was on the track this morning," Catherine explained as nonchalantly as she could. "He left before I did and I haven't seen him since."

"Commander Parker's looking for him."

"I'm sorry, I can't help."

Perkins left and returned a few minutes later after a flurry of activity from several others. Apparently Royce wasn't anywhere to be found, which was highly uncommon. Catherine worked hard at disguising her growing concern.

The phone rang; Elaine Perkins answered, routing the call. Her hand was still on the receiver when she turned to Catherine. "I didn't know Commander Nyland had a daughter. Somehow I can't picture old stoneface as a parent."

Catherine grinned. Not long ago she would have thought the same thing herself. But she'd seen Royce interact with his daughter, seen the love and pride shining through his eyes as he looked down at her. "She's ten and an absolute delight," Catherine said before she could stop herself.

"So you've met her?"

"Ah… I ran into them at the mall a couple of weeks back," Catherine explained, returning her attention to the case she was reviewing.

"If you've met her," Elaine continued, emotion bleeding into her voice, "then you might be interested in knowing where Commander Nyland disappeared to. Apparently his daughter was hit by a car on her way to school. She's at the Navy Hospital."

Catherine swore her heart stopped in that moment. She went stiff with shock, then completely numb. Slowly she rose to her feet and blindly looked around her as if the air circulating the room would tell her it wasn't so.

Oh my God. Oh my God. Not Kelly. Please not Kelly, Catherine's mind chanted. The phrase kept repeating itself in her mind, a prayer, an entreaty to the heavenly powers to watch over the child Royce loved so dearly.

"Catherine?" She couldn't look at Elaine, fearing she would read the stark terror in her eyes and know how much Royce and his daughter meant to her.

"Did…what's her condition?"

"I don't know. Are you all right?"

"I'm fine," she answered, reaching for her purse. "I'm… I'm taking my lunch hour."

"Sure thing," Elaine returned hesitantly. "I don't suppose you noticed it's only ten. It's a little early for lunch, don't you think?"

Catherine didn't bother to answer. She was already on her way out of the office. She rushed down the stairs and shot out of the building. It amazed her how calm she was. Outwardly, she was as cool and composed as

an admiral. On the inside she was quaking with fear so
stark and real the taste of it filled her mouth.

Please God, not Kelly. She must have repeated the
phrase a hundred times as she raced across the asphalt
parking lot to her car.

Catherine didn't remember any part of the fifteen-
minute drive to the Navy Hospital in Bremerton. One
moment she was at the Navy Base at Bangor, and the
next thing she knew she was pulling into the hospital
parking lot.

The emergency room receptionist must have recognized the urgency in Catherine's eyes, and after a few
preliminary questions, directed her to the third floor.

She took the elevator up, repeating the room number over and over in her head as she raced down the
wide polished corridor. The door was ajar when Catherine arrived.

Kelly, her face ashen against the sheets, was either
asleep or unconscious, the metal railing around the
bed raised. Catherine's heart, which had only recently
righted itself, tripped into double time. Once more she
prayed for the little girl who had come to mean so much
to her in so short a time. Tears filled her eyes, and she
bit into her lower lip in an effort to keep them at bay.

Royce was sitting in a chair next to the hospital bed,
his face in his hands, oblivious to her presence.

"Royce."

He lifted his head, turned and fixed his eyes on her.
He frowned as though he didn't believe it was her, as
though he desperately needed an anchor. His face was
ravaged with emotion, scored with myriad fears. Briefly
he closed his eyes before he stood and walked over to
her.

Thankfully Catherine had the presence of mind to

close the door. No sooner had it swung shut when Royce hauled her to him, lifted her from the floor and locked his arms around her waist. A shudder ran down the length of him as he breathed in deeply and buried his face in the gentle slope of her shoulder.

Catherine felt the moisture slide down her cheeks, and she held on to Royce with equal ferocity, her arms looped around his neck.

"She's going to be all right," Royce assured her several moments later, his words more breath than sound. As if he feared he was hurting her, he relaxed his hold and slowly, hesitantly lowered her feet to the ground. "She's asleep now. The doctor wanted to keep her overnight for observation. Oh God, Catherine, it was so close, so very close. A few more feet and I might have lost her."

His eyes continued to hold hers. The barriers were down now, and she understood so many things he'd never allowed her to see before. Though he wished she'd never been transferred from Hawaii. Though he wished she was in anyone else's command but his. Though he wished to hell she'd stayed outside his life. He needed her. He needed her because he couldn't endure seeing his only child hurt and stand at her bedside alone. He needed her then. He needed her tomorrow. The need wasn't ever going to go away.

Without thinking, Catherine did what seemed natural. She reached up and pressed her head to his chest, reassuring him the only way she knew how. His hands were trembling as his fingers tangled with her hair. Once again a tremor raced through his body.

"She's going to be all right," he said again.

"Thank God," Catherine whispered. She felt his heart pounding. Her breasts were flush against the hard wall of his chest, and it felt so incredibly good to be in his arms.

They might have remained like that forever if the sound from outside the room hadn't captured their attention. Even then neither one showed any inclination toward moving. Remembering all the unspoken promises they'd made to each other, Catherine gently broke away.

"Any broken bones?" was the only intelligent question she could think to ask. She ran her fingers down her cheeks, convinced her mascara was streaking her face. Using the back of her hand, she brushed the moisture aside.

"None," Royce said with a lopsided grin. "She was lucky that way. She has a bad concussion and plenty of scrapes and bruises."

"What happened?"

"One of the mothers was driving her kids to school when her brakes locked as she was coming to the school crossing. There wasn't anything she could do." Royce's eyes hardened as though he were picturing the frantic scene in his mind. The terror of the children helplessly scattering as the car slid toward them. The screams. The fear. The panic.

"Gratefully the car hit the curb before sliding into Kelly and Missy. From what I understand both were racing out of the way and were knocked hard to the ground."

"Was Kelly's friend hurt?"

"Cuts and bruises. The hospital released her to her mother."

Pressing her hands against the sides of Royce's clean-shaven jaw, Catherine closed her eyes, grateful that the accident hadn't been any worse than it was. Now that she was assured Kelly was going to be all right, she was more concerned about Royce. At one time she would have believed nothing could disconcert him, but Royce's Achilles' heel was his young daughter.

"Are you all right?"

He nodded, and offered her a weak smile. "Now that you're here, I am." He covered her hand with his own and roughly drew her palm to his mouth, tenderly kissing the inside. "Does anyone know where you are?"

Elaine Perkins had probably figured it out, but Catherine didn't want to worry Royce. "No."

"Good." His eyes were dark and intent. "Go back to the office."

"But…"

"And come back later this afternoon. Kelly will want to see you." His eyes revealed he'd want to see her again, too.

"All right," she said, reluctantly drawing away from him.

Royce reached for her hand, momentarily bringing her back to him, and pressed her fingertips to his mouth. "Thank you." He didn't need to tell her what for, it was there in his eyes for her to read. The eyes that had once seemed so hard and cold would never look the same again.

No man is an island. Royce had never completely understood those words until Kelly's accident. He'd been numb when security had come to tell him his daughter, his only child, had been taken by ambulance to the Navy Hospital. Numb with shock and disbelief. His heart had pounded so loud it sounded like a hand grenade exploding in his ears.

He hadn't said a word, but simply walked outside to his car, climbed inside and drove with a security escort to the hospital, praying, pleading with God for things to be different this time than they had been with Sandy's fatal accident.

Security Police had come to him then, too. All he'd known was that Sandy had been taken by ambulance to the Naval Hospital. The details with Kelly had been the same.

Only Sandy had been D.O.A.

Kelly had been spared.

Royce had loved his wife, at least in the beginning. He'd sensed from the first that she'd needed more love, more of him than he could ever supply. When they'd first married, the idea of being an officer's wife had excited her, but that novelty had quickly worn thin. She'd needed something more.

A career, she decided. One in which she would be appreciated and admired. One that would make her the envy of everyone she met.

Royce had encouraged her, which was his first mistake, but he hadn't expected her to become more involved with fashion than their lives together. After two years as a buyer for a major Seattle department store, she let it be known that if Royce were transferred, she'd stay behind.

In his ignorance, Royce had thought a child would help. Sandy had never been keen on raising a family. Insisting she bear him the child she'd promised was mistake number two.

After threats, tears and countless arguments, Sandy had agreed, but she'd never wanted Kelly. In some ways, Royce doubted that Sandy had ever loved their daughter.

Sandy worked up to a week before her delivery date and returned two weeks afterward. It was Royce who walked the floors when Kelly developed colic. It was

Royce who dropped her off at the day-care center and returned to pick her up after work. It was Royce who changed her diapers and sat in the medical clinic when she developed repeated ear infections.

As Sandy claimed, if Royce was so keen on having a family, fine. She'd done her part.

By the time Sandy had been killed, their marriage, indeed every aspect of their relationship, had long since died a slow, painful death. They hadn't slept in the same room for three years and hadn't made love in over a year. Their lives were as separate as they could make them and still remain married.

Royce hadn't asked for a divorce. He didn't know why Sandy hadn't. They rarely spoke in those days. Rarely communicated.

Nevertheless, when she'd died, Royce had suffered. With guilt. With regret. With doubts. He should have tried harder. Done something more to make her happy. Appreciated her more. Something. Anything. Everything.

He hadn't shed a tear at her funeral. Any emotion he felt for Sandy had long since been spent. He felt guilty about that, guilty enough to promise himself he would never make the mistake of falling in love a second time.

Then he'd met Catherine.

He cursed the day she'd been assigned to his staff. In the same breath his heart swelled with gratitude.

Royce had come to believe he was a man who didn't need anyone. People needed him. Kelly needed him. The Navy needed him. But he was an island, a man without needs.

He'd lived under that delusion until he'd seen Security approaching him that morning.

In that moment he'd needed Catherine. So badly that

he shuddered at the memory of the way her name had raced into his mind. He'd sat in the emergency room, wanting her with him so much that he could feel himself start to unravel. A woman he felt closer to in little more than a month than he'd ever felt toward the wife he'd buried. He needed Catherine, the woman he'd never held. The woman he'd never kissed.

Royce had waited, for what seemed like hours, but in fact had only been a matter of minutes before he learned Kelly had suffered only minor injuries.

His relief had been so great that it demanded every ounce of strength he possessed not to reach for the phone and call Catherine then and there and assure her everything was all right. His hand shook as the realization washed over him like cold November rain.

Still he wanted Catherine with him. He needed her warmth, her generosity, her support. The man who needed no one, needed her.

She must have known, must have sensed his desperation because she'd come. From out of nowhere, she'd walked into Kelly's hospital room like an apparition. When he'd first looked up and seen her standing there, Royce was convinced she wasn't real. His anguish had been so overwhelming that his troubled mind had conjured up her form to satisfy the deep craving he had for her touch.

Then her eyes had slid so hungrily to his, and she'd bit into her bottom lip and battled back the tears. Ghosts didn't cry, did they?

This one did. Somehow Royce found himself on his feet walking toward her. He half expected her to vanish when he reached for her. Instead she was warm and solid and real. And his.

Royce had been so grateful, so engulfed with gratitude that he hadn't been able to speak. His heart, which he'd taken such measures to protect, had heated with a love so strong, his throat had grown thick with emotion.

He'd held Catherine for the longest time, soaking in her strength, her love, her concern.

When he had been able to speak, he didn't know if what he'd said was the least bit intelligible. Catherine had started asking questions; somehow he'd found the strength to answer, strength she'd lent him without even knowing it.

Then they'd heard a noise outside the room and realized their perilous position. He'd had to send her away. He'd had no choice.

"Daddy." The fragile child voice rose from the bed as delicately as mist on the moors.

"Hello, sweetheart."

"I fell asleep."

"I know." He lifted her small hand and clasped it in both of his. "You're going to be all right."

"What about Missy?"

"Her, too."

"Did I ruin my new jacket?"

How like a woman to be concerned about her clothes, Royce noted, amused. "If you did, I'll buy you another one."

Kelly brightened enough to offer him a weak smile. "I thought I heard Catherine. Did she come? I wanted to wake up and talk to her, but I couldn't. I guess I was too tired."

Royce nodded. "Don't worry, Catherine will be back later."

Kelly's soft blue eyes drifted shut, and she yawned. "Oh-h-h good, I like her so much."

"I like her, too."

Kelly's smile was lethargic. "I know you do, and she likes you a whole bunch... I can tell. Remember what I said, okay?"

"About what, sweetheart?"

"A baby sister," she reminded him, and winced. "Don't forget."

Royce hesitated. Now wasn't the time to lecture Kelly, but if she were to say anything to Catherine, it might prove extremely embarrassing. "Let me handle that part, all right?"

"All right."

Within a few minutes, Kelly was sound asleep once more.

As promised, Catherine arrived later that evening, her arms filled with a giant stuffed panda and a large vase of bright flowers.

"Catherine!" Kelly greeted. His child was sitting up in bed, looking very much like her normal self, Royce thought. The ten-year-old held out her arms as though she and the lieutenant commander were close friends.

If the truth be known, Royce was having something of a problem keeping from holding out his arms as well. Catherine looked beautiful, but then he couldn't remember a time that she'd been anything less.

Catherine set the vase of pink, red and white carnations next to the flower arrangement Royce had brought.

"Dad said you were here earlier, but I was asleep." She hugged the panda bear and Catherine in turn. "Thank you. I didn't expect everyone to buy me gifts just because Mrs. Thompson's brakes didn't work."

"We're all so pleased you weren't hurt worse."

"It was real scary," Kelly admitted, eating up all the

attention she was receiving. "I tried not to cry, but it hurt too bad."

"I probably would have cried, too," Catherine confessed. She stood across the bed from Royce, who remembered the tears in her eyes as she'd rushed into the room earlier in the day.

"Wow, what happened to this place?" Catherine said with a grin, admiring the decorations. Her gaze briefly met with Royce's and seemed almost shy.

"My teacher brought me a poster," Kelly said, pointing proudly to the large sheet of brightly decorated butcher paper. "Everyone in the class wrote me a get-well message." The ten-year-old paused. "Everyone except Eddie Reynolds. He's never forgiven me for striking him out in baseball last year." She rolled her eyes as though to say men were all fools.

"Your friends did a beautiful job."

"Did you see the flowers Dad got me and the new cassette player?"

"Yes, they're very nice."

"I almost ruined my new jacket, but Dad says all we have to do is take it to the cleaners."

"Well, you're certainly looking chipper."

"I feel real good, but the doctor said I have to stay here overnight. Dad's going to come back early in the morning and bring me home. Then tomorrow night he's going to fix my favorite dinner. Will you come, too? Dad's a real good cook, and I have so much I want to show you."

Catherine's eyes shot to Royce's. It was clear she didn't know how to answer Kelly. It was also clear, at least to Royce, that she wanted to be there just as much as he and Kelly wanted her with them.

Five

"Okay, Dad, we're ready," Kelly called out excitedly from the family room.

Catherine shared a smile with the ten-year-old as Royce wiped his hands dry on a dish towel and wandered in from the kitchen. He was busy with the dinner preparations while Catherine was keeping Kelly entertained.

"See?" Kelly held out her arms, proudly displaying her fingernails. "Aren't they gorgeous?"

As a surprise for Kelly, Catherine had brought along press-on nails, and the two had spent an hour working the dragon-length fire-engine red nails onto the girl's fingers.

"How'd you do that?" Royce blinked and seemed genuinely amazed.

"We have our ways," Catherine said, smiling up at him.

"How long before dinner?" Kelly demanded. "I'm starved. Hospital food leaves a lot to be desired, you know." She was dressed in her pajamas and sitting on the L-shaped sectional with a thick feather pillow propped at one end. According to Royce, the doctor had given instructions to keep Kelly quiet for a day or two. A feat, Catherine was quickly learning, that was easier said than done.

"Hold your horses," Royce teased. "I'm putting the finishing touches on dinner now."

"Can I help?" Catherine offered.

"I want to help, too," Kelly chimed in, tossing aside the orange, yellow and brown hand-knit afghan.

"Stay put, the both of you," Royce insisted. "The table's set. All I need to do is dish up. It'll only take me a few more minutes."

The sight of Royce working in the kitchen had done funny things to Catherine's heart. If the wardroom could only see him now! A dish towel was tucked around his waist in apron fashion, yet it did nothing to disrupt the highly charged effectiveness of his masculine appeal. The sharp edges of his character were smoothly rounded when he was with his daughter, Catherine noted. Gone was the constrained, inflexible commander who ruled with a harsh, but fair hand. Royce Nyland was said to be a man with an iron will. Indeed, Catherine had bumped against it more than once herself. He was also said to be a man with an inner core of steel, but what few realized, what few saw, was that Royce Nyland also possessed a heart of gold. A man of iron. A man of gold.

Catherine had assumed she'd feel uncomfortable in Royce's home. She wasn't entirely sure that their being together like this didn't border on an impropriety, an indiscretion that could have serious consequences for them both. But Royce had been the one who'd seconded Kelly's invitation. They'd all wanted it so badly that Catherine had thrown caution to the wind.

"Dad makes marvelous spaghetti and meatballs," Kelly explained.

"Meat-a-balls," Royce corrected from inside the kitchen. "You can't eat Italian unless you speak it correctly. Try again."

"Meat-a-balls," Kelly returned enthusiastically. For someone who'd been hospitalized only a few hours earlier, the youngster revealed amazing vigor.

"Catherine." He pointed a sauce-coated wooden spoon in her direction.

"Meat-a-balls," she said, imitating his inflection perfectly.

"When are we going to stop talking about them and eat?" Kelly wanted to know. "I've been waiting all day for this."

"Now." Royce appeared and waved his arm toward the dining room. "Dinner is served."

The afghan on Kelly's legs went flying across the back of the sectional as she bounced to her feet. She sauntered into the dining room with her arms stretched out in front of her like a sleepwalker, her fingers splayed in an effort not to touch anything in case her nails weren't dry yet.

"Are you sure she can eat with those things?" Royce asked Catherine out of the corner of his mouth.

"I have a feeling she'll find a way."

Kelly had a problem eating at first, but once she got the hang of working her fork without her nails interfering, everything went smoothly. Although, Catherine had to admit, Kelly's first few attempts resembled something out of a Marx brothers movie.

After dinner, Catherine and Royce cleared the table and lingered over a cup of coffee in the family room.

"I can't remember when I've tasted better meat-a-balls," Catherine said, meaning it. "Kelly's right, you're an excellent cook."

Royce bowed his head, graciously accepting her compliment.

Sipping from her cup, Catherine's gaze drifted to the fireplace and the framed family photograph of Royce, Kelly and a dark-haired woman. It didn't take Catherine long to figure out the strong-featured female had been Royce's wife.

Royce's gaze followed hers. "That was taken a couple of years before the accident."

"She was beautiful."

Royce nodded, but it was clear to Catherine that the subject was a closed one. He didn't want to speak of his marriage any more than she wanted to summarize the details of her best-forgotten engagement to Aaron.

"There's a photograph on my fireplace mantel, too," she told him, struggling to keep the emotion out of her voice. She didn't often speak of her father, but she felt comfortable enough with Royce and Kelly to share this painful part of her life. When she'd finished, Catherine noted that Kelly was struggling to keep her eyes open.

"I think it's time I put her to bed," Royce whispered.

Catherine nodded, stood and took their empty coffee cups into the kitchen. Royce lifted a protesting Kelly into his arms.

"Good night, Catherine," Kelly said, covering her mouth as she yawned. When she finished, she held out her arms for a good-night hug.

Royce carried his daughter into the kitchen, and Catherine quickly gave Kelly a squeeze. Standing that close to Royce, however, feeling him tense as her breasts brushed against his forearm, did bizarre things to her equilibrium. She had barely touched him, in the most innocent of ways, and yet her body had sprung to life with yearning.

Danger. Imaginary red lights started flashing before her eyes, and Catherine knew if Royce and she were going to maintain their platonic relationship, she was going to have to find a way to get out of his home—and fast.

Royce disappeared, and not wanting to leave him with the dishes, she quickly rinsed and stacked them in the dishwasher. She was wiping down the countertop when he reappeared.

"Leave that," he said.

"I can't," she returned quickly, her eyes avoiding him. "My mother and I had this simple rule we followed for years, and now I'm a slave to tradition."

"What was this simple rule?"

Catherine continued wiping far more vigorously than was needed. "Those who cook shouldn't have to do the dishes."

"Catherine." His voice was low and seductive. "Come here."

She swore the tension in the air between them was so thick it could be sliced and buttered. "I think it would be best if I left now, don't you?" Slowly she raised her eyes to his, seeking confirmation.

"No, I don't." He said so much more in those few simple words. He told her he was weary of this constant tension between them. He was through waiting. His patience had reached its endurance level. So had hers, and he knew it. She wanted this, too. Sweet heaven how she wanted it.

Silence swelled between them, but for the first time in recent memory it was a comfortable silence unencumbered with misgivings and uncertainties. They both knew they were unwilling to wait any longer.

Royce took her by the hand and led her to the sectional sofa recently vacated by Kelly, pulling her down so they were side by side. They didn't speak, but there was no need for words, indeed words would have been a drawback.

Royce held her head between his hands and carefully studied her face. The look in his eyes, so earnest and intense, humbled her. They said she was the most beautiful woman in the world. His woman. Catherine wasn't going to argue with him, although she wasn't nearly as beautiful as he seemed to believe. His eyes smoldered with a blue light of yearning. Catherine was convinced his look was a reflection of her own. There was nothing between them. No pretense. No qualms. Only need. A need so honest, so comfortable, it seemed to flow between them like the peaceful waters of a rolling river.

Royce's mouth made a slow descent, and with a sigh, Catherine closed her eyes and raised her chin to be rewarded with what she'd waited so long to receive.

Catherine thought she was prepared. How wrong she was. How ill equipped. The moment his mouth met hers, she was assaulted with a swarm of warm sensations that came at her with the force of a bulldozer. He was gentle, so gentle. She hadn't expected that. Not when the hunger was so wild. Not when she'd been smothered in sensation long before his mouth found hers.

Catherine was enveloped in tenderness. She'd known from the first that Royce's kiss would be special; she hadn't expected to feel sensations so unbelievably potent that tears crowded the edges of her eyes. Sensations so powerful it was as though she'd never felt anything before this moment.

Royce groaned and slipped his mouth from hers. Burying his face in her hair, he drew in a deep, shuddering breath. He was about to speak, but she intercepted his action by directing his lips back to hers. They both seemed ready this time, prepared to deal with the wealth of sensation, eager to accept it. His tongue sought hers; she met his eagerly with soft, welcoming touches.

They found a rhythm with each other. A cadence. It was as though they were familiar lovers, enjoying a long series of deep, lengthy kisses full of hunger and desperate need. Soon Catherine was clinging mindlessly to Royce. Prepared for anything, for everything.

"I knew it would be like this." He braced his forehead against hers as he drew in several deep, even breaths as though he were struggling to believe all that was between them.

Catherine hadn't known it would be anything close to this wonderful. She hadn't a clue. Nothing could have prepared her for the fierce onslaught of feelings. Her body pulsed with desire, a need so great that she hurt in strange places.

Royce's hands shook slightly as he unfastened the buttons of her gray silk blouse. He peeled it open and released the clasp of her bra, then caught her breasts in his open palms as they sprang free.

Catherine moaned at the fresh onslaught of warm sensations. Her nipples were hard long before Royce caressed them with the callused pads of his thumbs. She thought it impossible, but they tightened even more. The feelings were unfamiliar, this being so needy, so wanting.

Slowly he lowered his mouth to the summit of her breast, capturing the tender nipple between his lips, laving it with the rough edges of his tongue. When Catherine was convinced she could endure no more, he drew it into his mouth and sucked gently. Catherine moaned and buried her fingers in his short hair, needing to touch him. She felt so close to him, closer than she had to anyone. She loved him so much in that moment, it was all she could do not to weep. Royce loved her, too. Catherine was as confident of that as she was of his love for Kelly.

Royce transferred his attention to her other breast, and Catherine groaned once more. She recognized the sound. It was the type of whimpering noise a woman makes when she's ready to make love, ready to receive a man.

Royce apparently recognized it too, and slowly raised his head. His gaze melded with hers, seeking confirmation.

Catherine's heart was in her throat. She wanted him. He wanted her. Oh, sweet heaven, how she wanted him. Royce must have read the need in her eyes and, responding to it, reached for her once more, his hands cupping the undersides of her face.

His mouth found hers in a hot kiss of savage frenzy. He thrust his tongue forward and swept her mouth with a wild kiss that told her he was fast reaching the point of no return. Even as he kissed her, his hands dropped to work open the zipper in the jut of her hip.

Some shred of reasoning, some ray of sanity grasped hold of Catherine's mind before Royce managed to succeed in opening her slacks. Had they both gone crazy? With their very careers on the line, they'd walked into this with their eyes wide open. In one blindingly clear revelation, Catherine knew they had to stop. It wasn't what she wanted. It wasn't what Royce wanted, either. But it was necessary.

"Royce...no." She scrambled from the sectional, her chest heaving with the effort. She had to escape before it was too late, before he kissed her again.

"Catherine?" Her name became a mixture of shock and need. "What's wrong?"

"Nothing," she assured him, so close to tears her voice wobbled like a toy top. "Everything," she amended. She couldn't stand so close to him and not be affected. It was either move away or fall willingly back into his arms. She couldn't resist him; she couldn't think when he was looking at her with such tenderness and concern.

She moved across the room from him, and braced herself against the opposite wall, needing its support. Her heart was beating so hard, the sound ricocheted around the room, each beat stronger, each beat louder. Surely Royce could hear. Surely he knew.

"We can't do it...we can't," she whispered, fighting back the tears. "Don't you understand how foolish it would be for us both..."

Royce moved off the sofa and walked purposely toward her. "Why not? Kelly's upstairs asleep...."

"Please, oh, please, don't argue with me. This is hard enough...so hard." Explaining would have depleted her of the strength she needed to follow through with her resolve.

Capturing her hands in his own, Royce lifted them above her head, and then, leaning forward, boxed her in with his muscled arms. His body was so close, she could feel the heat radiating off him.

"Royce," she pleaded once again, rolling her head to one side.

His thighs, taut and hard, pressed against her. It wasn't the only part of his anatomy that was hard, and that was pressed against her as well. Catherine moaned as the excitement shuddered through her, and dropped her head, weakening. It would be so easy to swirl her hips, to move against him. She longed to savor his strength, his power. It would be so easy to surrender to the gnawing need.

"Royce, what?" His mouth was so close, so warm. He nudged his nose against her earlobe, then took it gently between his teeth and sucked. Once again wild excitement seized her, and it was all she could do to keep from buckling against him.

"Don't...oh, please, don't." But her pleas lacked conviction. If anything they sounded more like a siren's call, an inducement to continue doing the very things he was.

"You taste so sweet," he murmured, dragging his mouth down the slope of her neck, then taking nibbling kisses at the scented hollow of her throat. Catherine moaned and rotated her head, granting him access to his desires. And he did desire her. It was as if a giant storehouse of need had been building in both of them, and had burst open all at once.

His mouth found hers, his kisses hot, filled with an untamed urgency, his hunger as raw as her own. His tongue swept her mouth, and before she realized what she was doing, Catherine pulled her hands free from his and grabbed at his shirt, demanding more and more, holding on. Royce answered by ravishing her mouth in a kiss so blistering, so carnal that any and all resistance in Catherine melted.

Pinning her against the wall with his hips, Royce started to move against her. Their kisses were so fiery, the air sizzled. The night sizzled. They sizzled.

Abruptly Royce dragged his mouth from hers. "Tell me you want this as much as I do," he whispered. His voice was thick and hot. So hot against her skin his breath alone was enough to scorch her.

That Royce would need her assurance touched something deep within Catherine. "Oh, Royce, yes…only…"

"What?"

"Only I won't be able to hide the way I feel if we make love. Not from anyone." Monday morning Elaine Perkins would guess what had happened between her and Royce. Catherine didn't doubt it for a moment. "I'm not nearly as good at disguising my feelings as you. It's hard enough now, but if we make love…if we do this… Everyone will know."

Royce went still for several heart-stopping moments before making a low, guttural sound of frustration and defeat. His shoulders heaved once as he rolled away from her and pressed his own back against the wall. "You're right."

"If I'm so right, then why is it so damned hard?"

"I don't know." He spoke through gritted teeth as he reined in his desire.

Catherine felt like weeping. "What are we going to do?"

Royce expelled his breath forcefully. "The hell if I know. I just hope to God the Navy appreciates this." Straightening, he heaved in one giant breath, squared his shoulders and with some effort managed to snap her bra closed. Then with deliberate businesslike movements he fastened her blouse, kissed her one last time sweetly, gently and whispered, "Now go, before I change my mind."

"Morning, Dad," Kelly said as she walked into the kitchen, dressed in her housecoat and slippers. She pulled out the chair and reached for a section of the Sunday paper. "What time did Catherine go home last night?"

"Early." Too damn early, Royce mused. Unfortunately it hadn't been soon enough. Royce couldn't believe how far matters had developed the night before. How far he'd *let* them develop. He'd never been closer to defying Navy regulations. If the commanding officer were to learn he was having an affair with Catherine Fredrickson, their lives would be ruined. Royce had seen it once before. An acquaintance had fallen in love with a woman in his command. They'd been discreet, or so they believed. Eventually it was discovered and they were investigated. No allowances had been made. No leeway given. Both parties involved had been immediately court-martialed.

Royce didn't know what the hell he'd been thinking. That was just it. He *wasn't* thinking. Thank God Catherine had the presence of mind to call an end to matters when she had. She was right. If they made love, neither one of them would have been able to continue with the pretense. True, Catherine was far more readable than he was, but Royce knew himself well enough to recognize there would be problems with him, too. Major problems.

"Can I call Catherine?" Kelly asked, reaching across the table for the comics.

"I don't think that would be a good idea."

"Why not?"

Royce wasn't in any mood to argue with his daughter, and his voice was sharp when he spoke. "Because I said you couldn't. I don't want any arguments about this, Kelly. Catherine is off-limits." To them both, unfortunately.

Kelly gave him an indignant look, scooted out of her chair and stalked out of the kitchen. Just before she reached the doorway, she bolted around and glared at him. "Sometimes you're an unreasonable grouch."

If Kelly thought he was bad now, give him another six months of working side by side with Catherine, knowing he'd never be able to hold her or kiss her again.

"What's with Commander Nyland?" Elaine Perkins questioned when Catherine returned from a session in court early Friday afternoon. Catherine had been in and out of the office all week acting as prosecutor on a series of criminal trials. If Royce's mood had been anything other than normal, she hadn't noticed.

"What's wrong?" she asked, setting a load of files down on her desk.

"If I knew that I wouldn't be asking you. He's been in a bad mood all week, making unreasonable demands on himself and everyone else. You would think once he found out his daughter wasn't badly hurt he'd be in a good mood. If anything it's gotten worse."

"If Commander Nyland has a problem, trust me, he isn't going to share it with me." Catherine did her best to maintain the pretense that she and Royce did nothing more than work together. She hadn't talked to him outside the office all week. The fact didn't trouble her; they both needed distance to put order to their thoughts.

Now that she thought about it, Catherine was willing to admit that Elaine did have a point. Royce seemed to be putting in plenty of hours, making too many demands on himself and consequently everyone else. He'd never gone out for any personality awards, nor was he in a popularity contest. If that were the case he'd lose hands down.

A couple of the other clerks rolled back their chairs. "Ever read much about arctic seals, Lieutenant Commander?" Elaine Perkins asked as the others slowly gathered around the secretary's desk.

"No." Catherine wondered what the men were up to.

"Apparently when danger is near they gather on a floating iceberg. The problem is they don't know when the danger has passed and so a sacrificial seal is thrown into the water. If he survives the others know it's safe to leave the iceberg."

Catherine stared at the small party of men gathered around Elaine's desk. A couple had leaned forward, pressing their hands to her desktop. "So?" Catherine demanded, not liking the sounds of this.

"We just voted you to be our sacrificial seal."

"What?" If she hadn't been so amused, she might have been concerned. Apparently she hadn't done as good a job as she'd hoped, hiding her feelings for Royce. The staff seemed to think she had some influence with their XO. A dangerous sign.

"It makes sense for you to be the one to approach him," Elaine explained before Catherine could ask why they'd bestowed the dubious honor upon her. "Commander Nyland may have all the sensitivity of seaweed, but he's still a man, and as such he's as susceptible as the rest of us to a pretty face."

"And what exactly am I supposed to say to him?"

"I don't have a clue. You're supposed to figure that out yourself. Just do whatever it is you do to put a man into a better mood."

"Please do it soon," Seaman Webster added. "I've had to type the same paper five times. He wants it perfect. The last time I had a comma out of place, and you would have thought the free world was in jeopardy."

"Sorry, fellows," Catherine said, walking back into her office, ignoring them as much as possible. She was staying away from this situation with Royce with a ten-foot pole. "You picked the wrong lady to do your dirty work for you. If Commander Nyland's in a foul mood, you'll ride it out together the way you always have. Furthermore I find your attitude highly chauvinistic."

"Oh, I agree," Elaine Perkins commented. "But we're desperate."

"I said no," she returned crisply. "And I mean it."

There was a fair amount of grumbling, but the staff gradually returned to their desks. Elaine Perkins, however, continued to study Catherine. "I thought you and the commander were friends."

"We are," Catherine said, doing her best to keep her tone light and unaffected.

"I understood that the two of you jogged together most afternoons."

Catherine wondered when she'd heard that and from whom. "Not anymore. I usually run in the mornings."

"Damn. I was hoping you might be able to talk to him casually some afternoon, find out what's bugging him. There isn't any need to make the rest of us suffer just because he's unhappy about something."

"Are you suffering, Mrs. Perkins?" Royce demanded from behind Catherine's secretary in a voice so cold, the words froze in midair.

Elaine went pale. "No, sir," she answered briskly.

"I'm glad to hear it." He hesitated long enough to look toward Catherine. "I'd like the Ellison report on my desk before you leave tonight."

"Yes, sir," Catherine returned just as crisply. She was hours from being anywhere close to finishing the report. Royce must have known it. Apparently she, too, was to receive the brunt of his foul mood, but then why should she be different from anyone else?

With that, Royce returned to his office and closed the door.

Elaine slumped back into her chair and released her breath in a slow exercise. "He wants you to have that report done by tonight?" she moaned.

"Don't worry, it won't take me long." Longer than she would have liked, but that couldn't be helped.

"Do you want me to stay and type it up for you?"

Catherine appreciated the offer, but it wasn't necessary. "No, thanks, it won't take me long."

"Aren't you furious with him?" Elaine asked under her breath, her gaze leveled on the closed door that led to Royce's office.

"No." Maybe she should be, but Catherine had learned long before that Royce's bark was far worse than his bite. She said as much to Elaine.

"Right, but you don't seem to be the one he's biting all the time."

The humor drained out of Catherine. The more she thought about Elaine's comment, the more concerned she became. Was it true? Had Royce given her more slack than the other members of his staff? Apparently they'd all felt the brunt of his bad mood in the past several days. But if what Elaine Perkins said was true, something had to be done, and quickly.

Catherine waited until later that same afternoon when Royce went down to the track. She gave him enough time to run several laps before she joined him. He looked over at her and frowned, his look so dark and uninviting that a shiver of apprehension moved over her. "The Ellison report is on your desk."

"Is there a problem?" He hadn't decreased his speed any, and she was having a problem maintaining his pace.

"Ah...ever hear of a sacrificial seal?"

"I beg your pardon?"

"Nothing...forget I said that."

They ran half a lap, then he turned to stare at her again. His eyes were cold, his look detached. That should have pleased her, should have assured her Elaine was imagining things, but it didn't. "We might have a problem."

"Is that a fact, Lieutenant Commander? Thank you so much for taking it upon yourself to inform me of this."

"More than...the usual problem."

"And what, tell me, is the *usual* problem?"

"There isn't any need to be so damned sarcastic," she said, affronted by his attitude.

"Isn't there?" he returned. "What do I have to do, order you off this track? I thought I'd made myself clear about the subject of us jogging together."

"You did, but..."

"Then kindly respect my wishes."

The wall was back in place, so firmly erected that Catherine was left to wonder if everything that had blossomed between them was a figment of her imagination. Royce was so cold. So caustic.

"What about my wishes?" she asked softly.

Royce came to an abrupt halt. His blue eyes had never been more piercing. "Listen, Lieutenant Commander, you have no wishes. If you didn't learn that early in your Navy career then we have a real problem. I'm your executive officer. You will do what I say, when I say it, without question. Is that understood?"

Catherine swallowed back a cry of protest. She blinked and nodded. "Yes, sir."

"Good. Now stay off this track from five o'clock

on." He made it sound like a direct order, when in fact he had no right to tell her when she could or couldn't be on the track.

"Is that clear?" he demanded.

"Very clear, sir." The "sir" was shouted.

"Good." There was no regret in his voice. No emotion. Only a wall so high and so thick, Catherine doubted she'd ever be able to scale its heights again.

Six

The phone was ringing when Catherine let herself into her apartment Saturday afternoon. Setting the bag of groceries on the kitchen counter and ignoring Sambo's protest over being ignored, she lurched for the receiver.

"Hello," she said, fighting breathlessness.

"Hi." It was Kelly, that much Catherine could tell, but it sounded like Royce's daughter was talking with her head inside a bucket.

"Kelly?"

"Yeah, it's me."

"What's wrong?"

"Nothing. It's just that I'm not supposed to be calling you, and if Dad finds out I'm in big trouble. I've got the phone cord stretched into the closet and I'm whispering as loud as I can. Can you hear me all right?"

"Just barely. Now tell me what's up." Catherine did her best to ignore the pain of Royce's most recent order.

"You still like me and my Dad, don't you?"

"Oh, yes, sweetheart, of course I do." But it was more complicated than that, and Catherine couldn't allow the youngster to go on thinking matters could continue the way they had. "There are problems, though."

"I know, Dad explained everything to me." Kelly paused, and Catherine could hear the frustration and disappointment hum over the telephone wire with every word the youngster spoke. "Sometimes I hate the Navy."

"Don't," Catherine pleaded softly. "Those rules were made for a very good reason."

"But Dad said we couldn't have you over to the house anymore and that we couldn't go to the movies or go out to dinner or things like that. He said it would be best if I forgot all about you because that was what he was going to do."

Kelly's words went through Catherine like a steel point. The pain was so sharp and so real that she swallowed hard and bit her lower lip.

"I don't want to forget about you," the ten-year-old whispered, her voice trembling as if she were close to tears, "I kept thinking that Dad and you...that you might be my mom someday. I asked God to send me a mom, especially one with pretty fingernails, and then Dad met you and he was listening to me when I asked him about getting me a baby sister and then all of a sudden..."

"And now everything looks so bad. I won't forget you, sweetheart, and the Navy doesn't have anything to say about the two of us being special friends."

"It doesn't?"

"Not in the least. We'll give your dad and me time to work matters out at the office, and once everything is settled there, I'll invite you over for the night and we can order pizza and rent a movie and we'll do our fingernails."

"Oh, Catherine, could we really? I'd like that so much."

"I'd like that, too."

There was a bit of commotion behind Kelly that

sounded like a door being jerked opened. "I've got to
go now, *Missy*," Kelly said deliberately loud, placing
heavy emphasis on her friend's name.

"I take it your dad just opened the closet door?"
Catherine asked, unable to contain a smile.

"Right."

"All right, sweetheart. Now listen, it probably would
be best if you didn't phone me again for a while. But I
promise I'll talk to your dad…"

"Only do it soon, okay?" she pleaded.

"I will, I promise," Catherine pledged, feeling more
depressed than ever.

The despair had grown heavier and more oppressive a week later. Royce hadn't spoken one unnecessary
word to her in all that time. It was as though she were
invisible. A necessary body that filled a space. Necessary to the legal department, but not necessary for him.
If Royce did happen to glance in her direction it was by
accident, and it seemed he looked straight through her.

The weekend hadn't been much better. Catherine
couldn't remember a Saturday and Sunday that felt more
empty. On Saturday she'd done busywork around her
apartment and answered mail. At least her good friend
Brand Davis from Hawaii was happy, she mulled, reading over the wedding invitation. Then on Sunday, after
church services, she'd attended a matinee and cooked
a meal she didn't feel like eating, and ended up giving
the leftovers to Sambo, who apparently wasn't interested, either.

Outwardly everything was as it always had been,
but inside Catherine felt empty. As empty as a black
hole. How stark her life felt, how barren. Until she'd
met Royce, she'd been blissfully unaware of the lonely

nothingness of her life. Royce had stirred her soul to life, and now she hungered for someone to share the everyday routine, someone to give meaning to her bleak existence.

The single red rose in a crystal stem vase was sitting on her desk waiting for her when she walked into the office Monday morning. Her heart quickened at the beauty of the delicate flower, but she knew immediately it couldn't, wouldn't be from Royce. He wasn't a man who would allow a rose to do his speaking for him. He wasn't a man to indulge in such romantic extravagances.

A card was pinned to the shiny red ribbon attached to the narrow vase. Catherine stared at the envelope for several moments, calculating in her mind who would have given her a rose.

"Aren't you going to read who it's from?" Elaine asked, much too casually to fool Catherine.

"In time." She unpinned the card and slipped it free of the small envelope. The name was scrawled across the face of the card in bold, even strokes. She grinned, somewhat amused. It was exactly who she thought it would be. Knowing Elaine was watching her, she replaced the card in the envelope, then set the rose on the edge of her desk.

"Well?" Elaine demanded impatiently. "Who sent it?"

"My, my, aren't you the nosy one?"

"If you must know, it's a little more than idle curiosity."

Catherine pulled out her chair and sat down. "I suppose you've got money riding on this."

"Ten bucks." Then without hesitation, she asked, "Commander Parker, right?"

Catherine grinned and nodded.

"I knew it all along," Elaine said, grinning broadly.

Catherine was pleased her secretary took such delight in the fact Commander Dan Parker had seen fit to flatter her with a red rose, but frankly, her secretary was more thrilled about it than she was.

Her lack of appreciation, Catherine realized, could be attributed to the fact she realized what was sure to follow. An invitation she didn't want to accept. It happened just as she suspected, just when she was preparing to leave the office that same afternoon. Commander Parker strolled into the room, grinning boyishly.

"Good afternoon, Catherine," he greeted, and struck a casual pose. He was tall and reasonably good-looking, his features well defined. From the scuttlebutt Catherine had picked up around the base, Dan Parker had the reputation of being a playboy.

"Good afternoon, Commander," she responded formally, wanting to keep it impersonal.

His gaze drifted over to her desk, where she'd left the rose. "I see you found my little surprise."

"It was very thoughtful of you," she said, eyeing the door, anxious to get away. The office was deserted, and she didn't want to get stuck in a long, boring conversation with a man she had no interest in cultivating a relationship with.

"I'm pleased you enjoyed it so much."

"It's lovely." She reached for her coat and slipped into it, doing her best to give the appearance that she was about to leave. Anything that would cut short this game of cat and mouse.

Commander Parker would ask her out, and she'd decline. Then he'd give her his well-practiced hurt-little-boy look, and she'd be required to spend the next ten minutes making up some excuse why she wouldn't go out with him. Something that would soothe the ruffled feathers of his substantial male ego.

"I don't suppose you have plans Friday night?" he asked right on cue.

"Sorry, I'm busy." Which was true. She planned on changing Sambo's litter box. Not exactly an exciting prospect, but it gave credence to her words. She looped the strap of her purse over her shoulder, determined not to play the game.

"I was hoping you'd let me take you to dinner."

"Another time perhaps," she suggested, heading toward the door.

"What about the Birthday Ball?" Every October the Navy celebrated its birthday with an elaborate ball. The celebration was coming later this year because the admiral had been gone. "It's two weeks away, and I was hoping you'd accompany me."

Catherine didn't have a single excuse. Her presence would be expected, but she hadn't given the matter of a date more than a fleeting thought.

The idea of spending the evening with anyone other than Royce didn't interest her. Her attitude was excessively stupid. They'd be able to dance once, maybe twice without raising suspicions. Risking anything more than that would be foolish in the extreme. The way matters were between them presently, it was doubtful Royce would go anywhere near her.

"Catherine," Dan prodded. "The Birthday Ball?"

She forced herself to smile as though it was a difficult decision. "I appreciate the invitation, in fact I'm flattered, but no thanks. I'm… I've decided to go stag this year. It's nothing personal, Dan."

Commander Parker's smile didn't waver, neither did the light in his dark eyes dim, if anything it brightened.

Slowly, without hesitation, he raised his hand and ran one finger down the side of her cheek. "I think I know why."

Catherine's heart thundered against her chest with alarm. She stared up at him and blinked, certain he could read everything she felt for Royce like a notice on a bulletin board.

"Don't worry," he whispered sympathetically, "your secret is safe with me."

Squaring her shoulders, Catherine's only choice was to pretend he couldn't be more wrong. "I don't know what you're talking about. I prefer to attend the Birthday Ball alone this year, and whatever connotation you put on that decision is of your own making."

Dan chuckled. "You're right, of course. Absolutely right." He straightened and was about to leave when he turned back, his friendly eyes suddenly somber and dark. "Good luck, Catherine, but be careful. Understand?"

Before she could continue with the pretense, Catherine nodded. "I will."

Royce was in a foul mood, but that wasn't anything new. He'd been in a dangerous one for nearly two weeks, and frankly he couldn't see it lessening anytime soon. The fact he'd recently spoken to Dan Parker hadn't improved his disposition any. Of all the foolish, mule-headed deeds Catherine had committed since he'd met her, rejecting Dan's invitation to the Birthday Ball took the cake. He'd like to wring her skinny neck.

"Ha," he said aloud, discrediting his thoughts. The last thing he wanted was to see Catherine suffer. Anytime he was within ten feet of her it was all he could do not to haul her into his arms and breathe in the fresh, womanly scent that was hers alone. He wanted to drink in her softness, savor her warmth and her love. He needed her so damn much, he was about to go out of his mind.

Royce didn't know what the hell he was going to do. One thing for sure, they couldn't continue like this much longer.

Royce had done everything he could think to do to forget her. He was working himself into an early grave, spending all kinds of extra hours at the office. Kelly was barely speaking to him, and he'd lost just about every friend he'd made in seventeen years of military service.

Something had to be done, and fast, before he ended up destroying himself and in the process, Catherine, too. He just didn't know what the hell the solution was.

A polite knock on his door interrupted his thoughts. Whoever it was possessed the courage of David facing Goliath to confront Royce in his current mood.

"Come in," he barked.

When Catherine opened the door, Royce's heart dropped to his knees. What now? He couldn't be any less encouraging than the last time they spoke. He couldn't have been any more sarcastic. No matter what he said, no matter what he did, she just kept coming back. By heaven, that woman was stubborn.

"Yes?" he demanded, giving the illusion of being busy, too busy to be intruded upon.

"I need to talk to you."

How sweet her voice sounded, how soft and feminine. Royce had lain awake nights tormented by the memory of her making delicate, whimpering love sounds. How close he'd come to breaking the very code of honor he'd sworn to uphold.

"There's nothing more to say," he said, forcefully

pushing all thoughts of her and that night from his mind. "I thought I made that fact perfectly clear." His voice was as brittle and hard as he could make it.

"It's about Kelly."

"My daughter is none of your business, Lieutenant Commander." Royce felt as though he'd been kicked in the stomach. Catherine had no way of knowing that Kelly continued to bring up her name night and day until he'd absolutely forbidden his own daughter to speak of her.

"If you have no objection, I'd like Kelly to spend the weekend with me and…"

"No." The word was edged with steel.

"Wanting to spend time with Kelly has nothing to do with you and me," Catherine insisted softly. "But everything to do with Kelly. She needs…"

"I'll be the one to determine my daughter's needs."

The silence between them stretched to ear-splitting proportions. Royce half expected the window glass to shatter under the pressure. Neither spoke. Neither daring. Neither willing to give an inch.

Royce feared an inch would soon lead to two and three, and before he could stop himself, he and Catherine would become lovers. The very word brought a tight hardening to his loins. It didn't take much for his tormented mind to envision her soft and willing beneath him, opening her life and her heart to him. The ache grew worse, but he wasn't sure which hurt worse: the pain in his loins, or the one in his heart.

"I understand you turned down Commander Parker's invitation to the Birthday Ball," he said when it became apparent she was going to continue with the same argument. His best tactic, he decided, was to change the subject.

"How'd you know that?" she asked, her beautiful dark eyes narrowing.

"Dan told me."

"Like hell, he did," she flared. "Commander Parker is a typical man. He isn't likely to tell anyone I refused his offer unless he was asked and..." She paused, and a deep shade of red seeped steadily up her neck and invaded her cheeks. "You...you asked him to invite me, didn't you?" She made it sound as though he'd attempted to involve her in treason. "You went to Dan and encouraged him to take me to...to the Birthday Ball." She closed her eyes momentarily, as though mortified to the very marrow of her bones.

"Listen, Catherine..."

Leaning forward, she pressed her hands against the side of his desk. "How dare you."

"You're out of order here, Lieutenant Commander." Royce could see he was digging himself in deeper than he intended. The most expedient way of extracting himself was to pull rank. Not the wisest means, but the most practical.

She ignored him as she straightened, then started pacing the length of his office, her steps clipped and angry. "You have one hell of a nerve, Royce. What makes you think you can rule my life?"

"Our discussion is over." He reached for his pen and commenced writing. He didn't know if a single word was legible, but that wasn't the point. Catherine, her eyes bright with unshed tears, stared at him with her heart on her sleeve. He had to get her out of his office before he did something foolish. Before he succumbed to what would, in the end, destroy them both.

"Why?" she asked. The lone word was saturated with emotion.

"You know the answer to that," he informed her stiffly, fighting back the urge to shout at her. She wasn't stupid; surely she could figure out his motives on her own.

"You honestly think it would help if I were to become involved with Dan?" Her words were low and disbelieving. When he didn't answer right away, she raised her voice. "Do you?"

"This discussion would be better left for another time," Royce informed her in his best military voice. "You may leave now." This was the tone he used often, expecting immediate and unquestioned compliance to his words.

"No way," she said, then stalked across the room and slammed closed the door, although they both knew they were alone. "We won't discuss this another time, because we're going to have this out here and now."

Royce bolted to his feet, as angry now as she. "If you value your commission, Lieutenant Commander, then I suggest you do as I ask."

She didn't so much as blink. "What exactly have you *asked*? That I date Commander Parker?"

"It certainly wouldn't hurt matters any," he said pointedly.

She knotted her fist at her side, and Royce had the impression she did so in an effort to hold on to her anger, and it required both hands.

"It may come as something of a surprise to you, Commander Nyland, but it's none of the Navy's business whom I date. It most certainly isn't any of yours!"

"In this case it is." Royce amazed himself by remaining calm, at least on the outside. Inside, he was a mess, something he wasn't willing to admit often, but Catherine had driven him to the outer edges of sanity.

"What makes you think dating Dan would help either of us? Answer me! I'm downright curious."

"Just do it, Catherine, for both our sakes."

"No," she cried, "if you want me out of your life, that's your business, but I refuse to make it easy for you."

A tear rolled down the side of her face, her precious sweet face, and it was all Royce could do not to reach out and comfort her. He slumped back in his chair and rammed all ten fingers through his hair in an urgent effort to regain control of himself. Shouting at each other wasn't going to accomplish anything. Neither was pretending.

"Sit down, Catherine," he instructed, motioning toward the chair.

"I prefer to stand." She was as stiff as plastic, eyes focused straight ahead. The evidence of that lone tear or any others had long since vanished.

"Fine. Have it your way." The fight was out of him, and he leaned back in his chair and braced his index fingers beneath his chin the way he did when he needed to think. "You were right," he stated after a while.

She blinked as though she wasn't sure she'd heard him correctly. "About what?"

"About what would happen if we'd made love that night."

Catherine's eyes briefly found his. "Even if everyone in the entire office hadn't guessed afterward, it would have been wrong."

"Only because the rule book claims it is," she argued. Her look told him the love between them was right, and always would be, no matter what the Navy decreed.

"No," he argued, gaining conviction. "Don't you understand? Can't you see? That night would have only been the beginning. Once we crossed the physical boundaries, there'd be no going back for either of us."

"I agree, but that doesn't make it wrong."

"We'd live in constant fear of being discovered, of someone, anyone finding out the truth," he continued with conviction. "We'd both make an effort, but it wouldn't be long before we'd be so desperate for each other that we'd be meeting in out-of-the-way spots—"

"We wouldn't," she cried, shaking her head in denial.

"Renting cheap hotel rooms," he added, and cringed inwardly at the thought. Catherine was too much a lady for clandestine meetings in dirty rooms. An affair would destroy the warm, generous woman he'd come to love. An affair would destroy them both. What had started out so pure and good would become tarnished and ugly. In the end it would devastate them both. He loved her too much to put her through that kind of heartache.

"No," she cried a second time, "we wouldn't let it go that far."

"Do you honestly think we'd be able to stop? Do you?" he demanded.

Catherine had gone terribly pale, so pale that Royce was tempted to take her by the hand and lead her to a chair before she collapsed. He was grateful when she chose to sit of her own accord.

"What about your transfer?" she asked, lifting her eyes to his.

Her gentle pleading was back, and it cut deep at his heart to deny her anything. If he had received the NATO assignment, although it meant they'd be separated by thousands of miles, the Navy restrictions would no longer apply.

"What I heard was a rumor," he reminded her, "nothing more. It's not going to happen." Kelly would be able to remain with him, but the blessings were mixed ones. His life with his daughter would go on without disruption, but he was going to be forced to drive the woman he loved out of his life.

"I see," she murmured, her words layered with defeat.

"What happened that Saturday night was entirely my fault." Royce felt he should admit that much. "I was so sure I was going to receive that transfer that I let matters go too far. Way too far. Monday morning I learned Commander Wayne Nelson out of San Diego had been given the assignment."

"It isn't necessary to assign blame."

In theory Royce agreed with her, but he wanted to accept the responsibility. He'd felt so close to Catherine that evening. Closer than he had to anyone ever. They'd kissed, and the sensation had struck him as powerfully as a bolt of lightning. It seemed melodramatic to compare her touch with the forces of nature, but Royce could think of no other way to describe it. His skin had felt branded by her gentleness, and his heart...his heart had swollen with a love so strong it left him weak and trembling. He'd never desired a woman more than he had Catherine that night.

It wasn't until later, after Royce learned that the NATO assignment had gone to an acquaintance of his, that he realized his mistake. He'd lowered his guard, allowed to happen what he'd promised himself never would. As a result, he was faced with an even more difficult problem than before.

"What about Kelly?" Catherine asked, her voice so thin he could barely hear her. Slowly she raised those same pleading eyes to his. She seemed to be saying how unfair it was to punish the little girl for something that was beyond Kelly's control.

Royce had learned early in life that the book on fair had yet to be written. He wanted to do what was right for his daughter, but he couldn't do or say anything that would mislead the ten-year-old into thinking there could be a relationship between him and Catherine.

"It's a delicate situation, and best left alone," he said reluctantly.

"No," Catherine argued with surprising strength. "I won't let you do it. I won't use Kelly…you have my word on that—but she needs a woman just now, and I… I seem to be the one she's reaching out to. Please, Royce…"

He hesitated. Saying no to Catherine was as difficult as refusing his own flesh and blood. "All right," he agreed, praying he was doing the right thing.

"We sat up all night and talked and talked and talked, and Catherine painted my toenails and she even let me paint hers."

"So you had a good time?"

"The best." Kelly squeezed him tight around the stomach. Friday night and all day Saturday the house had been as quiet as a tomb. Royce had aimlessly walked around feeling lost and alone. Kelly had spent the night with friends before, and he'd never felt as he had this time. This particular aloneness. Perhaps it was because he'd wanted to be with Catherine so much himself.

By noon, he found himself glancing at the clock every five minutes. When Catherine dropped Kelly off around three, it was all he could do not to run outside and greet her. Only it wasn't Kelly he was so eager to see.

It was Catherine.

Hell, he'd been a fool to think this was going to work.

"...I don't think she's feeling very well, though."

Royce heard the tail end of his daughter's comment as she blurted out the details of each and every minute she and Catherine had been together.

"What makes you say that?" Royce asked, trying to hide his concern behind a casual facade.

"We went shopping, and then...oh," Kelly cried excitedly, "I nearly forgot to show you, Catherine bought me a surprise. Just a minute and I'll go get it." Before he could divert Kelly back to his original question, she was racing up the stairs. Two minutes later, she returned wearing a pair of hot pink earmuffs. She put them on her head, then twirled around to show him the full effect.

"Aren't they cute?"

"Beautiful. Now what makes you think Catherine isn't feeling well?" Gone was the carefully concealed apprehension.

"Oh." Kelly frowned and removed the earmuffs. "After lunch we went out for Mexican food and Catherine ordered a chili something..."

"That explains it," Royce teased.

"No. She wasn't feeling bad until she got her mail. I think it had something to do with that. She opened a letter, and the next thing I knew she was staring out the window, looking real spacey. I think she might have been crying, but when I asked her, she said she had something in her eye."

The gutsy woman Royce knew wouldn't easily give in to tears unless something was drastically wrong.

Kelly hesitated. "I think she was crying, though...

I don't know. Catherine's not the type to let on about that sort of thing."

"What happened next?" he pressed, losing patience.

"Well, she made herself a cup of tea and said it was time to run me home. I didn't want to come back so soon, but I didn't say so because I knew she wanted to be alone."

"How did things go on the ride home?" Royce was beginning to feel like a detective, ferreting out each bit of information he could.

"She was real quiet. That's why I think she's not feeling very good."

Catherine was on Royce's mind for the remainder of the day. Hell, what was so unusual about that, he asked himself as he turned out the lights before heading up to bed. The beautiful Lieutenant Commander was in his mind about ninety-nine percent of the time, despite his best efforts to forget about her. Having Kelly chatter about her for hours on end certainly didn't help matters any.

Royce swore the kid had talked nonstop from the moment Catherine had let her off at the door. She'd repeated everything two and three times, so excited about every detail of their time together. Royce hadn't realized how much Kelly needed a mother's influence.

As was his habit, Royce read each night. It helped relax him. He expected to have a difficult time falling asleep, but as soon as he turned out the light, he felt himself effortlessly drifting off.

A phone call, especially one in the middle of the night, was never good news. It rang, waking Royce from a deep sleep. He groaned and groped for the receiver, dragging it across the empty pillow at his side.

"Yes?" he demanded.

Silence.

Royce scrambled into a sitting position. Something told him it was Catherine on the other end of the line. Some inner instinct.

"Catherine?" he asked, his heart racing. "Answer me. What's wrong?"

Seven

Catherine felt like an idiot, phoning Royce in the middle of the night. She didn't know what had prompted her to do anything so foolish, nor did she know what she intended to say once he picked up the receiver. As soon as he answered, she realized her folly and was about to disconnect the line when he called her name.

"H-how'd you know it was me?" She pushed the hair off her forehead and drew in soft, catching gasps in an effort to stop the flow of tears that refused to cease.

"It was a good guess," Royce admitted gently. "Now tell me what's wrong."

If only he'd been outraged, instead of caring. She might have been able to avoid telling him, but she needed him so desperately—as desperately as she'd ever needed anyone. "I'm fine, really I am," she lied. "It's just that I'm a little out of sorts and…" She couldn't admit to him she hadn't wept, really down-and-out wept in years, and once the tears had started, it was like a dam bursting over a restraining wall. Nothing she tried to do helped.

"Catherine, love, it's two-thirty in the morning. You wouldn't have phoned if everything was peachy keen."

She swallowed a sob and knew the noise she made sounded as though she were drowning, going underwater for the third and last time. "Thank you."

"For what?"

She gnawed on the corner of her lip and ran a tissue under her nose. "For calling me your love. I...need that right now." She was convinced he had no idea he'd used the affectionate term.

He hesitated, then gently pried again. "Are you going to tell me what's wrong?"

Catherine sat curled up on her sofa, her feet tucked beneath her. The pages of her mother's letter were scattered across the top of her coffee table. She'd moved the picture of her father down from the mantel and set it in front of her as well. For part of the night she'd held it to her breast and rocked to and fro in a frantic effort to hold on to him. The area around her was strewn with used tissues.

"Catherine," Royce repeated. "What's wrong?"

"I... I shouldn't have phoned. I'm sorry... I was going to hang up, but then you said my name."

"I'll be right over."

"Royce, no...please don't." She couldn't deal with him, not now. In addition, her apartment complex was full of Navy personnel. If anyone were to see Royce coming in or out of her apartment in the early hours of the morning, it could be disastrous.

"Then tell me what's troubling you."

Catherine reached for another tissue. "I got a letter from my mother..." she sobbed. A fresh batch of hot tears coursed down her face, streaking it with glistening trails of pain. Even now, hours after reading the letter, her mother's news had the power to wrench her heart. "You're going to think I'm so stupid to be this upset."

"I won't think anything of the sort."

"She's getting married. I don't expect you to understand...how can you when I don't understand myself... but it's like she's turning her back on my father after all these years. She loved him so much. She deserves to be happy but I can't help thinking...there'll be no one to remember...my dad."

"Just because your mother's marrying doesn't mean she's forgetting your father."

"I've been telling myself that all night, but it just doesn't seem to sink into my heart. I'm happy...for h-her." Catherine sobbed so hard her shoulders shook. "I'm really p-pleased. She's been dating Norman for ten years. It isn't that this is any surprise... I don't even know why I'm crying, but now I can't seem to stop. I feel like such a fool... I'm sorry I woke you. Please go back to sleep and forget I—"

"No," he whispered softly. "There's an old road off Byron Way. Just head north and you can't miss it. I'll meet you there in thirty minutes."

"Royce..." She meant to tell him to forget everything, that she was overreacting, behaving like an insecure child. Instead she found herself asking, "What about Kelly?"

"I'll have a friend come over. If he can't, I'll bring her along. Don't worry." The buzzing noise told her he'd hung up the receiver.

She shouldn't meet him. Catherine told herself that at least a dozen times as she drove down Byron Way. It wasn't fair to Royce to drag him out of bed in the middle of the night to an obscure road just because she couldn't deal with the fact her mother was marrying Norman. Dear, sweet Norman, who'd loved her mother for years and years, who'd patiently waited for her to love him enough to let go of the past.

Catherine managed to hold back the emotion while she struggled to find the road Royce had mentioned, but she felt as unstable as a hundred-year-old prairie farmhouse in a tornado. The first gust of wind and she'd collapse.

Royce was standing outside his car, waiting for her. The moonlight reflected off the hood, illuminating his face, which was creased with anxiety.

Catherine pulled off to the side of the road and turned off her engine. She didn't need a mirror to tell her she looked like hell warmed over, as her mother so often teased. Her eyes were red and swollen, and heaven only knew which direction her hair was pointing.

None of that seemed to matter when Royce walked over to her. He stared down on her as if she were a beauty queen, as if she were the most attractive woman in the world. His world. His eyes wandered over her face, and he raised his hand and caressed her cheek with his fingers.

If he hadn't been so gentle she might have been able to pull it off. She might have been able to convince him she was fine, thank him for his concern and then blithely drive away, no worse for wear. Royce destroyed her plans with his tenderness. He demolished her thin facade with a single look. Tears welled in her eyes, and she placed the tips of her fingers over her mouth in an effort to hold back the wails of grief and anguish that she had yet to fathom.

Royce reached for her then, pulling her into his arms. She went sobbing, banding her arms around his waist. She buried her face in his chest, not wanting him to know how hard she was weeping.

He led her to his Porsche and helped her inside, then joined her, taking her once more into the sanctuary of his arms. Again and again, he stroked the back of her head, again and again he whispered soothing words she couldn't hear over the sound of her own weeping. Again and again, he brushed his chin over the top of her head.

"It's all right," he whispered. "Go ahead and cry."

"I…can't seem to stop. Oh, Royce, I don't understand why I feel like this. I'm… I'm so afraid everyone is going to forget him. And it would be so unfair."

"You aren't going to forget."

"Don't you see?" she sobbed even harder. *"I don't remember anything about him."* Her throat was so thick she couldn't speak for several moments. "I was so young when he went away. Mom tried to help me remember. She told me story after story about all the things we used to do together and how much he loved us. As hard as I try I can't remember a single detail. Nothing."

"But he's alive here," Royce said gently, pressing a hand over her heart, "and that's all that matters."

Catherine wished it were that easy. But her emotions were far more complicated, as complicated as her love for Royce. Being in his arms, drinking in his strength and his comfort, helped to abate the tears.

"Kiss me," she pleaded, craving the healing balm of his love. "Just once and then… I promise I won't bother you again. I'll leave, and you can go back home."

He didn't hesitate. His hands were in her hair, his splayed fingers buried deep, angling her head so that his mouth could sweep down to capture hers the way a circling hawk comes after its prey.

Catherine sighed in appreciation, opening to him. Royce groaned, thrusting his tongue deep into the moist warmth of her mouth. She sighed anew and welcomed the spirals of heat that coiled in her stomach. Her hands gripped his shirt, holding on to him, needing the anchor of his love now more than ever before. The emotion that had been playing havoc with her senses all evening burst wide open and spilled over her like warm, melting honey.

Catherine whimpered.

Royce moaned softly, seeming to experience the same wonder. His hands roved over her back, dragging her forward until their hearts were pressed against each other's, each pounding out a chaotic rhythm of love and need.

When her breasts made contact with his chest, Catherine experienced a sensual hunger she had never known, a need that went beyond the physical. It was as if she were emotionally starved, as if the bleakness of her existence had been laid bare.

Royce's lips claimed hers a second time with an urgency that took her by surprise, his kiss of fierce possession, a deepening urgency, a ferocious hunger neither would be able to tolerate for long.

Royce must have sensed it, too, because he abruptly broke away, his chest heaving with the effort. Catherine longed to protest, but he raised his hand to her face and gently pressed his palm against her heated cheek. Her fingers covered his, and she closed her eyes, savoring this closeness.

When she looked up at him, she found him staring at her. Her eyes didn't waver from his. With unhurried ease, he bent forward and kissed her again, only this time his kiss was slow and tender, as slow and tender as the one before had been untamed and harsh.

"I want to taste you." The heat in his eyes and in his words caused her to shiver. His hands expertly parted her blouse, and when he discovered she wasn't wearing a bra, his eyes narrowed into blue slits. His hands cupped her breasts and lifted them until they'd formed perfect rounds in his palms. Her nipples had tightened even before he began stroking them with his thumbs. Catherine went still, afraid even to breathe, her eyes half-closed as she dealt with the intense pleasure his hands brought her. His mouth followed, and she rolled her head back and moaned even before his mouth closed over her nipple. With her eyes slammed shut, she arched her back. The impact was so keen, so intense, she longed to cry out.

All too soon his mouth returned to hers and she opened to him, greedily accepting what he was offering. Her hands slid along the curve of his back and up to the thickness of his mussed hair.

Royce's kisses were sweet and warm. Sweet and gentle; too gentle. He broke away completely and rubbed his face against the side of her jaw with a moist foray of nibbling kisses, working his way down her neckline.

"I want to make love to you," he whispered, then quickly amended. "I *need* to make love to you, but damn it all, Catherine, I refuse to do it in the front seat of a car."

With eyes still closed and her heart thundering like a Nebraska storm, she grinned. "Any bed will do."

"You're making this difficult."

"Has it ever been easy for us?"

"No," he growled, his hands continuing to caress her breasts. "You make me feel seventeen all over again."

"It's the car, trust me."

"Maybe." He shifted his weight and groaned, the sound rich and masculine. "I just hope the seamstress who sewed these pants took her job seriously."

Involuntarily, Catherine's gaze dropped to the bulge in his loins. Against her better judgment she trailed her knuckles over it, feeling the heat even through the thickness of his jeans.

The temptation was so powerful that she had to force herself to look away. She sighed, her shoulders lifted several inches with the effort.

Wrapping his arms around her, Royce pulled her toward him, until her back was cushioned by his chest. He leaned forward and slowly rotated his cheek over hers, nuzzling her ear with his nose. "Tell me about your mother."

Catherine grinned, content for the first time since the mail had arrived. "You'd like her. She's wonderfully witty and intelligent. To look at her, you'd never guess she's in her early fifties, almost everyone assumes she's at least ten years younger. The best part is that she's strikingly attractive and doesn't realize it. For the past fifteen years she's lived in San Francisco, and works at the corporate headquarters for this huge importing business. That's where she met Norman. He's a widower, and I swear he fell in love with Mom the minute they met. He's waited ten years for this day, and as much as I love my father, I can't begrudge Mom and Norman any happiness."

"It sounds like mother and daughter are a good deal alike," Royce murmured.

Catherine had to think on that a moment. "Yes, I suppose that's true... I just never thought much about it." Catherine hesitated, then added, "She loved my father."

"Loves," he corrected gently.

"Loves," Catherine agreed softly.

"You're close?"

"Always. She's incredible. If you meet her and still

think we're alike, then it would be the greatest compliment anyone could ever give me."

"I think you're incredible," he whispered, playfully nuzzling her neck. His arms were tightly wrapped around her middle, and she felt as though she were in the most secure place in all the world—in Royce's loving arms.

Content, Catherine smiled, folded her arms over his and closed her eyes. "What are we going to do, Royce?"

She felt the harsh sigh work its way across his chest. It was a question she was sure he'd asked himself a hundred times. One that had hounded them both for weeks, and they were no closer now to a solution than they had been before.

"I wish I knew." It went without saying that if they continued in this vein they were both going to be booted out of the Navy. "I never thought I'd be jealous of my own daughter."

"Of Kelly?" Catherine didn't understand.

"Yes, of Kelly." His grip around her middle tightened. "She, at least, can spend the night with you."

Catherine grinned and nestled back in his arms.

"How do you think I felt learning that you sleep in a little slip of lace that's all see-through on top?"

"She told you that?" Catherine asked, twisting around.

"Yes! Is it true?"

"Yes."

Royce groaned. "You could have lied… I wish you had lied."

"Did she also tell you I sleep on ivory-colored satin sheets?"

"No, she was merciful enough to skip over that part,"

he growled in her ear. "Oh, sweet heaven, it feels so good to hold you in my arms. I could get drunk on you."

Catherine was equally content, although she was likely to suffer in the morning. The console was digging into her hip, but it was a small price to pay for the pleasure of being in Royce's arms.

"You're going to be all right now?"

She nodded. "I don't know what came over me. Obviously I have a lot of unresolved feelings for my father."

"Don't get so philosophical. Your mother is letting go of an important part of your lives together. It's only natural for you to feel a certain amount of regret."

There was a lot more than regret in that raging storm of tears that overtook her, but Royce didn't know that. Catherine had yet to fully comprehend the blitz of feelings herself. Her emotions were hopelessly tangled. But it didn't matter, she could face anything or anyone as long as Royce was by her side, as long as the man she loved would hold her tight.

The orders Royce received to conduct an underway inspection aboard the USS *Venture,* a small service craft used by the base, seemed like a godsend. Royce needed time away from Bangor, and from Catherine. The time away was essential to his peace of mind. Three days aboard the *Venture* would help him gain some perspective on what was happening between them.

A hundred times he'd told himself to stay away from her. They were playing with a lit stick of dynamite. The fact they were both doing it with their eyes wide open frustrated him even more.

Royce had done everything he knew to get her out of his mind. He'd ignored her, pretended she didn't exist. When it came to dealing with her at the office, he made her a faceless name and tried to react to her that way. He'd had women under his command before without there ever being so much as a hint of a problem.

The difficulty was it didn't work. Royce couldn't ignore Catherine any more than he could jump over the moon. It was a physical impossibility. He couldn't look at her, even in the most impersonal way, and not hunger for the taste of her. It went without saying that a single taste would never satisfy him, and he knew it. He had to feel her, had to run his hands down the soft curving slopes of her body and experience for himself her ready response to his touch.

Some mornings he walked into the office and with one glance at her he'd been forced to knot his hands at his sides just to keep from reaching for her. The ache would start then and last all day and sometimes long into the night. Was it any wonder his men had come up with a few choice names for him while he was in his present state of mind?

The physical frustration was killing him, and as far as Royce could tell it was going to get a hell of a lot worse before it got better.

Just when Royce was foolish enough to believe he had everything under control, she'd called him, weeping in the middle of the night. If he hadn't been so starved for her, he might have been able to handle the situation differently. But the moment he'd heard her weep, the urge to take her in his arms and comfort her had been overwhelming. Already it was happening. What he swore never would. He arranged for them to meet in some out-of-the-way place where no one was likely to see them.

Royce justified the meeting, remembering how she'd been there for him when Kelly was in the hospital. Help-

ing her deal with the fact her mother was going to re-
marry was returning the kindness, nothing more.

To further vindicate his actions, he'd convinced himself that he'd have done the same thing for anyone under
his command. That might be true, but he doubted that
he'd meet them at the end of a long dirt road. Nor would
he hold and kiss them the way he did Catherine.

From that night forward, matters had only gotten
worse. Royce could feel his control slipping even more
than before. Twice he found himself looking for excuses
to call her into his office just so he could hear the sound
of her voice. It was coming to the point that she was
able to maintain protocol much better than he was. A
bad sign. A very bad sign.

Kelly wasn't helping matters any. If having to deal
with Catherine at the office wasn't bad enough, Kelly
talked about her constantly. The kid was crazy about
Catherine and had been from the moment they'd met.
At first Royce was convinced it was the fingernails, but
gradually, in a slow and painful process, he'd come to
realize how badly Kelly needed a mother figure. Why
she chose Catherine and not Missy's mom or any of the
mothers of her friends, Royce had yet to understand.
Instead she'd chosen the one woman who was driving
Royce slowly out of his mind.

This assignment aboard the *Venture* was exactly
what he needed. Time away.

Royce was packing his bag when Kelly wandered
into the bedroom. She plopped herself down on the
edge of the mattress and sighed as though she were
being abandoned.

"How long are you going to be gone?"

Royce had told her no less than four times, but she
continued to ask anyway. "Three days."

Kelly had wanted to spend the time with Catherine, but it made more sense for her to stay with Missy's family since the two girls were in the same class at school. Kelly hadn't been overly thrilled, but she hadn't argued. At least not any more than she usually did.

"When you get back, can we go for pizza?"

"Sure," Royce agreed, glancing up long enough to smile at her. He didn't know why she asked, they always went out to eat when he arrived home from an assignment. It had become tradition.

The phone rang, and Kelly leaped off the bed as though she'd received an electric shock. Even though Royce was less than three feet away, she screamed at the top of her voice, "I'll get it."

Inserting his little finger in his ear, Royce cleared the passageway and resumed packing.

Kelly appeared a minute or so later. "It's for you," she said, sounding disappointed. "It sounds like Captain Garland."

Royce nodded. "Tell him I'll be right there."

Royce finished tucking his socks into the corner of the bag and then went down the hallway. Kelly handed him the phone and leaned against the wall and waited until he'd finished.

The conversation with his commanding officer didn't last more than a couple of minutes. But each one of those minutes might as well have been a lifetime as far as Royce was concerned. What was it that was said about the best laid plans? He didn't know. Hell he didn't know much of anything anymore.

"What's wrong?" Kelly asked once he'd replaced the receiver.

"How do you know that anything's wrong?"

"Because you've got that look again."

Royce didn't know what she was talking about, and frankly he wasn't sure he cared to.

His daughter, however, was bent on telling him. "It's hard to explain," Kelly added on a thoughtful note. "It's a look you get when you're mad and trying not to show it. Your ears get red on the top and your mouth goes like this." She scrunched up her lips like an old prune.

"I never look like that," Royce told her with more than a suggestion of impatience.

"If you say so."

At least she was smart enough to know when not to argue with him, look or not. For that, Royce could be grateful.

He was halfway back to his room when he decided he might as well let Kelly know. "Catherine's coming along with me."

"She is?" Kelly sounded downright thrilled. "How come?"

"There's been a complaint of sexual harassment on board the *Venture* that she's going to investigate. Captain Garland felt it made sense to send us both up at the same time."

"He is the captain," the ten-year-old said with an air of great wisdom.

If Kelly thought to comfort him, she'd failed. Miserably.

It wasn't until they were both aboard the plane that Royce spoke to Catherine. She was sitting in the seat next to him, but he'd done his damnedest to ignore her. Not that it had done any good. Not that it ever did, but he liked to pretend otherwise.

"How'd you arrange this?" he demanded, his voice dripping with sarcasm.

"I didn't," she said, without looking up from the report she was reviewing. "I was ordered to accompany you." She made it sound as though she'd rather be anyplace else than sitting next to him.

Royce looked out the window, unexpectedly amused by her tart reply. Apparently she wasn't any more pleased about this than he was. Well that was par for the course as far as their relationship went.

"If it's any comfort to you I'll be away soon enough." There was a militant strain in her voice that challenged him.

Catherine was going away? It wasn't any comfort, in fact it was cause for alarm. "What do you mean?"

"I'll be attending my mother's wedding."

"I see." Royce hadn't seen the request yet, but he knew there wouldn't be any problem in granting her leave.

"Unfortunately that isn't going to help," he growled. The need to touch her, even in the smallest way, was so strong Royce couldn't fight it anymore. He moved his leg just enough so his calf could brush against hers. He nearly sighed in relief. Her skin felt silky and smooth, so smooth.

The movement, almost invisible to anyone else quickly captured Catherine's attention. She jerked her head up and frowned at him.

"Royce," she breathed, "what are you doing?"

"Looking for a way to get booted out of the Navy it seems."

She yanked her leg away, expelled a shuddering sigh and returned to the report she was reading. But Royce noticed that her hands were trembling.

Who was he kidding? If anyone was shaking it was he. It started that first afternoon on the track when

Catherine had refused to stop running, and it hadn't lessened since.

Royce laid back his head and closed his eyes. He needed to think. He'd come a hair's space from making love to her in the front seat of a car. He was meeting her on dirt roads. Now he was reduced to trying to feel her up while on a military transport.

He was in bad shape. Worse than he thought. Only a desperate man would have pulled that trick. Which said a lot about his mental condition. This assignment was going to be a hell of a lot more difficult than he'd imagined.

That thought proved to be more prophetic than Royce ever dreamed. The first day into the inspection he was so angry he walked around in a red haze. He wasn't civil to be around. It was so bad, he didn't even like himself. And for what reason? Because Lieutenant Commander Masterson had taken an instant liking to Catherine. The man had made his interest in her known from the moment they'd stepped on board the *Venture*.

Royce was making notes when he inadvertently happened upon Masterson talking to Catherine in the narrow hallway. He didn't like the familiar way in which the young lieutenant commander was leaning toward her. Nor did he appreciate the way the other man was looking at her as though he couldn't wait to get her into his bed.

"Are you finished with your report?" he demanded of Catherine.

"Not yet." She looked surprised that he'd even ask since the account of the complaint wasn't due for several days after their return.

"Then I suggest you start work on it."

"Yes, sir." She started to walk past him when Royce turned on Masterson, his eyes narrowed into dark slits. He couldn't remember a time he'd wanted to take a man down more.

"Problems?" Masterson asked innocently enough.

"This isn't the *Love Boat*, Lieutenant Commander," Royce said as scathingly as he could. "Captain Garland didn't ask Lieutenant Commander Fredrickson to accompany me for your entertainment."

The other man's eyes widened at the verbal attack.

"I suggest you keep your hands to yourself."

"But he didn't..." Catherine intervened, until Royce turned on her, making sure his eyes were hard enough to effectively silence her. She had no business speaking to him. No business defending Masterson, and that infuriated him even more.

"You're both dismissed," he said harshly, and waited until they'd retreated in opposite directions.

In the next twenty-four hours, Royce didn't say more than a handful of words to Catherine. In fact he was avoiding her. She was avoiding him, too. Like the plague. But then so was everyone else—not that he blamed them.

Royce was tired. Mentally and physically. But keyed up at the same time. Before heading off to bed, he decided to stop off in the galley for a cup of coffee. Caffeine sometimes helped to relax him.

He apparently wasn't the only one who needed something that night. Catherine sat at the table and glanced up when he appeared. She looked startled, as though she'd been caught doing something illegal.

"I'll leave," she said, slowly coming to her feet.

"No, stay," he returned crisply, walking over to the coffeepot.

"Is that an order?"

He had to think about it a moment. "Yes."

Her hands cupped the mug. Her gaze was centered on the steaming liquid as though something were about to leap out.

Royce poured himself a cup and sat down across from her. He didn't say anything for several moments, then decided now was as good a time as any to speak his mind. As bad a time as any for that matter. At least they were alone.

"I don't like the way Masterson's been looking at you," he admitted, frowning as he did so.

Catherine's head flew up so fast it was a wonder she didn't injure her neck.

"Lieutenant Commander Masterson?"

"Yes," he said roughly. He knew he sounded possessive, but he couldn't help himself. It had been eating at him from the moment they'd arrived. Mark Masterson had made a fool of himself over Catherine. Everyone had noticed. Certainly Catherine must have. Royce had even heard a couple of the men talking about the way Masterson had an eye for the ladies.

"You mean to say you've been acting like a...a..." Apparently she couldn't think of anything bad enough. "Like a moron because you're...jealous?" Her words were issued vehemently in a whisper.

"I have not been acting like a moron," he denied hotly, in the same low tones she used. "I have eyes."

"And what would you like me to do about it?"

Her words took Royce by surprise. He expected her to deny it, claim it was all in his head. He even thought she'd call him a fool for saying it. Okay, she'd called him a moron. That was close. What he hadn't anticipated was her acceptance of the problem.

"Well?" she demanded.

"What do I expect you to do about it?" he repeated. The answer came to him then, as profoundly as anything he'd ever felt. It was all so simple. It was all so complicated.

"Marrying me would settle it."

Eight

"You don't mean that," Catherine whispered, confident Royce's proposal had been prompted by a fit of jealous rage. She would never have guessed that Royce would be so insecure.

Sadly, Catherine couldn't deny that the lieutenant commander had gone out of his way to let her know he was interested. In what, she wasn't entirely sure. Mark Masterson had been more than attentive from the moment she and Royce had landed aboard the *Venture*. He hadn't done anything offensive, and under other circumstances Catherine might have been flattered. Certainly she'd done nothing to encourage his attention.

"The hell I don't mean it," Royce countered sharply, impatiently. His face was scowled in an intimidating frown that pleated his brow in thick folds.

"You don't need to shout at me."

Royce lowered his voice several decibels. "I am not yelling. Will you or won't you marry me?"

"I can't," she felt obliged to remind him. She was under his command, which was something he'd conveniently forgotten. Any relationship, other than one that involved Navy business, was strictly prohibited.

He knew it. She knew it. But for pride's sake Royce had chosen to overlook the fact.

Slowly Royce stiffened, as though anticipating a body blow, as if he were unsure of her and her love. "Would you marry me if it were possible?"

"Probably."

"Probably," he repeated, his eyes rounding. It was as though she'd issued him the greatest insult of his life.

"Yes, probably," she returned just as heatedly. "If the proposal weren't issued on the tail end of a fit of jealousy and…and if I were convinced to the soles of my feet that you loved me."

"I love you." This, too, was discharged as if he were tallying points in a heated debate. "So what's your answer? Yes or no?"

"Just like that?"

"Just like that." He made it sound as if there shouldn't be anything to consider, as if he were asking her out to dinner, instead of a complicated relationship that would involve disrupting both their lives, and Kelly's, not to mention their careers.

"Why?" she charged, "so I can inform Masterson I'm an engaged woman?"

"Yes," Royce confirmed without pause. His hands were cupped around his coffee with enough force to shatter the ceramic mug.

"Then thanks, but no thanks." Battling righteousness, Catherine stood abruptly, prepared to leave the room. How dare Royce offer her marriage in an effort to salvage his precious male pride. The only reason he'd even suggested it was out of concern she might be attracted to Mark Masterson. The ironic part of all this was that Royce had only recently tried to arrange a date for her with Dan Parker. In the space of a few short weeks, he'd gone from one extreme to another. Catherine didn't know what to expect next.

"What do you mean *no thanks?*" Royce demanded, leaping to his feet with enough force to topple his chair. Somehow he managed to catch it before it crashed to the floor.

"I don't know how much plainer I can make it, Commander. The answer is *no.*"

He looked positively stunned, as if she'd stepped forward and thrust a sword between his ribs. He'd been so sure of himself, so damned arrogant, as if it were a foregone conclusion she'd accept his offer of marriage without even needing to think it over. It hurt her pride that he'd proposed in such a callous manner with a complete lack of tenderness or romance.

"If and when I marry," she felt obliged to explain, "it will be to a man who doesn't behave like a jealous idiot. Someone who demonstrates his love with a tad more finesse than to shout out a proposal in a ship's galley because he's afraid someone else might do it before he gets the chance. Now, if you'll excuse me, I'm going to my stateroom." With that she stalked away.

To her dismay, Royce followed her down the long, narrow passageway. He was so close behind her, Catherine feared he was about to step on her heels. She hadn't a clue what he intended to say or how far he planned on following her. Outside her quarters, she vaulted around and confronted him.

"You wanted to say something?" she demanded.

"You're damn right I do."

In all the time Catherine had worked with Royce, she'd never seen him like this, as though he'd been driven to the very limit of his endurance.

"Might I suggest we discuss this at a more appropriate time, Commander," she said, her voice bordering on impertinence. She'd gone about as far as she dared with Royce, but she couldn't, wouldn't allow him to pull rank on her with an issue that was strictly personal.

"No, you may not." After looking both ways, he opened the door to her quarters and gently pushed her inside.

"What the hell do you think you're doing?" she insisted.

Royce didn't answer her. Instead he backed her against the bulkhead. His large, muscular hands settled over her shoulders, dragging her against him. Her struggles were of little good against his superior strength. Arching her back was a mistake as well. It only served to bring the lower half of her body in intimate contact with his. She was about to cry out in protest when his mouth smothered hers, his lips ruthlessly grinding over hers. Immediately his tongue was there, flickering softly over her lips, coaxing them open. Catherine fought him, fought herself for as long as she could hold out, which was a humiliatingly short time. With tears crowding her eyes, she parted her lips, welcoming the intrusion of his tongue, meeting it with her own. Royce groaned when she opened to him, and her moans of outrage and anger quickly became soft cries of bliss.

"Royce!" she cried, jerking her head to one side. Her shoulders heaved with the effort. "Are you crazy?"

"Yes." He didn't bother to deny it. Gradually he released her and took a moment to compose himself. "I have no excuse for this. Forgive me, Catherine." No sooner had the words been spoken when he was gone, leaving her to wonder if anyone had witnessed him coming out of her quarters.

* * *

Marilyn Fredrickson moved around the kitchen, her silk robe knotted at her trim waist. As Catherine watched her mother, she was struck anew by what an attractive woman Marilyn was. Petite, beautiful and intuitive, far more intuitive than Catherine remembered.

Marilyn brought the coffeepot around the kitchen counter where Catherine was sitting on a high stool. She, too, was dressed in her housecoat, her hair mussed. Catherine loved her mother's kitchen more every time she came to visit. It was painted a light shade of cheery yellow, with bright sunlight spilling in from the three skylights overhead. The counters were white with a huge wicker basket of dried flowers decorating the corner.

"So are you going to tell me about him?" Marilyn asked, slipping onto the stool next to Catherine.

She hadn't mentioned a word about Royce. Her flight from Seattle had landed late the night before. Her mother and Norman had picked her up at the airport, and they'd driven directly to the condo in San Francisco's refurbished Marina District. Catherine and her mother had stayed up half the night, but all the talk had evolved around her mother and Norman. Not once had Catherine mentioned Royce.

"About who?" she asked innocently, not sure even now she could talk about him.

Her mother's smile was chiding. She raised the coffee cup to her lips and took a sip, then sighed. "I remember the day Norman asked me to marry him. It wasn't the first time, mind you, but he hadn't pressed me in more than a year. I asked for more time, the way I always do. Ever the gentleman, Norman accepted that, but then he said something he never had before. He said he loved me, and always would, but he explained that a man only has so much patience. He was tired of living his life alone, tired of dreaming of having me for his wife one day. Then he asked me if I truly loved him."

"You do." Catherine already knew the answer to that.

"Of course I do, I have for years." Marilyn paused once more for another drink of her coffee, which gave her time to compose her thoughts, it seemed. "That night as I was getting ready for bed, I stood in front of the bathroom mirror to remove my makeup. As I stared at my reflection I realized there was a certain look about me, a certain... I hesitate to use this word, readiness."

"Readiness," Catherine repeated.

"Yes. Right then and there I realized what a fool I'd been to wait so many years to marry Norman. The time was right to accept his proposal, it had been right for a good long while, only I hadn't realized it. I couldn't even wait until morning, I phoned him right then." Her lips quivered gently with a smile. "I took one look at you this morning, Catherine, and there's a certain look about you not unlike the one I saw in myself."

"Readiness?" Catherine joked.

"No, not that. You have the look of a woman in love, but one who doesn't know what she's going to do. Do you want to talk about it?"

"I...don't know." Catherine had left for California shortly after her return to Bangor from the *Venture*. She hadn't seen Royce in three days prior to her departure, nor had she spoken to him since that one horrible night aboard the Navy vessel. Every time she thought about Royce's marriage proposal, she was forced to wade through a mine field of negative emotions, each one threatening to explode in her face.

Her mother was watching her closely, and Catherine realized she owed her some explanation. "There are difficulties."

"Is he married?"

Her startled gaze flew to Marilyn's. "Nothing that drastic."

"I take it he's in the Navy?"

Catherine nodded. "That's the problem. He's the executive officer, my boss."

Her mother knew what that meant without Catherine needing to explain it. The dark brown eyes narrowed slightly. "Oh, Catherine, sweetie, you do like to live dangerously, don't you?"

"It wasn't like I planned to fall in love with him," she cried, defending herself. No one in their right mind would purposely put themselves through this torment.

"Does he return your feelings?"

"I think so." After the night he'd met her on the dirt road, Catherine was convinced she'd never question the way he felt about her. Then he'd pulled that stunt aboard the *Venture* and she was left sinking with doubts.

"You think so?" Marilyn repeated slowly, thoughtfully. It seemed her mother was incredulous that Catherine wouldn't know something this important.

"He loves me," she amended.

"He just has a difficult time showing it?"

"Exactly." Catherine replayed the latest incident and how he'd followed her into her cabin. It had been a foolish risk that might have cost them both dearly.

"I take it you rejected his marriage proposal?"

"Of course I did. He asked for all the wrong reasons."

"But if he asked for all the right ones, what would you have said?"

"Honest to God truth?" Catherine asked.

"Honest to God truth."

"Yes. In a heartbeat. Oh, Mom, I'm so crazy about this guy—I don't know what's right anymore. I never dreamed I'd defy Navy regulations. It's simply not done. Yet here we are so crazy in love we're acting like complete idiots, risking our careers and our reputations and everything else I always thought was so important... I still think is important.

"I know Royce was upset that I'd been assigned to accompany him on the *Venture.* He'd wanted this time apart to gain some perspective about us and our relationship. At least I assume that was what he intended. Then I was ordered to accompany him, and it made everything much worse. Everything seems to be working against us."

"What's going to happen when you return?"

Catherine sighed and slowly shook her head. "I wish I knew."

"Royce...that's his name?" At Catherine's nod, Marilyn continued. "He'll have the time you seem to think he needs."

"But, Mom," Catherine said, feeling more miserable than ever, "if he does decide it would be best for us to marry, it won't help matters any. We'd both continue to paddle in the same leaky boat as before."

"But if you marry Royce, won't you give up the Navy?"

"No," she cried vehemently. "Why should I? I love the military. I'm not about to relinquish an eleven-year investment just because I happen to fall in love. And getting out of the Navy isn't all that easy, either. It takes up to a year, unless I were to find myself pregnant."

Marilyn's eyebrows shot toward her hairline.

"Oh, Mother, honestly. There's no possibility."

"I'm sorry, sweetie, it's just that I'd love to have grandchildren someday."

"I'll do my best—someday."

Marilyn rested her elbows on the counter and released an elongated sigh. "I hadn't realized getting out of the Navy would be such a hassle."

"I'm not leaving the Navy," Catherine reinforced.

"So what's going to happen?"

Her mother asked the question as though Catherine kept a crystal ball in her pocket and consulted it regularly. "The only thing either one of us can do is put in a request for a transfer."

"But you just moved to Bangor from Hawaii."

"I know. It isn't likely the Navy will look favorably upon shipping me elsewhere anytime soon."

"What about Royce? Can he put in a request?"

Catherine bit into her lower lip. It was a thought she'd entertained often, although she'd never spoken to Royce about it. "Yes, but I don't know that he will. He's been stationed at Bangor for several years now, and he'd hate to uproot Kelly. It's the only home she's ever known. Of course there's always the chance he'd be reassigned to one of the other commands in the Puget Sound area. We can hope, of course."

"Kelly? Who's Kelly?"

Catherine doubted that her mother had heard anything beyond the point that she'd mentioned Royce's daughter's name. "His daughter. She's ten and oh, Mom, she is such a delight. We get along so well. She's just at the age where she's discovering what it means to be a girl. It all started with me painting her fingernails when she was hurt in an accident. We've gotten so close. The last time we met, Kelly wanted her hair cut, so I took her to a salon and stood over the hairdresser like an old mother hen. When she'd finished, Kelly looked so cute."

"You're spending a lot of time with her, I take it?"

"As much as I can," Catherine said, and hesitated. "You're wearing that worried look again."

"I can't help it," Marilyn murmured. "I don't want to see you get hurt."

"I won't," Catherine assured her with more confidence than she was feeling. "Now quit being such a worrywart. This is your wedding day, and I certainly don't want you looking all serious and somber fretting about me." Catherine took a sip of her coffee and glanced at her watch. "Oh, my goodness," she said, sliding off the stool. "Look at the time! We've got to get ready, or you'll be late for your own wedding. Norman will never forgive me."

The wedding was lovely. Her mother made a radiant bride, Catherine mused during the plane trip on the way back to Seattle. Norman had never looked more distinguished or handsome. The two, backed with long years of steady friendship, were the ideal couple. Catherine had heard several people say as much as she wandered through the reception, making sure everyone had what they needed. Norman had insisted the affair be catered, but Catherine had made busywork in an effort to keep herself absorbed. If she'd sat back and relaxed, there might have been time to think about the young, handsome man in the photograph that rested on her fireplace mantel. The father she'd never known.

It was ironic that Catherine would be better acquainted with her new stepfather than the man who'd given her life.

When it came time for her mother and Norman to

exchange their vows, Catherine had felt a sudden rush of emotion crowd her eyes. A tear or two did manage to slip down her cheek as she stood beside her mother, clenching a floral bouquet. If anyone noticed, and Catherine prayed they didn't, she sincerely hoped they assumed it was a tear of shared happiness.

Catherine *was* happy for her mother and Norman. Even more so now that she'd experienced these few days with them. It was almost comical watching the two. They were like young lovers, so involved with each other the rest of the world didn't seem to exist.

In many ways Catherine was envious. Her love for Royce was so much more complicated.

As the Boeing 737 cut a wide path through the thick layer of clouds, Catherine couldn't help wondering what kind of reception Royce would have for her upon her return. Would he be pleased she was back? Would his eyes search hers out so she'd know how much he'd missed her? Would he find an excuse to be alone with her? Or would the brick facade he so often carried be tightly locked in place? So secure he'd look right through her and reveal little of what he was thinking and none of what he was feeling.

Catherine was exhausted when the plane landed at Sea-Tac. When she walked off the jetway into the airport terminal, she found her gaze scanning the crowds, hoping that Royce would be there waiting for her.

He wasn't.

It was ridiculous to expect him. As far as she knew, he wasn't even aware of her flight schedule. Then why, she asked herself, did she experience this heavy letdown?

"You're an idiot," she whispered as she walked down the concourse to the baggage claim area.

Again she reminded herself what a fool she was when she unlocked her apartment door over an hour later, after she'd picked Sambo up from the neighbor's. To her disappointment, there wasn't anything on her answering machine from Royce, either. Kelly had left two messages. The first call was to tell Catherine that her story about the Princess and the Dragon had been chosen by her teachers for the Young Authors Program. Kelly was so excited and had been talking so fast it was difficult to understand her. The second message had been made that afternoon, Catherine decided, and the purpose was to tell her Kelly missed her and wished she'd hurry back soon.

Catherine toyed with the idea of phoning the ten-year-old, then noted the time and realized Royce's daughter was probably already asleep for the night. It was unlikely that he'd appreciate the intrusion.

Nevertheless, she couldn't give up the idea. Five minutes later, against her better judgment, she found herself reaching for the phone.

It was Royce who answered. His voice was as rich and masculine as ever, and just hearing it sent goose bumps up her spine.

"It's Catherine," she said, managing to keep any emotion out of her voice, "I'm calling for Kelly."

He hesitated, as though she'd caught him off guard. "She went to bed about half an hour ago."

The tension crackled over the telephone wire like static electricity. "Will you tell her I phoned?"

"Of course."

Catherine closed her eyes against the lack of sentiment in his voice. It was as if he were speaking to a casual acquaintance and not the woman he'd once claimed

he loved. Once, only once, and then it had come as part
of a jealous rage.

"I... I won't keep you then," she announced stiffly.

"You aren't keeping me from anything more than
television." His control had slipped just a little, as if he
were reluctant to disconnect the line. For that, at least,
Catherine could be grateful.

"How was the wedding?" he asked, as though looking for ways to make polite conversation.

"Beautiful," she told him, meaning it.

"How were you?"

He didn't need to explain the question. He was asking how she'd dealt with the emotions she'd had so much
trouble accepting when she'd first learned her mother
intended to marry Norman.

Involuntarily, Catherine's gaze drifted to her fireplace mantel. "Fine," she whispered. She'd dealt with it
splendidly, far better than she'd expected. "Mom made
a beautiful bride." Once more there was a noticeable
silence. He'd done his part, now it was her turn. "How
did everything go at the office?"

"There weren't any problems."

"Good," she whispered. "I'll be back in the morning."

"So I understand."

Say something, Catherine pleaded silently. *Let me
know what you're feeling. Tell me you missed me as
dreadfully as I missed you. Tell me you regret that we
parted without settling our differences.*

Nothing. The line went so quiet that for a moment all
Catherine could hear was the sound of her own breathing.

"I'll see you in the morning," she said, when it became apparent Royce had no intention of continuing the stilted conversation.

"Right...in the morning." How clipped he sounded, how eager to be rid of her, but all changed abruptly when he said, "Good night, Catherine."

There was such hunger in those few words, such longing. "Good night," she responded softly.

She pressed the receiver more closely to her ear when she heard him call her name.

"Yes," she said, trying hard to disguise the eagerness in her voice. She sounded like a silly schoolgirl and couldn't have cared less.

"About Mark Masterson."

"Yes?" Her eyes drifted closed, ready to savor his words of apology, ready to apologize herself, anything that would dislodge this ten-foot wall between them. This wall of pride and pain.

"He phoned for you while you were away." Royce's voice hardened until each word fell like a chip of concrete against a hammer.

"Lieutenant Commander Masterson?" Catherine had trouble believing it. She'd done everything possible to discourage the *Venture*'s officer. Catherine couldn't understand why Mark, who had recently gone through a divorce, would turn to her.

"He left a number where you can get in touch with him."

"I have no intention of contacting him," she confirmed, in case Royce suspected she was even remotely interested in the other man.

"What you do or don't do is none of my concern." The hard note in his voice progressed to a savage undertone. "You're free to do as you wish."

"Do you honestly want me to date him?" she challenged, losing patience with Royce.

"What I want isn't a concern here. Masterson left a message for you. Why he chose to contact me to give it to you is anyone's guess. Apparently he's going to be in Bangor sometime soon. Heaven only knows how he arranged that, but he did, and he told me to let you know he'll be looking for you."

"What's that supposed to mean?" Catherine demanded.

"You can put your own connotation on it because I assure you I don't have a clue."

"I'll bet you don't," Catherine muttered.

"I beg your pardon."

"You heard me, Royce Nyland." The tension between them was stretched beyond the breaking point.

"Listen, Catherine, if you're waiting for me to tell you you're free to date Masterson, then you've got it. Feel free. There's nothing between us."

Catherine was so hurt and angry, she started to shake. "Is that a fact? Well, I must admit I find that interesting. One minute you're demanding I marry you, and in the next you're practically ordering me to date another man." She was so upset, she could feel her anger overwhelming her good sense. Sucking in a giant breath, she forced herself to stop before she said something she'd regret. "The dirt road off Byron Way," she said, as calmly as she could manage. "Meet me there in half an hour."

She didn't wait for him to confirm or deny his being there, but replaced the receiver.

She was walking toward the door when the phone started to ring. Ignoring it, she reached for her coat and purse and walked out of her apartment.

Forty minutes later, Catherine was standing outside her car, her hands stuffed in the pockets of her jacket, searching the night for Royce's headlights. She'd just about given up hope when she saw his car come barreling down the road. At least she assumed it was Royce.

He turned off the engine and leaped out of the car and stood there. For all his rush, he didn't seem to have a thing to say.

For that matter, Catherine didn't, either. They stood staring at each other, the moonlight cascading over them like a golden waterfall, splashing light on either side of them.

He looked dreadful, as though he hadn't slept in days. His face was stern and harsh, as austere as she'd ever seen it. Her gaze slid to his. It seemed for a moment that he wanted to avoid looking at her, but apparently something compelled him to meet her gaze, but he did so reluctantly. Catherine gasped softly at the way his deep, cobalt-blue eyes plunged into hers as though he would have drowned just looking at her.

"Oh, Royce," she whispered, stepping toward him, stretching out her arms. Her heart was so full of love she would cry if he didn't hold her soon.

He met her halfway, wrapping his arms around her waist and lifting her off the ground. With a growl, his mouth met hers in a frenzy of need and desire. They were so starved for each other that an eternity passed before either of them stopped to breathe.

Royce buried his face in the curve of her neck. "I'm sorry, so sorry," he chanted. "I've never been so insanely jealous in my life. I don't know how to deal with it. I've behaved like a fool."

Catherine's hands framed his face. "Just be quiet and kiss me," she ordered ruggedly against his lips.

She slipped her tongue forward to meet his, not giving him the opportunity to argue if that had ever been his intention.

If Royce was holding back anything in reserve, he gave it to her then. With a deep-throated moan, he tightened his arms around her, flattening her breasts to his chest. Catherine could feel every part of him, every fiber of his military issue coat, every button, every crease. The kiss was the most primitive they'd shared. The most punishing. Catherine opened to him, and his tongue met hers.

She coiled her arms around his neck and slid down his front. Apparently she became too heavy for him because he lowered her feet to the frozen ground. His hand ran down the length of her spine and then intimately over the curve of her hip. He continued to slide his hands up and down her sides as though he couldn't get enough of her, as though he couldn't believe even now that she was his.

Catherine felt as though the whole world was spinning. It didn't matter. Nothing did as long as she was in his arms.

In the middle of the sweetest, hottest, most intimate kiss of her life, Royce reluctantly tore his mouth away from her. She was gratified to note that his breathing was as labored as her own.

"This doesn't settle anything," he whispered, his breath mingling with hers. His eyes remained closed as though he didn't possess the strength to refuse her anything.

"You're right," she whispered, "but it sure as hell helps." With that she directed his mouth back to her own.

Nine

"**I** need to get back. I left Kelly at the neighbor's," Royce whispered close to Catherine's ear. They were snuggled up in the front seat of Royce's car, her back against his chest with Royce's arms draped around her. They'd spent the last hour just this way, savoring these stolen moments, not wanting to part for fear of how long it would be before they'd have the chance to hold each other again.

"I need to get back, too," Catherine admitted reluctantly, but neither of them seemed in any hurry to leave.

"One last kiss?" Royce suggested, while spreading nibbling kisses down the side of her ivory neck, pausing now and again to swirl the moist tip of his tongue around her earlobe.

"You wanted a single kiss a half hour ago," she reminded him in a low whisper, "and the next thing I know my bra is missing and you're cursing because you can't find the zipper in my pants."

"That was your fault."

"Mine?" Catherine was indignant. He'd been all over her. They'd been all over each other, so hungry with need it was a gnawing ache in the pit of her stomach still. If it hadn't been for the gearshift, Catherine was convinced they'd have made love several times over by now.

"Yes, your fault," Royce repeated huskily. "If you didn't have such beautiful, tempting breasts." His hands slid up from her midriff to rest against the undersides of her fullness. His hands were close enough to reignite the achy, hollow feeling within her. Her breath escaped in a trickle as his thumbs lazily grazed her throbbing nipples.

"All right," she agreed softly. "Just one kiss." She arched her back and strained upward until her mouth unerringly found his.

Royce claimed her lips roughly, reeling her senses into oblivion. As his mouth worked over hers, his hands roved under her sweater after what seemed like an excruciating delay. Catherine moaned at the sheer wonder of his touch. Royce's tongue breached the barrier of her lips, probing, promising, as his hands caressed the weighted fullness of her breasts, kneading the heated flesh.

Soon Catherine was panting with primitive needs that curled deep inside her. "We're steaming up the windows again," she told him, knowing full well it was their moans and sighs as much as their breaths that were misting the car windows. It was becoming increasingly difficult to rein in their desires, and each time they were together, it became more of a strain, more of a struggle. Catherine had never felt more wanton. Never more wanting.

"The windows are the least of our problems," Royce said in a husky murmur.

She threaded her fingers through his hair and arched

upwards, loving him so much she felt drunk with the emotion.

Royce lifted his weight, but his knee slammed hard against the gearshift. He cursed under his breath and rubbed the injured part of his leg. "I'm getting too old for this," he complained.

"We're both too old for this."

"I'm pleased you agree." His hands were at the band of her wool slacks. His touch was warm, and his lips, against the underside of her chin, were decidedly hot. A fluttery sensation rippled over her skin as he slipped the button at the side of her hip free and eased the zipper downward. The sound buzzed in the close confines of the car like a roaring chain saw. Catherine's heart was pounding just as loudly.

Royce was convinced there was a limit to how much sexual frustration one man could endure. He'd reached it the night before with Catherine in the front seat of his car. *The front seat of his car.* The thought was a sobering one. A man who'd reached the age of thirty-seven shouldn't be attempting to make love in a car seat. There was something ideologically wrong with that.

Only the physical restrictions had prevented him from taking Catherine. If he'd possessed any talent as a contortionist he might have been able to manage it, but he was long past the age of attempting acrobatics.

Royce, however, promised himself he'd never buy a two-seater vehicle again. Never. No matter how sporty looking it was.

That thought was sobering as well. Everything he'd predicted about his and Catherine's relationship was coming to pass. Everything he'd feared. They were already meeting in out-of-the-way places. The sad fact was, Royce knew he wouldn't be able to handle any more sessions like the one they'd recently shared.

The next step was the hotel room. He'd been ready for one the night before. He'd been so incredibly hot for Catherine, he hadn't given a thought to propriety. If the circumstances had been somewhat different he would have driven Catherine to the nearest hotel and damned the consequences. He'd needed her, had wanted her that desperately.

He hadn't, of course, and consequently he'd been trying to forget about his unspent passion for the past twelve hours, with little success.

Once they'd gotten past the physical aspect of their need, or as near to satisfying it as was possible, they'd held each other for another hour and talked.

Royce was amazed that they could find so much to talk about and not mention the one thing that was on both their minds.

What the hell were they going to do?

Royce didn't know. Catherine apparently didn't, either.

Sitting back from his desk, Royce rolled a pen between his palms as he pondered the situation between him and Catherine for the hundredth time that day.

The office was unusually quiet. Everyone had gone home for the day, which was just as well. Catherine was due back from a court session anytime. Royce had left word for her to come directly to his office.

He was anxious to see her. When the hell wasn't he anxious to see her, he asked himself caustically.

It was her eyes, he decided. She had the darkest, most expressive eyes of any woman he'd ever met. They were wistful eyes, that clearly spelled out her thoughts.

And, if he could read her thoughts, then surely everyone else could, too.

How were they supposed to combat that? Royce knotted his hands into tight fists of frustration. He wasn't any closer to finding a solution now than he had been weeks earlier when the problem first presented itself.

Catherine's eyes were also the most provocative ones he'd ever encountered. She'd look up and smile at him, that secret, sexy smile, and then her eyes would meet his, and Royce swore she told him everything she hungered for in a single look. Apparently she found her own thoughts embarrassing because she'd start to blush and her eyelashes would flutter and she'd quickly glance away. It was all Royce could do not to make love to her then and there.

If there was anything to be grateful for, Royce realized, it was that she'd yet to give him that look while in the office.

The polite knock at his door cut into Royce's thoughts. He recognized the short, abrupt rap as Catherine's.

"Come in," he called out.

She stepped inside the room and automatically closed the door. "You wanted to see me?"

He noted that her gaze just missed meeting his. Royce didn't know whether to be grateful or not. Matters being as they were, he probably should be.

"Sit down, Lieutenant Commander."

Her gaze briefly skidded to his, and he knew she was attempting to read his mood. Generally he didn't refer to her by her rank unless he was attempting to put some distance between them.

Catherine pulled out the chair and sat down.

Royce had spent a good portion of the day struggling

with the problems between them, trying to formulate a solution. He wasn't any closer now than the time he first accepted his feelings for Catherine weren't going to go away. It was either deal with them now or later. And later could prove risky to their careers.

"How are you?" he asked, not knowing exactly where to start. Asking about her health was a stall tactic and not one he employed often.

"Fine. And you?"

"Well." As well as could be expected under the circumstances, he amended mentally.

Her fingers were clenched tightly in her lap, and she flexed and unflexed them a couple of times in nervous anticipation. Royce wondered briefly why she should be so ill at ease. Then he realized that the only times he'd ever called her into his office it had been to reprimand her for one thing or another.

"Relax, Catherine," he said, lowering his own guard. "We need to talk, and this seemed to be the safest place." And the most dangerous, but Royce felt it essential to clear the air between them. To do it without the physical temptations clouding their judgments as had so often happened in the past. The only other place he could think to speak to her was the jogging track, and he couldn't be assured of privacy there.

"I was thinking we needed to talk, too," she said, her voice little more than a faint murmur.

"Then it looks like we've come to similar conclusions."

Her beautiful, expressive eyes shot to his, and he could read her alarm as clearly as if she'd spelled it out.

"W-what have you decided?" she asked outright.

If only Royce could reach a conclusion. "I haven't," he admitted with heavy reluctance. "I thought I'd have a chance to sort everything out while I was aboard the *Venture*. When that didn't pan out, I was hoping to have some time to think while you were with your mother." He'd soon discovered, however, that he missed her too much to be objective.

"I thought I might be able to do some thinking my-self," Catherine interjected softly.

"And did you come to any decisions?"

She hesitated, as though she wasn't sure she should voice them. "Only that the...way I feel toward you isn't going to change."

There was a grim sort of satisfaction knowing that. It didn't solve anything, but it soothed his battered ego to hear her admit this wasn't just a sexual thing between them, founded on good old-fashioned lust. He'd considered that aspect himself. He'd been without a woman since Sandy's death, and perhaps his body was starting to play cruel tricks on him. It had been a cause for concern, but one quickly dismissed.

"I want a month," he stated decisively.

"I beg your pardon?" She blinked and scooted to the edge of her seat as though she wasn't sure she'd heard him correctly and was straining to understand.

"I need a month. Right now our feelings for each other are running high." That was putting it mildly. A blacksmith's poker was less hot than they were for each other.

"H-how do you mean?"

"No contact except what's absolutely necessary here at the office. Nothing more. Not even a phone call. I want us to remain as separate as we can and still work in the same command."

Catherine considered the suggestion for a moment, then nodded. "That sounds fair."

"I realize it's going to be difficult for us both."

"But necessary," she added, sounding as reluctant as he felt.

"Unfortunately, it is necessary," Royce agreed. "We can't go on the way we have."

"Something's got to be done."

At least on that they were of one accord.

"What about Kelly?" Catherine asked, her beautiful eyes bright with concern.

"Kelly," Royce repeated in a slow exercise. His daughter was a problem. He'd never seen her take to anyone the way she had Catherine. If he was going to force Kelly not to see Catherine for an entire month, he was likely to have a revolt on his hands. Yet he didn't know how he could maintain his distance from Catherine with Kelly spending time with her. He considered the situation a moment longer, then decided. "As you were quick to remind me not so long ago, it wouldn't be fair to punish her for a problem between us."

Catherine lowered her eyes, and her shoulders sagged as though she were greatly relieved. "Thank you."

"We can set up a time now to talk in exactly one month." He leaned forward and flipped forward the pages of his calendar, finding the date and marking it.

She stood, her eyes somber and determined. "One month," she repeated on her way out the door.

Catherine had known from the moment Royce asked for a month's separation that it wasn't going to be easy. What she hadn't understood was exactly how difficult it would be.

She found herself watching him far more than she ever had before, hungry for contact with him. Each time they were in the same room together, her heart was bathed in a strange blend of emotions. On one hand he was her executive officer, the man she'd been trained to obey without question, without hesitation. On the other hand, he was the man she loved. Mere words were an injustice to describe the strength of what she felt for Royce. She ached for him emotionally and physically. Some nights she'd walk into her apartment so mentally exhausted from this silent battle of longing between them that it was all she could do to feed Sambo.

If this time apart was trying for her, and God knew it was, then it was equally difficult for Royce. They never spoke, not unless it was absolutely necessary. Yet they couldn't be anywhere close to each other without that throbbing awareness breaking out between them. They could be standing in a room filled with other people, yet the intimacy between them was as strong as anything Catherine had ever known. The air was thick and the sensations undeniable.

The first test of their self-imposed restriction came within the first week. Commander Dan Parker stopped Catherine outside the building one chilly afternoon. She'd stayed late working on a complicated case, knowing it was safe to do so since Royce had already left the office. Catherine assumed he'd gone down to the jogging track, as was his habit.

"Hello, Catherine," Dan greeted, strolling purposely toward her.

Catherine envied his carefree smile, and despite everything, found herself responding to it. He must have found encouragement in it, because he paused and asked, "Since you've already rejected my offer to the Birthday Ball, how about soothing my battered ego by agreeing to have dinner with me?"

To be honest, Catherine hadn't given the gala event

more than a passing thought since the first time he'd mentioned it. She should give some thought to the ball, but her thoughts were far from festive. "Dinner... when?"

"What's wrong with tonight?"

"I can't," she answered automatically. Dan seemed to be waiting for an excuse, but she had none to offer. "I'm busy," she answered finally. Busy missing Royce. Busy being miserable. Busy pretending how busy I am.

"It is short notice," Dan admitted. "How about tomorrow night then, after work? We'll unwind over drinks."

Catherine had no reason to refuse. She was convinced Dan had guessed her and Royce's feelings for each other, and although it would be out of the question to discuss the situation, Dan might be able to give her some insight into Royce's personality.

"All right," she agreed, but there wasn't a lot of enthusiasm in her voice.

"Five o'clock at the Yachting Club?"

"Sure, that sounds great."

"Come on, I'll walk you to your car," Dan offered, pressing his hand at her elbow. The comfort Catherine felt at his touch, however impersonal, was enough to bring a rush of surprising tears to her eyes. She managed to blink them away, embarrassed at the unexpected show of emotion.

They were walking toward the asphalt lot, when Royce appeared from out of nowhere. He rounded the corner in a dead run and nearly collided with them. He stopped abruptly, his breath coming in deep gasps.

"Sorry," he said, leaned forward and balanced his hands on his knees. "I didn't think there was anyone left around here."

"No problem," Dan assured him.

Slowly Royce straightened. His eyes avoided look-ing at Catherine. "What are you doing here so late?"

Dan chuckled and possessively moved his hand up Catherine's back to cup her shoulder. "Talking Cather-ine into having dinner with me, what else?" Dan joked. "You don't honestly believe I'd stick around this late for Navy business, do you?"

Although everything seemed perfectly normal on the surface, Catherine was well aware of the way Royce's body tensed. The undercurrent between them was so strong she was about to drown in it.

"I see," Royce said, his smile decidedly forced. "I take it our very capable attorney has agreed."

"Not without my having to twist her arm, but once again the Parker charm has won out."

Royce raised his hand in a friendly gesture. "Then don't let me delay you any longer," he said cheerfully. "Have a good time."

"We're going to have a great time," Dan returned, squeezing Catherine's shoulder.

"Good night," Royce said, looking away, but before his eyes left them, Catherine noted that he dragged his gaze across her lips.

"'Night," Dan murmured. The minute Royce was out of view, he demurely dropped his arm. "I'll meet you tomorrow," he said, grinning, and left.

Catherine stood exactly where she was for several seconds. She didn't know what game Dan Parker was playing, let alone the rules. All she did know was that she had to speak to Royce. Had to explain why she'd agreed to spend time with Dan Parker.

Royce had gone into the building, and not standing

around to debate the wisdom of her actions, she followed him inside.

She found him sitting at his desk, his back to her as he stared off into the distance.

"Royce," she said softly, wondering if it would have been better to greet him formally.

He didn't answer her. The silence seemed to stretch for a hundred miles.

"Royce?" she tried again. "Could we talk for just a minute? I know we agreed not to, but I feel… I wanted you to know why I…"

"I already know why," he said in a loud voice, then lowered his voice and swiveled his chair around. "There's no need to explain."

"But…" To her he looked so pale, beaten. Vulnerable.

"We agreed on one month," he reminded her, but the words didn't come easily from his lips.

"Yes, I know." Still she couldn't make herself leave. It felt so good to be in the same room with him, to talk even if it was only for a few moments on a subject that was painful to them both.

Blue eyes sparred with deep, dark ones in a silent, loving battle of wills.

"Catherine, for the love of God, just leave," he begged in a whisper.

"I can't.…"

"As your XO I demand that you go."

The silence returned, this time punctuated with pain. Knowing she was defeated, Catherine crisply saluted, turned and abruptly left.

Catherine didn't see Royce for the next three days. Her appointment with Dan, she hesitated to call it a date, was much ado about nothing. He was charming, undemanding and a perfect gentleman the entire time. Not once did he raise the subject of Royce, and for that, Catherine was grateful enough to agree to see him again sometime soon. They left the date open, another fact for which Catherine was thankful.

Time had never passed so slowly. Catherine had come to her decision the first week. She loved Royce, and wanted to be his wife. What they'd need to do to arrange their marriage, if indeed that was what Royce chose, was another matter entirely. She loved him, she loved Kelly, but she loved the Navy, too.

As did Royce.

Being a part of the military was more than their career choice, it was a way of life each had freely embraced. Her commission was just as important to her as Royce's was to him. Both their careers were bright, with room for advancement. Several years down the road, Catherine could easily envision Royce progressing through the ranks. For her part, Catherine hoped to become a judge. Falling in love, marrying and having a family shouldn't mean they had to jeopardize their careers.

It did mean changes would have to be made, however. Complex changes, as complicated as their love for each other.

Catherine's thoughts were interrupted by the phone. Sambo wove his furry, overfed body between her feet as she stood in the kitchen in front of the can opener. While still holding the can of moist cat food, she reached for the phone. Her intention was to continue feeding Sambo, who could be downright insistent, and talk at the same time.

"Hello."

"Catherine?"

She immediately recognized the small, trembling voice as belonging to Kelly.

"What's the matter?" she asked immediately.

"I'm not afraid."

"Of course you're not," Catherine said, abandoning the cat food entirely. "Tell me what's wrong."

"Dad's not here."

"Yes, I know." Royce was away at scheduled meetings for most of the week. "Isn't Cindy or one of the other neighbor girls with you?" Whenever Royce was going to be away, he paid one of the high-school girls in the neighborhood to come and stay with Kelly.

"Cindy's supposed to be."

"But she's not?" Catherine pried gently.

"Her mom's sick and needs her there. Cindy called and wanted me to go over to her house, but I didn't want to do that because I don't want the flu. I hate throwing up."

Catherine grinned, empathizing with that. "I don't blame you, but there really should be someone with you."

"I'm ten years old!" Kelly declared forcefully. "I'm not a baby anymore."

"I know, sweetheart, but there's no telling how long your father's going to be and it's much more fun to have someone stay with you than to be alone."

"Are you alone?"

That was a trick question if Catherine ever heard one. "Sambo's with me."

"A-are you afraid in the dark?" The question was made in the same trembling voice Kelly had used earlier.

"Sometimes," Catherine admitted. "Why?"

"B-because all the lights went out."

Catherine's heart tripped with concern. "You mean to tell me you're all alone in the dark?" Somehow she managed to curtail her anxiety.

"Yes." Once again Kelly's voice was small and weak. "I'm sure the electricity will come back soon, it's just that it's so-o dark."

"Your dad will be there anytime." Catherine hoped some confidence leaked into her voice. The thought of Kelly pretending to be brave brought out a strong motherly instinct in Catherine.

"Dad's probably on his way now," Kelly said, but she didn't sound any too sure of it. "But in case he isn't...do you think you could come over and stay with me until he gets here? I'm not afraid, really I'm not... I'm just a little bit lonely." She paused and sucked in a deep breath. "It wouldn't be too much trouble for you to come, would it?"

Catherine didn't so much as hesitate. "I'll be there in ten minutes." She hung up the receiver and had already reached for her coat when Sambo reminded her he had yet to be fed. Hurrying across the kitchen, Catherine placed the can of food directly on the floor. Sambo was appeased, but he let it be known he didn't appreciate her haphazard methods of serving him his evening meal.

When Catherine arrived, her headlights silhouetted Kelly, standing in the window with the drapes pulled back, waiting. The minute Catherine turned off the engine, the drape swished back into place. Kelly was standing at the front door waiting for her.

"Hello, sweetheart," Catherine greeted.

Kelly's small arms circled her waist and hung on tightly. "I'm glad you're here. I'm not scared or anything."

"Yes, I know," Catherine said, a smile curving the

corners of her mouth. The house was pitch-black. "When did the electricity go off?"

"Just a little before I called you." Kelly aimed the flashlight across the living room. "Dad keeps this one handy in the top kitchen drawer, and I found it right away."

"You were a clever girl."

"You really think so?" Kelly sounded proud of herself.

With her hand on Royce's daughter's shoulder, they advanced into the family room and sat down on the sectional together. Kelly chatted easily, as though it had been ages and ages since they'd last talked, which in fact had been several days.

There was a peacefulness that settled over the area, and the dark, which had once seemed so intimidating and uninviting, began to feel like a welcome friend.

Kelly must have sensed it, too. She placed the back of her hand against her mouth and yawned loudly.

"Are you tired?"

"Not really," Kelly answered just before she yawned a second time, but she snuggled closer to Catherine, propping her head in Catherine's lap. Within minutes the measured, even sounds of Kelly's breathing convinced her the girl was sound asleep.

Catherine must have drifted off herself, because the next thing she knew the lights were on. Straightening, she rubbed the sleep from her face just as Royce walked in from the kitchen.

He stopped abruptly and frowned. "What are you doing here?"

Ten

"Kelly was alone," Catherine explained in a husky whisper. "The lights went out and she was afraid." Royce looked shocked, as though he were viewing a ghost. She was certainly the last person he expected to stumble upon in his own home.

Carefully, so as not to waken the slumbering youngster, Catherine gingerly moved from the sectional. She reached for her coat and purse. "Now that you're here, I'll go." She removed the afghan from the back of the sectional and spread it across Kelly, who was dozing peacefully.

"What happened to Cindy?" Royce wanted to know before she left. His mouth had twisted into a tight line of impatience, and Catherine didn't doubt that the teenager was out of a job.

"Her mother came down with a bad case of the flu and she needed her there. She did phone and ask Kelly to walk over to her house."

"It's six blocks. I don't want my daughter traipsing around in the dark." Once more his mouth tightened.

"Kelly didn't go because she hates throwing up."

Royce frowned.

"She didn't want to catch the flu," Catherine explained.

The tight features relaxed, and the two shared a warm smile that seemed to arch between them like two ends of a magical rainbow. It had been so long since they'd shared something so intimate. So long since they'd lowered their guards to allow themselves the simple pleasure. Their eyes met and held for the longest moment. Their breaths seemed to echo each other's. Half a room separated them, and yet it was as though they were standing close enough to touch. A thought Catherine found infinitely appealing. There was security in Royce's arms. Security and love.

It was Royce who dragged his eyes away. His hands were buried deep within his pockets. Catherine would have liked to believe he'd placed them there to keep from reaching for her.

"It was good of you to come by," Royce said evenly.

"It wasn't any problem." The only problem was loving him so much and having to pretend otherwise, even when they were alone together. Such pretense went against the very core of her nature.

Royce followed her into the entryway, stepped ahead, then paused, his hand on the doorknob. His back was to her when he hesitated. "How was your dinner with Dan?"

The question caught her by surprise. Idle curiosity was the last thing she expected from Royce. In addition, she'd nearly forgotten that she'd ever gone out with the commander.

"Forget I asked that," Royce stated gruffly, and jerked open the door.

"Dinner was very good. The company, however, was charming, but decidedly uninteresting."

Royce raked his fingers through his hair and kept his gaze lowered. "Are you going out with him again?"

"No."

Royce's eyes, round and dubious, flew up to meet hers. "Why not?"

Catherine felt as though the weight of the entire world were pressing down upon her shoulders. Royce honestly seemed to need to know why she had no interest in dating another man. Had she been so lacking in communicating her love? Had she failed in letting him know that he was the very reason she lived and breathed? Didn't he understand that she was prepared to risk everything that was important to her for him?

"You want to know why I'm not dating Dan?" she asked, having trouble hiding how incredible she found the question. "Because, you idiot," she said, battling the urge to sock him, "I'm in love with you."

Royce stood directly in front of her, blocking the door. His eyes, his beautiful blue eyes, drank thirstily from hers, as if it had been years instead of hours since he'd last seen her.

"I shouldn't have asked that." His words were low and dark, laced with a thread of anger, as though he was furious with himself for his lack of control.

"It doesn't matter, really it doesn't," she countered softly, her voice as thin and delicate as the fluttering of her heart.

"Your love matters to me." His eyes lowered to linger on her mouth.

Catherine thought she'd go crazy if he didn't soon kiss her. She wanted him so much that she could taste the desire building within her. It circled her like a binding rope, imprisoning her.

Royce lifted his hand, and his movements were so

slow and deliberate. He touched her face, his fingers gently caressing her cheek as if he were blind and was acquainting himself with her. His touch, so light and tender, seemed to reach all the way to her soul. Nothing could have prepared her for the utter beauty of it, the sheer magnitude of these precious, silent moments.

Royce must have felt it, too, the intensity of it. The beauty of it. He was breathing hard when he pulled his hand away, much too hard for such a nondemanding task.

"Thank you for coming," he said, jerking the door open.

"Royce." She wouldn't let him send her away, not again. Not when she needed him so desperately.

"Please...just go." The words were wrenched from him. Sagging with defeat, Catherine did as he requested.

Catherine had dreaded the Birthday Ball all week. She wasn't in any mood to celebrate. Nor was she in the frame of mind to socialize and stand idly by while Royce waltzed around the room with one woman after another. Not when she so longed to be the one in his arms.

She hadn't talked to him since the night she'd gone to be with Kelly. These days were by far the most miserably long ones of her life. It was as if their brief moments together had been ripped out of time. Royce hadn't spoken to her, hadn't looked at her, hadn't acknowledged her.

Catherine had talked to Kelly only once on the phone, hungering all the while for some word from Royce. Something. Anything.

The situation didn't seem to be going any better for him. In the past few days he'd been in one bear of a mood. Half the time it seemed as if he was looking for an excuse to slam his fist through a wall. He wore his bad-boy image as tightly as a glove. It fit him well.

It had taken Catherine only one week of this trial time to make several valid perceptions. She now accepted the fact she was in love with Royce Nyland. But she'd known that before this self-imposed restriction.

She'd also realized that if he asked her to marry him, even if the proposal came on the tail end of a bout of jealousy, or a bout of anything, she'd accept.

What she hadn't anticipated was this heart-wrenching loneliness. The silence that had once fit so comfortably in her life, she now found deafening and painfully disturbing. The pleasure of her own company was sadly lacking. A hundred times, in a hundred different ways she found herself missing Royce even more than she had in the beginning. Since the night with Kelly, she missed the looks they'd often shared, the strong communication between them that made words superfluous. The throaty sound of his laughter. Oh, how she loved hearing him laugh.

She saw him every day, walked past him, spoke to him as if he meant nothing to her, as if they were little more than casual acquaintances. If she found it hard to continue the sham before, it was doubly so now. Painfully so.

Following through with this charade was difficult enough during the day, but to purposely expose herself to it for this Birthday Ball was a challenge she dreaded.

Catherine was forced to admit, however, how beautiful everything was. The orchestra was playing on the opposite end of the room while a mirrored ball hung overhead, casting reflections of warm light about the room. Romance, music, muted light surrounded the couples that circled the polished dance floor. From a distance they resembled graceful swans coasting on a mirrored lake. It was all so beautiful. So splendid.

Catherine stood on the outer edges of the crowd and looked on, admiring the handsome men dressed in either their dress uniforms or tuxedos. The women wore a variety of gowns. Catherine had chosen to wear the formal evening dress uniform with a long straight skirt of navy blue, with matching jacket.

It wasn't until she'd arrived that she understood her choice of outfit for the evening. She needed to remember she was in the Navy. All too often of late, she'd wanted to disregard the pledges she'd made when she accepted her commission. Love seemed far more important than the rules and regulations, which only went to prove how dangerously shaky her thinking was becoming. Royce was right. They needed this time apart, and since he seemed determined to use every one of these thirty days, she had no recourse but to stand by patiently until he'd come to a decision.

Catherine arrived. Royce noticed her the moment she walked in the door. It was as if everything came to a sudden, grinding halt. The music faded, the dancers went still, even the lights seemed to have dimmed. Royce stood, frozen. An air-raid alarm wouldn't have budged him. He simply stood and watched her, soaking in every delicate nuance of her. She was lovely, so breathtakingly lovely that she quite literally held him spellbound. He'd missed her. Dear Lord, how he'd missed her. He felt as though it had been a thousand years since he'd held her in his arms, a thousand years since he'd tasted her lips. Royce was so damned hungry for her that he would have gratefully accepted a few stolen moments alone even if it meant sitting in the front seat of his Porsche on a lonely deserted road.

"Evening, Nyland."

Royce turned to find himself face-to-face with Admiral Duffy. "Good evening, sir," he said, having trouble even then pulling his eyes away from Catherine.

Catherine found herself scanning the dancers, watching, searching. She wasn't fooling herself, she knew who she was looking to find. She didn't see Royce, at least not at first. It wasn't until later, after she'd gotten herself a cup of punch and was wandering around chatting with casual acquaintances that she found him.

He was across the room from her, involved in a conversation with two other men. The first was the admiral, she could tell that much. The second man was turned at an angle so Catherine couldn't identify him, not that it mattered. Royce captured her full attention.

She knew she was cheating on their promise to each other to be watching him the way she was. But the pleasure she found compensated by far for any feelings of guilt.

Royce was different from when she'd first met him, she mused, extraordinarily pleased by the realization. The changes had been subtle over the weeks, but nevertheless they were there. His features remained harsh, though they relaxed more often into a smile than they used to. He would always possess the same rugged appeal, that wasn't likely to ever change. But there was now a serenity about him, she noted, that had been missing when they'd first met, a tranquillity.

Again Catherine experienced a greedy sense of pride, knowing her love was what had made the difference.

"Lieutenant Commander."

The voice behind her was friendly and familiar. "Good evening, Elaine."

Her secretary was dressed in a red velvet gown and stood next to a tall middle-aged lieutenant, who Catherine recognized immediately as Elaine's husband. "This is my husband, Ralph Perkins."

"How do you do?" Catherine said, extending a hand to the man who played such a large role in her secretary's life. "Your wife is as valuable as my right hand."

"Oh, I know," Ralph said in a smooth Southern drawl that caused Catherine to think of antebellum homes with wide sweeping lawns and warm pecan pie fresh from the oven. "I couldn't get along without her, myself."

The three chatted a few minutes longer, before Elaine and her husband headed for the dance floor. For a few moments, Catherine watched them, envious of their freedom to express their love and enjoyment of each other. As she continued to hold on to her punch glass, Catherine's gaze drifted to the floor while she gathered her strength. She was going to need it if she were to make it through this night. When she felt strong enough, she looked over to where she'd last seen Royce.

He was gone. Experiencing a momentary sense of anxiety, she glanced around the room. She couldn't find him anywhere. She searched once again, scanning the crowded ballroom, her gaze moving from one area to another until she happened to catch a glimmer of dark hair and blue eyes when he swirled past her.

Royce was dancing, Catherine realized. Dancing. And it wasn't likely that it was the admiral in his arms.

Catherine had to stop and carefully analyze her feelings. Envy. She would have dearly loved to be the woman in Royce's arms. But she doubted that they would have been able to pull it off. Not tonight, not here with the admirals and captains and all the big mucky-mucks looking on. She was envious, yes, but not jealous.

Royce circled past her a second time, the music crescendoing to a loud climax. Immediately Catherine recognized the white-haired woman in his arms as Admiral Duffy's wife. She felt a little better, knowing the woman was happily married and had been for thirty years. It was little comfort, damn little, but it helped.

Her eyes were on Royce when she felt someone move next to her. "Hello, Catherine."

"Good evening, Dan," she greeted, doing her best to sound friendly. Despite the fact Dan enjoyed playing the role of devil's advocate, Catherine couldn't help liking him. He knew how she felt about Royce and was probably equally knowledgeable of Royce's feelings toward her. But the three of them chose to pretend otherwise. It was amazing when she stopped to think about it.

"Have you saved a dance for me?"

"I… I…"

"More excuses?" he asked with a knowing smile.

"If you don't mind, I'd rather sit this one out."

"My heart is mortally wounded, but I'm becoming accustomed to you knocking my ego around like a tennis ball."

Catherine grinned at the image that sprang readily to her mind. If anyone's heart had been abused, it was her own. And Royce's. Involuntarily, her gaze moved back to him. He really did look…

…she looked distressed. It was ridiculous to waltz around the dance floor with the admiral's wife in his arms and calculate every step so he could watch Dan

Parker make a move on Catherine. Ridiculous or not, that was exactly what Royce was doing.

At one time, he'd actually encouraged Dan to ask Catherine out. It had been a futile attempt to stop what was happening between him and Catherine. He couldn't believe he'd done anything so stupid. It wouldn't have worked. There'd never been the slightest possibility of that, but at the time he'd been desperate. He could still remember how angry Catherine had been at him, how she'd walked into his office, her eyes sparking with outrage and fury.

A good deal of water had passed under the bridge since then. The waters of discernment, the waters of perception. What he felt for Catherine was real. Strong. Heady. He hadn't meant to fall in love. He'd avoided love for years. Struggled with it, contested the fact it was possible for a man and woman to truly love each other. His first taste of it had left a bitter aftertaste, and he wasn't eager to experience it again.

"You needn't have turned Dan down, you know."

Breathless emotion clenched Catherine's heart when she realized it was Royce who was speaking to her. She whirled around to discover him standing only a few feet away.

"It wouldn't have mattered," he assured her.

Her heart beat mercilessly against her ribs. She blinked as though she wasn't sure she should trust herself not to have conjured him up. Her emotions were exhausted. Her nerves shot. This charade was killing her in inches.

"Shall we?" Royce held out his arms to her.

Catherine didn't question the right or wrong of them holding each other on the dance floor. Nor did she object when he slipped his arms around her waist. It was as though they'd been partnering each other for years. Their bodies were in perfect sync, they moved in flawless harmony, swaying naturally, rhythmically to the music.

Catherine's eyes held his, so greedy for the opportunity to study him that she didn't care what he could read in her eyes or who saw them. Nothing mattered but Royce. Her life had been a confused jumble from the time she'd first met Royce Nyland. Why should anything be different now?

"Why do you have to be the most beautiful woman here tonight?" Royce whispered the question close to her ear.

"It's in the genes, what can I tell you?" Catherine teased, and was rewarded by the feel of his mouth smiling against her hair. She knew he was holding her closer than he should, but she couldn't bring herself to ease away.

"I'd give everything I possess to be able to kiss you right now."

Catherine's response was half moan, half sigh. Unfortunately, she was feeling much the same thing herself. She dared to look into his eyes and was rewarded with the promise of sensual delights. For sanity's sake she quickly looked away, but it didn't prevent a hot flush to her cheeks.

"I don't think it's a good idea for you to say things like that...at least not here."

"Oh, and why's that?"

"Royce," she groaned, "you know why. Oh, stop, please stop...someone might notice." His hands were on her waist, and he was dragging her even closer, to a more solid intimacy. Her body was aligned with his in such a way, she could feel every subtle, and not so subtle, part of him.

"Let them look," Royce challenged, his words a low growl in her ear.

"But…"

His lips brushed her cheek. "Do you think I care?"

"Yes," she cried. "We both care."

"Not anymore." Once again his lips bounced lightly against her forehead.

"What…do you mean?"

"I mean there're reasons for us to do this sort of thing without worry, without fearing the consequences."

Catherine's heart clashed like two giant cymbals beating together. Holding her breath, she eased her head back so she could examine his face. His eyes readily met hers, and Catherine gasped softly at what she saw. Love. A love so strong and so determined that it would survive whatever they had yet to face. Royce loved her, with a love that defied logic, defied description. A love that was destined to be the moving force behind what remained of their lives. Neither one of them would ever be the same. Neither one of them would want to be the same.

"I love you so damn much."

Catherine closed her eyes to battle back a flood of feelings so strong they threatened to overwhelm her.

"We're getting married," he announced next.

The very eyes that had drifted shut only a moment earlier, shot open. "When? How?"

Royce laughed, that same throaty, hoarse laugh that had haunted her sleep for nearly two weeks. "I haven't got that part figured out yet, but I'm working on it. It seems, my dear, sensible wife-to-be that I'm about to be transferred."

"When? Where?"

"That's something else that has yet to be decided, but it's in the works."

He was so close, too close, but she needed that, needed the reality of him holding her in his arms even if they were supposed to be dancing. The fact their feet were barely moving didn't seem to concern either of them.

"When did you find out?"

"Tonight," he told her. "Shortly after you arrived. I was watching you, wanting you so much my heart was about to burst wide open when Admiral Duffy decided now was as good a time to tell me my request had been granted. He'd apparently been in contact with the detailers in Washington, D.C."

"You asked for a transfer...you never said—"

"I couldn't go on the way we were."

"Oh, Royce." She'd been watching him this evening, too. She longed to tell him how she'd looked for him the moment she arrived, hungry for the sight of him. But her throat was too thick. She'd tell him later when she could speak without the threat of tears.

"I want you, Catherine, by my side for the next fifty years. I want to make love to you so often they'll need another category in *The Guinness Book of Records*. When I wake up in the mornings, I want you sleeping at my side."

"Oh, Royce."

"Right now I want to kiss you so damn much that I'd be willing to risk shocking every man and woman in this room." His voice had grown reedy with impatience. "Let's get out of here before I do forget where we are and do exactly as my instincts demand."

"Oh, Royce."

"Frankly," he teased, his mouth tantalizingly close to her ear, "I don't remember you having such a limited vocabulary." The music stopped, but he didn't release her. If anything his hold grew more possessive.

"Royce," she hissed, "be good." She feared anyone even remotely glancing at them would immediately know what they felt for each other.

"I want to be bad," he whispered seductively. "Do you want to be bad with me?"

"Oh, yes…"

"Good, then we agree. Now let's leave before someone arrests me for thinking what I'm thinking."

Slowly, with enough reluctance to make her heart long to sing, Royce lowered his arms and released her. "Get your coat and meet me in the parking lot." A lazy grin slashed his mouth. "By now I'm sure you know which car is mine."

"Royce, I…do you honestly think…" Catherine pulled herself up short. "Just exactly how bad do you want to be?"

He chuckled. "I love it when you blush. I don't think I've ever found a woman more appealing than you are right this moment."

"I think you're crazy."

"We both are."

He left her then, hurrying across the room to make his excuses and gather his own coat. Catherine didn't linger. Within a few moments she was outside, searching through a sea of parked cars for Royce's. Before she could spot his black Porsche, he pulled to a fast stop directly in front of her.

The passenger door opened, and Catherine slipped inside. She had barely had time to sit down when Royce reached for her chin, directing her mouth to his for a surprisingly brief, but thorough kiss.

"Royce," she cried, alarmed. "What are you doing?"

"Kissing you." He took advantage of her open mouth by giving her a fleeting taste of his tongue. Despite the fact there could be several important people watching them who wouldn't take kindly to this public display of affection between two officers, one subordinate to the other, Catherine found herself drifting toward him.

"Hold on," he said, shifting gears so hard and fast they ground angrily. The car shot forward. Royce didn't take her far. Just to the other end of the parking lot where it was dark and private. "There's no need to be so impatient," he said, reaching for her even as he spoke. "You're going to have the opportunity to make love to me every night for the rest of our lives."

Eleven

"Have you gone out of your mind?" Catherine demanded with a free-flowing happiness that refused to be contained.

Royce eased to a stop at the red light, leaned over and kissed her soundly. Once more he used his tongue to tantalize and tease. His eyes were closed when he pulled away. "I am crazy," he murmured, unwilling to deny it, "crazy in love with you."

Catherine felt as though she were in a haze. "I can't believe this is happening."

"Believe it."

The light changed, but Catherine was convinced that, had it stayed red much longer, Royce would have reached for her a second time.

"Just where are you taking me?" The joy seemed to bubble out of her like fizz from an expensive bottle of champagne. If Royce had claimed he was headed for the moon, she would have held on for the ride.

"My house," he told her without hesitating.

"Your house," she repeated slowly.

"Kelly's going to want to be in on this. If we wait until morning to tell her, she'll be furious." Royce's gaze momentarily drifted away from the road, and his rugged features relaxed into a coaxing smile. "I'm convinced Kelly knew there was going to be something between us even before we did."

Catherine sighed and rested her head against the hard cushion of Royce's shoulder. It felt so incredibly good to be with him, so incredibly wonderful. There was nothing in this world to describe it.

A couple of minutes later, Royce eased his Porsche to a stop in his driveway. He turned off the engine and in one smooth movement reached for her. He kissed her hard and fast, and Catherine kissed him back with every ounce of her being.

Royce moaned as he deepened the contact. His tongue dipped to hungrily drink from her love. His hands were in her hair, and when he drew himself away, it was as though he were forcing himself to walk away from the gates of paradise.

"Let's go inside," he suggested, as though they'd best do it soon or else pay the piper.

Catherine nodded. At the moment, formulating words was beyond her passion-drugged brain.

The babysitter, a neighborhood teenager, was slouched across the sectional in the family room, watching television and drinking Pepsi. She looked mildly surprised to see Royce home so early. Her gaze left Royce and rested with candid curiosity on Catherine.

"Kelly's asleep," the teenager explained, her gaze drifting away from Catherine long enough to speak to Royce.

"Fine, thanks for coming, Cindy," Royce said, pulling out the money to pay her. He walked her to the door, opening it for her. "Goodbye, now."

"Bye." Cindy peeked around the door at Catherine

one last time. She raised her hand. "Bye," she said, directing the comment to her.

"Bye," Catherine said, raising her fingertips.

Royce eased the door closed and locked it after the teenager. When he turned back, his smile was gone. He murmured something Catherine couldn't understand. "I apologize for not introducing you, but there's a very good reason I don't want Cindy to know who you are." He rammed all ten fingers through his hair in an exercise of ill-gained patience. "Although heaven knows she's probably already guessed."

"Don't worry about it." Catherine stepped forward and pressed the tips of her fingers over his mouth. It didn't take much for her to figure out that Cindy was the daughter of someone who could make trouble for them. "I'm not going to let anything or anyone ruin this night."

Gripping her by the shoulders, Royce braced his forehead against hers. "Have I told you how much I love you?"

"Yes, but I'd be willing to listen to it again if you're inclined to tell me."

"I'm inclined," he murmured, his mouth brushing hers. "Get ready because it's going to take me a lifetime to say it properly."

They kissed again. The moment was gentle and sweet, so sweet that Catherine had trouble believing everything that was happening between them was real.

"I better get Kelly," Royce said, unwillingly easing himself from her. "While I still have the strength to pull away from you."

Catherine didn't know who found it more difficult, Royce or her.

"Wait here," Royce said, positioning her at the bottom of the carpeted stairs. "I'll be back in just a moment." He kissed her once more and raced up the stairs, taking them two and three at a time. Catherine could hear Royce talking to Kelly, but as far as she could tell the conversation was strictly one-sided.

Royce appeared at the top of the stairs a few moments later, a sleeping Kelly draped over his shoulder. The youngster had on her robe, one patterned with the faces of her favorite rock group, and her feet were dangling with hastily donned fuzzy slippers.

"Kelly?" Catherine coaxed softly. "Your father and I have something important to tell you."

Yawning, the sleepy-eyed girl slowly lifted her head from her father's shoulder. "Catherine?"

"I told you she was here," Royce reminded his daughter.

Rubbing her eyes with small fists, Kelly straightened. "But you said Catherine couldn't come over anymore. I'm not supposed to phone her or even say her name unless you tell me it's all right first."

Royce looked downright chagrined. He cast an apologetic glance to Catherine, cleared his throat and explained, "Your name came up far too often."

"No, it didn't," Kelly denied, placing her head back down on Royce's shoulder as he carried her down the stairs.

"That's all going to change," Catherine told the youngster. "Real soon."

"I asked Catherine if she'd marry me, and she's agreed," Royce said. A brilliant smile sat contentedly at the edges of his mouth.

Kelly's head came off Royce's shoulder so fast it was downright comical. "You're going to marry Catherine?" she cried, then squeezed her dad around the neck. Royce's shining eyes met Catherine's, and he stuck out his tongue as though he were in danger of being strangled.

"Oh, Catherine, I'm so happy." Kelly broke away from her father, twisted around and reached for Catherine, squeezing her equally hard. "I can't believe it! This is the happiest day of my whole, entire life. I'm not dreaming, am I?"

"No, sweetheart," Royce said, sharing an intimate look with Catherine, "this is very real." He set a squirming Kelly down on the carpet.

"This is great. This is *really* great." Kelly slapped her hands hard against the sides of her legs. "What I want to know is what took you guys so long?"

"Ah..." Catherine hesitated.

"I realize there were a few minor problems, but as far as I could see you both stretched everything way out of proportion. Heaven knows how long it would have taken you to come to your senses if it hadn't been for me."

"That's true," Royce agreed, looking to Catherine and poignantly rolling his eyes. He moved to her side and slipped his arm around her shoulder with a casual easiness that suggested he'd been doing so for a good long while. "The thing is, sweetheart," Royce said, his eyes dark and serious, "we're going to have to keep this a secret. Understand?" The entire wedding would need to be handled discreetly.

Kelly nodded, then pretended to zip her lip closed.

"When?" Kelly demanded.

Royce's gaze caught Catherine's. "Soon, I hope."

"Great. Now, listen, we don't have a whole lot of time to waste with this." The ten-year-old stalked into the living room, sat down and crossed her legs. "Well, come here," she said, gesturing for them to follow her.

Catherine and Royce stared blankly at each other.

"Come here," Kelly repeated when they hesitated. "We don't have all night, you know."

"Exactly what is it you want to talk to us about?" Royce demanded.

"What else is there to discuss?" Kelly cried. "My baby sister!"

"Ah..." Catherine's gaze darted to Royce, who did a good job of looking as stumped as she. Children. Kelly wanted to discuss enlarging their family when they hadn't decided on a wedding date. Good heavens, Catherine had yet to figure out how they were going to pull this whole shenanigan off without anyone from the base finding out, and Kelly wanted to discuss a baby sister.

Royce's arm circled Catherine's waist as they moved into the formal living room. "What's the matter, darling, has the cat got your tongue?"

"A baby sister," Catherine repeated slowly, thoughtfully. She didn't want to burst Kelly's bubble, but at the same time the ten-year-old needed to be aware that there were several things to consider before they discussed a pregnancy.

Catherine sat down on the bronze velvet sofa. Royce sat slightly behind her, his arms circling her waist. "I was hoping we could talk about other matters," Catherine suggested, thinking of a tactful way of changing the subject.

"We could." Kelly was willing to concede that much. "I can be the flower girl, can't I?"

"Anything you want." Catherine hadn't gotten around to thinking that far ahead, but she certainly didn't have any objections if that was what Kelly wanted.

"I was thinking pink."

"Pink?" Royce repeated as though he'd never heard the word before. "Pink what?"

"For the wedding colors, of course." Kelly tossed him a look that suggested his presence wasn't at all necessary, at least not right then. "You look real pretty in pink, Catherine, and it's a nice omen."

"Omen?" This time it was Catherine who couldn't find her way around Royce's fast-talking daughter.

"For my baby sister."

"Of course, how silly of me." Catherine was beginning to feel that Kelly wasn't so much interested in gaining a mother as she was looking for a vehicle to deliver her long-awaited sibling.

"What if we have a son first?" Catherine wanted to know. She should find out these things just in case Kelly intended to boot her out of the family for having delivered something other than the specified request.

Kelly wrinkled her nose as if she found the mere suggestion distasteful. "I suppose a boy would be all right. I've heard lots of talk from the girls at school about how dads really like having sons. Personally, I'd much prefer a sister, but I guess this is just one of those things that we'll leave up to God."

"I have no idea where she comes up with this stuff," Royce whispered for Catherine's benefit.

"Does this mean we're moving?" Kelly wanted to know next, her look pensive.

Royce went tense behind Catherine. She realized this was the part Royce dreaded most. Bangor was the only Navy base Kelly had ever known, although Royce had been stationed in other Puget Sound bases. Uprooting his daughter had been Royce's primary concern about the two of them marrying. "More than likely we'll be moving."

After having a good deal to say about everything else, Kelly simply nodded.

"Does that bother you?" Catherine asked.

"Not really. Lots of other kids in my school have lived all over the world. Everyone says that if you join the Navy you get shipped everywhere. I think it's our turn. Actually, when you think about it, it's time we left Bangor."

"I don't know where we're going yet."

"But where do you think?" Kelly pressed.

"I'm hoping to be assigned to the Navy station in Bremerton, but we can't count on that."

"Really!" Kelly jumped off the couch and clapped her hands. "That'd be great. We could move to Catherine's apartment and Sambo could sleep with me and it'd hardly be moving at all."

"But we can't count on that. Admiral Duffy's promised to see what he can do."

"Where else?"

"There's always a chance I'll go to Pensacola, Florida."

Once again Kelly was on her feet clapping wildly. "All right, Disney World here I come."

"Sweetheart," Royce said, looking more than a little surprised by his daughter's reaction to the possibility of moving across the country. "Just remember, I haven't a clue where we're headed. So we should be prepared for anything."

"Does it matter where we move?" Kelly asked with a sanguine smile. "Catherine will be with us."

"Maybe," Royce corrected.

Kelly's bright blue eyes narrowed suspiciously. She set her fists against her hip bones and glared across the room. "Exactly what do you mean by that?"

"First we have to find out where your father's going to be stationed," Catherine explained, loving the expressive way Kelly had of letting her feelings be known. "Then I need to request a transfer there myself, or at least to a base close to where your dad's stationed. We still won't be able to be in the same command, but—"

"What happens if the Navy decides to send Dad one place and you another?"

It was a distinct possibility, and one Catherine prayed they'd never have to consider.

"We'll cross that bridge when we come to it," Royce assured the three of them.

Kelly's nod was profound. "Good thinking." She crossed her arms and leaned back against the sofa. "Now that we've got that out of the way, there are a couple of other things we need to discuss."

"Is that a fact?" Royce said, but the look he shared with Catherine suggested that he was as much at a loss as she.

Kelly cleared her throat, and her face grew dark and serious. "No hanky-panky."

"I beg your pardon." Royce was indignant.

"You heard me." Kelly's index finger shot out in a way that would have made teachers across America proud. "Not until you're married at least. I'm not a little kid anymore," Kelly informed them with a righteous tilt to her chin. "I know what kind of stuff goes on between men and women. I watch MTV."

"I don't believe this is any of your concern, young lady." Royce was frowning, but Catherine wasn't entirely sure what was bothering him; the fact Kelly watched racy music videos, or that she was insisting on curtailing their romantic involvement.

"You wouldn't want to taint my young mind, would you?"

"If I'm going to taint anything, it'll be your backside," Royce announced loudly.

The threat was real enough for Kelly to sit on her hands to protect her posterior.

"This is the same kid who was afraid in a power outage," Catherine whispered to Royce.

"That was a trick."

"She turned off all the lights herself?"

"No," Royce said, and shook his head for emphasis. "She called you over knowing I'd be back any minute, thereby forcing the two of us to deal with each other."

"You always told me it's impolite to whisper," Kelly said indignantly from across the room. She stood, yawned once and headed for the stairs. "I'll be back in just a moment."

"You'll be back?" Royce repeated.

"Of course. I'll need to go with you when you take Catherine home. You don't honestly expect me to stay here alone, do you?"

"Ah…"

"What's the matter, love?" Catherine murmured, flexing her long nails against Royce's arms, which were wrapped securely around her waist. "Has the cat got your tongue?"

"I'll only be a minute," Kelly said, rushing up the stairs.

"Which means…" Royce said, drawing Catherine back on to the thick sofa cushions. He felt solid and strong, and just the feel of him was enough to ease the terrible loneliness that had haunted her for nights on end.

Catherine raised her arms to link them around his

neck. His eyes were on her. "So much for us being bad." He lowered his mouth and feasted.

"Ho hum." Kelly coughed loudly, disrupting them a few minutes later. "Not a good idea," she announced. "There's plenty of time for that sort of thing later. Right now we've got a wedding to think about."

"A flower girl," Royce murmured, slowly untangling his arms from around Catherine. "I have a feeling that by the time this wedding takes place, Kelly may be in a boarding school in Switzerland."

The following week was impossible. That was the only way Catherine could think to define it. Knowing Royce was being transferred, but not knowing where made any planning impossible. They couldn't arrange for a wedding until several factors were figured into the equation. First and foremost they needed to know when Royce would be dispatched. The news of his new duty assignment could come at any moment, and Royce could be ordered to ship out with as little as twenty-four-hours notice and as much as six months.

The restrictions upon them were just as stringent as before. As Kelly had so eloquently put it, *no hanky-panky.* Catherine would have paid anything just for the opportunity to "be bad" with Royce, but that, too, was prohibited. They'd come too far to risk everything now.

Catherine was sitting at her desk when Royce strolled into the office. "Lieutenant Commander, could I see you in my office, right away?"

"Yes, sir."

Elaine Perkins scooted back to her chair as Catherine left her office, her secretary's gaze following Royce. "Ol' stoneface seems to be in a pleasant enough mood lately, don't you think?"

"I wouldn't know," Catherine said before she let something slip that she'd soon regret. She'd long suspected that her observant secretary was aware of her feelings for Royce, but it was a subject neither dared broach.

"How can you not have noticed?" Elaine demanded. "I actually saw Commander Nyland smiling the other day. Smiling. Not that I could see there was anything to smile about, but that's not my concern. Up until recently I assumed it would take an act of Congress to get that man to so much as grin. Lately that's all changed."

Catherine didn't comment. "Do you want me to ask him what he found so amusing? I'll tell him you're curious to find out."

"Funny, Catherine, very funny."

Amused herself, Catherine walked into Royce's office and closed the door. "You wanted to see me?"

"How do you feel about living in Virginia?" he asked without warning. "I've been assigned to Submarine Force, Atlantic Fleet at Norfolk."

"Virginia," she repeated slowly. Her heart was pounding hard. "I'd love Antarctica if I could be there with you."

Royce grinned, and their eyes held each other. "I feel the same way."

"How much time do I have?" She arched her brows expectantly, waiting for him to respond.

"Two weeks."

"Two weeks." Catherine's heart sank as she lowered herself into a chair and closed her eyes. Her mind started buzzing. It wasn't possible. It simply wasn't possible.

But it had to be! She'd do whatever she must to arrange it so they could be married before he was deployed.

"Catherine?"

She was on her feet again and not quite sure how she got there. She blinked once, then smiled over to Royce, confident her smile covered her entire face. "Two weeks," she repeated, and nodded once, willing to accept the challenge. "I've got a whole lot of planning to do."

Royce looked concerned. "I don't want to postpone the wedding." It went without saying that the ceremony would have to be discreet. For the two of them to marry so quickly after Royce was detached from the command would be a problem. They'd discussed it at length and had agreed to fly to San Francisco for the ceremony.

Catherine cast him a look that assured him otherwise. "I don't want to wait, either." They were both well aware that it would be better for them to let several months pass. But neither found that acceptable. "I'll contact my mother right away. She'll help with the arrangements. Personally, I doubt that I'd be able to pull this off without her."

"You can contact the whole state of California if that's what you want. Just as long as you're at the church on time."

"I'll be there, don't you worry."

"Mom, it's Catherine."

"Sweetheart." Her mother's voice was elevated with pleasure. "It's so good to hear from you."

"How's work... I mean, you're not into anything heavy, are you?"

"No more than usual."

"Good." Catherine hesitated. She really would be

asking a good deal of her mother, who was a newlywed herself, but there was no help for it.

"Good? Why's that?" Once again her mother's voice was raised with curiosity.

"Because I need you to do something for me…"

"Of course, whatever you need."

"I need your expertise—" She wasn't allowed to finish.

"Catherine, you're a fine lawyer, I'm sure you don't need my opinion, and furthermore I don't think the Navy would take kindly to my interfering in something that has to do with the military."

"Not in the courts, Mom." Catherine couldn't keep from grinning. The happiness was oozing out of her. "Royce asked me to marry him."

"I thought he'd already done that."

"He wasn't serious then, only jealous."

"I take it he's serious this time?"

"Very serious. He arranged for a transfer before he proposed. He's been assigned to the submarine base in Virginia. I've put in for a transfer there myself."

"And?" The question came after a noticeable pause.

"And I haven't heard yet. But we want to be married as soon as possible. We can't let anyone know, at least not right away. The whole thing has to be handled delicately."

"Of course. But once you're married, the Navy wouldn't separate a husband and wife, will it?"

"You're joking, Mom?" Catherine asked with a light laugh. "I thought you knew the military better than that. The Navy does what's most convenient for the Navy. Royce and I have no right falling in love in the first place."

"But he'll be in Virginia, and you might well end up stationed in Washington."

"We don't know that yet. Royce is pulling every string he can to make sure that doesn't happen. Even if worse comes to worse and I do have to stay here, it won't be forever. Eventually we'll be together."

"I don't like the sound of this, Catherine," her mother said in low, concerned tones.

"Trust me, it's essential for right now."

"Not necessarily. Sweetheart, don't you think you should consider resigning from the Navy?"

It was an argument Catherine had been having with herself for several days. She'd talked it over with Royce, and they'd batted the idea back and forth several times, but she'd been adamant and he hadn't pressured her. "I'm not leaving the Navy," she argued forcibly with her mother. "I'm not giving up my career just because I happened to fall in love."

"You'll always be an attorney, and frankly, I've never understood why you don't simply join a law firm, you'd do much better financially."

"That's an old argument and not one I'm going to get involved with now. I've come too far to resign now. Besides, of all the people in the world, I would have thought you'd understand my feelings about the Navy. Resigning isn't even up for consideration. Royce knows that and accepts it."

"But, Catherine, sweetheart, be reasonable, what man wants to be separated from his wife by thousands of miles?"

"You're making it sound like a foregone conclusion that I won't be transferred with him. In every likelihood I will, so quit worrying about it," Catherine stated heatedly. She immediately felt contrite. Her mother wasn't telling her something she hadn't already debated long and hard. The Navy was important to both her and Royce. Catherine noted, however, that no one suggested he resign his commission and become a civilian because he wanted to marry her.

"What about children?"

"Mom, I don't think we're going to accomplish anything productive going over this now. I've got less than two weeks to make all the necessary arrangements. Royce is detaching from his command here, which helps. Can you send us whatever it is we need to file for a wedding license in California?"

"Of course."

"Good." But her mother was right. What about children? Catherine didn't know if she was being greedy to want it all. A career, a family and the Navy. That was a question she had yet to face.

The next few days passed in a whirlwind of frantic activity. Catherine barely saw Royce, barely talked to him. Late in the week he and Kelly flew to Virginia to make the necessary arrangements for housing.

Friday after work, Catherine returned to her apartment in a haze of concern. Over the next two days she spent hours on the phone with her mother, arranging for the florists, photographers and trying on every wedding dress within two counties.

Royce called her late Sunday evening. "Hello, beautiful," he greeted in a soft, sexy voice that curled her toes.

She was exhausted physically and mentally. "Hello yourself," she answered, fighting back a powerful need to have his arms around her. Instead she forced herself to ask all the right questions. "Did you and Kelly find a house?"

"Within the first day. It's perfect. Three bedrooms, nice family room, a large kitchen and all for a reasonable rent." Royce hadn't been able to obtain housing on the base, which made the move just a little more difficult. Kelly had considered it important to accompany him on this trip so she could scout out the schools and choose the right kind of neighborhood, which meant one with lots of girls her age.

"What did Kelly think of Virginia?"

"It was radical this and radical that. At least that's what I seem to remember her saying. Right now everything's new and fun. I don't think she's going to have any problems making the adjustment."

Catherine snuggled up on the sofa, the phone cord stretched as far as it would go from the kitchen wall. Her gaze rested on the photograph of her father, lingering there for several moments. "Kelly's going to be making a whole lot of adjustments in the next few weeks." It worried Catherine that Royce's daughter was suffering the brunt of the sacrifices they each were forced into making for this marriage.

"Kelly's resilient. Trust me, she would have willingly moved to the jungles of darkest Africa if it meant you were going to be part of our family."

"I love you." Catherine felt the need to say it. It suddenly seemed important for her to voice her feelings.

"I love you, too." After the hectic craziness that had surrounded them for what seemed like months on end, it was good to sit in the solitude of her home and cherish the words she'd longed to hear for so many weeks.

"I didn't want to love you, at least not at first," Royce admitted roughly. "God knows I tried to stay away from you."

"I tried, too."

"I'd give anything to have you in my arms right now."

"That's all going to change soon, and I'll be in your arms for the rest of our lives." She said it as a reminder to herself, wiping the moisture from her cheek. She should be the happiest woman in the world. Within a matter of days she and Royce would be man and wife. Yet the envelope sitting on the corner of her desk was a constant reminder of how quickly that happiness could be tarnished.

Royce paused, and although he must be exhausted, Catherine realized he'd picked up on the fact she was miserably unhappy. She tried so hard to hide it behind busy questions and a cheerful facade.

"Are you going to tell me?" he demanded softly.

"There's no need to spoil everything now. You'll find out soon enough.... You're back safe and sound, and that's what matters. Mission accomplished. Kelly's happy. What more could you possibly want?"

"You."

"Oh, my darling, you have me. You've held on to my heart for weeks on end, don't you know that?"

"I already know, Catherine," he told her softly. "You don't need to hide it from me."

She sucked in her breath. "When did you find out?"

"Friday before I left."

Her request for transfer had been denied. The worst scenario. Her worst nightmare. She was going to be stationed in Bangor while Royce and Kelly were on the other side of the country.

"Oh, Royce," she asked softly, "what are we going to do?"

"Exactly what we're planning. I'm marrying you, Catherine, come hell or high water."

Twelve

The wedding ceremony took place Friday evening in a small San Francisco chapel with the pastor from Marilyn Fredrickson-Morgan's church. The altar was decorated with brilliant red poinsettias, and although Royce wasn't much into flowers, he was impressed with the traditional Christmas flower that crowded every square inch of floor space around the altar. Catherine and her mother had done a beautiful job. Even Kelly who'd first suggested a pink color scheme approved of the festive red bows and other complements.

As for the ceremony itself, Royce remembered little of what progressed. The moment he'd stepped over to join the reverend and viewed Catherine slowly marching down the aisle toward him, he'd been so lost in her loveliness that everything else around him had faded.

Even the small reception afterward with both families and a few close friends remained hazy in his mind. Catherine fed him a piece of heart-shaped cake bordered with red roses and sipped champagne. They even danced a couple of times.

There had been gifts, too. Royce couldn't get over

how many when there were less than fifty people at the entire wedding.

Kelly had been in her element. Royce's parents had flown in from Arizona, along with a couple of his aunts and uncles. Even his younger brother and his family had managed to make it up from the southern part of the state. Kelly had basked in all the attention. She'd taken to Marilyn and Norman almost as quickly as she'd taken to Catherine herself.

His daughter delighted in announcing to any and everyone who would listen that he and Catherine owed everything to her. She'd also sounded like something of a parole officer when she admitted to Catherine's mother that she'd personally seen to it that no hanky-panky had been allowed before the wedding ceremony.

At the moment Catherine was changing clothes, something she'd done once or twice already since the wedding. He couldn't understand why she insisted on dressing when he fully intended on undressing her the minute they arrived at the hotel room he'd booked.

Royce would much rather have chosen someplace romantic for their honeymoon. Unfortunately they weren't going to have a whole lot of time together before he assumed his duties in Virginia. With a limited time schedule, Royce quickly decided he'd rather spend it in bed with Catherine than on the road seeking out the perfect romantic hideaway.

A private room on one of the beaches might have worked out nicely, but the San Francisco hotel offered one advantage the others didn't. Room service.

Royce had two short days with Catherine, and he sure as hell didn't plan on spending any of it sightseeing.

It seemed to take the taxi forever to reach the hotel. They chatted about the wedding, teased and even managed to kiss a couple of times. It wasn't until they'd registered and were on their way up to the honeymoon suite that it hit Royce.

He was nervous.

Royce Nyland jittery! It was almost enough to make him laugh. Marriage wasn't a new experience to him. He'd been through it all before. If anything was different it was the fact he and Catherine had yet to make love.

Sandy had been sleeping with him for months before they'd seriously discussed getting married. Royce wished to hell he'd made love to Catherine before now. It might have eased the knot twisting his gut.

No it wouldn't, he amended promptly. When it came right down to it, he was glad they'd waited. It hadn't been easy, even with Kelly wagging her finger under their noses at every opportunity.

He didn't need his daughter reminding him to be good, or anyone else for that matter. The Navy had seen to it all on its own. He'd followed the law book, with only a few minor infractions. He'd made the best of a sticky situation. But, by heaven, Catherine was his wife now, and he was ready to attempt a new world's record for lovemaking!

A warm sensation softened his heart. He was doing everything right this time. Right by Catherine. Right by himself. Right by the Navy. There was a gratifying sort of comfort knowing that.

"Are you hungry?" he asked.

"A little." Royce swore she sounded as on edge as he did, which pleased him. At least he wasn't the only one experiencing qualms.

"Do you want to order something from room service?" He found a menu by the phone and scanned the list of entrées. Nothing sounded particularly appetizing, but if Catherine was interested, he'd order something for her.

"I'd be willing to eat something," she said lightly, but Royce wasn't fooled. Dinner was a delay tactic for them both.

They ordered a fancy meal, but Royce noted that neither of them seemed to have much of an appetite once the food arrived. So his gutsy Catherine was nervous, too. Royce found that endearing, and he was charmed by her all the more.

What they really needed to get things rolling, Royce decided when he set the food tray outside their door, was the front seat of a car. The thought produced a wide grin, one he suspected would have made a Cheshire cat proud.

"You're smiling," Catherine said when he returned. "What's so amusing?"

"Us. Come here, woman, I'm tired of pussyfooting around this. I want to make love to you, and I'm not waiting any longer." He held his arms open to her, and she walked toward him, slipping tidily into his embrace. They fit together perfectly. Royce believed they had been created for each other. For a cure for all the lonely, barren years he'd spent alone. Years she'd spent alone.

He kissed her once gently and felt her breath, hot and fiery, against his throat. One kiss and Royce was suddenly as weak as a newborn kitten. It didn't help matters any to have her snuggle against him, her skin silky and warm.

Royce's hands were trembling as he reached for the zipper at the back of her dress. Catherine straightened and raised her arms so he could lift the silky garment over her head. It slipped right off, and she rewarded him for his efforts by trailing her lips over the corded muscles of his neck and shoulders, her tongue slipping over the hollow of his throat.

Royce closed his eyes to the deluge of feelings. His heart started to pound, but that wasn't his only reaction. His whole body had started throbbing. He couldn't remove his clothes fast enough. Once his shirt was free of his waistband, Catherine took over for him, slowly, too slowly to suit him, unfastening the buttons one by one. She sighed softly and fanned her hands across his chest, her nails innocently tugging against the hairs of his chest like a kitten yearning for attention.

"Oh, Royce... Kiss me, please kiss me."

He caught his breath and then did as she asked, spreading hot kisses across her delicate shoulders, then up the side of her exquisite neck until their mouths met in a burst of spontaneous combustion that was so fierce it threatened to consume them both.

Her tongue shyly met his, and he groaned, the sound rough and masculine to his own ears. Catherine moaned, too, and it was the most sensual, erotic whimper Royce had ever heard. He had to touch her, had to feel for himself her excitement, had to taste it and know she wanted him as desperately as he hungered for her.

His hands massaged her back, and he was gratified to realize she'd removed her bra. She leaned into him, absorbing what little strength he possessed, and looped her arms around his neck. Royce's hands cupped her breasts. They were soft and full, so marvelously lush and round. The nipples instantly pearled, and the feel of them puckering, hardening, then scraping against his palms as she moved against him sent a wave of molten sensation over him.

Royce raised his head and judged the distance to the bed. Lifting her into his arms, Royce stalked across the carpet like a warrior hauling his conquest into the middle of camp.

He pressed Catherine onto the mattress and then joined her, being sure he didn't suffocate her with his weight.

He kissed her again and again, so many times he lost count, so many times that she melted against him, her eyes pleading with him for the completion they both sought.

Royce couldn't wait another moment, another second. His hands caught the sides of her lace panties and dragged them down her silken legs. He rolled aside long enough to glide open the zipper of his slacks and ease them over his own hips.

Once they were both free of restrictive clothing, he knelt over her. Her eyes were golden, hot with need. Royce nearly groaned just looking at her, just feeling the heat radiating from her smooth ivory skin.

She raised her hand to his face, her fingertips grazing his cheekbone. "Love me," she whispered. "Just love me."

Her words, her touch were all the inducement Royce needed. He positioned himself over her, using his thighs to part hers. She opened to him without reserve, without restraint.

By all that was holy, Royce didn't know where he found the strength to go slowly, to linger, prolonging the moment. Her eyes held his as he pushed forward, gliding the throbbing, aching staff of his manhood into her.

If he were ever going to die from pleasure, it would have been at that moment. Catherine was ready for him, waiting for him, so sweet and hot and moist, Royce knew in a heartbeat that he dare not move.

His eyes returned to hers, which were half-closed

as she, too, drank in the exquisite tumult. After giving her a moment to adjust to him, Royce continued easing himself into her until she had taken in all of him.

Breathing hard, Catherine raised her knees and bucked beneath him. Royce groaned aloud as a flash of white-hot pleasure shot through him. Unable to endure much more, he pushed forward and was nearly consumed with the second wave of moist, hot bliss. When his eyes connected with Catherine, he noted that she was biting hard into her lower lip.

"I'm hurting you?" He didn't know if her reaction was one of pleasure or pain.

"No...oh, no," she whispered. "I never knew anything could feel this good."

"This is only the beginning," he promised. He closed his eyes in order to savor every sensation, drink in every fiery aspect of their lovemaking.

He honestly meant to go slow. He had to, he felt, in order to fully appreciate the magic between them. But once he started to rotate his hips, he was lost. Lost in pleasure. Lost in the storm, but he wasn't alone. Catherine clung to him, answering each bold thrust with one of her own.

It was a storm. One of need. One of fury and frenzy. It came on quickly, with such intensity that Royce was pitched from one world to another until he realized there was no slowing down, no going back. No stopping. Not for heaven, not for hell. For pain or for pleasure.

His climax came as a searing completion, far too quickly to suit Royce. He didn't want it to end, not now. Not so soon.

Catherine's labored breathing matched his own, and the sound of it was the only thing that shattered the silence as they both burned in the wake of the sweetest tempest Royce had ever known.

Royce woke around three to the sounds of Catherine singing. She was taking a shower. In the middle of the night no less.

Grinning, he rolled onto his back and raised his arms, cupped his head beneath his hands. They'd made love twice and then fallen into an exhausted sleep. The last thing Royce remembered was Catherine snuggling close to him, berating the fact she had yet to put on the special lace nightie she'd bought for their wedding night.

She came out of the bathroom and was bent over, briskly rubbing a towel over her wet hair. When she raised her head, she noted that Royce was lying in bed, watching her. Something he was sure she'd enjoy doing for many more years yet to come.

"I didn't wake you, did I?"

"As a matter of fact, you did." She had on the skimpiest nightie he'd ever seen. Although he was exhausted and physically drained, seeing her in that slip of black lace seriously threatened his composure.

"I apologize. I guess I shouldn't have started singing, but I just couldn't help myself... I don't know when I've been so happy. I don't think I ever want to leave this room."

Royce was thinking much along those same lines himself. He held out his arms. "Come here, woman."

Surprised, she glanced toward the bathroom. "I was going to blow-dry my hair."

"Later. You woke me, and there's a penance to be paid."

"But, Royce, it's the middle of the night. We've already...you know...several times."

"Come here." He grew impatient waiting for her. He rolled off the bed, walked over to where she was standing and removed the towel from her head, letting it fall to the carpet. He threaded her wet hair through his splayed fingers, cherishing the feel of her, so warm and moist. That caused him to think of other places on her delectable body that were warm and moist, too.

"What are you doing?"

"What am I doing now or what do I intend to do later?" he asked, wiggling his eyebrows provocatively.

"We've already done everything there is to do," she announced primly.

"Is that a fact." He kissed her, sweeping his mouth across hers and giving her a taste of his tongue.

"Well, maybe not everything," she amended. He nibbled his way across her jaw to her earlobe and whispered seductive promises to her. He smiled, loving it when she responded with a sharp gasp.

"Royce... Why that's indecent."

"Oh, really." He kissed her a second time, sliding his tongue across the parted seam of her lips. Once more he captured the lobe of her ear between his teeth and sucked lightly. Then he whispered what he intended to do to her in a very short while.

"Royce!" Her eyes went wide. He loved watching her cheeks turn a fetching shade of pink.

Royce couldn't help it, he laughed. "And not just once, either. I have a lot of time to make up for, and you, my dear, sweet wife, have fallen right into my hands."

"But I...oh, Royce," she moaned as he traced a row of moist kisses across her face until he found her lips. The kiss was wet and wild. Wild and sweet.

His hands were busy trying to figure out how to take off the flimsy black nightie she wore. He eased the satin straps down her shoulders. She worked her arms free for him until he could remove the top completely, liberating her luscious breasts. He slid his palms over their fullness. Up and down, savoring her softness. Her femininity.

Unable to wait a moment longer, he lifted her into his arms and carried her to the bed, pressing her into the mattress. His body followed, covering hers. Instinctively she opened to him, and he entered her in one swift movement.

Catherine moaned.

Royce sighed.

Then the storm took over and they moved as one to hold back the torrent, or perhaps to bring it on—Royce didn't know which. The world went spinning out of control, a hurricane of wild need that consumed them both.

Catherine woke slowly. A serene smile lifted the corners of her mouth, and she rolled onto her back and raised her arms high above her head, as content as Sambo stretching after taking a long nap in the sunlight. Instinctively she rolled onto her side, seeking the warmth and comfort of Royce's body.

The space beside her was empty, however. And cold. Her eyes opened, and sadness settled over her, blocking out the early-morning sunlight.

They'd spent less than five nights together. Five nights out of a lifetime, and she continued to search for him. At night she tossed restlessly in her sleep, seeking his warmth, seeking his strength. No one had warned her how dangerously addictive it was to sleep with a husband.

Royce and Kelly were in Norfolk and had been for two weeks. They communicated often. Letters arrived nearly every day, and their phone bill rivaled the defense budget. Yet Catherine found the grating loneliness inescapable.

She didn't know which was worse. Loving Royce and being forced to hide the way she felt behind a deluge of Navy regulations or being married to him and separated by two thousand endless miles.

It wouldn't be any worse if Royce were stationed aboard one of the submarines, at least that was what she told herself. They'd be apart for months on end. Just the way they were now.

Before he and Kelly had left for Norfolk, they'd made plans for Catherine to join them over the Christmas holidays. That wasn't so long to wait.

A few days. Surely she could hold on to her peace of mind for a few more days, especially when they were said to be the shortest days of the year.

Catherine did manage to survive, but just barely. Royce and Kelly were waiting for her at the airport when her plane touched down. The minute Kelly saw her, she flew into Catherine's arms, hugging her as though it had been years since they'd last seen each other.

"Oh, Catherine, I'm so glad you're here."

Catherine was glad, too. She raised her head, and her eyes connected with Royce's. His were warm and welcoming. She stepped into his embrace and squeezed tight.

"We've got everything ready for you," Kelly told her excitedly. "Dad and I worked real hard putting up the Christmas tree and wrapping presents. I even helped him clean the kitchen and everything."

"Thank you, sweetheart. I appreciate it so much." She

gave the ten-year-old a second bear hug. She'd missed Royce's daughter, too, more than she'd thought possible.

"Can we do my nails again?" Kelly asked, holding out her hands for a visual inspection. "They look just wretched, don't they?"

"Of course we'll both work on our nails."

"Shopping, too. Dad's simply impossible, but then he always was."

Royce collected her luggage and led the way through the terminal to the parking garage. The ride into Norfolk took only a few minutes. The weather had cooperated beautifully, and the sky was crisp and clear with a sprinkling of stars scattered boldly across the horizon of black velvet.

The colonial house was exactly as Royce had described. Catherine liked it immediately and felt its welcome the minute she walked through the wreath-covered door.

"Did you miss me?" Kelly asked, clinging to Catherine's arm. "Because I sure missed you," Kelly said, and then her voice lowered. "Dad missed you, too."

"Oh, sweetheart, I missed you both so much."

"What about…" Kelly paused and darted a look toward her father. Once more she lowered her voice several decibels. "You know."

Catherine didn't know. "What?"

Losing patience, Kelly clenched her fists against her hipbones. "A baby. Are you pregnant yet, or not?"

"Not," Royce informed his daughter crisply.

"Not," Catherine echoed in a far more gentle tone. Unfortunately. Catherine had given a good deal of thought to the idea of them adding to their family. True, Kelly wanting, or rather demanding a baby sister, had been the catalyst, but when Catherine analyzed it, she had to admit the ten-year-old had a valid point. Royce was already in his late thirties, and she was at the age when all the internal female workings were at their peak.

Catherine wasn't keen about going through a pregnancy without Royce being close to love and pamper her during the discomforts she was likely to encounter. Yet Navy officers through the ages had suffered no less. She wasn't an exception.

Beyond all the other token reasons, Catherine longed for Royce's child. The matter had been on her mind every minute that she'd been separated from Royce these past two weeks. She might be rushing matters, but the idea strongly appealed to her. She planned to approach her husband about the subject during this brief visit. If everything went according to schedule, this might well be a bonus Christmas.

Kelly chatted for the next hour, telling Catherine all about her school and her new friends. Catherine had heard it all before, but gave her rapt attention to Kelly while Royce brewed hot-buttered rums.

"All I get is hot butter," Kelly said with a grimace when Royce delivered the steaming drinks.

"The only reason you get that is so you'll go up to bed the way you promised."

"Dad!" Kelly exclaimed. "It's Christmas Eve's eve. You don't honestly expect me to go to bed at the regular time, do you?"

"It's two hours past your bedtime already," he reminded her. "Now drink up and hit the sack."

"You just want time alone with Catherine," the youngster accused as she sipped from the edge of her mug. "But," she added with an expressive sigh, "I can understand. People in love need that."

"Thank you, Dear Abby," Royce teased. "Now scoot."

Kelly took one last sip of her drink, then set it on the counter. She gave both Royce and Catherine hugs, then dutifully marched up the stairs.

Now that Catherine was alone with her husband, she watched as he stood and turned out the lamps until the only light illuminating the room came from the ones blinking on the Christmas tree. Although dim, the beautifully decorated tree gave off a soft glare, enough for her to realize Royce was studying her. His cobalt-blue eyes said all sorts of things that words could never express. They told her how much he'd missed her and how he woke each morning searching for her. He'd been left to confront a cold empty space just the way she had. His eyes also told her how much he needed her. Physically. Emotionally. Mentally. Every which way there was to need a woman, he needed her.

Slowly, never taking his eyes from her, he removed the steaming mug from her hands, setting it aside. He reached for her then, gently taking her into his arms and kissing her with a hunger that told her his nights had been as achingly lonesome as her own. While his mouth was hotly claiming hers, he was working at opening her blouse and bra. He was so eager to love her, his hands shook.

"Royce," she pleaded, "the bedroom's upstairs."

"We can't, at least not yet," he argued. "Kelly won't be asleep."

"But she might come down here."

"She won't. I promise." His voice was a low growl, heavy with impatience.

"Don't you think we should wait?"

"I can't. Not a second longer. Feel me." He grabbed hold of her wrist and boldly pressed it to him. "I need you," he said, his voice strained as she took the initiative and moved her open palm back and forth.

"I need you, too," she returned in a husky murmur, closing her eyes to the loving way in which he sought her breasts, lifting them, scoring the undersides with his thumbs. If she hadn't been so fascinated with touching him, with receiving his touch, she would have been rushing to remove her clothes.

"I've thought of nothing else but this from the moment we parted."

"Oh...yes."

"I want you so damn much I can't think straight."

"Me, too."

"I want you more than I ever believed it was possible to want another human being."

"You know what I want?" She didn't wait for him to answer. "I want you to stop talking about wanting me, and hurry up and carry me to bed so we can make love."

He laughed, and Catherine swore it was the most wonderful, melodious sound in the world. He reached her hand and hurried her up the stairs. They tiptoed past Kelly's bedroom with Catherine clenching her blouse closed.

The instant they were alone, his mouth sought hers in a fierce kiss that sent her senses reeling.

The winds of their passion were building, gaining momentum. Royce scooped her into the shelter of his arms and pressed her against the mattress. Then, without hesitation, he removed her clothes with a few agile movements.

Catherine raised her arms, waiting to curl them around his neck as he quickly removed his own clothing.

"Come here, husband," she whispered wantonly. "Let me show you exactly how much I missed you...."

Catherine woke several hours later. She was in bed with Royce cuddling her spoon fashion as though they'd been sleeping together for years. He really was a romantic creature, but it would have embarrassed him had she told him so.

The flight across the country had exhausted her. A smile scooted across her lips. Perhaps it had, but not nearly as much as the session with her husband.

Royce rolled onto his back, giving her the opportunity to study him in the dim moonlight. His features were relaxed in slumber, and the musky scent of their lovemaking lingered. Her heart felt full, open wide to receive all the love he had to give her. It was a good feeling.

"Catherine?"

"Did I wake you?"

"Yes," he said, yawning, "and you know the penalty."

"Oh, Royce," she whispered, grinning, then gave an exaggerated sigh. "Not again."

"Oh, yes...'again' as you so eloquently put it."

Elevating her head, she leaned over and kissed him gently. "Can we have a talk first?"

"Must we?"

"Yes." Her lips briefly touched his. "Please."

"This sounds serious."

She kissed him again, cherishing the taste of him.

His hands held her face away from his. "Either we talk or we kiss. We can't do both."

"All right. One kiss and then we talk. Seriously." His hands were in her hair, unerringly directing her mouth to his for an intimate kiss that was slow and familiar.

"Enough," he whispered, dragging his mouth from her. "Now talk."

"Royce," she said, drawing in a deep breath. "What would you think if I were to become pregnant?"

The air went cold and still. "Are you?"

"No, but I'd like to be."

His eyes closed briefly as though he were greatly relieved. "Not a good idea."

"Why not?" His attitude stung more than she ever thought it would. She expected some hesitation on his part, but nothing like this.

"As long as you're in the Navy there won't be any children for us. I thought you understood that."

Thirteen

"What do you mean?" Catherine demanded, sitting up in the bed and grabbing the sheet by her fists to cover her bare breasts.

"Exactly what I said." Royce was frowning heavily. "There won't be any children for us as long as you're in the Navy. I thought you understood that."

"I want to know when the hell I agreed to that." She was angry, but damn it all, she couldn't help it. How arrogant. How high-handed of him. She was the one who was willing to go through with the pregnancy. The one who'd offered to balance both her career and a family. It was what she wanted, what she'd planned all along. She'd swallow a gallon of seawater before she'd ever agree to no children.

"We talked about it before we were married," Royce announced coolly.

"The hell we did."

"Catherine, think about it. We had several serious discussions about what we would do if you weren't transferred to Norfolk with me. Remember?" His patience was as grating as his words.

Various conversations they'd had about her transferring did come to mind, and she reluctantly nodded. "Yes, but I certainly don't remember us saying anything about children."

"Trust me, we did."

"Wrong," she returned heatedly. "You're making the whole thing up... I would never have agreed to it. I want a baby, I've always wanted a baby. Two babies." That should really outrage him. Imagine her being greedy enough to want more than one!

An ironic grin quirked the edges of his mouth. "Fine, if that's what you want, we'll have three or four children. More if you want."

"Good." Apparently he wasn't going to make as much of a fuss over this as she'd originally thought. The outrage slowly drained out of her.

"We'll work hard on getting you pregnant," Royce added purposefully, "just as soon as you resign your commission."

"What?" Catherine was on her knees, the protective shield covering her nakedness long forgotten. She was so furious, she leaped to her feet and started traipsing across the mattress in giant steps. Leaping onto the carpet, she searched for something to cover herself with and grabbed a shirt of Royce's that was hanging in the closet. She jerked it so hard the hanger clattered to the floor.

It didn't help matters to have Royce casually sitting up in bed, propped against two fat pillows. "Is there a problem with that?"

"You're damn right there is."

"Then why don't we sit down like two civilized people and discuss this rationally."

"Because," she cried, hands braced on her hips, "I'm

too damn mad. I never dreamed...not once that you'd do something like this."

"Catherine, if you'd cool off for a moment we could talk this over rationally."

"I'm cool," she shouted, holding back her hair with both hands. "Answer me one thing."

"All right."

"Do you want a baby?" The whole world seemed to stop. It was as though their marriage, indeed their relationship, hung on a delicate balance, weighed by his answer.

"Yes," he whispered with enough feeling to convince her it was true. "I've tried to tell myself it didn't matter. That I'd leave everything up to you, but damn it, yes, I would like another child." He said it almost as if he were admitting to a weakness.

Catherine was so grateful, her knees weakened. "Oh, Royce, I do, too, so much."

"Apparently the communication between us isn't as good as I'd thought."

"Why are we arguing?" she asked softly.

He grinned. "I don't know. Damn it, Catherine, I love you too much to fight with you."

"I'm glad to hear that." The long-sleeved shirt she'd so hastily donned silently slipped to the floor. With an unhurried ease, she walked over to the side of the bed, her head held high and proud. "As far as I'm concerned the sooner we make a baby the better, don't you think?"

"Catherine?" Royce sounded unsure, which wasn't like him.

"I want to make love." She sat on the edge of the mattress and sought his mouth, kissing him so lightly that their lips barely touched.

Royce groaned, grabbed her by the hair and plunged

his tongue deeply into the moist hollow of her mouth. The kiss was so hot it threatened to blister them both.

"We need to finish our talk first," he murmured breathlessly, but even while he was speaking, he was kissing her. He groaned and shook his head. "Catherine...we can't do this."

"Later... We'll talk later."

"I don't think that would be a good idea." He firmly grabbed hold of both her wrists in an attempt to push her back, but the maneuver didn't work. Instead of fighting, she leaned into him, taking full advantage of the fact his hands were occupied. Murmuring words of love and sexual need, she seduced him. Whispering to him between kisses, she told him all the things she planned to do for him. All the things they'd do for each other.

"Catherine..." He didn't sound nearly so insistent as before. "I don't...we need to talk before we do anything...first."

"If that's what you really want," she whispered, taking his earlobe between her teeth and biting lightly. "Touch me," she pleaded softly. "Oh, Royce... I need you so much."

His hold on her wrist slackened. "Catherine, I don't think it would be a good idea—"

"I do..." She was kneeling over him, her thighs spread wide, anticipating the contact, knowing it would play havoc with them both. This was what she wanted, what she needed.

Royce hesitated; his face was hard, his eyes closed, blocking her out, because that was the only way he had of resisting her. The power she felt was strong enough to intoxicate her.

Neither moved. Neither breathed. The pleasure was too intense for either. There was no beginning. No end.

The pleasure, once it started, only grew better. The joy burst forth in Catherine's heart until it filled every ounce, every pore of her being.

Joy. Pleasure. The tenderness so sweet it was violent. The beauty of their lovemaking transcending anything she had ever experienced.

When they'd finished, Royce cradled her in his arms. Neither spoke. After what seemed like forever, Royce reached for the blankets, covering them both. His arms held her close, nestling her head against his hard chest. He kissed the crown of her head, and whispered that they would talk in the morning.

Morning. Catherine's eyes slowly drifted open, and she snuggled against Royce's cozy warmth. He must have sensed that she was awake, because he ran his hand over the top of her head, smoothing her hair.

"Are you going to argue with me again?" he whispered.

"That depends on how unreasonable you intend on being," she said, rolling onto her back and arching her body, yawning. "I'm…sorry about last night." She was embarrassed now at the brazen way in which she'd come at him. Using their physical need for each other as a weapon to twist his will was not a tactic she'd ever intended to employ. But he'd made her so furious, she hadn't been thinking properly.

"I want a child, Royce," she told him, her voice low and determined.

"It's not a problem," he assured her, "as long as you're out of the Navy."

His stubbornness stunned her. "Why should I be the one to give up my commission?" she asked, in what she hoped was a reasonable tone. Her emotions were pitch-

ing around like a small rowboat upon a stormy ocean.
The waves of righteousness slapped roughly against
the sides. It was all so unfair. She had to make Royce
understand that.

"How about if you give up your commission first?"
she offered, hoping he'd see the foolishness of his logic.

He didn't answer her right away. "You agreed before
we were married. We discussed it and—"

"We didn't," she denied vehemently.

"...and you chose to stay in the Navy," Royce finished as though she'd never spoken. "Obviously it wasn't
as clear as I'd thought it was, and that's unfortunate,
but the fact remains..."

"I'm going to have a child, Royce, and I'm going to
be the best mother you ever saw. I'm going to prove
to you that I can also be a damn good lieutenant commander as well—"

"No." His voice was gruff and angry.

"Why do I have to be the one to resign?" She wasn't
being flippant this time, but she honestly wanted to
know.

"Because a child deserves a mother."

"What about a father?"

"One of us has to accept the majority of the responsibility."

"We can't share the duty?"

"No," he argued, more heatedly this time.

"Why are you being so stubborn about this?" she
demanded. Royce might be a lot of things, but she'd
always found him to be fair.

"Because Sandy—"

"Now just a minute," Catherine said, struggling into
a sitting position. She narrowed her eyes as she stared
down on him. "Get this straight right now, Royce Ny-

land. I refuse to be compared with your first wife. I'm not Sandy, and I won't have you holding me up to her." She climbed off the bed and stalked across the room, heading for the bathroom to take a long hot shower and cool off her indignation. She paused, her hand on the doorknob. "There's something you should know." She didn't dare look at him. "I woke up…in the middle of the night last night…" She wasn't proud of this and refused to turn around and look at him as she admitted what she'd done.

"And what?" Royce demanded.

"I… I flushed my birth control pills down the toilet."

She heard his muffled curse as she stepped inside the bathroom.

The shower was running, and Catherine was standing under the stinging spray when the door was thrust open and Royce stepped inside.

"What the hell did you do that for?" He didn't need to explain what he was asking about.

"Because." Catherine was well aware her answer didn't make sense.

"It won't make a whole lot of difference. All I have to do is make a trip to the drugstore."

"Fine. Do it." She reached for the bar of soap and lathered the washcloth. "I'm tired of having everything rest on my shoulders. It's time for someone else to take responsibility."

Royce frowned at that. The water pelted down around him, splashing against the sides of the cubicle. "I'm not going to argue with you. These days are too precious to spend fighting. Even if we were to agree about you getting pregnant, it's too soon. Let's wait a year and talk about it then. A lot could change in that time. There's no need for either of us to get caught up in our disagreements when there's so much we do agree on."

He shouldn't make this much sense. It should be black-and-white. Cut-and-dried.

His hand was under her chin. "I love you, Catherine, I'd much rather be making love to you than standing here debating a subject I assumed was closed." He leaned forward and gently brushed moist lips over hers.

Heaven help her, but she couldn't resist him. Not like this. She stood on her tiptoes and looped her arms around his neck, easing her softness against his hard, lean strength. Steam fogged the windows and mirrors, but Catherine was convinced it had nothing to do with the hot spray of water and everything to do with the way Royce was kissing her.

As it happened, the water turned cold a whole lot sooner than either of them did.

Catherine was frying bacon for Kelly's breakfast when Royce came bolting down the stairs. He grabbed his jacket and was heading toward the front door when Kelly stopped him.

"Where're you going, Dad?"

He hesitated and cast a dark frown in Catherine's direction. "Shopping."

"It's too early in the morning for anything to be open," Kelly informed him with perfect logic.

"A drugstore will be," he muttered, and moved out the front door, slamming it behind him.

Smiling contentedly to herself, Catherine continued to fry the bacon.

It wasn't supposed to happen like this, Catherine told herself a month later. A woman didn't flush her birth control pills down the toilet one minute and, bingo, turn up pregnant the next. This was one for the record books. Something like this was supposed to take weeks. Months.

Not seconds.

As far as Catherine could figure it out, she was more fertile than the Napa Valley.

She didn't know what she was going to tell Royce. Or when. Not soon, she decided. This pregnancy was something that would demand diplomacy and tact. Good grief, only a handful of people in Bangor even knew she was married.

If only she weren't so thrilled about it. So excited. Of course being separated the way they were, she might even be able to have the baby without Royce knowing.

But that was ridiculous. He was the father. He deserved to know. Kelly deserved to know.

She waited all day for his phone call, deciding to play it by ear. At precisely six, her time, just after she'd poured herself a cup of coffee, the phone rang.

She grabbed it off the hook, holding the receiver tight against her ear. She reminded herself that she was an accomplished attorney who knew her way around the courtroom. She could argue with the best of them. Her arguments had swayed more than one judge. All she needed to do was remain collected and poised. This child, although unexpected, was a welcome gift. Once Royce saw things from her point of view, he'd change his mind. He didn't have any choice. The deed was done.

"Catherine?"

"Hi," she answered cheerfully. "How are you? How's Kelly? Not much happening around here except that the strip turned blue." Catherine couldn't believe she'd blurted it out like that, although it was unlikely that Royce knew she was referring to the home pregnancy kit she'd picked up at the pharmacy.

"What are you talking about?"

"Oh, nothing. Just a bit of local humor. Are you missing me?"

"You know I am." His words were low and seductive.

They talked for a half hour, the longest thirty minutes of Catherine's life. The minute they were finished, she rushed into the bathroom and hung her head over the toilet. She was never going to be able to pull this off. Royce would guess by the end of the week. She didn't know what would infuriate him more, the fact she hadn't told him right away or that she was pregnant in the first place.

Catherine gained two important lessons from her thirty-minute conversation with Royce. First, that she would need to confide in someone, and second, she wasn't going to be able to drink coffee for the next nine months.

"Hi, Mom," Catherine greeted.

"Sweetheart, what's wrong?"

"How did you know anything was?"

"You mean other than the fact you're phoning and it's past midnight? Don't worry, I wasn't asleep. Norman went to bed hours ago, but I'm up reading one of Mary Higgins Clark's mysteries."

"Midnight. I didn't realize it was that late."

"You always call late when you're upset."

Catherine didn't realize that, either. "Say, Mom, what would you say if I told you the strip turned blue?"

The pause was only slight. "Is this a trick question?"

"No... I'm dead serious."

"A strip turned blue. I don't know, sweetheart, probably that you should see a doctor."

"Right answer," she said on the tail of a breathy sigh. "Now comes the difficult part. Can you guess why I need a doctor?"

Again there was a semi-lengthy pause. "I'd say it was because you were pregnant, but I know that's not the case."

"Wrong answer."

"You mean… Catherine, do you honestly mean to tell me you and Royce are… But you've only been married a short while, and he's in Virginia and you're in Washington state. Honey, how did it happen?"

"You want me to explain it to you?" Catherine asked incredulously.

"You know what I mean." Catherine could almost see her mother blushing.

"Christmas," Catherine whispered.

"You don't sound like you're sure you're pleased about this."

"I'm thrilled, Mom, honest I am."

"Are you going to leave the Navy?"

"No!"

"But, Catherine, can't you see how impossible it will be? You and Royce live two thousand miles apart. A child deserves to know his father."

"Royce will see the baby."

Her mother must have sensed the argument brewing just below the surface of Catherine's stubborn pride, because she diplomatically changed the subject.

"I'm going to tell you something I never have before," Marilyn said softly, gently. "You, my darling daughter, were a surprise."

"I was?"

"Actually, you were more of a shock."

Catherine grinned. Her sense of timing never had gotten straightened out, it seemed.

"Your father and I were in college. Young. Idealistic. Foolish."

"Do you mean to tell me you and Dad *had* to get married?"

"No, but as best as I can figure you were born nine months and one day after our wedding. I didn't know how I was going to tell your father. As it turned out, he was delighted. I was crying—the hormones really did a trick on me. I'll never forget how gentle he was, how pleased. It was as though I were the only woman in the world who'd ever endured a pregnancy." Her mother paused, and Catherine could hear the slight quaver in her voice.

"In those days the father wasn't often allowed in the delivery room. But Andy refused to leave me. For a minute there I thought he and the doctor were going to come to blows."

Catherine enjoyed hearing these loving details about her father. Her gaze rested tenderly on the fading color photograph that rested atop her mantel.

"When you were born, I was afraid he would be disappointed with a daughter. But not Andy. The delivery room nurse placed you in his arms, and he sat beside me and wept for joy.

"After they wheeled me into the recovery room, I was exhausted and fell asleep. But Andy was too excited to stand still. The nurses told me he dragged everyone from the janitor to the hospital administrator up to the nursery to take a look at you. Not once did he regret that I'd become pregnant so soon." Her mother paused, and Catherine could hear her voice tremble with soft emotion.

"I love hearing stories about him," Catherine admitted, discovering she was close to tears herself, which probably meant this pregnancy was going to play havoc with her emotions.

"Royce doesn't know yet, does he?" her mother pried softly.

"No."

"When exactly do you plan to tell him?"

"Next year when it's time to figure our income taxes?"

Her mother's laughter echoed softly over the long-distance line. "Oh, Catherine, you remind me so much of myself, and so much of your father. Royce is a good man, I don't think you have a thing to worry about."

They spoke for a few minutes more, and then Catherine hung up. Slowly, thoughtfully, she walked over to the fireplace and gently ran her finger along the top of her father's picture. It was something she did often when she needed to feel close to him. She prayed her mother was right and that Royce would be thrilled. Her gaze rested on her father's handsome features. A lone tear streaked her face as she regretted once again her inability to remember him.

Royce was weary as he drove down the maple-lined street and pulled into his driveway. He missed Catherine. It had been nearly three months since he'd last seen her, and it could well be another three before he did again. He tried not to think about it.

They were close, as close as any two married people could be that were separated by the width of an entire country. If anything troubled him it was the fact she was so content with their arrangement. They talked two times a week and wrote nearly every day. Only on rare occasions did Catherine reveal any regrets on their being so far removed from each other.

Not so with Royce. He wanted his wife with him. If he was being selfish, inconsiderate, then so be it. The nights were lonely. Friday nights were always the worst. Kelly usually spent it with a friend, which left him to fend for himself. He was pleased his daughter had such an active social life; his, however, was wrapped around a woman two thousand miles away.

He really knew how to pick them, he mused darkly. Career women. First Sandy and now Catherine, both so eager to make a place in their chosen profession.... No, he wasn't going to dwell on it. He'd done that too much lately. He'd gone into this marriage with his eyes wide open. From the first he'd known how important the Navy was to Catherine. He'd married her still, loving her enough to place a distant second in her life if that was all she was willing to give him.

His life was good. He had only a few complaints. He liked Virginia much better than he ever expected he would. He enjoyed his job, and over the past few months had developed several interests. He wasn't much into hobbies—at least he hadn't been until he married Catherine. Now he had to find something to fill the time or go crazy thinking about how much he missed her.

He just wished there was some way he could get her transferred out to the East Coast. Even if she were stationed in Florida, it would be a whole lot closer than Washington state.

The lights were on in the house, and Royce was trying to remember if Kelly was going to be home or not. Home, he guessed.

He opened the front door and removed his jacket and hung it in the hall closet. Someone was cooking in the kitchen. Whatever it was it smelled like heaven. Royce was going to have to say something to Kelly about fixing dinner. She was too young to be attempting it without adult supervision.

"Kelly?" He paused to sort through the mail.

"I'm in the kitchen, Dad." She sounded downright pleased about something. Probably that she'd managed to cook his dinner without burning down the house.

"What smells so good?"

"Yankee pot roast, mashed potatoes, steamed baby carrots and fresh-baked apple pie."

The mail dropped out of Royce's hands as he slowly turned around. He was dreaming. He had to be, because it was Catherine's honey-sweet voice that was talking to him and not Kelly's. She stood in the kitchen doorway, a towel tucked into the waistband of her jeans, holding a wooden spoon in one hand.

"Catherine?" He was almost afraid to reach for her for fear she'd vanish into thin air. Either real or imaginary, he had to hold her. Two steps later, and she was in his arms.

He closed his eyes and breathed in the warm, familiar fragrance of her, intoxicated within seconds. His arms were wrapped around her so tightly that he'd lifted her half off the floor without even realizing it.

"Are you surprised?" Kelly asked.

"You knew?" He couldn't believe that she'd managed to keep it a secret from him.

"Only since yesterday."

He kissed Catherine with a hunger that quickly stirred awake dormant fires. "How long can you stay?"

Mentally he was tabulating how many times they could make love in three days.

"How long do you want me for?"

A lifetime! Fifty years or whichever came first. "How long have you got?" No use aiming for the stars. He'd take what he could get and be damned grateful.

"A while." She kissed him, tantalizing him with the tip of her tongue, and then casually sauntered back to the stove.

"A while," Royce repeated, not understanding.

"Now?" Kelly demanded, looking up at Catherine.

Catherine nodded mysteriously. Royce's daughter held up her two hands. "Ten minutes," she said. "That's all the time I'm giving you."

"It shouldn't even take that long," Catherine assured her.

Kelly was gone in a flash, racing up the stairs.

"Ten minutes," Royce repeated once Kelly was out of the room. "Honey, I don't know what you've got in mind, but I'd appreciate a bit more leeway than ten minutes."

"I want you to read something." She walked over to the table and handed him an official-looking envelope.

Royce stared at it for several moments, not knowing what to think.

"And while I've got your attention, I think you should know we killed a rabbit."

"What?" The woman had become a loony tune. A three-month separation had driven her over the edge. He knew it had him, so it shouldn't come as any big surprise.

"Actually I don't think it's officially a rabbit these days."

"Woman, what are you talking about?"

"You mean you honestly don't know?" He clearly seemed to not know.

He wouldn't be standing there with his mouth open, looking like a fish out of water if he did. "I don't have a clue," he admitted reluctantly.

"We're pregnant."

Royce shook his head, convinced she was playing a practical joke on him.

"It's true, Royce." Her eyes met his, shyly, as though she were honestly afraid of his reaction. She was studying him closely, judging his response, watching him for any signs of emotion.

Royce felt the sudden need to sit down. "When?"

"As-s best I can figure, sometime over Christmas. My guess was that morning...in the shower."

He nodded. He felt too numb to do much of anything else. He started figuring dates. It had happened at Christmas, and they were already into the second week of March.

"But that was..."

"A few months ago now," she finished for him.

"You're three months pregnant?" She'd kept it a secret for all those months.

She nodded. "Aren't you going to say anything? Oh, Royce, please don't keep me in suspense any longer. Are you happy?"

He struggled for words, but the emotions had jammed in his throat. He swallowed and slowed his breath before nodding. "Yes." He reached for her, taking her by the hips and drawing her to him. He flattened his hand over her stomach and closed his eyes. It was impossible for him to speak.

"Read the letter," she whispered, and tears slipped from the corners of her eyes and ran unrestrained down her cheeks. She brushed them aside. "Don't worry, I'm terribly emotional these days. I start weeping at the drop of a hat, but the doctor said it wasn't anything to be concerned about."

Royce withdrew the paper from inside the envelope. He scanned the contents twice, certain there was some misunderstanding.

"You're leaving the Navy?" he asked, his voice incredulous.

"Yes, but I'm still in the Reserves."

"Why?" After all her arguments about keeping her commission, he couldn't believe that she'd voluntarily give it up.

Catherine's arms circled his neck, and she lowered herself onto his lap. "Because I finally figured out why the Navy was so important for me."

Royce stared up at her, not understanding.

"I was searching to know my father, looking to find him in Navy life... I know it all sounds crazy, but having no memory of him has troubled me for years. Hanging on to the Navy, especially now, was like grasping at straws, because I wanted to find something about him to hang on to."

"But what changed your mind?"

"Our baby. I realized I could do it. Raise our child and everything else when we were so far apart. Then it dawned on me how silly I was being, grasping to find my own father and denying my own child the privilege."

Royce kissed her, worshipping her with his mouth, loving her until they were both trembling.

"Have you told him yet?" Kelly demanded from the top of the stairs.

"She told me," Royce answered.

Kelly raced down. "What do you think, Dad?"

He grinned and held out his hand to his daughter, bringing her into the circle of their love. It was more than he ever dreamed, more than he deserved. Taking Catherine's hand, he pressed her fingertips to his lips. Their eyes held, and in hers Royce saw the warm promise of tomorrow.

Epilogue

Royce was whistling a catchy tune when he pulled into the driveway and turned off the engine. The station wagon was parked alongside of his black Porsche, a baby seat strapped in the rear seat.

Andy was fast outgrowing the padded chair, which worked out well since Jenny would soon be needing it. His three-month-old daughter was growing like a weed.

Pushing a tricycle out of the way, Royce opened the front door and hung his hat and jacket on the brass coatrack. "I'm home."

Four-year-old Andy let out a cry of glee and came tearing around the corner at top speed. Royce swept his son high above his head and hugged him close.

"How's Daddy's little man? Did you help your mother today by being a good boy?"

"Aye, aye, sir." Andrew Royce Nyland saluted sharply, then squirmed, wanting back down. The minute his feet hit the floor, Andy was back to whatever it was that had captured his attention in the first place.

"Royce," Catherine greeted, coming into the entryway, holding their daughter. A smile came automatically to his lips. It never ceased to amaze him, after all

these years, all this time, how his heart quickened at the
sight of her. She was in a blue business suit with a fancy
silk blouse, and Royce vaguely remembered her telling him she'd had to go into the office later than usual.
He was proud of the way Catherine had found a position in a prestigious law firm. Proud of her for showing
him it was possible to mix a career with a family. She
worked three days a week now, but when the time was
right, she would eventually take on a forty-hour week.
Frankly, Royce felt his wife had something of an advantage over other attorneys. She was so damn beautiful and intelligent he couldn't see a jury in the land
disagreeing with her.

"Oh, Royce, I'm glad you're home." Catherine
paused to give him a quick but satisfying kiss, handing him Jenny. No sooner was his daughter in his arms,
when Catherine was reaching for her coat.

"Where are you headed?"

She turned around and chastised him with a smile.
"I told you about the Navy wives meeting this evening,
don't you remember?"

"Oh, right." Royce recalled nothing of the sort. He
had trouble keeping track of his own schedule, let alone
everyone else's.

"Kelly will be home within a half hour," Catherine
informed him. "And she's bringing a young man home
with her."

"A boy?"

"Royce, she's almost sixteen. This is important to
her, so don't make a fuss. All she asks is that you give
her a little privacy."

"Hey," he grumbled, reaching for his wife. "How
does she rate? If anyone deserves a little privacy, it's
us." He kissed her along the side of the neck, savor-

ing her special fragrance. "What time are you going to be home?"

"Not late," she promised, rubbing her mouth over his lips in a slow, erotic exercise. "I promise."

Royce reluctantly released her. "Good, because I've got plans for tonight."

"You've got plans for every night," she teased, "which is a good thing because if you didn't, I would have." She grabbed her purse, started for the front door and turned back around.

"Forget something?"

"Yes." She patted Jenny's sleeping brow and then raised her mouth to his. The kiss was one for the record books. Teasing. Coaxing.

Royce felt his knees grow weak, and if it hadn't been for Jenny, he would have wrapped his arms around Catherine and hauled her up the stairs right then and there.

Catherine sighed and hesitantly broke away from him.

"What was that for?" he asked breathlessly.

"Just so you'd know how much I love you. How grateful I am that you were patient enough to allow me to come to my own decisions. About the Navy. About my joining the law firm. About having Jenny."

"I sincerely hope you intend on thanking me again later."

"You know I do." She grinned and started for the door. Royce turned toward the kitchen, whistling contentedly.

* * * * *

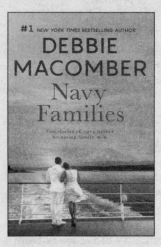